Romancing
Waikiki

C. J. Johnson

Novelstokeep@gmail.com

Romancing Waikiki

CJ Johnson

MILL CITY PRESS

Mill City Press, Inc.
2301 Lucien Way #415
Maitland, FL 32751
407.339.4217
www.millcitypress.com

Printed in the United States of America

Paperback ISBN-13: 978-1-6628-1052-7
Ebook ISBN-13: 978-1-6628-1053-4

Dedication

I dedicate this book to everyone who has experienced love.
In these stories, I have tried to show the many dimensions of love.
If pressed, I would define love as not the electrifying passions
of a fresh romance, but what remains when the flames
have subsided, leaving embers of empathy,
commitment, and a willingness to forgive.

Acknowledgments

*T*his collection of stories is infused with ideas and suggestions from countless visitors to Waikiki Beach, whom I met on my sunset walks along the iconic beach. I listened to stories from visitors from Asia, Australia, Canada, Europe, and the United States, including an ex-Miss Hawaii. I was surprised and pleased by the number of women who offered to share their stories of falling in love, while their partners shrugged with wry smiles.

I could not produce a publishable novel without editors that care deeply about their craft. I wish to thank Dr. Mara Miller for her editing and suggestions on how to improve the stories. In addition, I greatly appreciate the thorough edit of *Romancing Waikiki* by Tom Wallace.

I am grateful for constructive suggestions from those who have experienced the joys of romance as well as the pains of lost love, including Gary Bowersox, David Burson, Lisa Gundling, Aaron Johnson, Katie Johnson, David Jordt, Dr. Ingrid Jordt, Kay Kolt, Penny Macaulay, Li Wang, Michelle Johnson-Wang, Dr. Xiaodong Wang, Tami Wellman, and Dr. John Wiltshire. Suggestions came from across the age spectrum—from a sixteen-year-old published author to a romantic couple in their eighties.

Prologue

*F*or two decades, I frequented Waikiki Beach on weekends and discovered much more than the powdery golden sands, the iconic Diamond Head backdrop, and the multihued blue ocean that flowed seamlessly into the sky. The romance it evoked as far back as the opening of the elegant Moana Hotel in 1901 to welcome well-heeled travelers who arrived by steamship has continued to the present.

Lying on the sand, I overheard sunbathers whispering about the attributes of the women and men who strolled along the beach and frolicked in the surf. There were murmurs, carried on wisps of wind, of romantic encounters in the beachside bars that came alive at dusk. I was frequently asked to take photos of couples, newlyweds, and families; some just handed me their expensive cameras or smartphones, and posed. Over the years, I thought about the stories that could be told if the famous beach could reveal its secrets. That led to writing *Romancing Waikiki*.

The daily rhythm of Waikiki Beach begins before the sun clears the Koʻolau Mountains. The beach is swept smooth by the tide, a process helped by ghostlike machines that appear after midnight and are gone before sunrise. Mornings are the quietest, with a sprinkling of joggers, swimmers, surfers, and walkers, mostly older, strolling the two-mile strip of sand.

By midmorning tourists stream onto the sand, and by noon the beach is a checkerboard of straw mats and beach towels embracing a mélange of people from around the world. Families with children share the beach with singles displaying swimwear in a myriad of colors and sizes, like the tropical fish around the offshore coral reefs. As sunset nears, parents shepherd tired children back to their hotels, and singles transition to the beachfront bars, leaving the beach sparsely populated by those seeking solace with the setting sun. Later, especially when the moon is full, silhouettes of couples can be seen strolling at surf's edge, sometimes merging into one.

This selection of love stories, written in Waikiki coffeehouses, spans the period from the Second World War to the present. It covers all ages, from a coming-of-age teen romance to senior citizens who discover love has no expiration date. The chapter titles give clues to the plots but not twists. While the stories are fictional, they have threads in the sands of Waikiki and beyond. Matters of the heart can be found in the footprints in the sand, a letter fluttering across the beach, remnants of a sandcastle, an army nurse waiting, and in a homeless woman blowing out a candle. The takeaway from these stories on my favorite beach is that love blossoms when least expected. And it changes everything.

Table of Contents

The Promise

A gentle breeze swayed the potted palm fronds as Matt
Turner strolled through the lobby of the New Otani
Kaimana Beach Hotel to the Sunset Lanai. Sandy, the cocktail
waitress, waved and gave him a welcoming smile and turned to
the bartender. She briefly primped, using the mirrored cocktail
tray, then carried a bottle of Kirin and a dish of Japanese rice
crackers to his table.

"How's my favorite teacher?"

He shrugged and waved the pile of exams. "Half my students still think they're on summer vacation, not taking col-
lege-level biology."

"Don't be too hard on them. It's only the third week of
school. Remember, the pace of everything is slower in paradise." Her closeness and fragrance distracted him from his
papers as she tipped his glass and deftly poured the beer until
the foam just reached the rim. "But there's a reason you've
stayed here in Hawaii and not gone back to the Mainland."

Matt had been in Hawaii for almost four years, teaching at
Kapiolani Community College, on the north side of Diamond
Head, ten minutes from Kaimana Beach at the east end of
Waikiki Beach. On most Fridays, he came to the Sunset Lanai
cocktail lounge at the New Otani Kaimana Beach Hotel around

1

five thirty to grade papers, and he remained until well after sunset. The Kaimana Beach Hotel, as locals called it, stood at the far end of Waikiki, away from its crowded center, near the foot of the iconic Diamond Head. The cocktail lounge was close enough to the beach to let in the melodic sounds of the surf, yet a few steps too far for the beach bar crowd. Here he could sit for an hour or more nursing a beer, sometimes two, watch the sunset, and not feel rushed to free up his table.

Sandy's relaxed attitude and cheerful service were as important to him as the setting in drawing him back on Friday evenings. A transplant from Southern California, the lithesome blond drew more than passing interest from Asian men in the Japanese-owned hotel. She skillfully rebuffed suitors and had told Matt before he had a chance to ask her out that the hotel prohibited after-hours fraternizing with patrons.

Just before sunset, the modest decor of the Sunset Lanai was transformed into an exotic place, as the sun's rays, splintered by palm fronds, cast tropical wavy patterns across the lounge. Sandy set a second plate of Japanese rice crackers on the table and leaned close. "If you can take your eyes off the exam papers for a moment, you'll notice the attractive lady in a stunning green silk dress who's been stood up."

He looked over at a twenty-something woman with coiffed ginger hair, his gaze lingering.

"What makes you think she's been stood up?"

"No wonder you're single. There're two Mai Tais in front of her, and she's sipped only one over the past hour. The other is untouched. She's glanced toward the entrance every couple of minutes and at you several times. Why don't you go over and introduce yourself? Could be a lot more stimulating than grading papers."

"Sandy, have you ever seen me hit on a woman? I don't pick up women in bars."

"Really? I've seen you give me that look many times, and that's why I told you I don't date patrons." Sandy turned and walked over to the woman and leaned close and whispered. The woman glanced his way with a cautious smile, and Sandy beckoned him with a flick of her head and a devilish grin.

He gathered his papers and beer and walked over. "Hi, I'm Matt Turner. Mind if I join you for a drink?"

"Well . . . I suppose so. The waitress told me you wanted to meet me. I'm Karen." She extended her hand as he set down his papers and beer and wiped his wet hand on his shirt before taking hers.

"I'm a teacher here in Hawaii."

She gave a wry smile. "I thought you might have flown over from the mainland just to grade papers at sunset on Waikiki Beach."

Sandy arrived with two fresh Mai Tais. "These are on the house," she said with a wink.

Karen had noticed him when he entered the hotel lounge and was cheerfully greeted by the waitress. He looked very masculine, with a face more chiseled than rounded and a couple days' growth of whiskers. His well-worn, wrinkled aloha shirt and the bundle of papers in his hands suggested he had not been looking for a pickup. As soon as he'd sat at his table, he'd begun marking papers with a red pen, turning pages as his expression fluxed between smiles of approval and frowns. His peculiar behavior had piqued her curiosity, but she had come to meet someone else—someone *special*.

"I've never met a man grading papers in a bar."

He grinned. "Well, there's a first for everything," he said, and he took the tiny decorative umbrella from his drink and set it aside. Karen lifted her glass to meet his, and they said cheers in unison. She noticed he wasn't wearing a wedding band, nor was there an untanned band on his ring finger.

There was an awkward silence after the toast, then he picked up the tiny umbrella and twirled it in his fingers. "These decorative pieces that makes our drinks special have taken a long journey to reach our glasses. Somewhere in Asia, a tall bamboo plant was cut down, probably by someone from a hill tribe. Did you know that bamboo is the miracle material of Asia, with hundreds of uses, from buildings to this tiny umbrella?" Before she could reply he continued. "Bamboo has personal and political significance to the Chinese, as it embodies strength and can bend and not break in strong winds. Skilled fingers crafted this umbrella to smoothly open and close, then covered it with rice paper and painted it, and all for maybe two or three cents. Amazing, isn't it?"

Karen wasn't sure she'd made the right decision to let him join her for a drink. She had met many single men but never one who began with a lecture about irrelevant minutia. "You, ah, really like bamboo," she replied with a forced smile.

Matt set the umbrella aside and shrugged. "You mean I'm boring? I'm not good at meeting women in bars."

She mused, *Okay, he's rusty at pickup lines. But he could be interesting. Better than drinking alone.* "I've always wanted to travel to Asia to see the exotic sights I've only seen in travel magazines. But trips to Hawaii are as close to Asia as I've been so far."

"So, you've been here before."

"I came with my parents when I was thirteen and had a Shirley Temple in this lounge. In college I came back with my girlfriend and stayed in the heart of Waikiki. We had a ball on Waikiki Beach and enjoyed the nightlife."

"I bet you had to fight off the beachboys?"

Karen smiled and twisted a dangling jade earring. "I had fun. I'm older and more selective now."

He laughed and took a gulp of his drink before shaking his head. "You can't be over twenty-five."

She laughed. "At least you've learned to always underestimate a women's age. I'm twenty-eight. And you're probably in your mid-thirties?"

"Thirty-four next month." He picked up the tiny umbrella and opened and closed it a couple of times before looking into her eyes. "So, if you don't mind my asking, who's the guy who stood you up?"

"I doubt you want to hear a really dumb story about a teenage promise."

"Can't be dumber than some of the excuses my students give me for not doing their homework."

She held her glass with both hands, avoiding eye contact. "Bobby was my high school sweetheart. He was so handsome. He had swimmingly blue eyes and cute dimples when he smiled. A star athlete with solid B-plus grades—pretty good for someone who lettered in football and basketball. We were hoping to go to the same university, but a football scholarship took him to the University of Nebraska, while I stayed near home and attended San Francisco State.

"The night before Bobby left for Nebraska, we made a blood pact." She pulled a three-by-five-inch card from her purse and handed it to Matt. He scanned the note.

If we, Bobby Hunter and Karen Peterson, are still single ten years after high school graduation, we agree to meet at exactly 6:00 p.m. on September 24, 1999, in the cocktail lounge of the New Otani Kaimana Beach Hotel on Waikiki Beach, and try again.

"That's a most unusual promise. I suppose you contacted him to confirm he'd be here?"

"That's the dumbest part. We stopped communicating when we began dating others in college. I checked our high school alumni website, and he had posted a note in July that he was still single and would like to renew contacts with classmates. He couldn't have forgotten our blood promise, could he?"

Matt shrugged. "No. But I'm not Bobby."

5

"My thinking was that if I was still important to him, he would come. And if not, my consolation prize would be a holiday in Hawaii."

Matt gazed into her green eyes. "I would have come." He paused. "Consider me your consolation prize."

She nodded. "That's a much better pickup line than describing the wonders of bamboo."

"What made you choose this cocktail lounge?"

"I had my thirteenth birthday here. The cocktail waitress gave me a small cake, and everyone sang Happy Birthday. Thirteen-year-old girls remember things like that."

"Boys also have childhood memories."

Karen twisted her napkin. "Enough about me. Tell me a little about yourself."

"I grew up in Virginia City, Nevada, a restored mining town a little more than an hour's drive from Reno. My dad was a bartender in an old-time saloon, and Mom worked in a gift shop. I had lots of time to roam the hills and explore old mines with my best friend. Terry and I collected rocks and even found a few specimens with silver. Enrolled in the Mackay School of Mines at the University of Nevada in Reno with plans to become a mining engineer, but one class in biology changed my mind, and I transferred in my second year to UC Davis to study biology. I did my grad studies at UC Santa Barbara, then got a position at Kapiolani Community College in Hawaii. I do some hiking and kayaking, and I've been back to Thailand and Laos twice to do research."

"You didn't mention any romances in your life."

"Ah, I don't reveal such things to strangers unless they agree to have dinner with me."

She smiled. "That's doable. If I have dinner with you, what are your expectations?" Her eyes drilled into him.

He shrugged. "Depends on whether your high school boyfriend shows up."

"If he was coming, you wouldn't be sitting at this table. Where do you suggest we eat?"

"Karen, the Hau Tree Lanai in this hotel is the nicest setting on Waikiki and an easy escape if you change your mind."

"I think I can trust you."

The historic Hau Tree Lanai, nestled under a canopy of ancient flowering hau trees, was just a couple of steps down to beach level, and although it was fully booked, they were given an ocean-side table once he told the hostess that Karen was staying at the hotel. Matt had to duck to be seated under a gnarled hau tree, whose limbs were festooned with Christmas-tree lights that added intimacy to the setting at the edge of the beach.

"Did you know Robert Louis Stevenson, who wrote *Kidnapped* and *Treasure Island*, might have sat under this tree when he was in Hawaii?"

"What makes you think so?"

"It says it on the back of the menu."

She grinned. *He's funny, in a quirky sort of way.* "Matt, I remember having breakfast with my parents under this tree. I had poi pancakes with pineapple syrup and a bird in the tree pooped on our table."

"You must have a photographic memory."

"No, I keep a diary. This place is as magical as I remember."

"I sometimes come here for breakfast and their Kona coffee. I came once for dinner and thought the meal was average, but a date makes a big difference."

"This isn't a *real* date, but, Matt, you've turned a depressing evening into something memorable. The fresh fish entrees all look good. Any suggestions?"

"Hmm . . . we could share two seafood dishes—shutome, with a sweet ginger wasabi sauce, and opakapaka, with buttered shiitake mushrooms. In case you're not familiar, shutome is swordfish, and opakapaka, pink snapper. For wine, I suggest

Iron Horse's Sangiovese with a touch of cabernet sauvignon that gives it a Tuscan style."

Karen smiled as she gazed into his eyes. "Seems Professor Turner knows a lot more about food and wine than he does about how to meet women in bars."

"Remember, I went to UC Davis, the premier university for studying viniculture. My roommate's parents owned a small vineyard in Napa County, and I got to taste a lot of wines."

As was often true on first dates, the meal, superb as it was, was secondary to their conversation, which revealed pieces in the montage of their lives. Hours vanished, along with the other diners, until they found they were the last to leave.

Karen paused at the elevator, giving Matt time to embrace her with a kiss, then she disappeared into the elevator. He stood watching the elevator lights—one, two, then stopping at three—and waited to see if the elevator would descend. As he turned to leave, he spotted Sandy sitting at a cocktail table with a cup of coffee and his exams.

"Sandy, you didn't have to wait just to give back my papers."

"What would your students think if you lost their exams? And I wanted to see if you would join her in the elevator."

"I don't do one-night stands."

"Really. What if she asked you to her room?"

"Well, she didn't."

"She wanted to."

"Sandy, you don't know that."

"I've seen hundreds of first dates here, and when the chemistry is right, the two enter the elevator. You two had that look. Hopefully you offered to show her some sights."

"Yes. She's been to Hawaii twice before, so she's seen the popular tourist sites. Any suggestions?"

"If she's a good swimmer, you could drive to Waianae and swim out to meet the dolphins. They usually show up early in the morning and can be quite playful."

"She's terrified of sharks."

"Then hike through the rainforest to the crest of the Koʻolaus, where you'll have fabulous views of the craggy windward side. A pretty sweaty and muddy hike, especially with yesterday's rain, so on your return you can stop in her room for a shower."

"Sandy, you're reading too much into a simple dinner with a woman who was stood up. I was the consolation prize. Even that's thanks to you."

"Or more like the knight in shining armor who saved a damsel in distress."

Matt shook his head as he walked over to get his exams. "Thanks for waiting with my exams. You'll be disappointed when you see that I'm just a tour guide for Karen."

"Tourists don't kiss their tour guides on the lips."

Karen was waiting on the entrance steps of the hotel when he pulled up in his open-topped Ranger Jeep. She waved and picked up her beach bag, then hurried to the passenger side. Matt liked the fresh college-student look of her pink polo shirt, tan shorts, and bouncy ponytail.

"Aloha. I was worried you might come with your coiffured hairdo that wouldn't survive five-minutes in my open-topped Jeep."

"This is the real me. Where have you decided to take me that's not too touristy?"

"If you agree, we'll head to the North Shore to visit Waimea Valley, a place sacred to the Hawaiians, who populated the valley for hundreds of years. It's a tropical paradise, and at the end of the valley, we can swim under a waterfall. It's rarely crowded."

"I've never been there. Sounds great."

Her ponytail spun like a windmill in the wind as they sped west on the H-1 Freeway past Pearl Harbor, where they had a distant view of the white memorial above the sunken USS *Arizona*.

9

"Matt, I cried when I visited the memorial with my parents. When the Japanese attacked Pearl Harbor, my grandfather joined the army and was sent to the Pacific. He survived for two years before being killed. Several times, I found my grandmother sleeping with his framed photo on the pillow next to her. She never remarried."

"I'm sorry. I tell all first-time visitors that they should visit Pearl Harbor and remember the sacrifices in the last great war that touched every American family."

They swung north on the H-2 Freeway, then took Highways 80 and 99 past the Dole Plantation and its crowded parking lot. "Unless you have a desire to look at hundreds of pineapple-themed trinkets, I suggest we continue to Hale'iwa and get coffee and muffins at the Coffee Gallery."

"I remember the Dole Plantation pretty well. I stopped there with my parents and had a soft pineapple ice cream cone that made quite an impression. It was tasty, but coffee and a muffin at the Coffee Gallery sounds better."

The route they took was the quickest to their destination but the least picturesque, with arid landscape and scattered monotonous pineapple and sugarcane fields interspersed with the small towns of Mililani and Wahiawa.

An hour from Honolulu they pulled into Hale'iwa, where Hawaiians, tourists, and surfers—both native and international—crossed paths. The one-street town was struggling to keep its local laid-back identity of single-story clapboard buildings that harked back to the days before passenger jets brought six million tourists a year to Hawaii. Matt turned into the North Shore Market Place and parked under one of the large shade trees.

The fresh coffee aromas spilled onto the boardwalk, drawing them to the open door of the Coffee Gallery where they had to step over a dog to enter. The line of people in T-shirts, shorts, and flip-flops moved slowly as regulars stopped to chat. The coffee was quite good, but the pièce de résistance was the warm muffin packed with pumpkin and sesame seeds, shaved coconut, and grated carrot, and infused with Hawaiian honey.

"The atmosphere seems to invite people to slow down and linger," she commented. "Back home, I grab a coffee at a Starbucks as I rush to work. It's an efficient and quick caffeine fix, but it doesn't reduce stress levels like here."

"I drive up here every month or two for the coffee and muffins but most of all for the calming atmosphere. Sometimes I take the slow route back to Honolulu, following the windward side of the Ko'olaus, like we'll do later today. That is, unless you happen to have a hot date waiting for you at the Kaimana Beach Hotel."

"Not likely. I guess I misjudged Bobby's interest."

"His loss. There are roadside stands along the way where we can buy fruit and corn picked the same day, plus we'll find nearly deserted beaches and breathtaking views of the tropical side of Oahu."

Karen toyed with her ponytail. "But don't you get a little lonely without someone to share the experience with?"

"I didn't say I came alone." He smiled. "Lisa sometimes rides with me."

"And who, may I ask, is Lisa?"

He laughed. "My neighbor's dog. I look after her when they're traveling."

"You're a tease."

"I have a date today, and I'm not sad that Bobby didn't show."

Karen smiled and reached over to lightly stroke his forearm.

After paying the entrance fee to Waimea Falls Park, they were given a brochure and map of the valley showing the locations of interesting sites on the three-quarter-mile meandering road to the waterfall. The valley was a vast botanical garden covering almost three-square miles, with its native Hawaiian history going back hundreds of years to before Captain Cook discovered Hawaii for Europeans. The lush valley had a dizzying array of five thousand species of plants from Hawaii and around the world, and dozens of different bird species — some rare.

There were little diversions where visitors could watch Hawaiians weaving grass matts, see hula performances, and have questions answered about Hawaiian culture, plus *keikis* (children) could take lessons on flower lei-making. The sacred valley had been populated by Hawaiians, including royalty, back to the fifteenth century, but only a few remnants of their society remained, including a stone Hawaiian *heiau* (temple). The ubiquitous presence of termites in the islands had destroyed all *kauhale* (thatched Hawaiian living sites), and the one in the park was a replica, though accurate and full-size.

"Matt, why are there so few people here?"

"My guess is because of its location and lack of the kind of attractions that bring people to Hawaii. Most tourists come for the beach experience and stay in Waikiki. Waimea Park is basically a botanical garden that has little appeal to most visitors — particularly families with children. I believe it's important for visitors to understand a little about Hawaiian culture, because that's the elixir behind the friendly aloha spirit of the islands. Enough of my opinions. What I'm most looking forward to is swimming under the waterfalls with you."

"Then what?"

"You'll have to wait."

"Your mind should be on this beautiful park with its abundance of tropical plants and flowers, and the sound of the brook and the peacocks running about. It reminds me of a painting of paradise I saw as a young girl, except that one had lots of wild animals."

"Mmm. Probably Rousseau. You know, unlike Gauguin, he never even saw the tropics."

"When did the Polynesians discover Hawaii?"

"The islands were first inhabited about 300 AD, when the first Polynesians arrived from the Marquesas Islands. I've read that the Portuguese were the first Europeans to discover the islands, but they kept it secret from their British rivals for over two hundred years, when Captain Cook arrived in 1778 on his ill-fated voyage. The early Hawaiians did a pretty good job of preserving their natural environment until the arrival of Europeans, who exploited everything that was of commercial value, particularly the hardwood forests, and converted the land to sugar cane and pineapples. This valley is a very important preserve, as it has so many rare species."

"Being a biologist and teacher, you must feel strongly about preserving the natural environment of the islands?"

"Yes, but I try to get my students to look at both sides of issues, as one-sided solutions are unsustainable. I've seen other Pacific islands that blocked economic development, with the result that there are few good jobs, so people leave or live in poverty. There needs to be sustainable economic growth for growing populations, as well as protection for critically important aspects of the environment. Waikiki is an example of overdevelopment, but we must work with what we have today and not try to return to a past that no longer exists. These days the Hawaiian government has started doing a better job of considering Hawaiian rights issues in evaluating future developments, but it's pretty slow at taking action."

"You must be a good teacher."

"You'll have to ask my students," he said, chuckling, and he took her hand. "I have a special place I want to show you." They detoured to the right, off the main winding paved road. The dirt path ended in a small grassy meadow surrounded by lush tropical vegetation and bird-of-paradise flowers, their pointy orange and blue blossoms adding a regal touch to the setting. Along one side of the meadow were crimson hibiscus blossoms, and ferns blanketed the hillside.

"Matt, this is a perfect place for weddings."

"My thinking, too. When I get married, I want it here with a Hawaiian quartet singing the 'Hawaiian Wedding Song' as my bride comes down those steps on the hillside."

"Why is such a romantic still single?"

"I suppose I'm too focused on teaching, and, as you discovered, I'm not good at pickup lines. Grading papers in a lounge on Waikiki on a Friday night is not the path to meeting available women."

"But you met me."

"Only because Sandy took the initiative. I might not have even looked up to notice you. Sandy's the main reason I go there."

"I'm glad someone's looking after you." She leaned in to kiss him on the cheek, but he quickly turned, and their lips met and lingered before she slowly pulled away. She mused, *It isn't shooting stars, but it has possibilities.*

They held hands a little tighter and continued to the falls, the laughter of children signaling they were close. They swam in the refreshingly cool jade water below the falls, their voices drowned out by the cascading water and squeals of teenagers and younger children. As she expected, Matt pulled her close for a kiss under the waterfall—a memorable touch to their visit to the valley. They dried off sitting on boulders along the shore and watched a bronzed Hawaiian make a graceful swan dive from the forty-foot-high falls.

The drive back along the winding two-lane highway provided glimpses of secluded beaches on the left and rural Hawaii and mountains on the right. The rainforest swooped down from the Ko'olaus and, in places, arched across the highway, branches entwined from both sides. Most small valleys had simple, single-walled plantation houses nestled among coconut palms, papaya trees with clusters of pear-shaped green-and-yellow fruit, and towering monkeypod and banyan trees. As soon as they stopped at a roadside fruit stand, a barefoot teenage girl came dashing down a trail to greet them and give the daily prices of the sweet finger-bananas, papayas, coconuts, and *lilikoi* (yellow passion fruit).

Back in Waikiki, they ate at Duke's, a ten-minute walk from Karen's hotel, and planned the next day's outing. Again, he left her at the elevator, but the goodnight kiss was longer.

Sunday morning Matt picked up Karen before sunrise, and they took the Pali Highway over the Ko'olau Mountains to Kailua, where they rented a two-person kayak a half-block from Kailua Beach. The Kalapawai Market, at the entrance to the beach, supplied takeout coffee, almond croissants, plus sandwiches and canned drinks for their lunch on the Mokulua Islands. Although less than a mile off Lanikai Beach, the two tiny islands were two miles from Kailua Beach and not for those unfamiliar with ocean kayaking. They had their coffee and croissants on picturesque Kailua Beach, edged in ironwood and palm trees as the sun rose above the horizon.

"If we weren't kayaking to the Mokulua Islands, I would have driven to Lanikai Beach, where we could see the sun rising between the islands."

"It's hard to imagine a nicer spot than right here. Ironwood and palm trees lining the beach instead of concrete hotels, and the ocean is smooth, and perfect for kayaking."

"Mornings are best for kayaking. In the afternoon the wind comes up and the water gets pretty choppy."

Karen surprised Matt when she adjusted quickly to paddling, and as they passed Flat Island, they overtook another couple that had launched their kayak several minutes earlier. The smooth water allowed them to view the extensive coral gardens, some within two feet of the surface. They changed course twice as protected green sea turtles surfaced on their bow, seemingly unconcerned about the kayak. But their landing on Moku Nui did not go as planned, as waves sweeping around the islet from both sides collided under them and flipped their kayak.

Matt jumped up, his arm around their inverted kayak and the small ice chest held to the kayak by a bungee cord. "Karen, you okay?"

"I guess so. The wave caught me by surprise." She helped Matt flip the kayak over, then grabbed the bow rope handle to help pull it onto the small beach, a third of which was already claimed by a seven-foot-long Hawaiian monk seal.

"Well, Karen, there's five hundred pounds of blubber blocking the trail around to the other side of the island, where we could have more privacy."

"I like our little beach right here, where I have a rather large chaperone."

Their sandwiches had been spared the sea water but were crushed by the canned drinks when the ice chest had turned upside down. Karen didn't seem concerned and said it reminded her of the smashed sandwiches when she went on hikes as a kid. Within half an hour, six more people in kayaks arrived—a crowd for a tiny beach, so they headed back, stopping at Lanikai Beach to see the postcard view toward the Mokulua Islands.

They returned to Waikiki early, as Matt had to prepare for Monday classes. After Matt left, Karen lingered in the Sunset Lanai, chatting with Sandy, who was as inquisitive about her as she was about Matt. Sandy asked if Karen's interest in Matt was likely to extend beyond the vacation.

"Probably, but I have to admit, I'm still bothered by the no-show of my high school flame. I was sure he'd show up, after he posted that he wanted to get back in touch with classmates."

Over the next few days, Karen explored local sights during the day while Matt was teaching and met him in the evenings to try different Waikiki restaurants, then stroll along the beach. They watched hula performances while having drinks at a couple of the beachside hotel bars, and Matt explained the importance of hula, which was deeply woven into the Hawaiian culture and not just to entertain tourists. "Some of my students have devoted years of their childhood to learning hula." On Thursday they went to a live play at TAG, The Actors' Group, near Chinatown, and had dinner at one of the Irish pubs nearby. Each evening, the goodnight kisses at the elevator were longer and Matt held her tighter.

For her last night in Hawaii, they decided to reenact their first meeting in the Sunset Lanai cocktail lounge. Matt wasn't sure how the evening would turn out, but on the chance that he wouldn't be driving home, he left his Jeep in overnight parking. At the hotel entrance he paused, waiting until exactly six p.m., then strolled in past the registration counter, catching a whiff of jasmine in the faint ocean breeze. He couldn't suppress a broad grin as his eyes settled on Karen in her stunning green dress with her ginger hair done up exactly as he had first seen her five days earlier. She looked regal as she turned to gaze his way, her delicate fingers touching an earring, two Mai Tais waiting on the table. His heart pounded as he fought the urge to dash over and sweep her up in his arms. He was halfway to her when she exclaimed, "Oh, my God!" and put her hand over her mouth.

Matt hesitated as he tried to process the unexpected outburst and her astonished expression. Sandy also appeared startled as she looked his way.

A man in a smart, off-white linen suit swept past Matt, holding a luxurious orchid lei, and Karen jumped to her feet and shrieked, "Bobby!" Moments later, he encircled her head in the lei and engulfed her in his arms. Over his shoulder, Karen silently mouthed, *I'm sorry.* Pulling away, she tearfully said, "You didn't come on the twenty-fourth, as we agreed."

"It's the twenty-ninth, isn't it?" He pulled the water-stained card from his wallet and showed her. "I've carried it all these years. Look at the date."

She studied the card. "The *four* is smudged and looks like a *nine*. This is so embarrassing. When you didn't show up on the twenty-fourth, I thought you didn't want to keep our promise to try again. Matt Turner kindly stepped in and showed me the sights of Oahu and saved me from a disastrous vacation."

Bobby thrust out his hand. "I'm Bobby Hunter. Thank you for turning my mistake into a memorable vacation for a woman we both know is very special. I insist that you join us for dinner at La Mer, in the Halekulani."

Karen reached for Matt's hand. "Please come."

Matt smiled graciously. "Thank you for the kind invitation. My job is done and you two have ten years of catching up. My mother warned me that third wheels are for tricycles. And anyway, I have exams to grade. I wish you two my very best."

Karen embraced Matt, her eyes glassy as she whispered, "I'm sure there's a special woman out there waiting to share a Mai Tai with you."

Matt stood, hands to his sides, eyes transfixed in their direction after they were gone.

"Matt, have a seat. You deserve a drink."

He shrugged and slumped into his usual table and waited for Sandy to bring a Kirin beer and dish of Japanese rice crackers. She strolled over and sat two Mai Tais on his table.

He looked up at Sandy. "Two drinks to compensate for being dumped?"

She slipped into the chair across from him and took the delicate umbrella from her drink. "Matt, I want you to tell me all about the wonders of bamboo and how it became this beautiful little umbrella."

Takeout French Chef

aikiki Beach woke slowly on Saturday mornings, as the
younger beach set trickled in, subdued after the previous
night's celebrations and fireworks. Midway along the beach
was the iconic Royal Hawaiian Hotel, with its charming old-
world Spanish-Moorish architecture. Among Waikiki's high-
rise cookie-cutter hotels, the flamingo-pink Royal Hawaiian
maintained the elegant and staid atmosphere that appealed to
mostly wealthy older travelers and honeymooners, particularly
from Japan.

Wellesley College grads Judy Richardson and Courtney
Winthrop were staying at the hotel, an extravagant graduation
gift from their parents. They spent the first day on the shaded
lounge chairs within the roped-off area for hotel guests only,
separated from the rest of the youthful beach crowd. On the
second day, they stepped over the rope and laid their beach
towels on the sand just above the reach of the surf.

Judy, the more outgoing of the two, had luxurious blond
hair that rained down over her shoulders, while Courtney's
brown hair frizzed in the slightest breeze and touch of humidity.
Judy's bikini invited second and third looks, while Courtney's
more modest one barely attracted a glance. Courtney wasn't

jealous, preferring the more daring and experienced Judy to take the lead when they met men.

They had just lathered each other's backs with their new environment-friendly sunscreen when two tanned young men altered course and headed toward them. "Courtney, a couple of testosterone-laden hunks are veering our way."

"Aloha, ladies, and welcome to the friendly islands," said the more muscular man, with dirty-blond hair.

Judy pushed her Louis Vuitton sunglasses up into her hair to reveal her blue eyes. "Is it that obvious?"

He grinned as he swept back his hair and squatted close to Judy, his shark's tooth dangling over the *shaka* Hawaiian greeting on his T-shirt. "Your skin is as white as Chinese porcelain, and your pink towels are from Royal Hawaiian Hotel. We're here to offer you free surfing lessons."

Judy laughed. "So that's your best pickup line?"

"The surfing lessons come after you join us for drinks so we can get to know each other better. We're free until three o'clock, when my friend must leave for his chef duties and I head to my job with Hawaiian Airlines."

"A pilot no doubt," Judy teased.

"I'm Keith Apina, a flight attendant on Hawaiian Airlines, and my friend is a French chef."

"I'm Jean Martel from Marseille, France."

"We need a minute to discuss your proposal." The men backed a few feet away. "Courtney, sounds interesting. Keith didn't get those muscles from passing out napkins on Hawaiian Airlines, and Jean reminds me of young Jimmy Stewart with a French accent."

"Judy, you're letting their bodies blur your thinking. I can believe the flight attendant line, but a twenty-something French chef in Hawaii is a stretch. I want to ask a couple more questions before we decide."

The women looked toward the men and they stepped forward. Courtney took off her sunglasses and stared at Jean. "I get the French accent but a French chef at, let me guess, twenty-five is impossible."

Jean gazed into Courtney's eyes, his expression enigmatic. "Does it matter?"

"Not really. I suppose you don't really have to be a French chef to give surfing lessons."

Judy cut in. "Let's talk over iced tea."

Jean pointed down the beach. "If you don't mind a short walk, the Moana Surfrider Hotel is a perfect spot for spiced iced tea under a shady banyan tree."

As they followed the men along the beach, Courtney whispered, "I'm still not sure this is a good idea."

"Courtney." Judy's voice held a hint of exasperation. "We agreed that we'd have fun in Hawaii, and that means taking a little risk. What happens here stays here. Your uptight Harvard boyfriend doesn't need to know. Look at those butts."

Courtney adjusted her sunglasses and smiled.

The setting under a massive banyan tree in the courtyard of the historic Moana Surfrider Hotel was a rare remnant of the bygone era of whaling ships, brigs bringing missionaries, and steamships with a few upper-class travelers. The fragrant iced tea came with a pineapple spear in each glass and a dish of taro chips. Judy stirred her drink with the pineapple wedge, then slowly sucked the tea-infused spear. "So, Keith, did you grow up in Hawaii?"

"I was born here when my father was stationed at the Kaneohe Marine Base. We moved a lot, and lived in Guam, Japan, and Germany, and I got the bug for travel and living on a tropical island. The Hawaiian Airlines job gives me both."

"Do you have a favorite place you like to visit?"

"Asia's most exotic, but it's impossible for me to pinpoint just one favorite place. Depends on my mood. The Angkor Wat ruins in Cambodia clearly rank near the top. China has the most sites I like—the Great Wall, the Forbidden City, Guilin, and the terra-cotta warriors in Xian, to name a few."

21

Courtney turned to Jean. "Your French accent suggests you're from France. I wouldn't think Hawaii would be promising for a young French chef."

He grinned. "No competition here! Seriously, I grew up in Marseille and moved here three years ago when I had the opportunity to prepare meals in a fine restaurant and surf—my two great loves."

"Where do women fit into your list of great loves?"

"Of course, every Frenchman adores women." He reached for her hand, but she quickly pulled away.

"Where are the surfboards?" Judy asked.

"Just a few steps away. Are you ready?"

"Yes," Judy quickly replied.

Courtney hesitated, then nodded.

On the side of the police substation, less than a minute along the beach, were racks of surfboards, each with a private padlock. It was a city service to residents and particularly useful for surfers with long surfboards that were difficult to store in small apartments and carry through crowded Waikiki.

The surfing lessons began on the beach, Keith pairing with Judy and Jean with Courtney as they demonstrated the various positions on the longboards. The men showed them where to place their feet on the boards and how to jump quickly to a standing position to ride waves. It looked pretty easy until they reached the waves beyond the barrier reef. With the help of strong hands to push them onto their boards and launch them at the crest of waves, they were able to catch a few waves. Courtney was the first to stand for over five seconds, which they all took as a major milestone. She enjoyed the surfing but had mixed feelings about close physical contact with a stranger. Judy never got the hang of standing on her surfboard, but clearly enjoyed tumbling into Keith's arms.

Returning to the beach, exhilarated from the water and exercise, and pink from the sun, the two women found the men proved as skillful in applying sunscreen lotion. But at three o'clock. both men gave brief hugs and cheek kisses, then jogged away.

"Courtney, that's our ticket to a memorable week. I gave Keith our room number."

"Judy, I'm not sure it's a good idea to give out our hotel room number to someone we barely know. They could be married, as far as we know, and a twenty-nine-year-old with a French accent does not make a French chef. Did you notice how he avoided telling me where he worked?"

"Who cares? You're not going to marry the guy. It's your last chance for a little fling before you marry your rich boring lawyer and lead a very proper life."

"My parents adore Gerald!"

Judy drew a question mark in the sand with her finger. "But do you?"

"I love him and can see a good life ahead, and . . . he adores me."

"So why didn't you invite him to come to Hawaii instead of me?"

Courtney tilted her head as she twisted a few strands of hair. "It's the last chance for an unscripted vacation. So maybe giving out our room number is okay."

"Now you're starting to make sense. Your French chef—or, more likely, short-order cook—is handsome, and he's ready to show you a good time."

"Out there surfing, his hands were all over me."

"Are you complaining or bragging?"

When the anticipated call didn't come the following morning, Judy and Courtney rented surfboards to try it on their own and maybe meet other beachboys. Without helping hands, catching a wave proved much harder, and being pretty conferred no status with the experienced surfers. After Judy got a verbal reprimand for failing to follow surfing etiquette, they abandoned the ocean to explore the shops on Kalakaua Avenue.

Courtney wanted to try the Ono Hawaiian Takeout that Jean had suggested in the International Market Place—a bustling, chaotic mix of over a hundred stalls in the center of Waikiki, where owners hawked tourist goods that ranged from cheap knock-offs to a few genuine articles. They had to ask directions three times before finding the takeout café that Jean had recommended. Their $7.95 kalua pig plate lunches were tasty and came with sides of steamed rice and macaroni salad. As Judy had hoped, the message light was blinking when they entered their hotel room.

"Hi. This is Keith. How about a swim with dolphins tomorrow morning? Jean and I are free until mid-afternoon and would feel privileged to have you two accompany us to the Waianae Coast. The dolphins usually arrive around eight to eight thirty in the morning, so we need to pick you up at the entrance to your hotel at six forty-five. Give me a call if you two are up to a real Hawaiian adventure."

"Courtney, I told you they would call. Imagine swimming with dolphins."

"And sharks," Courtney added as she opened her Oahu travel guidebook. "Let's see where they want to take us. It's pretty far from here on the northwest part of Oahu. Hmm, it says the Waianae area is arid. And tourists should be careful not to leave valuables in their cars and not to stay on the beaches after dark. Doesn't sound safe."

"We'll be going with two muscular men who live here. They're our bodyguards."

"But can we trust these guys taking us to a secluded beach?"

"I'm willing to take a chance."

Judy and Courtney were sitting on the entrance steps when Keith pulled into the roundabout and stopped behind a stretch limousine. A half-dozen Japanese tourists poured out of the limo, and for a few minutes, their heads bobbed as three porters loaded their baggage onto luggage carts. As soon as the limousine pulled away and Keith drove forward, the smartly dressed doorman opened the rear doors for Judy and Courtney. "Keith, where are you and Jean taking our guests today?"

"To the Waianae Coast to swim with dolphins."

Courtney leaned over to the open window. "Can these guys be trusted?"

The doorman laughed. "I wouldn't let them date my sister."

Keith frowned. "Eddie, don't scare our dates. Tell them what nice guys we are."

"Yeah, they're okay. You wouldn't want to go there alone, and these guys will look after you."

A black Mercedes pulled up behind them. "Gotta get back to work. Enjoy your day, ladies."

As they pulled away, Courtney said to Keith, "Why did Eddie say he wouldn't let you date his sister?"

His answer was hardly to the point. "Eddie's an only child. I went to high school with him and we played football together. He went through a rough patch but cleaned himself up and is taking night classes at a community college. We're tight."

Jean handed out coffees and croissants as they took the ramp onto H-1 West, and thirty minutes later they swung north onto Farrington Highway, which hugged the dry, stark Waianae Coast. The uncrowded beaches were inviting, but the homes and small businesses had an unplanned, shabby appearance the two women found unnerving. Vehicle traffic on the Waianae Coast had transitioned from cars and buses in Honolulu to pickups with oversized tires.

Keith pointed to a cluster of shabby houses set back from the Farrington Highway. "That's where Eddie lives with his parents, wife, and two boys in one house, and he commutes every day to Waikiki. Many native Hawaiians live here, as housing costs in Honolulu are prohibitive, and Hawaiian families are often too large to fit into the cramped apartments in Honolulu. The best students attend private schools in Honolulu—Kamehameha if you have Hawaiian blood. The cream of the crop, like Barack Obama, attend Punahou and Iolani, stepping stones to elite universities on the mainland. Sadly, not many Hawaiians make it."

Keith ran through the procedures for swimming with the dolphins. "They are protected, so we wait for them to come to us. Always remember they're wild animals and you're meeting them in their environment." He grinned. "They like pretty women, so they'll want to come close and check you out."

Past Makaha, they parked by a speck of beach bounded by angular basalt boulders. "You'll need these," Jean said as he pulled out two sets of fins, goggles, and snorkels.

"Jean, how did you know our sizes?"

Keith laughed. "Didn't you know Frenchmen are into women's feet?"

Jean shrugged as he picked up the cooler and beach matts and headed down the path to the beach. Waist deep in the surf, Jean and Keith checked the face masks and fins of their dates before giving a thumbs-up. Judy swam alongside Keith, while Courtney paired with Jean a few yards back. A hundred yards offshore, they treaded water for several minutes and scanned the ocean for signs of dolphins. Keith wasn't helpful in telling them that a dolphin's dorsal fin is only visible briefly as it surfaces—but if a fin stays above the surface it's a shark and they should make a dash to shore.

Courtney pulled out her snorkel mouthpiece. "I'm heading back."

Jean grabbed her hand. "Please stay just a few minutes more. I've never seen a shark in this area, and we're safer together."

"Ladies, our entertainment has arrived." Keith pointed north to four dolphins heading directly toward them. For several minutes they dove under their human guests and circled them, then one jumped over Judy, and they headed south.

The four treaded water, watching the dolphins until they disappeared, then they turned toward shore, trying to judge the wave surges and swim between the sharp boulders. Keith, the most experienced swimmer, led the way, but he skinned his knee trying to keep Judy from the rocks, winning him extra attention when they reached the shore. Jean held Courtney's hand tightly as he timed the wave surges and they washed up on the beach unscathed.

Jean laid out a spread of iced tea, mango, pork laulau, and *poke* (diced raw fish). Judy and Courtney were cautious about the raw cubes of tuna until they tasted a morsel, then it was a battle of chopsticks chasing after the slippery delicacies. Keith was the liveliest, with local stories and jokes, while Jean was reserved, choosing his words carefully.

On the drive back to Honolulu, Judy sat in front, Keith and Courtney in the rear. Courtney bit her lip as Jean caressed her hair and kissed her earlobes, his day-old whiskers brushing her sensitive cheeks. She was glad they were far from Boston, and Gerald would never know the feelings streaming through her. By the time they reached the Royal Hawaiian, they had agreed to meet early the following day for a sail around Kaneohe Bay on a friend's sixteen-foot catamaran and lunch on a mysterious island that would magically appear in the afternoon.

After the men dropped them off, each getting meaningful hugs and kisses, they spent the rest of the afternoon around the pool, sunbathing and talking about their morning adventure and what might be coming. There were a few older couples around the pool and two middle-aged men pretending to read thick reports while frequently glancing at them with inviting smiles.

"Judy, don't make eye-contact or they'll come over. One looks old enough to be my father."

"Courtney, we already have our fresh catches for the week."

"I still feel guilty about cheating on Gerald."

"You haven't tied the knot yet. This week, let your heart rule and not Gerald's pedigree. Dogs have pedigrees and Frenchmen have—"

Courtney cut her off. "Enough! I know, but I don't want things to get out of hand. They may be thinking about getting us in bed, and you're not considering *that*, are you?"

Judy giggled, "It never crossed my mind."

"Judy, I want to ask Eddie a few questions about our dates before things go any further."

"What do you think he'll tell you?"

"We're hotel guests, and without Keith and Jean around, he can be more truthful."

"Suit yourself."

After changing, they stopped at the hotel entrance so Courtney could ask Eddie about the men. "Eddie, we're wondering if you could tell us a little more about Keith and Jean."

Eddie paused to adjust his white gloves. "Are you two looking for a serious relationship or a week of fun and no commitments?"

Judy cut in, "Lots of fun with two handsome guys and no commitments."

"Then all you need to know is what they tell you. Excuse me ladies," and he quickly rotated to open the door of a limousine.

"Judy, do you think he's hiding something and maybe they're not as nice as we think?"

Judy dismissed her concern. "You worry too much. Eddie's just protective of his friends. But I'm sure he's also protective of his job. He's not going to send hotel guests off with criminals and jeopardize that."

They browsed among the hotel's pricy shops, ending up at the Mai Tai Bar to have cocktails and watch the sunset. A trio belted out old Hawaiian songs as they strummed a ukulele and two slack-key guitars, and after one drink the two women returned to their room.

The blinking message light wasn't from the men but Courtney's mother. "I really don't want to call her back, as Mom's so noisy, and anyway, it's after midnight on the East Coast."

"So, don't."

Moments later, the phone rang, and Courtney waited until the fourth ring. "Hello, Mom. You're up very late."

"Sweety, I couldn't sleep. I just wanted to make sure you and Judy are okay."

"We're having a good time. Took a tour to see dolphins today, and we'll go out on a catamaran tomorrow."

"Make sure you go with a reputable tour group recommended by the hotel. I want you to be safe."

"Yes, they're recommended by the hotel."

"Good. Maybe, your dad and I will try the same tour company when we meet you in Hawaii next Saturday. Make sure to call Gerald tomorrow, as you know how much he misses you. Be careful of the beachboys who might take advantage of you."

"Ah, we're just fine. You don't have to worry. I better not keep you up. It's so late there. Luv ya."

Courtney hung up and flopped back on the bed and crossed her arms over her chest.

"Courtney, don't let your mom ruin our week of freedom. You can go back to being straitlaced when they arrive next weekend and I'm gone."

"I know, but Mom makes me feel so guilty."

"Courtney, save your guilt until after I leave. Good night."

They left at eight o'clock and took the Likelike Highway over the Pali to Kaneohe Bay. Near the peak of the Ko'olau

Mountains, they passed through the half-mile Wilson Tunnel, emerging into sweeping views of the ocean and Kaneohe Bay, its turquoise-blue water mottled with white splotches.

"Keith, what are those white spots in the bay?" asked Judy.

"Submerged coral reefs and sandbars. Our destination is *Ahu O Laka*, also called the Sand Bar, which, hopefully, will appear at low tide."

They zigzagged down the steep windward side of the Ko'olau Mountains to the small dock at the edge of Kaneohe Bay, where Keith's friend kept a sixteen-foot catamaran. Jean secured the ice chest to the boat, then the four of them launched the catamaran, and Keith immediately hoisted the sail. "Breeze is already good for sailing, so this afternoon, when the wind whips up, we'll have some fast sailing," he said.

"Mind if I take the rudder?"

"Go ahead, Courtney. Now head in that direction, and I'll tell you when to adjust course."

Courtney didn't listen, but tacked at an angle that doubled the speed, and when she skillfully came about, Keith hollered into the wind, "Where did you learn to sail like that?"

"My grandfather raced small yachts, and I joined him every chance I could, and I belonged to a sailing club in college."

They circled the bay, waiting for the sandbar to appear, and were briefly joined by two dolphins swimming alongside. At Pyramid Rock, Jean took the helm and demonstrated his sailing skills, skipping across breaking waves at the entrance to the bay, and as the sandbar began to appear, he brought the catamaran in for a smooth landing.

"So, Jean, you didn't spend all your time learning to be a French chef," Courtney teased.

"Both require skillful use of the hands and exact timing," he replied as he unfastened the ice chest.

The sandbar, above the surface only at low tide, wasn't much to look at. But the views of the Ko'olaus were even better than from the Mokulua Islands, and the distance softened the man-made features to give a more pristine view.

Jean served fresh ahi sashimi as an appetizer with a fruity chenin blanc, followed by crispy huli huli chicken and avocado salad. Jean offered the toast. "Waikiki Beach brought us together. We must embrace the moment, for today will never return." After lunch, Keith brought out a foam-rubber ball for a game of touch football that turned into full body contact in the shallow water. Later, as they dried in the sun, Judy flipped off her top before lying on her stomach so Keith could apply lotion, while Courtney lay facedown before letting Jean unfasten her top.

The women dozed during the drive back to Waikiki Beach, Judy's hand resting on Keith's thigh, and Courtney's head on Jean's shoulder. Only Keith was available that evening, so Courtney declined the invitation to dine with Judy and Keith.

For the women, every day was a new adventure, always ending in mid-afternoon, when Jean or both men left for work. They hiked along trails fragrant with the scents of wild ginger, guava, and lilikoi, and swam below water falls in cool jade pools. High in the Ko'olaus, they explored thick groves of towering bamboo and listened to the melodious song of the white-rumped shama.

On their last night together, before Judy's flight to Boston and Courtney's parents' arrival, they dined on Jean's yacht moored in the harbor in front of the Ilikai Hotel—a welcome treat, as Jean normally worked on Friday nights.

He had purchased the forty-three-year-old, teak-paneled yacht at half the price of a Waikiki condo, and it came with a coveted slip in the Ala Wai Yacht Harbor. The meal began with sashimi and a sauvignon blanc from the Loire Valley, followed by braised prawns in a garlic-wine sauce, a pilaf of wild rice, and lilikoi-infused vinaigrette, drizzled on vine-ripened local tomatoes. At seven forty-four Jean raised his wine glass to propose a toast. "Ladies, may your lives be filled with romances that light up the sky." As they clinked their glasses, the Friday-night fireworks commenced from behind the Hilton Hawaiian Village, decorating the sky with red, white, and blue sparkles and loud booms.

Judy didn't return to the Royal Hawaiian with Courtney, promising to reappearance the next morning in time to pack before checkout at eleven. Courtney declined Jean's invitation to stay overnight on his yacht, but lingered on the steps of her hotel, their arms entwined, passionately kissing. The carefree week had come to an end, and Courtney knew there would never be another such week for her. Her eyes glassy, she told Jean not to try and contact her.

Judy returned at nine twenty-five the following morning, glowing from the night with Keith and full of plans to return soon. After packing, Judy and Courtney took a short walk along Waikiki Beach and reminisced about the week and the men who made it memorable. Courtney gave an unconvincing no when Judy asked if she was having second thoughts about marrying Gerald.

At the airport, they were surprised when Keith and Jean showed up with leis. "How did you know which flight I was on?" Judy asked as Keith embraced her and draped a lei around her neck..

"Perks of working for an airline."

Jean also gave Courtney a lei and a kiss. "Thank you, but you didn't have to. I'm not leaving for another week."

"This is the last time I'll see you, unless you change your mind."

"I'll be busy with my parents, but I'll never forget this week."

After Judy boarded her flight, Courtney told the men to leave before her parents arrived. Jean embraced her, holding her against his hard chest. "Gerald's a lucky man. You know where my yacht is moored if things don't work out as planned." A lingering kiss, then he turned away.

Courtney wiped a tear as she watched to see if Jean would look back for a final wave, but he didn't. She felt drained and walked aimlessly among the airport shops, her thoughts flipping back and forth between her romantic feelings toward Jean and deciding what she would reveal to her nosy mother. She feared her uncanny mother would ferret out the truth about her fling with another man just weeks before her engagement party with Gerald. Gerald had everything her mother wanted for her—a Harvard degree, blue-blood linage dating back two centuries, a generous inheritance, and charm that compensated for his flashes of arrogance. The key would be keeping the focus on her parent's twenty-fifth wedding anniversary, the main reason for their coming to Hawaii. The forty-minute flight delay gave her enough time to compose herself and go over what she would tell them.

Her parents came off the flight with the first-class passengers and overdressed for Hawaii. "Aloha," Courtney called in a cheery voice as she hurried to them with a lei for her father and two for her mother.

"Honey, you didn't have to buy me two leis."

"Ah, the lei salesperson gave me an extra one."

"You must have really charmed him."

"I did."

"I can't wait to hear all about your week. Judy's mom told me Judy was having a splendid time with a flight attendant with Hawaiian Airlines, but nothing serious. Hope you weren't bored with Judy spending so much time with someone else."

"How could anyone get bored in beautiful Hawaii?"

They took a limousine to the Royal Hawaiian Hotel. Courtney suggested that she stay in a separate room, but her mother insisted she join them in the two-bedroom suite. She kept the conversation focused on things they would do in Hawaii and away from details about her week. After changing into casual clothes, she took them to the Mai Tai Bar for sunset drinks.

"Mom, I recommend the fruity Mai Tai with rum, grenadine, and pineapple juice."

"You order, sweety."

When the drinks arrived, Courtney took the tiny decorative umbrella from hers and stuck it into the bun at the back of her mother's hair. "Now you look like a local Hawaiian princess."

Her mother took a sip, then held the glass hovering near her lips as she stared into her daughter's eyes. "Judy's mom told me a young man was flirting with you. Was he your tour guide?"

"Yes, a nice young man with a French accent who claimed to be a French chef. I'm sure he's French, but a French chef he's not. Nothing serious, just a friendly guide."

"Did you tell him you were about to become engaged to Gerald?"

"Yes, of course."

"What would bring a French chef all the way to Hawaii?"

"He loves surfing. Anyway, he was most helpful in giving us tips on things to see."

A familiar irritating smile appeared on her mother's face. "Why wouldn't a young man want to be helpful to a rich girl staying at the Royal Hawaiian Hotel?"

"I'm not rich. You are!"

"Yes, but you're about to marry into money, and eventually there'll be an inheritance." Her mother reached across the table and patted her hand. "Maybe we'll all have to try a French meal while we're in Hawaii. Is his restaurant near?"

"He didn't tell me where he works, because then I'd find out that he's not a French chef."

"I was a little concerned that some suave beachboy might take advantage of you."

"I'm old enough to know what I'm doing."
Pat's eyes narrowed. "Hawaii's a romantic and seductive place."

Her father had booked several tours, including a circle island helicopter flight over Diamond Head crater, Hanauma Bay, the Pali Cliffs and hidden waterfalls, followed by a luxury dinner cruise and full day at the Polynesian Cultural Center. Courtney enjoyed the deluxe tours, but after the past week, she felt she was now in a bubble, isolated from the real Hawaii. In the mornings before they left on the day's tour, Courtney scanned the beach for Jean, and again in the late afternoons when they returned. She wanted to see him walking the beach and maybe wave from a distance—maybe blow him a kiss.

The seventh day was unplanned, as her parents wanted to stroll through Waikiki Beach the way they had on their honeymoon twenty-five years earlier. Courtney suggested showing them parts of Waikiki Beach popular with locals, and her mom thought that would be fun. They walked as far as Ala Wai Yacht Harbor, stopping for a local breakfast in the Harbor Pub, where locals and the yacht crowd gathered. The restaurant showed its age, as did their waitress, yet she gave excellent service, and the food was above average. As they walked past Jean's yacht, Courtney looked for any movement inside, but there was none.

They strolled back toward Diamond Head, stopping at several stores, including one of the ubiquitous ABC convenience stories, ending at noon in the International Market Place. Her parents remembered shopping among the clutter of tiny stalls and were disappointed to discover that the thatched treehouse in the large banyan tree was gone. Courtney suggested they eat at a local favorite takeout café she had discovered, not mentioning that Jean had recommended it. She guided them to the small food court with wobbly tables and chairs. The Ono Hawaiian Takeout had a long line in front of the order window.

"Darling, we don't know the local food, so you order for us. Your dad and I need to rest our feet."

Courtney joined the line of well-dressed professionals and locals in *slippahs* (flip-flops) and T-shirts. As she moved closer to the window, she spotted the sign: Chef Jean Martel Serving from 12 to 2 Today. At the pickup window stood Jean, engaged in a lively conversation with a muscular Hawaiian man. *So, this is where French Chef Jean works.* She quickly turned away.

"Mom, the line is moving too slowly, and I don't really feel like Hawaiian food. So, let's go back to the hotel for lunch."

"I was thinking the same thing."

For their twenty-fifth anniversary dinner, her father had pulled strings to get reservations at the exclusive, members-only Kipuka 888. Courtney had suggested that her parents celebrate alone, but her mother insisted they make the special evening a family affair.

They rode a koa-paneled elevator to the penthouse restaurant, where they were greeted by the tuxedoed maître d'. "Mr. and Mrs. Winthrop, we are most pleased that you and your daughter have chosen to dine with us this evening. We have a window table reserved for you that will afford you a view of the ocean and the evening fireworks."

Each table had a spray of orchids in a delicate Chinese vase, and inside the black leather folders, embossed in gold, were menus printed on parchment—the stratospheric prices listed on only her father's menu.

For starters, they ordered Sydney rock oysters, flown in that day, paired with an Australian Hunter Valley Sémillon. Courtney followed her mother's choice of fresh opakapaka in a ginger-infused white wine sauce and a pilaf of jasmine rice with black truffle flakes. Her father ordered the New Zealand rack of lamb in a lilikoi-laced cabernet sauce.

Later, after the exquisite dinner and fireworks, the gold-and-crystal dessert trolly was wheeled to their table. The centerpiece on top was an anniversary cake with their names across the top. The pastry chef had secured sculptured dolphins around the side of the cake, with orchids to highlight their names.

"Henry, you continue to surprise me even after twenty-five years of marriage."

"Pat, I'm surprised too. I didn't tell them it was our twenty-fifth anniversary."

She reached across and took his hand. "I love you now more than when I married you."

As they shared a slice of their anniversary cake, the chef entered, wearing a crisp white uniform, his mushroom-shaped hat adding a foot to his six-foot height. He moved slowly among the tables, exchanging a few words with diners at every table. At the adjacent table, they heard him assure the governor that he was available as head chef at the annual governor's ball. The governor shook his hand and complimented him for volunteering at small eateries in Waikiki to boost local interest.

Courtney was gazing out the floor-to-ceiling windows when he stopped at their table. "Mr. and Mrs. Winthrop, I wanted to personally thank you for having your twenty-fifth anniversary dinner at Kipuke 888. I believe you came from Boston, a city of exceptional food. I hope your meal met with your high standards."

"Pat and I were just saying that we've never had a better meal in Boston or, for that matter, anywhere."

Courtney turned from the window and gasped, putting her fingers to her lips.

"Good evening, Courtney. You were right. You have a striking resemblance to your mother."

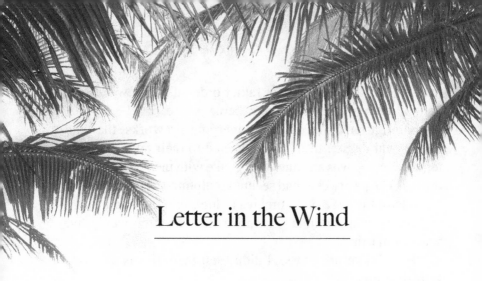

Letter in the Wind

*A*lan Fletcher stepped onto the balcony of his room in the Hilton Hawaiian Village and gazed over palm-tree-studded Waikiki Beach, its sand brushed golden in the morning sun. He was glad he had booked an extra week after the four-day conference. The combination of the special conference room rate and his Hilton points had reduced the daily rate by fifty-five percent.

The beach and multi-hued azure water were too enticing for him to remain holed up in his room finalizing his conference speech, so fifteen minutes later, he strolled across the broad beach and spread out his towel. He was about to smear on some SPF 30 lotion when a gust of wind sent beach mats and inflatable toys tumbling across the sand. A sheet of white paper and three green bills twisted in the air and landed a few feet away. He sprang to his feet and picked up the $100 bills and letter and looked back for the owner. No one was looking his way, so he brushed the sand from the letter and read it.

Dear Zoe,
    I trusted you to remain on the pill and you didn't. Now you're pregnant. You know I'm not ready to settle down and have children—and maybe never

will be. Enclosed is $300 for an abortion. I know you don't agree, but to me it's the best solution. Jack and I are leaving tomorrow on a three-month backpacking trip through the Alps. Do what's best for both of us.
Sincerely,
Brandon

Alan scowled. *What a scumbag.* He continued his search for a young woman who might be Zoe but saw only couples and children. Then, turning his gaze to the ocean, he spotted several possibilities. A redhead caught his attention as she stood knee-deep in the surf looking out to sea, her arms gesturing as if she were talking to someone. He moved closer and called out, "Zoe."

She turned, a bewildered look on her face. She didn't appear pregnant.

"Are you Zoe?"

"Yes. How do you know my name?"

"It's on the letter I picked up on the beach along with three one-hundred-dollar bills."

She scowled. "Damn him!"

"Despicable bastard! I read the letter."

"Were you snooping in my things?"

"No . . . a gust of wind blew them to me."

"Thanks. I suppose a lot of people would keep the money. How can I repay you?"

Alan scratched his day-old whiskers. "A drink over there at the Hau Tree Bar would be nice."

"I can't drink alcohol."

"I know. You've got a baby onboard."

She smiled weakly. "I guess we should introduce ourselves."

"Alan Fletcher from Raleigh, North Carolina."

She took his hand. "Zoe Webb. I just moved here last month from Santa Cruz, California."

He tried not to stare at the slender figure—one that would look good in any swimsuit. She had a high nose, wide-set green eyes accented by auburn eyebrows, and smallish breasts. He guessed her age between twenty-five and thirty. The letter was proof that she didn't have a boyfriend.

The beachside bar had shaded tables and views of the beach and ocean. Zoe ordered a lemonade and Alan a local Longboard. She studied him as she pulled the green scrunchie from her ponytail, smoothed her hair, and replaced the silky band. Even though he didn't have a tan, she liked what she saw—a handful of hair on his chest, firm abs, and light-brown hair matching eyes that were slightly enlarged by his frameless glasses. He was a couple inches taller than her five eight.

"Here on vacation or business?"

"Conference plus a few extra days to see sights."

"What's the theme of the conference?"

"Beyond Fossil Fuels. The focus is on options for transitioning to renewable energy to reduce the rate of climate change. I'm giving a talk on natural gas as a substitute for coal to generate electricity—what I call a transitional place-holder until renewables can fill the gap between supply and demand."

"What a coincidence. At UC Santa Cruz, I was studying oceanography and the rate of ocean temperature increases resulting from climate change. A lot of computer modeling stuff, but now my education is on hold until after the baby comes and I sort out the issues of money and my parents. My parents are climate change deniers and will support only practical studies like nursing," she added drily.

"What brought you to Hawaii?

"I needed to get away from my parents, who would never accept my getting pregnant out of wedlock, and I was offered a job as an assistant lab technician in the Hawaii State Aquatic Resources Division. The pay is low, but they provide health coverage that includes maternity leave."

"If you're interested, I might be able to get you into the conference at a student rate."

"I'm pretty sure my boss would give me time off for the conference, given its topic, but I'm on a really tight budget."

"Maybe I can get the organizers to waive the fee. Then would you come?"

"I'd love to come if that can be arranged and it's not too much trouble. If you'll give me your number, I'll call you later today, and you can let me know if my registration fees can be waived."

They chatted for the next hour and a half, revealing thumbnail sketches of their lives and important events. Zoe had grown up in Santa Cruz, not far from the beach, and her life was centered around ocean and beach activities. She had spent a summer with her university advisor in the Gulf of California, collecting data on the distribution of corals, and she'd met Brandon in La Paz, where their fateful romance blossomed.

Alan had grown up in historic Alexandria, Virginia. He'd loved exploring the collections in the Smithsonian Museums in the National Mall and the National Geographic building. He had earned degrees from Georgetown and Johns Hopkins Universities and was married for three years until he discovered his wife still had an intimate relationship with a previous boyfriend. Marriage counseling revealed her inability to end the extramarital affair, and they divorced. The divorce was amicable, and Alan admitted he took part of the blame for not giving enough attention to his marriage while he was in grad school.

Zoe took the slice of lemon from her drink and sucked it as she eyed him. "A good-looking professor should have little problem finding eligible women to date at your university."

"Thanks for the compliment. But I'm only an assistant professor, and becoming a full professor is a decade away. As for dating, faculty-student dating is frowned on and strictly forbidden for anyone in my department. I admit to occasionally imagining a date with an attractive graduate student, but that's as far as it goes."

Before they parted, he agreed to find out if he could get her a fee waiver as a student and his guest and would let her know when she called in the evening.

Alan knew there wouldn't be a fee waiver, and he paid the $45 student registration fee. When Zoe called, he told her she was registered at the conference, and all she needed to do was to fill out personal details at the registration desk in the morning. His intentions were not entirely innocent, as he looked forward to deepening the friendship at the luncheons and banquet.

He was waiting next to the registration desk when Zoe arrived the following morning wearing a fashionable, if staid, blue business suit with a white silk blouse. This was over-dressed for Hawaii. Few people who lived there, men or women, wore suits, except for the most formal business situations, but she would turn heads at the conference. After Zoe completed registration, they strolled over to the speakers' room and shared coffee and croissants.

"Alan, my registration indicated the student fee was paid. You didn't need to do that."

"It's my gift to you. I was a struggling student once."

"Thanks, I really appreciate that." She touched his forearm. He wasn't sure if she meant it as a caress or a simple pat.

They attended different sessions during the morning, making plans to sit together at the luncheon. But when they entered the room Alan was escorted to the speakers' table, and Zoe was left to find a seat with the other attendees. He watched as a man in a linen suit pulled out a chair so she could sit on his right, then graciously shook her hand and presented his business card. Alan, couldn't concentrate on his meal knowing that an interloper was chatting with the woman he had planned to have sitting at his side. After the luncheon, Alan rose quickly to go to Zoe but was distracted by a friend right away, and when he looked back, she was gone. It was unsettling. He had been planning to ask her to accompany him to the governor's banquet.

Alan didn't like giving his talk immediately after luncheon because attendance was usually low, as people lingered to talk with new acquaintances and colleagues. The room that he was speaking in was only half-full, and people trickled in throughout his talk. He didn't notice when Zoe arrived during his talk, only that she wasn't there when he was introduced and he began speaking. He spotted her and the mystery man at the conclusion of his talk, but again, she was gone by the time he finished meeting people and exchanging cards. He was disappointed that she had so quickly found someone else to escort her around.

After the conclusion of the last afternoon session, Alan was talking to the cochairman of the conference and his wife, when he spotted Zoe entering the room in the company of the man she had met at the luncheon. "Dr. Fletcher, I want you to meet Alberto Pasolini. He has kindly taken me under his wing and introduced me to some useful contacts for the future."

Alberto was immaculately dressed; beneath the off-white linen sport jacket, he wore a Tori Richard aloha shirt, open at the neck to reveal a heavy gold cross nestled in curly chest hair. With his swarthy face and neatly trimmed beard, he had a slight resemblance to the opera singer Luciano Pavarotti. "Dr. Fletcher, I enjoyed your talk on the role of natural gas as a transition fuel." His handshake was firm—too firm—as the two eyed each other.

"Alberto is taking me to the governor's reception and banquet. Alberto, would you mind if Dr. Fletcher joins us?"

"Would love to have the professor come, but it's by invitation only, and I can only bring one guest."

"I fully understand," Alan replied with a touch of sarcasm. He was not interested in spending the evening competing for Zoe's attention, and he didn't need mention what seemed obvious to him—all speakers had invitations to the governor's reception and banquet.

Alan decided to skip the reception and banquet; he didn't want to watch Alberto fawning over Zoe. He took a leisurely stroll along the beach, past Fort DeRussy Beach Park, stopping to catch the sunset and watch two turtles in front of the Outrigger Reef Hotel. Then he continued, finally ducking into a noisy beach bar for a beer and mahimahi sandwich. He pushed Zoe from his mind, reflecting on the talk he'd given and the new professional contacts.

He was most pleased to have met two professors from Tsinghua University, in Beijing—China's MIT—and received an invitation to visit their university and give a series of lectures. He would need to pay for his flight, but all costs within China would be paid by his hosts, and they promised to show him sights, such as the Great Wall of China and the Forbidden City.

The reception and banquet were over when he returned to the Hilton Hawaiian Village, the beach deserted, except for a couple standing near the water's edge. He thought about returning to the beach the next day at the exact time and spot where the letter and money had landed. Although not a believer in serendipity, it had seemed a most fortuitous encounter with an alluring young woman. He had not anticipated a handsome Italian swooping in and disrupting his plans to spend more time with Zoe. Yet he had just met her the previous day and had no claim to her time. Back in his room, he gazed out over Waikiki Beach, closed the curtain, and crawled into bed.

He woke early, still not having adjusted to the six-hour time difference, and took a jog around the yacht harbor and along the beach, then he returned for a shower before dressing for the conference. The speaker's hospitality room was open to the speakers only on the day of their talks, so he walked over to the Starbucks in the lobby of Kalia Tower, where he met another conference attendee, taking his mind off of Zoe. He knew he would see Zoe in the first morning session, as it was the talk she had marked with two stars. He sat near the back so he could see her when she came in, but she didn't show up. He was perplexed as to why she would skip the session she most wanted to attend. Maybe, after the first day of talks, she had decided they weren't that interestingly, and she had more immediate things on her mind, with a baby on the way. He found himself hoping that was all it was.

As he left the luncheon for the afternoon session, he spotted Alberto with another young woman hanging on his arm. "Alberto, have you seen Zoe today?"

He paused, cocking his head toward Alan. "Maybe she found the conference overwhelming. You know, she's rather naïve and out of her depth here." He quickly turned back to his new companion. "Ronda, we don't want to miss the opening to the next session."

Alberto's dismissive comments about Zoe set off alarm bells in Alan's head. Something had surely gone wrong, and he was going to find out what it was. He hurried over to the registration desk, hoping she had checked the box indicating her address was public, and she had. The taxi dropped him off in front of a rundown, three-story apartment building in Moiliili, a few blocks beyond the Ala Wai Canal. He knocked several times, but there was no answer. Then he called out, "Zoe, it's me, Alan Fletcher. I came to see if you're okay."

"I don't want to talk to anyone!" came an anguished reply.

"I'm not leaving until you open the door. I'm here to help."

Alan stood by the door for ten minutes, then called out again that he wasn't leaving, and sat on the concrete floor, his back against the wall. Another ten minutes, then a rattling of the safety chain, and the door opened enough for Alan to see she was a mess—bloodshot eyes, puffy cheeks, and tangled hair drooping down to her chin.

"Zoe, what happened?"

"You want something from me, just like Alberto. Just leave me alone. Go back to the conference?"

"Look, Zoe, I admit to being attracted to you, and was hoping the feelings might be mutual. I promise I would never do anything to hurt you."

"Are you thinking about forcing me into bed like Alberto?"

"Please don't think that way. I'm here to help you, and anything more is entirely up to you."

The door opened wider, and Alan stood and brushed his hands off. He smiled. "That concrete is hard on my butt."

"You can come in." Zoe backed away from the door as he pushed it open and stepped inside. She didn't pull away as he took her into his arms, letting her head rest against his shoulder. "Alberto is a beast," she said. "He just wanted sex."

"Did he hurt you?"

"He put his hand up my dress and I kicked him. He dragged me to the door and threw me out of his room so hard I fell and hit my head on the wall." She pulled back her hair to show the bruise.

"That *son of a bitch*. Did you report him?"

"No. I can't prove it. There's no physical evidence, and I voluntarily went to his room. With no proof, what would the authorities do? Alberto seemed genuinely interested in helping me. He told me he had a folder full of useful contacts in his room and even knew the president of a foundation that might provide a scholarship for my university studies. I should have realized it was too good to be true."

"Not all men are like Alberto. Have you eaten anything?"

"Some crackers and peanut butter."

"Get dressed. We'll go out and get something in your stomach."

She nodded. "I need a few minutes to shower and change."

"Take your time. I have all day."

Forty-five minutes later Alan watched with amusement as she downed a large bowl of Vietnamese pho noodle soup with beef, fresh basil leaves, lemon, and bean sprouts. When she pushed the bowl away, she licked her lips. "That was delicious."

"Do you feel like returning to the conference with me?"

"No. I can't bear the thought of seeing Alberto's face. You go without me."

"I would much rather stay with you, unless you want me to leave. How about seeing a few sights together? You can be my guide."

Zoe studied Alan's face. "I'd like that."

The next morning, they drove to the North Shore and spent the day exploring the mostly deserted beaches along the windward side of Oahu, stopping for lunch of garlic shrimp at Giovanni's Aloha Shrimp Truck, in Kahuku. Their pace was unhurried, as they held hands and strolled along beaches looking for seashells, avoiding the occasional purple Portuguese man-of-war. They spent a half-hour watching a green sea turtle use his flippers to move sluggishly up onto the beach.

Each evening, they planned the following day's activities, and grew closer. She introduced him to local favorites—Spam *musubi*, chicken *katsu*, laulau (tender pork wrapped in ti leaves and steamed), kalua pig, ahi sashimi, and poi (steamed taro root pounded to a smooth paste). On the fourth evening, Zoe leaned in to give Alan the first serious kiss on the lips, and he responded. Each night, he struggled to fall asleep, his arms hugging a pillow as he thought about her.

Days seemed to speed up, with each one a reminder of how soon they would part. On the last night before Alan's return to California, they had drinks and pupus on an outdoor terrace and watched the nightly hula performance. Alan was surprised when Zoe asked to go to his room to watch the lights over Waikiki, telling him she didn't want what happened with Alberto to steal away her trust in men. They sat together holding hands on his balcony, watching the play of lights on the surf as the moon rose above Diamond Head. It was after midnight when they drove back to her apartment and clung together at her door until Zoe finally pulled away.

"Alan, I want to see you off at the airport tomorrow."

"Zoe, I'm falling in love with you."

"I hope so."

The next morning, she called Alan to tell him she was staying in bed and wouldn't see him off at the airport. She assured Alan that it was just morning sickness and that she'd call him in Berkeley, where he had a stopover for two days to meet scientists at UC Berkeley and the Lawrence Livermore Laboratory.

As soon as he arrived at his hotel in Berkeley, he called Zoe but got no answer. Then called her office. Her boss was also concerned, because she hadn't come to work or called in sick. He was worried but tried to be optimistic, telling himself she would call him that evening and say she was fine. He jumped when his cell phone rang. Recognizing the Hawaii area code, he quickly answered. "Hello, Alan Fletcher speaking."

"This is Dr. Jay Shibuya, at Straub Hospital. Ms. Zoe Webb gave you as the emergency contact when she was admitted six hours ago."

"Is she okay?"

"Yes, but she had a close call. Ms. Webb had a softball-sized tumor that burst and she was within an hour of dying when she arrived by ambulance. We were able to remove the tumor but could not save her pregnancy. We believe the tumor is benign, but we won't know for sure until we get the lab results."

"Can I speak to her?"

"She's sedated and asleep but should be able to talk to you tomorrow. She needs emotional support from loved ones."

"I'll catch a flight and be there tomorrow."

"I was hoping you'd say that."

Alan stepped from his taxi at two twenty-three p.m., handed the driver three twenties, and rushed into Straub Hospital without waiting for his change. The attentive receptionist checked with Zoe's physician then directed him to the open door to her room. She was on her side looking toward the window.

"Zoe," he said softly. "I came as soon as I could get on a flight."

"I lost my baby," she sobbed.

"I know. Dr. Shibuya told me the location of the tumor made it impossible to save both you and the baby. I should have listened to my heart and stayed longer."

She rolled over to face him. "I didn't want to call you. You have your life to live and it was just a one-week fling in Hawaii, huh?"

He pulled a chair close to her bed. "Zoe, when I picked up that letter on the beach and read it, I trembled, as if something momentous was about to happen, and it did." He slid from the floor onto his knees and took her hand. "I'm not very good at this."

She gazed into his eyes. "Yes, you are."

Under the Banyan

*K*enny Choi gazed out the window of the military transport as it descended through the clouds. The sight of the emerald tropical island made his heart race. Growing up in Chicago, he'd heard stories from his uncle about the beauty of Hawaii and the aloha spirit. His degree in Asian Studies did not lead to a job in his chosen field, until an army recruiter told him they needed people with his skills. He enlisted as a US Army Intelligence Officer, and after boot camp he was sent to Hawaii for four months of advanced training before his transfer to Seoul, Korea.

On his first twenty-four-hour leave, Kenny left his army buddies on Hotel Street, famous for its raunchy bars and prostitutes, and headed for Waikiki Beach. The main street, Kalakaua Avenue, was full of tourists and the stores that welcomed their dollars in the aloha spirit. In the middle of Waikiki, he discovered the International Market Place, with its clutter of tiny stalls selling cheap tourist goods in a distinctly Asian atmosphere. Near the entrance was a thatched bamboo hut perched on the limbs of a giant banyan tree. He stepped inside to get a closer look at the fairy-tale treehouse that could have been snatched from the pages of his favorite childhood novel, *The Swiss Family Robinson*. He studied the treehouse, moving closer beneath its expanse of limbs that provided shade to a dozen small stalls. He was about to continue into the maze of stalls, when he caught sight of a beautiful Asian woman kneeling at the base of the banyan, her fingers deftly stringing blossoms on a string. Her jet-black hair, accented by a scarlet hibiscus flower over her left ear, tumbled to her waist. He moved closer, and she looked up, her wide-set eyes locking on him as she gave him a welcoming smile.

"You wan' buy fresh flower lei?"

"Ah . . . yes . . . of course," he said as he stood breathless, taking in her beauty.

"You military?"

"Yes, I'm here taking a short course on Chinese and Korean culture." There was something about her. "May I ask if you're from Korea?"

"I born in Seoul, but come America when Communists invade South Korea in 1950. Without brave American soldiers, there would be no freedom in South Korea today." She wiped a tear from her cheek, then stood, taking a white plumeria lei from her display and looping it around his neck and giving him a feathery-light kiss on his cheek. He was mesmerized by the petite woman who barely reached his chin.

"How much is the lei?" He would have paid anything she asked.

"No charge. You good military man."

"Thank you. I'm Kenny Choi from Chicago."

"My name Jin Lee, but most people call me Jinny. Have wonderful stay Hawaii." She turned away, kneeling next to her basket of flowers, and continued stringing the delicate petals as she hummed a melody that he didn't recognize but that reminded him of Mozart. He remained transfixed, watching her until she looked up. "Why you look at me so much?"

"I was thinking that I'd like to take you to lunch."

"You kind man, but I must stay at my stand."

Ten minutes later, he reappeared with two Korean plate lunches and tea. When he offered her one, she hesitated, then she took it with both hands and bowed her head. "Very kind. Thank you." They had little time to talk as tourists kept pausing to enquire about her leis.

A family of three stopped to look at the display. "Honey, I would like a lei, if it's not too expensive."

"How much do they cost?" Her husband's tone was demanding, but Jinny showed no reaction to it as she told him the prices. He opted for the cheapest lei and handed it to his wife.

"Daddy, I want one too."

He frowned at his preteen daughter. "Christina, I told you before we left the hotel not to ask for anything frivolous."

Jinny picked a matching lei and looped it over the child's head.

"Didn't you hear me tell my daughter we're not buying another lei?"

Jinny smiled and nodded. "My gift to pretty keiki."

The girl shrieked and hugged Jinny, then skipped alongside her parents as they walked off.

As Jinny returned to eating her barbecue beef plate lunch, Kenny said, "You can't make any profit giving away leis."

"I give aloha, and that means love. Keiki never forget gift and maybe return someday with her family. I get back more than I give." She held up a morsel of her lunch with chopsticks, and grinned. "I give you one-dollar lei, and you give me three-dollar lunch."

Kenny laughed. "Umm, are you married?"

"Why you ask personal question?"

"I was thinking, if you weren't married, maybe you'd accept my invitation to dinner."

Jinny studied his face. "No time. I close late every night, except Sunday, when I close at six."

"I'll meet you here next Sunday at six, okay?"

He scouted the Waikiki restaurants for one nearby with a view of the ocean. He decided on the seaside restaurant at the Moana Hotel, only a three-minute walk from the International Market Place. Jinny complained that it was too expensive, but it wasn't hard to see she was thrilled to be treated with such beautiful elegance. Over their seafood dinner they shared stories that filled in the mosaic of their lives. Jinny was attentive, frequently laughing when he said something funny.

They didn't kiss until their third evening together. At every opportunity, Kenny returned to meet Jinny under the banyan tree, always bringing two cups of tea. He was tall for a Korean-American and had a smile that Jinny said made him more *resistible* when he laughed.

"I hope you mean *irresistible*," he said. Born to Korean immigrant parents, he'd grown up in two worlds—traditional Korean at home and an all-American boy with his mostly Caucasian friends at school and socializing. Kenny had wanted to fit in with his American friends, until he reached college, where he decided to major in Asian Studies and fell in love with a Korean-American girl. His passion for Korean culture was sustained, but not his first romance.

Jinny's story couldn't have been more different. She grew up in Seoul under Japanese occupation, when Korean women and teens were not safe on the streets after dark, and even during the day, females were accosted by Japanese soldiers. Jinny wore no makeup, dressed in shabby clothes, and concealed her long hair under a floppy hat that covered part of her face. She escaped to America at the end of the Second World

53

War and was befriended by a Hawaiian woman who taught her the craft and art of lei making.

Their first kiss came at twilight on Waikiki Beach, behind the Moana Hotel. There were many more to follow. Jinny grew more fearful as their romance blossomed—and his departure grew closer. The Korean conflict was still in full swing when Kenny boarded his ship for Korea. He had spent the last night at her small apartment, where they made love passionately, laced with Jinny's tears that he would never return. She clung to the taxi door until the driver said, "Mister, either tell the missus to let go or get out. I can't wait all day."

"Jinny, I promise to return and marry you." She waved as the taxi pulled away then stood long after he was gone. A passerby asked if she was okay.

"I don't know." She turned away.

Now Kenny pressed his face to the window as the islands came into view, the early morning sun brushing gold across the crest of the Ko'olaus. His two-year assignment in Seoul in the '50s had turned into thirty-seven hard years in North Korea. It was Jinny's promise to wait for him that kept a thin thread of hope alive. Even during his darkest hours in brutal captivity, when he considered suicide, the memory of her face remained clear. He knew such promises were made by thousands of women before their loved ones left for war, but surely no woman would wait this long. Many men would never return, and women moved on with their lives. After so long, Kenny was prepared to find that Jinny had married and probably would have grown children. A thousand times he had thought through what he would find in Hawaii, and he was sure he was prepared to wish her the best when he discovered she was married. Still, she would remember him, and he needed to let her know that he had survived, to end the decades of her wondering, of not

knowing. He would give her the small pendant he had meticulously carved from a bone fragment, then catch the next flight
back to his hometown of Chicago. He wasn't sure how much
he would tell her about his ordeal. Would she want to hear his
story? Would she ask him to stay for dinner? Would she cry? So
many questions that would be answered in a few hours, questions he had hardly dared allow himself to ask himself, though
she'd been constantly in his thoughts.

He didn't have an address, so he told the Filipino taxi driver
to drop him off at the front entrance to the International Market
Place. He couldn't imagine her lei stand would still be there,
but perhaps someone would remember her and could give him
directions to her home. If that didn't pan out, he would work
his way through the five hundred–plus Lees in the telephone
book and hope one would be her. Could she afford a phone?
Stoically, he reminded himself that, of course, she could have
taken her husband's surname.

Kenny ran his fingers through graying hair as he stood in
front of the International Market Place. The banyan tree was
still there, but the bamboo thatched hut was gone. A clutter
of carts blocked his view of the base of the banyan. He took
a deep breath and walked inside, around a glitzy cart selling
pearl oysters, and he froze as his eyes settled on a petite, gray-
haired woman sitting on a plastic stool, threading blossoms
on a string. Unkempt hair hung across her face, and a wilted
red hibiscus flower dangled at a cockeyed angle from her left
ear. Next to her, on a flimsy bamboo rack, were three leis, the
blossoms wilted. She was not wearing a wedding band, but
his hopes fell as fast as they'd risen; it didn't necessarily mean
anything. Many Asian women didn't wear them. He waited
until she lifted her head to be sure it was Jinny. Then, as if he
had said something, she looked up and pushed her hair from
her face. Her wide-set eyes locked on him as a tentative smile
touched her lips.

"Hello, Jinny. Remember me? Kenny Choi? I came back as promised." His heart pounded and his legs felt weak.

"You want to buy lei?" She held up one she had just finished. Her look was innocent. Too innocent—something was missing from her gaze. Her words were soft and tentative—unsure.

"Remember me? I'm Kenny Choi. We met a long time ago before I went to Korea."

She tilted her head and put her hand on the side of her face. "I'm waiting for my Kenny. He's in Korea and will return soon."

He stepped closer and squatted and stared into her eyes. "I'm that Kenny. I'm the Kenny Choi you've been waiting for."

Jinny seemed not to hear his words as she leaned forward and encircled his head with a wilted lei. "You remind me of my Kenny. But gray hair. Older . . ." She didn't ask to be paid and returned to stringing wilted blossoms and humming the tune he could never forget.

The Vietnamese woman selling live pearl oysters at a nearby cart stepped over to him. "Mister. Jinny has Alzheimer's. Are you the Kenny Choi she's been waiting for?"

"Yes," his voice shaky. "I'm too late."

"Please sit. I'm Tien Long. How come you not return as promised?" She poured a cup of tea from her thermos and handed it to Kenny.

He took the warm drink and looked at Jinny as she struggled to string blossoms. The leis were so poorly made that he wondered how she could sell any. "Does anyone buy her leis?"

"Maybe one or two a day, then we add money to her cash box when she's not looking. She doesn't remember how many she sells, but meeting people and waiting for her Kenny keeps her going. Over the years, men ask her out, but she faithful to you. Now too late. Why you not come as promised?"

Kenny told Tien Long his story. He'd been captured by North Koreans shortly after his arrival in South Korea. For several months, he was interrogated and beaten and thought he would die. Then he was offered a choice—teach English, or go to a hard labor camp. He took the option to survive. There was no opportunity to escape, as he always taught in secure military facilities. Then a year ago, he was transferred to a chemical factory adjacent to the Yalu River that separated North Korea from China. Months later, an accident and violent explosion caused a fire, and in the chaos, he was able to escape across the Yalu River. Chinese guards immediately arrested him, but after two weeks of interrogation, turned him over to the American Embassy in Beijing. At first the embassy personal didn't believe his story, suspecting he had defected to North Korea during the Korean war. He passed two polygraph tests and, after a month of debriefing, was allowed to fly back to America, with Hawaii his first stop.

Tien Long revealed how Jinny had become a friend to everyone in the International Market Place and was always ready to help out those in need, until Alzheimer's slowly erased her memory. The shop owners had returned Jinny's decades of generosity by helping her during her time of need.

Tien, like most of the Vietnamese shop owners, had come to America as a refugee in 1974, with the fall of South Vietnam. Jinny had been the first person to help that influx of refugees, even though she had little extra money from her small lei business. She had friends with army connections who had relentlessly pestered the army for information on Kenny on her behalf. But all they could ever tell her was that he was missing in action and presumed dead.

"We notice Jinny's failing memory about two years ago, and in recent months she often arrives with empty basket, forgets to buy blossoms for make leis. We bring blossoms so she make four or five leis, then put few dollars in money box to keep her going."

That night, Kenny lay in bed, struggling with what to do until after midnight, when he drifted off to a restless sleep. He woke at dawn and took a long walk to the base of Diamond Head Crater before turning back. It didn't come as a spark of inspiration but slowly took shape in his mind. He had sufficient retirement funds from the military and a small inheritance, so there was no need to be concerned about living expenses. It was his commitment to return and marry Jinny that had kept him from committing suicide during the long, harsh years in North Korea. He had been ready to accept that she had married and moved on. But she hadn't, and that made all the difference. He couldn't abandon the woman who had faithfully spent almost her whole life waiting.

It was midmorning, when he arrived at the International Market Place. Jinny was sitting under the banyan, wearing the same wrinkled muumuu, struggling to thread blossoms onto a lei string, broken flowers scattered on the pavement. He knelt beside her. "Jinny, it's Kenny. Kenny Choi. I'm here to help you."

She stared at him with a quizzical expression then handed him the needle and string. She watched him thread plumeria blossoms and started humming the Asian melody he remembered from so long ago. As the days passed, lei-making became the thread into Jinny's vanishing world, as she revealed fragments of her past. Often, in the late-afternoon, she would lay her head against his shoulder and doze. When she woke, she would ask, "Did my Kenny come?" Sales increased to a dozen or more leis on most days. Jinny would gaze for hours into Kenny's face, frequently telling him how much he reminded her of her Kenny. He would gently tell her that he was her Kenny, and she would smile and say that was her Kenny's name. When Kenny would lean over and kiss her on the forehead or cheek, she would smile, and sometimes she would reach up to gently move her fingers over his face, like a blind person seeking to identify someone.

He began coming to her apartment each morning to accompany her on TheBus to Waikiki. The driver always greeted her with a cheery aloha and waited until she was seated before pulling away. In the evening they repeated the journey in reverse.

The day he dreaded came too soon; he found her unconscious, sprawled on the floor of her apartment. The ambulance arrived quickly, but two hours later the attending physician told Kenny that Jinny was in a coma and unlikely to regain consciousness. He sat at her bedside throughout the day and into the night, talking to her as if she were awake and listening. He had just adjusted Jinny's head on a pillow and was stroking her hair when she opened her eyes. Cupping her hand, he whispered, "Jinny, it's me, Kenny. Your Kenny Choi."

She gazed into his eyes with the enigmatic look he had seen daily for five months, but something was different—tears had appeared in the corners of her eyes. "Kenny, I knew you would return." She closed her eyes and he kissed her, his tears joining hers.

The lei stand is long gone. Sometimes, it is said that an old man appears with two cups of tea and sits at the base of the banyan and hums a strange Asian lullaby that sounds vaguely like a piece from Mozart.

Sandcastle

"*M*ommy, will you help me build a sandcastle like that one?" At the fluid edge between the reach of the surf and the beach the nine-year-old girl watched a young boy waging a battle to keep the rising tide from washing away his castle.

"Sweety, why don't you go help the boy save his sandcastle."

"I don't know him," whined Mandy.

"That doesn't matter. He'll lose his castle if he doesn't get help."

Mandy kicked off her sandals and ran across the beach, stopping a few feet from the blond boy and his castle. "Can I help?"

He looked up. "Sure. You put sand on the other side of the castle."

With four hands shoveling sand, they were able to hold back the surf and add a pigeon feather and shell decoration before a rogue wave splashed over them; in seconds the castle was gone. Mandy's mother raced across the beach. "Mandy, are you okay?"

Mandy giggled as she pushed soggy hair from her face. "I'm fine, just soaked." Mandy stood as her mother wrapped her in a large beach towel.

Seconds later, a trim man reached them. "Hi. I'm Greg Knight, Billy's dad. They were a good team until the wave hit." Billy jerked his head away when his father ran his fingers through his wet hair. "Dad, I'm fine."

"I'm Laura. Our kids built quite an impressive sandcastle before the wave struck. Mandy, it's getting late. We need to return to our hotel to shower and change for dinner, and I need to call the office."

"Mommy, can I play a little longer? You're always calling work, and anyway, it must be midnight in New York."

Laura pursed her lips as she crossed her arms over her chest. "Mandy, you know better than to talk to me in that tone."

"Sorry, Mommy." Mandy looked down, making squiggly lines in the sand with her toe.

"Laura, why don't we get together tomorrow so the kids can build another castle?"

She looked up at the six-foot frame now blocking the sun from her eyes. "We'd love to, but it's not possible. We leave at seven in the morning for Maui."

"Mommy, I really like this beach."

"We already have hotel reservations on Maui, and you'll make new friends there."

Mandy looked at Billy, then she turned away and wiped her eyes.

"Laura, I have two extra discount tickets for a buffet dinner tonight. I would love to have you two join us."

Mandy turned to her mother, hands clasped together. "Please, Mommy. I love buffets."

"I suppose I can cancel our dinner reservations."

Billy and Mandy shrieked and high-fived each other.

They agreed to meet at five thirty in the lobby of the Royal Hawaiian Hotel and walk to the buffet. Greg was surprised that Laura and Mandy were staying in such an expensive hotel; he knew it cost two or three times what he was paying at the Sheraton Princess Kaiulani.

Greg and Billy arrived wearing shorts and inexpensive aloha shirts from an ABC Store, while Laura and Mandy stepped from the elevator in matching tailored aloha dresses. "You two look great," Greg said, trying to conceal the twinge of embarrassment he felt for suggesting the cheap buffet for dinner.

The kids skipped ahead, pausing to point in windows, then dashing on, oblivious to their parents. When the group reached the buffet restaurant on Kuhio Street, they discovered a line of people snaking out of the front onto the sidewalk. With the exception of one elderly couple, the wife in a muumuu, Laura was the only woman wearing a dress. The long line gave Greg an excuse to suggest they go elsewhere, but Laura shrugged and said, "The kids are already in line, so best to wait."

The discount coupons listed snow crab, shrimp tempura, chicken teriyaki, rice, a choice of salads and eight deserts. But by the time they were seated, there was no snow crab or shrimp tempura left, and the chicken teriyaki was heavily picked over. Laura stuck to the salads, and Mandy and Billy were able to get away with extra deserts.

Laura sipped a watery Mai Tai, grimaced, and set it aside.

"Pretty awful buffet and drinks," Greg said as he put down his chopsticks. "I'm sorry."

"Well, the children are having fun. Greg, what do you teach at San Diego State?"

"Art history—Italian Renaissance and the history of European art. I got hooked when I was an exchange student in Florence. My dad wanted me to study something more marketable, like business or accounting, but after taking a class in accounting, I switched to art history and never looked back, though the salary of an assistant professor is, let's say, on the meager side. What do you do, Laura?"

"I work at LS Investments, in Manhattan. We manage accounts for clients who have over twenty-five million to invest in stocks and bonds. I got my MBA from Columbia and started as an investment analyst at the company."

"Sounds impressive. I'm sure it's more rewarding financially than teaching. It must be difficult raising a daughter and working in a high-pressure job at the same time."

"Of course, but that wasn't the plan. I married a stunningly handsome, charismatic man while at Columbia. He could charm the panties off any woman, and he did."

"So, he cheated on you and you divorced him?"

"You're half right. He cheated all right, but then he got himself killed skiing in Switzerland with his girlfriend before I had a chance to divorce him. He left me with a pile of debts." She grimaced. "End of story. And you?"

"Married my high school sweetheart. She was from Lebanon and wanted to be an investigative reporter. We both knew when we married that I would be sharing much of the child-rearing responsibilities. She was killed in Lebanon six months after Billy was born. She tried to save a child who had run into the middle of a firefight between Christian and Muslim factions and took a bullet to the head." Greg picked up his weak Mai Tai and chugged it down. "We were married six years."

"I'm sorry." Laura reached across the table and squeezed his hand.

They followed behind the children on the way back to the Royal Hawaiian. "Sorry about the lousy meal."

"The meal wasn't as important as seeing Mandy happy, and it was nice having adult conversation."

Saying good-bye in the lobby of the Royal Hawaiian was awkward. Suddenly the chatty kids were tongue-tied as they looked at each other. "Mandy, you can write to each other."

"It's not the same," said Mandy, and she turned away and walked to the elevator, not looking back.

"Mandy's at that emotional age," Laura said. "Maybe Billy can call her tomorrow night at the Hyatt Regency Maui Resort and Spa."

"He's never called a girl before, so I can't promise. Anyway, enjoy your vacation in Maui." Laura remained rigid as he gave her a quick hug, their cheeks brushed.

"Daddy, wake up!"

"Huh? What time is it?"

"It's almost six, and Mandy leaves for the airport in an hour."

"I know. We said our good-byes last night."

"I want to give her the treasure shell from our sandcastle."

"Billy, I'm sure she'll find other shells in Maui."

"Daddy, you don't understand. It's a special shell, and you're already awake."

He set up on his elbows and looked at his son. His frown quickly dissolved to a smile. "Okay, I guess we better hurry."

"Thanks. You're the greatest, Dad."

They were the first customers at the lei stand under the banyan tree in the International Market Place. The elderly Asian woman gave him a special price for two plumeria leis. They reached the entrance of the Royal Hawaiian Hotel just as a sleek limousine pulled away. Mandy's face was pressed to the window. Billy ran after the car waving his arms and shouting, then the taillights came on and the limousine backed up. The right passenger window came down and Mandy's head poked out. "Billy, you came!"

"I have the treasure shell from our sandcastle."

The door opened and Mandy jumped out and carefully took the olive-size spotted cowrie from his hand. "Thanks. I'll keep it forever."

"Billy, don't forget to give Mandy her lei," said his dad.

The lei caught on her hairclip, and he awkwardly untangled it, their faces inches apart. Greg looped the second lei over Laura's head and gave her a brief hug and a peck on her cheek. The sendoff was over in two minutes, then the limo pulled away as the children waved at each other.

"Happy now?" said Greg.

"Thanks, Dad. Mandy really was excited to get the shell."

They strolled next door to the rear of the towering Sheraton Waikiki Hotel and bought juice, coffee, and muffins at a tiny takeout café. Greg felt slightly melancholy as he sipped his coffee on the terrace overlooking the ocean, his mind on the woman he had met. It didn't make sense to read more into their brief meeting than a playdate for Billy and Mandy. Billy seemed happy, but later that day, the halfheartedness of his attempt at building a sandcastle suggested he missed his playmate.

The half-hour Hawaiian Airlines flight gave Laura and Mandy views of Oahu, Molokai, and Maui, including Maui's Haleakala volcano with its crown of clouds glistening in the morning sun. They were met at the Kahului Airport and driven in the hotel limousine across the island to the luxurious Hyatt Regency Maui Resort and Spa, on Ka'anapali Beach. Laura had chosen the resort because of its lavish Garden-of-Eden-themed children's play area.

The Disneyland-like jungle-paradise was as advertised — water slides, a meandering pool, a rope bridge, and a swim-through grotto set in a rich tapestry of verdant palms and vines splashed with tropical flowers. The caws of brilliant green and red parrots were drowned out by the squeals of children romping through the magical playland. Mandy approached a girl near her age, but she was already playing with another girl and didn't let her join in. By early afternoon, she was back in their ocean-view suite reading the *Magic Tree House*, a children's adventure set in Hawaii.

"Mandy, we're in Hawaii. The real thing is outside, not in your book."

"I know, Mommy, but I'm tired today and just want to rest."

Laura coaxed her daughter onto the balcony to see the sunset and the ocean liner passing on the horizon. They dined in the Hyatt's romantic tiki-torch-lit Son'z at Swan Court among palms and a waterfall. Mandy poked at her keiki meal of opah fish sticks and Maui potato chips, while avoiding eye contact with her mother.

"Honey, what's wrong?"

"Mommy, I know you picked this place for me. I tried to make friends with a girl my age, but she already had a friend and didn't want another. And when I asked a boy if he wanted to play, he said he didn't play with girls."

"Maybe tomorrow you'll find a playmate."

"Mommy, if you call Billy's daddy, maybe they'll fly over to see us. I think he kind of likes you."

"Yesterday was a playdate for you kids. Billy's dad and I are from different worlds. Honey, I can call Billy, and you two can have a chat on the phone."

"Yes, and maybe they'll come."

Laura toyed with her one-carat diamond earring. Greg was handsome, with nice abs that didn't develop from lecturing about art history. She placed the call. "Hello, Greg, it's Laura." She skipped any further greetings. "Mandy would like to talk to Billy."

"I'm so glad you called. I think Billy misses his playmate. I'll put him on."

At first, the two were at a loss for words, but within a few minutes, they were chatting and laughing. Billy kept motioning in the air with his hand, as if she could see him. A half-hour later, Laura told Mandy to say good-bye to Billy and let her have a few words with his dad.

"Greg, I was wondering if there's any chance of you flying over to Maui so our kids can play together. They seem to get along so well. And there's a super jungle playland at the Hyatt."

"I was thinking the same thing, but the Hyatt is out of my price range. Let me make a few calls to see if I can find a nearby hotel suitable for a struggling art history professor."

Laura would gladly have paid the difference but knew her offer would be rebuffed and didn't want to hurt his male ego. "I'm sure you can find something in your price range."

"I may not get back to you until tomorrow morning. Don't say anything to Mandy until I confirm hotel and flight arrangements."

None of the hotels in the Ka'anapali area had available rooms in Greg's price range. As a last resort, he went to the front desk of the Sheraton Princess Kaiulani and asked to speak to the reservation's manager. The general manager happened to be talking to one of the receptionists and turned to Greg.

"I'm Ted Martin, the general manager of this hotel. Can I help you?"

Greg explained his situation as Martin viewed the computer monitor for details about his guest. "Dr. Knight, do you happen to teach at San Diego State?"

"Yes, I teach art history."

"I almost went there, but money issues kept me here in the islands where I studied at the University of Hawaii. I sometimes wonder where I would have ended up had I gone there."

Greg grinned. "General manager of a major hotel in Waikiki sounds pretty good to me."

"I like it, but sometimes wonder where the path less traveled would have taken me."

"Sounds like you've read some of Robert Frost's poetry."

"One of my favorite poets. I'll check on availability at our Ka'anapali Sheraton. It's at the other end of Ka'anapali beach from the Hyatt."

"That would be great. I have budget constraints."

Martin's ambiguous expression was between a grin and a smirk. "If there's a room available, I think I can get you a good rate." He called the general manager at their Maui property, and in two minutes Greg had a room at the same low rate. "Dr. Knight, it's not an ocean view, but you're steps from the beach."

"That's perfect. I appreciate your help." Greg handed him his business card. "If you ever get to San Diego, give me a call and I'll show you around the campus—the road not taken."

They flew standby on the six a.m. flight to Maui—too early to call Laura. On arrival at the Kahului Airport, Greg rented a four-door Toyota Corolla, hoping that the four of them would be seeing sights together. He called Laura at seven twelve as they pulled out of the airport, and she answered on the first ring. "We're just leaving the Kahului Airport and have a room at the Sheraton at Black Rock. Where do you want to meet?"

"That's wonderful! Mandy will be thrilled. You're at the other end of Ka'anapali Beach, so how about meeting in the middle, at Whaler's Village at, say, nine o'clock?"

"We'll be there. Are you sure you remember what I look like?" he jested.

"No, but Mandy will recognize Billy," she teased.

After check-in and changing, Billy raced out, kicking up sand and pausing several times to shout for his father to hurry up. When Laura and Mandy came into view, he sprinted, hands waving as Mandy ran toward him. She did a near-perfect cartwheel, followed by a failed attempt by Billy, who landed on his butt. They excitedly embraced like teammates after a goal in a soccer match. Mandy launched into the description of the wonderous jungle play area at her hotel.

"Greg, I'm so glad you could make it. Mandy really misses Billy."

"It's a great age, where boys and girls can become close friends without romantic complications."

Laura nodded. "That's for sure."

They took a brief stroll through Whaler's Village, stopping under the massive sperm whale skeleton. "Mandy, it's big enough to swallow both of us whole. Like in *Moby Dick*."

"No need to worry. The humpback whales found around Hawaii prefer small fish and krill to humans. The great white sharks would find you a couple of tasty morsels, though," Greg said.

Laura nudged Greg. "Don't scare them. They'll have nightmares."

As they strolled back to the Hyatt, Laura mentioned how competitive men were in Manhattan. "I always have to be on guard."

"So, an assistant professor of art history must be no threat," Greg replied.

She flipped a lock of hair from her forehead. "More dangerous, because his tactics are unknown."

Mandy and Billy dodged the pulses of the surf as they followed the beach to the Hyatt, dashing close to the receding water, then shrieking as they raced to beat the next wave surge. When Billy slipped and fell into the surf, Mandy ran back to help, and both were knocked down by a wave. Soaked and holding hands, they were giggling as they waded back to the beach.

"I can't remember when Mandy had so much fun."

The two had to rinse in the outdoor shower before Laura would allow them to enter the Hyatt's tropical playland. While the kids explored their jungle-world, Laura and Greg sat in lounge chairs, sharing fragments of their lives, slowly revealing vulnerabilities. Mandy had been unplanned, Laura confessed, and had accelerated their plans to marry. "As I mentioned in Waikiki, my husband's infidelity destroyed our marriage.

Ultimately, Mark was killed on a sky slope in the Alps with his girlfriend."

"Are you dating anyone now?"

"No one seriously. I just don't have the time or interest right now. My job's exhausting and consumes most of my energy. And then there's Mandy. I want her to have a happy childhood, but it's challenging being a single parent. As you can see, I spoil her, like on this vacation, because I feel guilty for my long hours away at work."

"Being a teacher, I have pretty long vacations and more flexibility to spend time with Billy. But I know I'm a poor substitute for a mother. I need to try harder to find someone to love who will also be a good mother for Billy."

"So, are you looking for someone?"

"It's been so long that I don't even know where to start."

"Maybe you're afraid to reveal your vulnerabilities to another woman."

He looked away from her penetrating gaze.

Mandy and Billy made their appearance when their parents' sandwiches, chips, and iced tea were served, flinging drops of water over the grown-ups. "We're starved."

"We'll order food for you." Laura picked up the menu.

"No time." They took bites out of their parents' sandwiches, grabbed a handful of chips, and dashed back to the water slide.

"I send Mandy to a private school where they're supposed to learn manners, and this is what I get." Laura shook her head, but her eyes were smiling.

"If we were their age, we'd do the same thing."

It took several warnings before the children bounded out of the pool to dry off. "Billy and I want to have dinner together."

"Laura, sounds good to me. What do you think?"

"Do I have a choice?" Laura smiled again. "I'm already outvoted."

They agreed to meet at five thirty at the beachfront Hula Grill, in Whaler's Village. When Laura jokingly asked if Greg had discount coupons for dinner, he grinned. "No, do you?"

Greg and Billy were waiting next to the entrance to the Hula Grill when Laura and Mandy arrived, Mandy in pink shorts and a Burberry polo shirt with a distinctive black plaid overlaying a pink background. Laura was wearing a beguiling sarong, snug and artfully wrapped around her body and accented with a necklace and earrings.

"Wow!" Greg remarked. "You've outdone us again."

Laura smiled, pleased that he noticed.

They were early enough to be seated at a table on the sand under an umbrella of coconut palm fronds. Mandy and Billy kicked off their sandals and leaned forward in their chairs, digging their toes into the warm sand. The tiki torches and thatched umbrellas gave a 1950s Hawaiian feel to the setting, enhanced by nostalgic Hawaiian songs belted out by a handsome Hawaiian.

Greg and Laura had tasty ahi katsu and panko-crusted ahi, and the children had breaded chicken nuggets with mango sauce. But the main draw was the tropical ambiance on the beach. Greg and Laura talked mainly about their children, usually a killer on a date but not with them. Both felt cautious about revealing feelings about each other with their children within listening range. As darkness closed in, the tiki torches cast a soft glow over their faces, and the children quieted, heads nodding.

"I think Billy and Mandy are ready for a good night's sleep," whispered Laura.

"No, we're not," replied Mandy, her eyes half closed.

The loud squawking of mynah birds woke Mandy. "Mommy, where are you?"

"Honey, I'm having coffee on the balcony. I don't want to miss a moment of this beautiful day."

Mandy jumped out of bed. "Is Billy coming back to play?"

"We're going to meet them at their hotel after breakfast and go snorkeling at Black Rock. It's a good place to see lots of fish and green sea turtles."

Greg and Billy were waiting in the lobby of the Sheraton when Laura and Mandy arrived on the Ka'anapali Trolley. Billy grabbed Mandy's hand, and they dashed off, while Greg and Laura lugged the snorkeling gear, towels, and lotions.

"They must think their snorkeling gear will magically appear on the beach."

"Laura, they're right," he said with a chuckle. "Payback comes when they have kids. A year ago, Billy wouldn't have anything to do with a girl. Now, she's all he talks about."

"He's in Hawaii, and he's found a playmate his age—it's so much better than playing with adults. It's a special time in life, before puberty, when everything changes," Laura mused, thinking back. "Do you remember when you first noticed girls as more than a nuisance?" she asked with an inquisitive smile.

"I always liked to play with girls, but I first started noticing the difference in the sixth grade. Her name was Trudy Gait. She sat behind me in class, and when she leaned over to talk to me I could see down her blouse, and I had a strange feeling."

"You were aroused?"

"I didn't know why it happened and was embarrassed. I wanted her to be my girlfriend, but I was too shy to tell her my feelings."

Laura thought, *You still are*.

On the beach, Laura laid out the towels while Greg helped the kids adjust their face masks. "Billy, stay close to Mandy when snorkeling, and don't get too far ahead of us."

"Okay, Dad."

Greg and Laura snorkeled a few yards behind the children along the south side of Black Rock, a lava peninsula that blocked the waves and quieted the sea, providing good viewing of tropical fish and green sea turtles. At first, Billy and Mandy snorkeled side-by-side, then Mandy took his hand and pointed to a green sea turtle grazing on the seaweed. Laura and Greg didn't hold hands but kept brushing against each other as they swam behind the children.

Even with sunscreen, they had to abandon the beach by midmorning, and they drove to nearby Lahaina, once a port for whaling ships and now the most popular tourist town on Maui. Front Street was lined with quaint-looking shops and seafood restaurants sporting nineteenth-century wooden facades and inviting menus of ahi, mahimahi, opah, onaga, and tiger shrimp prepared with fresh tropical ingredients and Asian spices.

Laura's thoughts of a lunch in one of the seafood restaurants was foiled when Greg stopped at the century-old banyan tree that covered most of a square block. Several children were climbing along the lower limbs that spread out over seventy-five feet from the massive trunk.

"Dad, can we climb the tree?"

"Mommy, that will be so much fun."

"Honey, it's lunch time and it looks dangerous. Greg, what do you think?"

"I wish I was a kid and could climb with them."

"You're not much help. Okay, Mandy, but only on the lowest limb. Fifteen minutes, then we need to go for lunch."

Thirty minutes later, Greg walked to the corner takeout café and bought sandwiches and sweet guava drinks for a picnic under the banyan. As he handed Laura a tuna sandwich he said, "You never get much of a meal when you're with me."

She grinned. "You're such a softy with the kids. I tend to be too rigid with Mandy and you're, uh, more flexible."

"Diplomatic answer. What you really mean is the kids can manipulate me to get whatever they want. We'd be a good balance for Billy and Mandy . . . uh, I mean, hypothetically."

They returned to the Hyatt in midafternoon so Billy and Mandy could build a sandcastle, but the coarser sand didn't stick together as well as the sand on Waikiki Beach, and they returned to the Hyatt's jungle playland and pretended they were on a lost island. That evening, Greg and Laura let the kids have room service and watch a kids' video, while Greg was Laura's guest at the Son'z at Swan Court, surrounded by waterfalls and the soft flickering glow of tiki torches. Greg and Laura stayed on neutral ground, talking about their day with the children and making plans for their drive to Hana. Greg slid his hand around Laura's lower back as they neared her room, about to turn her into him for a meaningful kiss, but a scream from inside the room interrupted the romantic moment. Laura rushed in, finding Billy and Laura standing on separate beds having a pillow fight. Greg forced a smile, regretting he'd waited too long.

Laura was worried about getting carsick on the drive Greg proposed for the next day along the windy, cliff-hugging Hana Highway, with its 617 turns and fifty-six one-lane bridges. But she agreed to try it when Greg assured her he would drive slowly and stop if she felt woozy. He pointed out that it was the most tropical part of Maui, adding that scenes from *Jurassic Park* were filmed there. Plus, they might see rare, brightly colored finches and maybe a monk seal on the beach. He embellished descriptions about cascading waterfalls and passion fruit that could be picked from the car window, and mysterious grottos with red water.

Laura wasn't keen on leaving at six thirty in the morning but again was outvoted by the others. She and the children dozed on the forty-five-minute drive across the isthmus between Maui's two major volcanoes, waking when Greg called out, "Anyone want fresh coffee or hot chocolate and muffins?" Maui Coffee Roasters was offbeat, with lively music, T-shirts emblazed with

Corporate Coffee Sucks, and bold coffee to back its claims. They indulged in oversized muffins, large cappuccinos, and whipped-cream-topped hot chocolate—perfect, unless one is headed off on a three-hour drive on a very curvy road. The narrow Hana road was moody, changing frequently throughout the day depending on the weather and the angle of the sun. On the makai side (the seaward side) of the serpentine road, precipitous cliffs plunged to crescents of sand, some golden and others black, tucked into inaccessible coves. On the mauka side (or upland side), jungle-clad cliffs disappeared into the mist, and waterfalls plummeted so close that spray boiled across the road. In mist-filled glens, vague silhouettes of Hawaiian bungalows emerged from among papaya, banana, and taro patches like Impressionist paintings.

The unblemished beauty was dulled by the endless turns swaying them back and forth. Laura and Billy were wishing it would end soon. Stops at lookouts gave but a few minutes of reprieve from the nausea, and Laura sighed with relief as they finally pulled to a stop in the Wai'anapanapa State Park. This was the spot Greg hoped would most impress everyone—lava caves filled with spring water that occasionally turned pink, and one of Hawaii's famous glistening black-sand beaches.

"Everybody ready to explore a mysterious water-filled cave and walk down to the beach and maybe see a monk seal?"

"Greg," Laura moaned. "The curvy road has made me woozy. I'd rather stay in the car and not move until my stomach settles."

"Dad, I'm a little car sick too. I think I'll stay with Laura."

"Mandy, how do you feel?" Laura asked.

"I'm fine, and I want to see the magic caves."

Mandy liked the extra attention from Greg as they walked to the water-filled lave tube, the entrance draped in lush ferns and a profusion of flowers.

"Mandy, it's like the entrance to a magical grotto where mysterious beasts lurk. Are you ready to enter?"

"Yes." She took his hand.

Greg switched on his flashlight, and they stepped inside. The water was so clear they could see the bottom. "It's not red like you said it would be."

"It's only red on special moonless nights when bats fly about and blood seeps from the rocks into the water," Greg said in his best haunted-house voice.

"Not real blood?" Mandy replied.

Greg laughed. "No. An ancient legend is that a princess and her lover were killed here, and on certain nights, when there's no moon, their blood turns the water red. But the truth is it's caused by millions of tiny, red shrimp appearing from cracks in the lava and turning the water red."

"I wouldn't go in the water when it was full of shrimp."

"It's okay today. You can go in for a swim."

She waded in slowly until she was to her knees, but she shuddered. "Brrrr. It's so cold."

"Billy will be jealous because you braved the cold water."

That was all it took to persuade Mandy to briefly go in and paddle around for a few seconds before jumping back out of the water. Greg quickly wrapped a towel around her shoulders. "You'll warm up fast when we get to the beach. The black sand soaks up the sun's heat and can get quite hot."

The beach was as Greg said—too hot to walk on in bare feet. They found a shady spot to spread out their towels. "Greg, what's that big thing over there on the beach?"

"You have sharp eyes, Mandy. It's a Hawaiian monk seal. They're rare, and you spotted it before me." He gave her a high-five. She leaned back against his shoulder.

"Mandy, coming all the way to Hawaii must be a great treat."

She shrugged and raked her fingers through the warm lava sand. "I like traveling with Mommy, but I'd be happier if our family was complete."

"You miss your daddy?"

"Yes, even though I was too young to know him. He was very handsome in pictures, like you. And Mommy cries at night when she thinks I'm asleep. I think she's lonely."

"Oh. Mandy, a family can be just two. But I understand what you mean. Billy feels he's missing out, not having a mother. Your mother is smart and pretty, and I'm sure she'll find the right man someday."

She shook her head, her wet ponytail flipping from ear to ear. "I don't think so. She thinks all men are after her money. The company she told you she works for—she owns it. She's rich. Don't tell her I told you, or she'll get very angry at me. Do you know she likes you?"

"I suppose so. But just as a friend doing playdates with you and Billy."

"I saw a piece of paper in the waste basket with your name on it."

"Oh?"

"She wrote *Laura Knight*, and drew a smiley face next to the name."

Back in the parking lot, Laura and Billy sat in the front seat of the car, with the windows down and the seats reclined as far as they would go. Both sipped Cokes that Greg had brought along and claimed would settle their stomachs, as it did his stomach on bumpy flights.

"Laura. Umm, what do you think about my dad?"

"Well, he's smart and nice and likes to do fun things that I wouldn't think of doing. I know he cares a lot about you."

"He's not that smart. He knows nothing about women."

"Why do you say that?"

"I don't remember him ever going out on a *real* date. He's still paying off his college loans and doesn't have much money. He's really nice to everyone, even women that I think would like to go out with him. I can tell when they flirt with him and he does nothing. Zilch! I think he likes you but, just like with all the others, will do nothing. We'll fly home and he'll go back to teaching."

Laura smiled but said nothing.

Mandy's revelation had emboldened Greg, and he reached for Laura's hand before they pulled out of the parking lot. Later, after an early dinner at the Hyatt, Greg suggested the kids watch another movie while he went for a walk on the beach with Laura. They returned two hours later, soaked and giggling like children.

"What happened to you two?" Billy and Mandy asked in unison.

"Greg, you explain."

"Well we were walking along the beach, and this gigantic wave came and knocked us over like bowling pins—a perfect strike."

"Dad, that's a made-up story!"

"Mom, what's the real story?"

"Mandy, my lips are sealed," said Laura, and she zipped her pinched fingers across her mouth.

Mandy cried at the airport as Billy walked with his dad onto their flight. Laura and Greg had had hopes that this was the start of a lasting romance, and tentative plans were made to meet in the Bahamas over the children's Christmas break.

Then came the long email telling Greg she had met someone.

Years melted away. Greg's book, *Sleuthing Art History*, had been well reviewed and become a best seller in the art world; eventually he was offered and accepted a full-professor's position at San Diego State. He was in a coffeehouse along San Diego's Mission Beach Boardwalk when his iPhone chimed. "Hello."

"Greg . . . it's Laura Sutherland. I read your most interesting Facebook page and bought a copy of your best seller, *Sleuthing Art History*. I was wondering if I could get you to autograph it?"

"Of course. It will be my pleasure. Send it and I'll sign it along with a special note to you."

"Or, Greg . . . how about you autographing it on Waikiki Beach? I'm planning a trip there alone, and I'd enjoy having a playmate to help me build a sandcastle."

Haku Lei

*A*lex had just opened the sliding glass door to his second-story lanai when the doorbell rang.

"I'll get it, Daddy," yelled his eight-year-old daughter. He paused, holding the whale-tail-shaped handle of his coffee mug, and listened, trying to catch snippets of the conversation at the door. At eight, Ellie was old enough to answer the door in their neighborhood during the day, as long as Alex was within hearing distance. He gazed down Manoa Valley to Waikiki Beach and the Pacific Ocean. The older three-bedroom home had been a financial stretch when he'd bought it in 1998, but it had turned out to be a good investment.

"Daddy, it's a woman who wants to speak to you about something. She said it's important."

"Tell her we're not buying anything or doing any surveys."

"She says it's about a poem you wrote."

Alex was bewildered. He hadn't written any poetry since college, two decades earlier. "Ellie, tell her I'm coming down." He gulped the rest of his coffee and descended the stairs into the living room. A young woman with red hair was turned away, looking at photos on the wall. "You want to see me about a poem?"

She turned, and he gasped, "Suzanne!"

"I'm Jill Smith. Suzanne's my mother."

"Of course. You . . . you look just like her," Alex stuttered.

"Yes, when she was twenty. She's forty now and has a few streaks of gray in her hair."

"How did you find me? And *why?*"

"You wrote a poem, titled *Haku Lei*—Crown of Flowers— for my mother. It's in her scrapbook along with your photo. I used Google to find poems titled *Haku Lei* and got seven hits. One lead me to yours, published in an issue of *Hawaiian Arts and Poetry*. It took me a little sleuthing to find your picture on the webpage of your company, Tourist Analytics, in Honolulu. Except for your hairstyle and glasses, you look the same as the photo in Mom's scrapbook."

"Is it something about Suzanne? Is she okay?"

"It's about you and my mother. And yes, she's fine. We arrived yesterday from New York. Mom's in our room at the Outrigger Reef Hotel, in Waikiki."

"Does she want to meet me?"

"Definitely not!"

"So, why are you here?"

Jill gazed into Alex's eyes. "Because you're my father."

Alex took a step backward shaking his head. "That's impossible!"

"So, you're saying you didn't sleep with my mother when she was in Waikiki in August, 1994?"

Alex scratched the back of his head. "Um, well . . ." Alex's defensive demeanor softened, his mouth open as he gazed at Jill. "There may be other possibilities."

"I've always wondered who my father was, but Mom wouldn't tell me anything except that you were a deceitful jerk. This is what you wrote on the back of the poem you gave her."

August 10, 1994
Dear Suzanne,
The love we shared during the past three weeks is beyond my ability to express in words. I hope this poem I wrote for you conveys more than I could express when you were in my arms and our hearts beat together. You will be in my mind every day, every minute, and every second until we meet again.
Love always,
Alex

He nodded. "I wrote it and meant it at the time, but that was twenty years ago, and a poem and love note do not prove I'm your father."

"The date of your note was August tenth, 1994, the day she left Hawaii. Mom's diary indicated that she was in Hawaii from July eighteenth to August tenth. I was born full-term on May eleventh, 1995, so I had to be conceived around August fifth, give or take three or four days. Mom's diary tells what she did each day in Hawaii and who she was with. She wrote that you two made love on Waikiki Beach on the night of August fifth. You are the only man she mentions meeting in Hawaii. And look at Ellie, she's a copy of me at her age. I brought mom's diary, if you want to read her exact words."

Ellie moved to Jill's side. "Daddy, I do look just like Jill."

Belatedly, Alex remembered that Ellie was still there, listening to it all. He studied the two girls, then nodded and grinned like a Cheshire cat. "Seems to me that I've just gained another beautiful daughter who's a heck of a good detective."

"Daddy. This means I have a big sister!" Ellie screeched.

Alex rubbed his day-old whiskers. "Yes, and I have a grown daughter." He opened his arms and embraced both. Tears shook loose from his eyes as he kissed Jill's wet cheeks then the top of Ellie's head. He stood back, holding Jill at arm's length. "We have a lot of catching up to do."

"So, you don't mind if I call you Dad?"

"I insist."

"Dad." She tried it out. "When I was little, I would talk to you and pretend you had come back. I was nine or ten when the fantasy went away, I thought forever. But I never gave up hope that someday you'd knock on our front door. I never dreamed I would be the one knocking on your door."

"Jill, I'm so glad you didn't give up looking. I must see Suzanne. I have a lot of explaining to do."

"Dad, I want you two to get together. But Mom emphatically told me she doesn't want to try and contact you and she warned me not to try."

"But I can't have her so close and not meet her."

"I was hoping you would feel that way. I have a plan. It must seem to be an accidental meeting—a total surprise. Remember, Mom has twenty years of anger built up. So be prepared for a rough start to any meeting. You've got to have a good explanation for not contacting her as you promised."

"I have a good explanation, if she'll listen. You know your mother best. So, what's your plan?"

"Mom and I are meeting at eleven thirty for tea in the Beach Bar of the Moana Surfrider Hotel. I suppose you know where it is?"

"I know it well. So, I'll arrive with Ellie before eleven thirty and will be sipping tea when you two arrive."

Jill shook her head. "No, because I don't know where Mom will decide to sit. Better that you come later, then you can be sure to sit at a nearby table. Don't stare at us—just wait for Mom to recognize you. Then it's up to you to engage her in conversation—and you better have a really good reason for dumping her."

"What if she doesn't recognize me?"

"I go to Plan B."

"And what is Plan B?"

"I don't know yet."

Ellie jumped around on her toes doing a pirouette. "This is like a Nancy Drew mystery."

Jill helped dress Ellie to look the way she looked at her age, even using her green scrunchie for Ellie's ponytail. Alex shaved and slipped into a polo shirt and shorts like the ones he'd worn during his college years. The main differences were the frames of his glasses and shorter hair, graying now at the temples.

Alex and Ellie strolled through the Moana Surfrider lobby a few minutes before noon and paused on the back veranda overlooking the Beach Bar, scanning the dozen or so people seated in the courtyard under a sweeping banyan. Suzanne and Jill were at a table to the right of the main trunk and engaged in conversation as Alex and Ellie took seats at a table a few feet away.

Ellie giggled and leaned over to her father. "She's really pretty."

He put his finger to his lips. "Shhh."

Several times over the next half-hour, Suzanne looked their way but showed no sign that she recognized Alex. She finished her tea and signaled for the bill.

"Daddy, she doesn't recognize you, and they're leaving."

Jill silently mouthed the words *get ready*, then she knocked over her iced tea, spilling it onto the table and into her mother's lap. Suzanne jumped up as Alex leaped from his chair, throwing his cotton napkin on the wet tabletop as his shoulder brushed her.

"Jill, you should be more careful!" She shrieked. Then she turned to Alex. "Thank you." She extended her hand. "I'm Suzanne Smith."

He wiped his hand on his shorts and took hers. "Alex . . . Alex Storm."

She froze, eyes locked on his face and lips pursed. She paused a moment. "You . . . you lying, two-faced, devious scoundrel. You abandoned me!"

"Suzanne, I'm here to explain everything. I didn't know you were pregnant."

"You're twenty years too late! Jill, we're leaving." She grabbed her purse and hurried away.

Jill ran after her mother. "Mom, please stop and listen to what Dad has to say."

"He's doesn't deserve to be called your dad."

Alex watched as they disappeared into the lobby of the hotel, then he turned to Ellie. "Well, so much for Plan B."

The waiter approached their table with the bill. "Is the lady returning?"

"I don't think so. I'll take care of her bill."

Ellie put her arm around her father's waist. "Why wouldn't she listen to you?"

"I guess there's too much anger inside for her to want to hear what I have to say. I didn't know she was pregnant, or I never would have given up looking for her."

"I know, Dad." She hugged him. "Maybe Jill can get her to come back."

"I hope so. It won't hurt to stay a little while longer."

They were both watching the entrance when Suzanne and Jill reappeared on the terrace. Alex quickly stood and pulled out a chair as they descended the steps and walked over to their table. "Suzanne, thank you for coming back."

"You can thank Jill for that."

"I took care of the bill."

She slumped down in the chair. "Okay, I'm listening. But spare me your deceitful and self-serving excuses. Just the truth."

"Where do you want me to start?"

"You could try explaining why you didn't call me as you promised. And you gave me a bogus telephone number."

He leaned back, reeling from her accusations. "I had just finished my shift selling at the beachside café and walked out to the spot on the beach where we had made love in the moonlight."

"I don't remember any moon that night," Suzanne replied sarcastically.

"Anyway, I was at the surf's edge, thinking about you, when a Japanese woman screamed that her husband was drowning. I dashed into the surf and was able to pull the man to shore. Later, when I took out the contents of my soaked wallet, your telephone number was illegible. I was only able to save your photo." He opened his wallet and showed her the discolored photo.

She smirked. "How convenient. I suppose you never heard of a telephone directory?"

"I remembered you told me you lived in Philadelphia, and I called information. There must have been a hundred Smiths in Philadelphia, and I called every one and found maybe a dozen Suzannes and Susans. But they were all dead ends. I waited for you to call me, as I'd given you my number, but you didn't. So, I assumed you didn't want to continue with a long-distance romance. There was nothing more I could do."

"I actually lived north of Philadelphia in the village of Ardsley, which nobody's ever heard of. Okay, I accept that you couldn't find my number. But that doesn't explain why you gave me a phone number that was out of service. I wanted to call you as soon as I arrived home, but my girlfriend told me you would call if the romance was for real. Then, when I discovered I was pregnant, I tried to call you immediately, but you'd given me an out-of-service number."

"Suzanne, I wouldn't have done that." He leaned back and closed his eyes for a few moments then sat up, eyes wide open. "I think I know what happened. I don't recall the dates, but I remember changing my number because I was getting too many calls meant for Queen's Hospital."

There was a silence that Jill rushed to fill. "Mom, I believe Dad's story."

Ellie chimed in. "Daddy always tells me to tell the truth, and he never tells big lies. Well, he did fib about Santa Clause until I got him to fess up."

Suzanne's pursed lips melted into a smile as she tapped the table with her fingernails. "Jill, I'm sure you're behind this accidental meeting that's complicated our relaxing vacation in Hawaii."

"Mom, did you really think I would come to Hawaii and not try to find my father? And aren't you glad that you know that Alex didn't abandon you as you always thought?"

Suzanne took a deep breath. "I need something stronger than iced tea. We have a lot to talk about."

Alex clapped his hands and Ellie and Jill joined in. "Ellie, why don't you take Jill for a walk on the beach and show her where the turtles hang out behind the Outrigger Reef Hotel."

Alex wasn't sure where to start, so he began with the easy part, graduating from college and launching his career, leaving his failed marriage to the end.

He had reluctantly taken his advisor's advice and written his master's thesis on the bakery industry in Hawaii. He found a struggling company with a large facility that was heavily in debt and producing bakery goods at far below capacity. He quickly discovered that the company was failing on all fronts—overpriced baked goods, poor quality control, underutilization of their facilities, and little effort to expand sales. Four months later, he handed a draft copy of his 184-page thesis to the owner, who said he didn't have time to read it, Then he said, "If you're so smart, you can buy the company. A hundred and fifty thousand dollars—and you assume the company's debts."

Alex jumped at the offer. With the help of a loan from his grandfather, and after he managed to obtain a contract to supply two of the major airlines servicing Hawaii, he was able to double production in the first year. Ten years later, he sold the company for a nice profit and started his consulting firm,

Tourist Analytics, to help other companies adapt to Hawaii's evolving tourist industry.

"Alex, that's amazing that you turned a thesis project into such a profitable business, and at only twenty-six."

"The real credit goes to Dr. Asiel Gordon. He's the one who convinced me to study a boring bakery company. But my business success sure didn't carry over to my disastrous marriage that ended up in divorce."

"My marriage was a mess too."

"I dated several women, none seriously, until I met Gail Palmer at an avant-garde movie, *Educating Rita*, being shown at the Honolulu Museum of Art. Gail had auburn hair and a strong resemblance to you, but a different personality. She was a social worker involved with abused woman, and she was a health addict, swimming an hour every day. We hit it off right away, and within two months she had moved in with me. Gail took the initiative on the third date, when she reached over and unzipped my pants."

"Did you stop her?"

"No, but I should have."

"I doubt that," Suzanne said as she licked the salt from the rim of her margarita.

"The problem was that sex came before there was love, and I blindly ignored issues that would emerge as problems after we married. That was in 2003. She didn't want children, and I did. Her pregnancy was a surprise, and she wanted an abortion, but I convinced her she would bond with our baby. But Gail had serious postpartum depression as she struggled to adjust to motherhood. She began seeing a psychiatrist, and I missed the signals that she was getting more out of the sessions than help with her depression. She filed for divorce and signed over all her parental rights to Ellie, and I've raised her since she was two. She's everything to me. Now I have another daughter, and perhaps another chance with you."

Suzanne drained her margarita and carefully set it on the table. "The only thing for sure is you have two daughters. Whether we can rekindle the flames that went out twenty-years ago is yet to be determined."

"Suzanne, what about your life? Did you finish your marketing degree?"

"No. I remained with my parents, who were immense help with Jill while I was in college. I took an introductory painting class and was hooked on art. My parents warned me that it would be a struggle to earn a living as an artist, but still they supported me through college. For the first four years, my day job was designing advertising posters and I managed to begin selling my paintings on the side."

"Which career won out?"

"A whimsical drawing of a treehouse in one of Jill's illustrated story books gave me the idea that turned my art hobby into a profitable career. I knew every child fantasized about living in a treehouse, so why not adults? The key was to produce original oil paintings that could be marketed as fine art in upscale art galleries. I completed twenty-seven different paintings trying to find a style that would appeal to the fine-art market. I convinced the owner of an art gallery in Philadelphia to have a showing. Over fifty people came and sipped champagne and wine, and I sold one painting—a total failure, I thought. I was ready to give up painting, but my dear dad, who knows nothing about art, said to me, "Failure is when you give up." The following year, I won third place in the new artist's category at the Annual Manhattan Art Show, and sales took off."

"Suzanne, you must meet a ton of charming, suave, eligible men at your art showings."

"Yes, of course. I dated many men in the early years, then I met Marcus Rutherford, the kind of man who drew attention from both sexes whenever we went out. He was especially kind to Jill and very attentive to my feelings. I convinced myself that he would make a good husband, but months stretched into years with no mention of marriage. Then I accidentally saw a photo on his iPhone of a male model sans clothes. I confronted him and he admitted to being bisexual. I told him I needed an exclusive relationship, something he couldn't promise. We remain good friends and occasionally meet for a dinner, but there's no romance. The art community is full of gay and bisexual men who make great friends but not husbands. I've recently begun dating a divorced professor at New York University, but it's too early to know if it will go beyond an occasional dinner and Broadway play."

"I should be sorry about your bad luck with men, but right now I'm not. What made you decide after so many years to return to Hawaii with Jill?"

"Jill strongly wanted to come and told me that if I didn't come with her, she'd come alone. Also, I kind of wanted to go back to the place where Jill was conceived on Waikiki Beach. Those three weeks in Hawaii were among the happiest in my life. But the beach has changed a lot, and I'm not sure where that spot is. You know, if only my phone had rung, maybe everything would have been different."

"Suzanne, let me show you the spot where we made love."

"I might cry."

"I'll hold you."

"That's what I'm afraid of."

The beach had receded to half its former width, and the spot where they had made love was now ten yards offshore. Suzanne didn't resist when he knelt and removed her sandals, then took her hand and led her into the surf, the water soaking them to their waists. She didn't pull away when he gently stroked her face and pulled her against him. Their lips touched, tentatively at first, then the memories flooded back.

"Mom, Dad, you're soaked!" Jill and Ellie shrieked when they saw them coming up the beach, arms hooked together. "What happened?"

"Suzanne and I were just walking near the surf when a big wave splashed us."

Ellie turned to Jill. "He's telling a big fat fib."

Every morning, the four of them set off on new adventures around Oahu and up into the tropical forest, hunting for trees to inspire Suzanne, and each day they grew closer, as broken threads were reconnected. The foreshadowing of their budding romance was the frequency of fresh stories and laughter that they knew would subside with time and familiarity as their stories and experiences were retold.

Alex wanted Suzanne to experience something unexpected, exhilarating, and memorable, and he arranged for a helicopter tour of the Na Pali Coast, on Kauai, without telling them. He only told Suzanne and his daughters that they were flying over to Kauai for two days to see the Na Pali Coast, the most picturesque coastline in Hawaii and, some claimed, in the entire Pacific. They had all seen photos of the crenellated three thousand–foot verdant cliffs, so they thought they knew what to expect. Suzanne anticipated that they would take one of the many catamaran boat tours to see the iconic coast. As soon as she realized they were going on a helicopter tour, she said to Alex, "It's too expensive."

"Suzanne, I had twenty-years to save for this."

Their pilot, Ben O'Leary, was more than experienced; he had five years of combat experience flying Black Hawk helicopters and sixteen years flying helicopters over Kauai. He was cheerful but exacting in giving them safety instructions before takeoff. He warned about the cloud cover over part of the Na Pali Coast and decided to check out Waimea Canyon first, but it was also socked in with clouds, and he turned seaward, skirting the coast. As they turned east along the Na Pali Coast, a double rainbow appeared, arching over the entrance to Kalalau Valley.

Ben exclaimed, "That's only the second time in sixteen years I've seen a double rainbow." Then he hovered so everyone could take photos. Alex was relieved that the flight had produced something memorable, even if they couldn't fly into Wai'ale'ale Crater, usually the climax of the helicopter tour.

They continued along the Na Pali Coast, dipping lower to watch a rigid-hull inflatable boat with a dozen people zoom into a sea cave and emerge a few seconds later from another cave entrance. They spotted a monk seal with her baby on a small beach and, high on the cliffs, a wild goat.

As they swung south to head back, Ben announced, "The clouds have pulled back, so maybe I can get into the lost world of waterfalls."

They flew high above and over the Na Pali cliffs then swooped down into the Wai'ale'ale Crater, lined on three sides with pleated velvet cliffs and twelve waterfalls plunging over a thousand feet to the valley floor.

"Oh, my God!" Suzanne exclaimed. "I never believed such a place could exist."

"Miss, that is my feeling every time I can fly into the crater. Most days, it's shrouded in clouds, and I'm unable to show the crown jewel of Hawaii's natural wonders. It's not publicized well, and that's good, because it has a spiritual quality that demands respect and tranquility."

Suzanne turned Alex's face toward hers and kissed him, the roar of the helicopter drowning out her words and the giggles of the girls seated behind.

The second day was spent hiking the rugged, narrow Kalalau Trail, along the Na Pali Coast, giving them a closeup view of the rugged cliffs and birdlife. They climbed down the rocky trail at the two-mile mark to Hanakapi'ai Beach, which they had hoped to have to themselves. But a large Hawaiian monk seal had already staked out the prime spot, opening an eye to check out the intruders before dozing off in the sun. Alex and Suzanne laid out the bento boxes of barbequed chicken, steamed rice, and macaroni salad—an island favorite—while their daughters explored the beach for shells.

"Alex, this feels like a real family outing."

"Suzanne, no matter what happens tomorrow, today is real."

Back on Oahu, the day began with breakfast at the popular and noisy Eggs 'n Things, then the girls opted to stay and explore Waikiki Beach while Alex and Suzanne went to the Honolulu Museum of Art. Alex hoped Honolulu's little-publicized but world-class art museum would impress Suzanne, who was familiar with the more famous art collections in Manhattan. He told her to close her eyes, and he led her into a room to show her works of his favorite painter.

"Now open your eyes."

She said nothing as she gazed at the two golden-brown Tahitian women standing on a beach against a backdrop of white-crested waves.

"Well, what do you think?"

"Alex, it's by Paul Gauguin! I love his work—his use of color, his portrayal of Tahitian women in lush tropical settings. I didn't expect to see such important works by Gauguin in Hawaii."

"There's much more."

As they moved among the rooms, Suzanne was enthralled by the works of Cezanne, Monet, van Gogh, Matisse, and Picasso. Then they entered the Asian collection, with thousands of pieces spanning five thousand years, including calligraphy, exquisite painted scrolls, ceramics, Japanese woodblock prints, and statues.

They had their lunch in the Pavilion Café, in the museum's airy tropical courtyard with its gardens, immense stairway mural, impressive sculptures, and gigantic ceramics. It reminded Suzanne of outdoor restaurants in Italy. "This is the best lunch I've had in Hawaii, Alex. And I never expected to see such valuable works of the great European painters on a tropical island. This is a must for anyone who loves art. But where are the visitors?"

"They do little advertising, plus most tourists are in Hawaii for the sunny beaches. I've thought about offering to help them with their advertising. But I can't bring myself to do it. Turning it into a crowded tourist attraction would take away its peaceful serenity." He smiled. "But it would be easier than turning around a bakery business selling goods with a five-day shelf life, since art doesn't go stale."

They spent the rest of the afternoon looking at the thirty-two galleries and had only scratched the surface of the twenty thousand works of art when it closed at five. They had an early dinner with their two girls in the oceanfront Outrigger Reef Bar & Grill, where patrons cooked their own fish and steaks that were accompanied by a buffet salad bar. Jill and Ellie took over the cooking chores, while Suzanne and Alex waited, holding hands across their table, their mood mellowing as they discussed what they would do on their last day together.

The final day was spent on the beach in front of the Outrigger Reef Hotel, snorkeling and relaxing on chaise longues under beach umbrellas. Alex and Suzanne had started the week with no idea of the changes ahead, and as the week closed, there was still no clarity about the way forward. Both had deep roots where they were, and they were a continent apart. While Suzanne had forgiven Alex, forgiveness and an enjoyable week together couldn't bring back the missing twenty years of life. Maintaining a long-distance relationship was fraught with danger, especially with Suzanne already dating someone in Manhattan. Yet that was the plan.

The sun was setting as Jill and Ellie took cold showers on the beach, Jill helping her new sister rinse sand from her tangled hair.

Alex handed them towels after they turned off the faucet. "What do you two want for dinner on your last night together?"

"Daddy, I want Jill to spend the night with me. We'll make our own dinner and stay up late playing games, and you and Suzanne can go out and have a dinner without us as chaperones."

Alex laughed. "You have it all planned out. Suzanne, do you think you can trust being alone with me without our chaperones?"

"I'm not so sure. But at least this time I've got the right telephone number," she joked. "If we can get a reservation, I'd love to dine next door at Orchids, in the Halekulani. It's a little pricy, but it has five-star reviews."

They returned to Alex's Manoa Valley home so he could show Suzanne where he and Ellie lived. At the entrance, they stepped over an assortment of shoes, sandals, and slippers and into a cluttered home where tidiness was clearly not a priority. Books and magazines were piled everywhere, and mismatched dishes and pans covered the kitchen counter. Even the paintings and prints on the walls were a mismatch, with an abstract Miro print next to a painting of a beach scene on the Big Island. The spare bedroom had boxes of Christmas decorations, a full laundry basket, and an ironing board next to a rack of clothes. Ellie pranced around the house excitedly, showing Jill her things. A child's touch was everywhere: drawings and finger paintings taped to the refrigerator, the doors, and her bedroom walls, a school project on the kitchen table, dolls on the couch.

"Pretty messy, huh?"

"Alex, it's a home with lots of love, but it could use a little order."

"Wait until you see the view from the upstairs lanai." He led her up the stairs to his bedroom and onto the lanai. "How would you like to wake up to this view every morning?"

She leaned on the railing as she looked down Manoa Valley to Waikiki Beach and the ocean beyond. "My view in Manhattan is of skyscrapers, but what I like most about your home is I can see love for Ellie in every room. You've made it a real home."

Ellie shortened the home tour by yelling, "You two can go anytime. I want to be alone with my sister." As they reached the front door, Ellie said, "Dad, stay out as looong as you want. Jill and I are going to play games and watch some videos."

"I might not be back until almost midnight. Are you sure you'll be okay?"

"Dad, I'm almost nine, and Jill is with me. You need to make sure Suzanne's last night in Hawaii is special. You know what I mean?"

He smiled and kissed both daughters on their cheeks.

He wasn't surprised to see the kitchen light still on when he pulled into the driveway at five seventeen the next morning. Ellie often fell asleep with lights on, even in her bedroom. He quietly unlocked the front door and stepped inside, slipping off his shoes. He had on one sock—the other lost on the beach. He tiptoed to the kitchen to switch off the light and froze. Ellie was standing, holding a tray with coffee mugs and toast.

"Ellie, what are you doing up so early?"

"Dad, we need to talk." She pushed aside the papier-mâché school project on the table, put down the tray, and handed a mug to her father.

"Did you and Jill quarrel?"

"No. We had lots of fun, and we didn't go to bed until midnight. She's the sister I always wished for." Ellie paused—her eyes focused on her dad. "I couldn't sleep."

"Worried that I didn't come home last night?"

"No. I hoped you would stay with Suzanne."

Alex cautiously sipped his coffee, wincing at the bitter taste. "Too strong?"

"A little, but a good first try," he said as he put down the mug. "I'm sure you didn't get up at five just to make me coffee."

"I want to know about you and Suzanne. My friend at school told me that when a man spends the night with a woman, they make babies and will get married. Is that true?"

He clasped his hands together on the table as he considered his daughter's probing question. "Ellie, it's more complicated than that. Last night, Suzanne and I had a long talk about our future."

Ellie licked the jam on her toast. "Are you going to marry Suzanne?"

"You're getting ahead of things." He beamed at Ellie and leaned over and kissed her forehead. "Suzanne's decided to change her flights. I hope you don't mind sharing your room with your big sister."

Tangled Leis

*K*elsey looked forward to her twilight swims off Waikiki Beach, especially after school on Fridays, when she didn't have to rush home to correct student papers and prepare for the following day's classes. After six years teaching Chinese at a high school in Los Angeles, she had jumped at the opportunity to move to Honolulu and teach at the prestigious Iolani School. She happily gave up a comfortable two-bedroom apartment in the LA suburbs for a one-bedroom condo and a mortgage fifty percent higher. The trade-offs were worth it—a ten-minute walk to Iolani School compared to an hour drive in LA, and the opportunity to swim year-round with much healthier air quality. Her main regret in leaving LA was that she couldn't drive over to see her parents in nearby Anaheim. Her Irish-American father had met her Chinese mother while on a United Nations mission to Beijing, China, and after two years of secretly dating, they had married.

At five foot nine, she was the tallest woman in her family, and only an inch shorter than her father. Her rounder eyes, lighter complexion, and brown hair were a giveaway that she was not pure Chinese, but hapa, as mixed-race groups were called in Hawaii. She felt strongly about preserving her

Chinese heritage, an important reason for becoming a Chinese language teacher.

Two-mile-long Waikiki Beach was divided into a series of beaches, with her favorite, Sans Souci, near Diamond Head. It was popular with locals because there was free parking, and it was less commercial, so the crowds were smaller. Kelsey regularly went to the beach because the offshore channel through the coral reef provided the best place in Waikiki for serious swimming.

The crowds thinned in late afternoon, and by the time she arrived, shortly before sunset, there was only a handful of people on the beach. Kelsey adjusted her Speedo goggles as she gazed out at her destination, the red flag marking the entrance to the channel. A few yards offshore stood a man in a new aloha shirt and Bermuda shorts, his head bowed, and flower leis in his hands. She sometimes saw people tossing leis into the ocean on their final day in Hawaii or in memory of a loved one, so she waded around him, checked her goggles, then began her swim to the red flag.

Depending on the tides, the current through the channel could be strong and not for weak swimmers, but today she could barely feel the current, a sign that it would be a fast swim. She paused at the red flag to check her time, then set off, stroking harder to cut off a few seconds on the return trip. Almost to shore, her arms flailed in the water and she stood up, pink and white petals floated around her as she untangled a lei from her arms. She looked up into the eyes of the man that had cast the leis into the surf.

"I'm so sorry, I didn't see your leis."

His pensive expression was replaced by a gentle smile. "No apology needed. It was just an accident." He paused. "The blossoms are kind of pretty spread over the water."

She was surprised by his forgiving remarks and waded toward him, taking in his height, his sturdy build, the generous lock of hair across his forehead, and his tanned face. As she moved closer, she could see a two- to three-day growth of whiskers and gray around his temples, suggesting he was older than his otherwise mid-thirties appearance.

"I'm Kelsey O'Brian." She extended her hand. "I hope you don't mind a wet handshake."

"Not at all." His hand embraced hers more firmly than necessary. "Jason Abbott, from Menlo Park, California. I'm a geologist working with the US Geological Survey."

"I feel I owe you something for ruining your ceremony."

He shook his head. "It was my fault for tossing the lei in front of you and messing up your swim. I owe you an apology."

Kelsey smiled as she picked a petal from her shoulder. "Let's call it a draw as our apologies cancel each other's. Have a nice evening."

Jason's gaze followed her as she crossed the beach to the outdoor shower. He stood mesmerized, watching the spray dance off her body, producing a halo effect in the setting sun. He waded ashore and walked toward her. "Miss O'Brian, would you care to join me for a drink in the Kaimana Beach cocktail lounge? I feel a bit melancholy and would feel better having a drink with you."

She hadn't heard that line before, but she didn't immediately reply as she toweled off. "I have a date with Pikake at seven, so it will have to be a quick one."

He grinned. "That'll be fine."

"I'll change in the hotel restroom and meet you in the cocktail lounge." As she combed her hair in front of the mirror, she mused, *If he's interesting, I'll give him my number, and if not, I'll make a speedy exit to meet Pikake.*

He smiled and quickly stood when she entered the lobby. "That was a fast transformation. What would you like to drink?"

"A Kirin draft would be fine."

He ordered the same, then there was an awkward silence. "You also like Japanese beer?"

"Yes, particularly in a Japanese-owned hotel where it tastes better. Have you been to Japan?"

"I visited Tokyo during my research on volcanoes around the Pacific Rim," he said. "I climbed Mount Fuji along with hundreds Japanese tourists. More exciting was climbing a volcano in Papua New Guinea and almost getting cooked."

"By the natives or the volcano?"

"The volcano. My taxi driver in Port Moresby told me there's actually a law against eating humans in PNG."

"So, there must be a reason that they had to pass a law," she said.

"My thinking also. Cultural reasons, they say." He raised his glass. "Cheers." There was another long pause. "Hawaii is a dream location for a volcanologist. That's a geologist that studies volcanoes."

"So, you're a volcanologist?"

"Yes," he enthusiastically replied.

"Interesting," she replied in a monotone voice.

"My dissertation was on the chemistry of Hawaiian volcanoes to determine why they're less explosive then those around the Pacific Rim."

"They have the friendly aloha spirt," she jested.

He missed her bit of humor. "They are deficient in silica, because the Hawaiian lava doesn't pass through the silica-rich continental crust like those along the edges of continents. Interesting how such small amounts of silica in basalt can make such a huge difference."

To you, she thought. She took a gulp of her beer and gave a forced smile as she put the half-empty glass on the table. "Sorry, but I have to run. Can't be late for my date with Pikake."

Jason continued to look toward the hotel entrance after she disappeared. He shrugged and touched his glass to hers. *What was I thinking, talking about the chemistry of volcanoes?* He hadn't had a date since Doris had died eleven months earlier, following an eighteen-month battle with cancer. It had been painful watching her decline, and his feelings of helplessness had almost overwhelmed him. They'd reminisced about their eleven years together and their honeymoon in Hawaii until the final days, when she was too sedated to be aware of what he was saying. He had kept on talking to Doris until the nurse entered the room, looked at the straight-line on the monitor screen, checked her pulse, and told him she had passed away. He nodded, then continued talking to Doris until the nurse took his hand and led him away.

He knew his courting skills were rusty, and he had trepidations about dating again. Doris had been emphatic that he must move on in life, and that would include falling in love again. After her death, he had dealt with his grief by turning his energies to work. But that wasn't enough. Increasingly he had trouble sleeping; he'd wake, aroused and lonely. Finally, he made the decision to begin dating. But first he needed to fulfill a promise to Doris—the purpose of the trip to Hawaii.

His sister had insisted that he would have to bring closure to his past with Doris before he'd be able to open his heart to love again. He had booked the Hyatt Regency Waikiki Resort and Spa, where they had stayed on their honeymoon. It was more expensive than other hotels, but on their wedding night in Waikiki, Doris had made Jason promise that they would return someday. He deeply regretted not bringing her back until it was too late. He hoped the symbolic gesture of tossing the two leis into the surf would bring a degree of closure. But the solemn ceremony had been interrupted by Kelsey accidentally becoming entangled in the leis. He laid back in bed, wondering if it was serendipity. But if it was, he had blown his chance. He flicked off his bedside light, punched his pillow, and turned onto his side.

Kelsey stood on her balcony stroking Pikake's soft fur as she gazed over Waikiki at the towers of the five-star Hyatt Regency Hotel. She had been surprised to see the hotel's magnetic room key in Jason's wallet, thinking a government geologist would most likely be staying in a less pricy hotel. "You know, Pikake, he's quite handsome and took an interest in me, but his conversational skills would put anyone but another geologist into a coma. Hopefully, Pikake, his interests go beyond volcanic rocks. Maybe he was just nervous, and I was too abrupt. What do you think?"

Pikake, continued licking his fur. She'd had two dates with handsome and suave men in the last year—both a disappointment. Calvin Farley, a pilot, was so enamored with himself that he couldn't stop looking past her at himself in a mirror. At least Jason kept his eyes on her from the moment they met in the ocean until she got up to leave. She'd bet he'd watched her all the way to the door.

At 7:18 a.m., Jason stepped from the elevator into the lobby, carrying a battered bag on his way to catch the hotel bus to the airport. The scent of flowers filled the air, and the indoor waterfall added a soothing sound that muffled people's voices.

"Aloha," Kelsey called out in a cheerful voice, as she glided across the polished floor—her white muumuu, patterned with delicate pink orchids, flowing after her. She looped a tuberose lei over his head and gave him a hug and brushed a kiss on his cheek. Her fragrance was intoxicating.

"Kelsey, what are you doing here?"

"Driving you to the airport. I would hate for you to miss your flight to see a volcano," she quipped.

"But how did you know where I was staying and when I was leaving for the airport?"

She laughed. "I don't know you well enough to reveal my secrets."

"I'm really glad you came. After last night, I was sure I'd never hear from you again."

"Your pickup lines need some work."

"Where are you parked?

"Right in front."

Between a Jaguar and a Mercedes was a dusty white Nissan. The Asian bellman opened the driver's side door for Kelsey, then held back a limousine so she could pull out onto Uluniu Street.

"The bellman must be a friend?"

"I've never seen him before, but he's an Iolani graduate and saw the Iolani School staff sticker on my bumper. There's a special loyalty to one's high school in Hawaii; it can be almost as important as your university degree in getting a job or running for public office. Put Punahou or Iolani school on your job application, and you are already ahead of others."

"What's that sweet smell?"

"There's a box of malasadas in the back seat. They're a treat the Portuguese brought with them. I thought we could have a coffee and pastry at the airport before your flight. Have you ever tried a malasada?"

"No, but my guidebook says it's a donut minus a hole and has a sweet jam filling."

"Yes, and not very healthy. But I still like them on special occasions."

"So, it's a special occasion driving me to the airport?"

"Too early to tell."

They only had time for a quick cup of coffee and a guava-filled malasada before the boarding announcement. "How can I repay you for the ride and pastries?"

She laughed. "Don't fall in the volcano."

Kelsey took the slow route back to Waikiki along Nimitz Highway and parked in the free parking area next to the Ala Wai Yacht Harbor. She strolled along the dock, reading the hopeful names on the yachts—Intrepid, Liberty, My Passion, Free Spirit, Second Wind, Destination Unknown. She thought about the kind of people that owned the yachts. These were not the luxury yachts of the very wealthy but of people of more modest means. She'd had dreamed about sailing to enchanted islands in the South Pacific but had chosen security instead. Jason was the type that she could envision on such an adventure. Was that what made him appealing?

Kelsey was pleased that she'd surprised him at Hyatt Regency and driven him to the airport. It made up for walking out on him the previous evening, and now the ball was in his court. But he wasn't like most men and might not know how to volley. She returned to her apartment and discussed the issue with Pikake, who refused to take a position on the matter.

As soon as his flight leveled out and coffee was served, he opened his box with the remaining two malasadas. The young girl next to him stared back and forth between the pastries and him.

"Keala, don't bother the man," said her Hawaiian mother.

"Would you like the last two malasadas?" said Jason. "I had all I can eat at the airport."

He sipped his coffee, trying not to inhale the intoxicating smell of the pastries he had given away. From the right side of the plane, he watched snowcapped Mauna Kea and Mauna Loa appear as faint white clouds that gradually materialized into the massive volcanoes that dominated the Big Island. The volcanoes, just under fourteen thousand feet above sea level, were the highest mountains in the world when measured from their base on the sea floor. Though the scientific installations were hotly contested by Hawaiians, they supported telescopes with the clearest land-based views of the solar system and beyond, as well as an observatory taking samples of atmospheric gases, including carbon dioxide concentrations.

Hilo International Airport was humid, the air laced with the scents of tropical flowers. His rental car was waiting, and a scant forty-five minutes later, he was at the entrance to Hawaii Volcanoes National Park. His US Geological Survey ID got him in free, and a minute past the main gate was Volcano House, the historic inn perched on the lip of the Kilauea Caldera. The hotel was the only one in the park and well worth the price for the view into the large caldera. From the hotel terrace, visitors could see the occasional eruptions of lava, and the plumes of sulfurous smoke and steam billowing from the Halema'uma'u Crater, located on the far side of the Kilauea Caldera.

Jason easily spotted Heather Madison sitting near the rugged stone fireplace, reading a US Geological Survey report. Even in her khaki shirt and pants, she was quite attractive, something he'd noticed daily when they'd worked together in Alaska. Since he had been dating Doris at the time, he'd never revealed his attraction to Heather, but they did become good friends. It had been six years since he'd seen Heather, and the streaks of gray in her hair, now cut short, added a sophistication he found appealing.

"Welcome to my playground," she said, rising to shake his hand and lean in for a quick hug. "But, Jason, I have some bad news. I got a call two hours ago to fly back to the USGS headquarters in Reston ASAP. I had to have at least one day with you, so I booked a flight out tomorrow. Seems a conservative congressman from Kentucky wants to slash our budget for research on predicting volcanic eruptions—*again*. Probably because there are no volcanoes in Kentucky." She shook her head in disgust. "I was hoping we'd have more time together so we could catch up on more than geology. But at least I have today to give you a cook's tour. For the rest of the week, you'll be on your own."

Is she implying more than a professional interest in me? "Heather," he said. "I was also hoping for more time together, but I understand. Protecting your budget takes priority."

"Thanks for understanding. As soon as you check into your room, I'll give you a tour of the park. This evening, we'll drive to the coast to watch lava flowing into the ocean and the memorable fireworks it produces."

To most tourists, the Hawaii Volcanoes National Park was good for a one- to two-day visit, including the nightly fireworks display caused by molten lava pouring into the ocean. To Jason it was much more meaningful than that; the visit to the Hawaii Volcanoes National Park was about as good as it could get in field research. A fellow volcanologist had described his visit to the Kilauea volcano as "achieving nirvana."

They started behind the Volcano House Hotel on the terrace overlook, where they had an intriguing view of the barren caldera floor of buckled lava flows. Two hikers appeared as ants, inching across the moon-like landscape of the three-mile-wide caldera. Heather told him that, decades ago, before the mission to the moon, astronauts practiced walking in the caldera to get the feel of what it would be like on the lunar surface.

They rode in the USGS Jeep southwest around the chasm, stopping at the overlook and Thomas A. Jaggar Museum to study the multimedia displays, maps, and artifacts. Then they headed to the adjacent Hawaii Volcano Observatory to view the seismographic activity and historical measurements.

"Heather, I see on the seismograph record quite a bit of activity over the past two weeks."

"Yes, Pele's getting restless, but no eruptions are expected while you're here. More likely it'll be a few months away before we'll see any surface expressions. Fortunately, thanks to close monitoring these days, we'll have enough warning before an eruption to clear the park of tourists." She explained the updates in the monitoring equipment. "Next we'll drive around to take a look into Pele's home in Halemaʻumaʻu Crater.

Pele, as Jason knew from his reading, was the goddess of Hawaiian volcanoes, revered by many Hawaiians who still left flower leis and other offerings around Halemaʻumaʻu Crater. The parking lot near the Halemaʻumaʻu Crater was full, but the parking restrictions did not apply to official park vehicles. A seven-minute walk brought them to the overlook and the plumes of heavy smoke and sulfurous gases he'd seen from Volcano House. They covered their mouths with handkerchiefs as they peered down into Pele's brew of the bubbling red and yellow magma.

"I've looked into the magma chambers of five volcanoes, Heather, but I've never had the opportunity to be so close."

"Most people don't realize that this is the best spot in the world to have a closeup look into the throat of an active volcano. Pretty cool."

They bypassed the popular six hundred–foot Thurston lava tube, which was large enough for a small car, and explored one of the dozens of lava tubes closed to the public. Heather had brought along a large flashlight and pointed out the geological features on their hour-long walk inside the lava tube.

"Some of these extend more than twenty miles to the coast and contain rare molds and insects that have evolved in isolation for tens of thousands of years," she told him. "The extreme remoteness of the Hawaiian Islands and the lack of predators have allowed the evolution of thousands of molds and insects that exist nowhere else in the world. My thinking is there are important drug possibilities in these molds and fungi that should be investigated."

"Sounds logical to me. Maybe send some samples to some of the pharmaceutical companies."

"I contacted the biological research center at UH, but that's as much involvement as I can take on."

"Heather, I've read that over fifty species of finches evolved in the Hawaiian Islands from a single pair of finches blown across the Pacific from the Americas. Here they developed into bright-colored honeycreepers. But today, over half of the honeycreepers and two-thirds of the native species of birds have become extinct."

"Yes. The isolation of the Hawaiian Islands without predators produced vulnerable species that were less adaptable to change and invasive predators. Birdlife extinction is going on at a faster rate here than anywhere else in the United States. It's because of a combination of factors: loss of their original forest habitat; introduction of mongooses, rats, and malaria by Europeans; and, to a lesser extent, native Hawaiians who prized their bright plumage for decorative purposes, especially for royal regalia—like capes and kahili, those royal standards with the feather plumes."

"Didn't I read that the native Hawaiians had conservation practices that prevented over-harvesting of feathers for decorative purposes?"

"Yes, and there's evidence of conservation among native populations across most Pacific islands. I suggest you visit the Bishop Museum's collection of kahili and capes. I go there when I'm on Oahu for their lectures, workshops, and, of course, their astronomy events—not to mention their light shows. They even have concerts at the planetarium. And you must see the arts of Hawaii exhibits. They're amazing."

Jason had always been impressed with the way Heather was a fountain of knowledge that went well beyond geology. They frequently brushed against each other as they climbed over fallen slabs of lava on the cave floor. Up close, he detected the scent of Heather's perfume and wondered if she had put it on for him.

They had lunch outside the entrance among human-sized ferns and under the shade of a large 'ohi'a tree, with feathery red blossoms.

"You know, Jason, sometimes I have to pinch myself for being so lucky to work here on a living volcano surrounded by so much beauty."

"It does sound great. But don't you ever get lonely?"

She handed him an orange. "There's a friendly community in nearby Volcano Village, but a scarcity of men I would date." She reached across and gently squeezed his hand. "Jason, I was sorry to hear about the passing of Doris. Are you seeing anyone? Or is it too soon?"

He paused to peel the orange. *Should I mention Kelsey and squelch the chance that Heather is interested?* He wasn't dating her, so no reason to mention her. Yet Kelsey had aroused him after he returned to his room in the Hyatt Regency Hotel, sending him to a cold shower. How seriously should he take this?

"I, uh, met an interesting woman on Waikiki Beach. I asked her for a drink, but once I got talking about silica in lava, she almost ran for the exit. Still, she picked me up this morning and drove me to the airport. Think she might be interested?"

Heather smiled. "If she came back after you bored her to tears, then she's interested. I think you're a good catch, Jason. Seems our timing is always a little off," she mused aloud.

"Heather, I had hoped to find out if there might be something more than friendship between us. But whatever we might have, it must be based on honesty." He handed her an orange wedge.

It was midafternoon when they turned down the Chain of Craters Road, leading to the coast. The nineteen-mile two-lane road was etched into multiple lava flows, monotonous and uninteresting to most tourists but fascinating to geologists. Along the road were textbook examples of cinder cones, different kinds of lava flows, both *pahoehoe* (ropy) and *'a'a* (blocky), and kipukas, the isolated islets of native forest that appeared to float on the frozen river of lava. They made several stops to examine slabs of lava banded with green olivine crystals, proof of the deep source of the lava, and in crevices, Heather pointed out the bristling glass needles called Pele's hair.

They reached the parking area near the ocean at twilight and proceeded beyond the roped-off section that kept tourists from getting too close to the river of lava pouring into the ocean. Nowhere else in the world could people come to view thousands of tons of 2,200-degree lava flowing into the sea. It produced explosions that hurled fiery lava bombs hundreds of feet into the air, lighting the sky in a continuous fireworks display. As they neared the molten river, Jason thought about Kelsey's quip that he shouldn't fall into the lava.

It was after ten when they arrived back at Volcano House, and Jason invited Heather in for a nightcap around the massive stone fireplace. He knew she couldn't stay long; she had to pack and get ready for her morning flight. The day had been as important for the geology as for the chance to become reacquainted with each other at a personal level.

As Heather rose to leave, she reached for Jason's hand and pulled him close. "If I were you, I'd hop on the first flight back to Honolulu. Goddess Pele is millions of years old and patient, but what you found on Waikiki Beach may be fleeting." She kissed him firmly on the lips, before quickly walking to the door. Then she turned. "If Waikiki Beach doesn't pan out, there're more interesting things we can uncover back here in Volcanoes National Park." She blew him a kiss and, moments later, was gone.

Jason was up before sunrise, standing on the balcony of the Volcano House Hotel, gazing toward the shadowy plume of steam from Halema'uma'u Crater. At any other time, his heart would be pounding in anticipation of a day examining the treasure trove of volcanic rocks. But, like static on a shortwave radio, his research plans kept being interrupted by thoughts of Kelsey—and Heather's warning. The first flight with available seats was at nine thirty-five a.m., giving him time for a breakfast of eggs, Portuguese sausage, and pancakes with local 'ohi'a preserves made from a cranberry-like berry that grew high on the slopes of Kilauea.

Minutes seemed to drag by during the hour-long flight back to Oahu. He hurried to the baggage carousel and waited impatiently for his bag, then dashed out to the curb and flagged a taxi. He reached the New Otani Kaimana Beach Hotel just before noon, forgetting to request the government rate until the receptionist asked. In his room, he threw down his bag and called Iolani School, but he was told Miss O'Brian was on personal leave and would return the following day. The school receptionist wouldn't release her unlisted telephone number but took a message for her to call him the following day.

He wasn't about to sit in his room in Waikiki, and he decided to swim out to the red flag, as Kelsey had done. Swimming out was easy, then he discovered how difficult it was to swim back to shore against the outgoing tide. Exhausted, he sat on his towel enjoying the kaleidoscope of colors and shapes of bikinis on the beach. He was about to return to his room when a newlywed Japanese couple, photographer, and two assistants crossed the beach to the water's edge. The couple looked so young and innocent as the photographer and assistants adjusted their poses between shots, the bride's smile unwavering throughout the half-hour photo shoot. The carefully arranged stoic poses reminded Jason of mannequins in a clothing store window. He hoped they would have fond memories like his of his wedding day on Waikiki Beach. Back then, he couldn't afford a professional photographer and had asked a passerby to snap a couple of pictures. Those two photos were enlarged and remained on Doris's dresser until she died. They'd finally moved to a photo album the day before his trip to Hawaii.

He returned to his room to shower and change, then he went back to the beach to catch the sunset, Birkenstock sandals in hand as he strolled toward the main section of Waikiki Beach to find a beachside restaurant for dinner. The crowds had dissipated, leaving legions of footprints to be erased by the incoming tide. Hawaiian melodies wafted from the hotels, blending with the timeless swish of the surf, and the whiffs of succulent dishes quickened his pace.

Among the high-rise hotels lining the beach was the flamingo-pink Royal Hawaiian Hotel. Its classic tropical architecture harkened back to an era when only the most prosperous or adventurous travelers ventured to the islands, traveling by steamship. He paused to listen to a tenor's voice as the man strummed on his slack-key guitar. Jason casually gazed over the mostly older crowd, then froze as the young woman in a scarlet dress came into focus. It was Kelsey, wearing a double-strand flower lei, fawning over a strikingly handsome man twice her age, their hands entwined as she leaned across the cocktail table. Jason spun around and hurried away, angry with himself for reading so much into their brief meeting on Waikiki Beach. It was obvious why she hadn't given him her telephone number—she didn't want him to call.

When he reached Sans Souci Beach, he waded in at the spot where he had tossed the two leis in memory of his deceased wife. He stood for several minutes gazing toward the horizon, not seeing or hearing the beauty of the ceaseless ocean. A flash of white fluttered past his right shoulder and settled on the water. For an instant it was a bird; then it materialized into a double-strand flower lei. He turned as Kelsey waded toward him, her dress wicking up the water, her red shoes scattered on the beach.

"Why did you run away?"

"You were with your lover."

"He's my father, and I haven't seen him for over a year. Why aren't you on the Big Island studying volcanoes?"

Jason stood, arms to his side, staring at Kelsey. "Some things are more important than volcanoes." Gently scooping up the lei, he waded to her and looped it over her head.

Kelsey slowly pulled back from their embrace and lifted off her lei, lovingly kissed the petals and tossed it into the surf. "Doris, thank you for letting Jason fall in love again."

Nurse Waiting

Japan's surprise attack on the Pearl Harbor on December 7, 1941, changed the lives of every American, including Helen Walker and Tommy Bowden, in Maple River, Iowa. A week after the devastating strike on the US Pacific Fleet, Tommy joined the Army, and two months later, Helen joined as a nurse. They were high school sweethearts and were planning to marry as soon as Helen completed her nursing degree.

With Tommy temporarily stationed at Schofield Barracks, in Central Oahu, Helen's first choice was to be sent to Tripler Army Medical Center, overlooking Pearl Harbor. Leaves were short, and Tommy proposed to Helen on Waikiki Beach two days before his deployment to the Western Pacific. She proudly showed off her tiny quarter-carat diamond ring to the other nurses. After the war, they would return to their hometown for their wedding, then take over the farm from Tommy's ailing grandparents.

Tripler Hospital was perched on the lower western slopes of the Ko'olau Mountains, with views of Pearl Harbor below. At a distance, the sunset-pink hospital could be mistaken for a majestic hotel, not the destination for thousands of wounded soldiers. The tearful parting when Tommy boarded his troop ship was quickly replaced by long hours attending to soldiers pouring into the hospital, many still in their teens.

Often, Helen would hold a soldier's hand in his final moments and talk to him softly, like a mother with her child. One dying patient with barely enough whiskers to shave penetrated the professional barrier Helen was trained to maintain. Delirious, he smiled as he reached out with both arms and asked if she was an angel sent to take him home. She held both of his hands and whispered yes, and he smiled and closed his eyes. The peaceful expression remained on his face as she pulled the sheet over his head. Helen stood stoically as his body was wheeled away, holding back her tears until she reached the bathroom. Ten minutes later, she was smiling at the bedside of another wounded soldier.

Helen was in her eleventh month at Tripler when her name was announced over the intercom. She thought it must be one of her patients calling for her, but at the nurses' duty station, she was told a new arrival in bed 183 had asked for her. She rushed to the bed, heart pounding, fearing it might be her Tommy. Who else would know her name? The soldier's head was covered in bandages, and one leg was elevated. She grabbed the clipboard at the end of the bed and was relieved to see the patient's name was not Tommy, but Ray Griffin. Age twenty-six, from Seal Cove, Maine.

"I'm Nurse Helen Walker. You asked for me?"

There was a long pause. "I knew Tommy," the man said in a slurred voice.

Helen struggled to remain calm as she reached for his hand. "Tommy's okay, right?"

He moaned under the bandages as his head wobbled from side to side. "I was with Tommy when he got hit."

"But he survived!" she shouted, tears flooding her eyes.

116

Silence, except for the metallic ticking of a clock on the wall and the distant voice of someone calling for a doctor. He squeezed her hand. "Tommy didn't make it." His voice was barely audible.

"No! It's a mistake. Tommy promised to come back and we would get married, take over his grandparent's farm and have children. He promised!"

"Miss, every night, Tommy knelt in our foxhole and repeated his promise to you and to God."

Stella Dowling, the head nurse, took Helen back to the nurse's quarters and consoled her and gave her a pep talk. "Helen, nothing you can do will bring Tommy back. But you can save other men like Tommy—men who also have loved ones waiting back home. That's what Tommy would want, and that's what you signed up for. I've seen how you give comfort and hope to the wounded. Take the day off to mourn your Tommy, but tomorrow at 0600, I expect to see you back tending wounded GIs."

Helen returned the following morning, stopping at bed 183, where she checked his medical record: "Three bullet wounds, one in lower left shoulder and two in right leg, plus three pieces of shrapnel removed from his face. Recovery expected and patient likely to be suitable for desk job."

"Good morning, Helen."

"How did you know it was me?" she said as she checked his pulse.

"You have a slight limp."

"Yes, I crashed riding my brother's bike when I was nine. Anyway, I wanted to come back and thank you for being with Tommy when he . . . uh, died. I need to know what happened."

"I'm so sorry. I met Tommy the day we landed on Guadalcanal, and we quickly became buddies. We shared

foxholes over the next nine months and seventeen days. We
had fought and pushed the Japs back from Henderson Field
and remained to defend it. We had to always be on alert as the
Japs could charge out of the jungle at any moment, day or night.
And they'd never retreat."

"What about Tommy?"

"He talked about you incessantly and wrote you many letters. Did you get them?"

"Yes, they were beautifully written and showed me a
romantic and poetic side of Tommy that I didn't know existed.
Each letter made me fall more deeply in love with him. I need
to know how he died and if he suffered."

Ray cleared his throat.

"It was dusk, the most dangerous time of day. I had just
delivered some extra ammo to two GIs in a foxhole about
twenty yards from ours and was returning, when all hell broke
loose. There was a barrage of gun fire from maybe sixty yards
away. I got hit with three bullets and collapsed on the ground,
and then mortar shells began exploding around me. I had no
chance of survival lying in the open. It was too dangerous for
anyone to try and save me, but your Tommy ran into a hail of
enemy fire and dragged me back to our foxhole. Blood was
everywhere. I thought it was mine until Tommy slumped in
my arms. His final words were, 'Tell Helen I love her more
than anything.'"

Ray choked up, and Helen struggled to hold back tears as
she stroked the back of his hand.

Helen checked on Ray daily in the weeks ahead and was
there when Dr. Woodburn removed the bandages covering his
face, revealing a bird's nest of matted whiskers that hid his features, except for his piercing hazel eyes.

Ray touched his tangled whiskers. "I look pretty scruffy, huh?"

"Yes, but a shave and bath will have you looking human again."

"Nurse Walker, do I look as handsome as you imagined?"

"That's classified."

"Nurse Walker, I knew you were pretty from the two pictures Tommy showed me. But you're gorgeous!"

"You're still shell-shocked and delusional. Better calm down so Orderly Hargrave can bathe and shave you."

"I really mean it. You have sea-blue eyes and hair spun from gold."

Dr. Woodburn shook his head and turned to Helen. "Should we give him a shot in the butt to calm him down?"

"I'm sure Orderly Hargrave can handle him."

The doctor snickered. "Mr. Griffin, follow Nurse Walker's orders and you'll be up and walking in no time." He jotted comments on the clipboard and handed it to Helen, then briskly left the room.

She leaned close and picked bits of the bandage from his whiskers. "My hair is in a bun under my cap. So, what makes you so sure it's golden?"

"A strand of pure gold is sticking out from your cap. I would love to see your hair down."

"That's officially out of bounds. I'll check on you later, when you've been bathed and shaved."

"I'd love to have you do it."

"I bet you would," she teased, "but Orderly Hargrave is quite experienced. Did I mention that Orderly Hargrave's a man?"

Over the following two months, Helen continued to stop by to check on Ray. Usually she could only stay for a few minutes before dashing off to another patient. But occasionally she had enough time to wheel him out to the hospital terrace, where they could watch the beehive of activity at Pearl Harbor—sunken navy ships being raised and facilities repaired and expanded.

As Helen got to know Ray, she recognized similarities to her Tommy. Both were handsome outdoor types from hardworking blue-collar families, humble and romantic. She hadn't realized Tommy's romantic side until she began receiving his letters from Guadalcanal. While Ray claimed to be a simple fisherman from Maine, he also had a romantic way with words and loved to recite his favorite poems. She was not surprised about his growing attraction to her, as it was common among lonely male patients far from loved ones on the mainland.

Ray was still wheelchair-bound when he was released from Tripler Hospital and transferred to a desk position at Fort DeRussy, on Waikiki Beach. He invited Helen to visit him, but she declined, claiming to be too busy at the hospital. It was true enough, but the main reason was it just felt too soon after Tommy's death to begin seeing other men. Safer were telephone calls with updates on Ray's recovery and listening to his poetic descriptions of Waikiki Beach.

Ray knew that Helen was free every other Friday evening, and he was determined to get her to visit him in Waikiki. His call was carefully rehearsed. "Helen, I have two tickets to a special fund-raiser for wounded soldiers tonight in Waikiki, and I'm hoping you can come as my guest. I'm still in a wheelchair, so you can easily outrun me if I get too frisky."

"Give me a moment." She covered the phone and turned to her roommate, Jill. "Ray wants me to come to Waikiki tonight for a fundraiser. What do you think?"

"If you don't want to go, tell him I'm available," she teased.

"Jill, you're no help." She turned back to the phone. "Okay, Ray, as long as it's for a good cause. I need a couple of hours to see if I can get a ride."

It was almost six when an open jeep with two Navy men in front and Helen in the rear screeched to a halt in front of Ray. "Nurse Walker, is this the guy you're looking for?"

"Yes. Thanks for the lift." The jeep zoomed away as soon as she touched the pavement. "It was hard getting a ride that didn't include a date. They're heading to Hotel Street for some excitement, whatever that means, and said they will return for me at ten."

Ray stood and gave her a plumeria lei followed by a brief hug. "I love your fragrance."

"My girlfriend let me use her perfume to mask the smell of hospital disinfectant. Where did you find the pretty lei?"

"A woman in my office gathered them from the plumeria tree outside our window and showed me how to string them."

"Have you asked her for a date, yet?"

"She's really cute but engaged to a marine, and I'm attracted to a nurse at Tripler."

"You're still delusional, I see." She pushed his wheelchair to the tables by the band under a large army tent next to the beach. There was a crowd of about a hundred, mostly men in uniform but few women. Before Helen had even sat down, she was asked to dance, and Ray encouraged her to have fun. Sitting in his wheelchair, he struggled to maintain a smile as he watched soldiers dancing with Helen, holding her closer than he would like. For an hour and a half, she barely had time between dances to nibble a snack and sip a drink. Finally, she turned to Ray. "I need a break. Is there somewhere quieter we can go?"

"There's a little pier a few minutes from here." He pointed the way as she pushed him along a path and to the end of the narrow wooden pier. She helped Ray from his wheelchair, and they sat with their bare feet dangling inches above the water. For security, the hotel windows were blackened, leaving haunting silhouettes of the famous Waikiki hotels—and privacy for couples, along with breathtaking views of the star-studded sky.

Helen felt comfortable enough to open up about how she had met Tommy in high school and their coming-of-age romance. "Tommy was the first boy I ever kissed on the mouth, and I really did see stars. I was only fifteen, too young to be allowed to date. But we secretly went steady through high school, and I wore his ring on a chain under my blouse. We sometimes snuck off to an old barn on his grandparent's farm to talk and make out. Because of my religious beliefs, I wanted to wait until we got married to have sex. And now it doesn't matter." She paused before looking at him again. "What about you, Ray? Is there a special girl?"

"I'm with her right now."

"I'm serious. You know I'm not ready to date yet."

"My dad's a fisherman and always needed me to help on his boat, so there was little time to date. Annie was the first girl that I kind of liked, in the eighth grade, but she liked someone else. I dated Caroline near the end of my junior year in high school, but she moved away that summer. Most of my romantic encounters have been in books I read and my writing."

"You write romance stories?"

"Just simple short stories about romances that blossom like spring flowers in the most unexpected places. My dream is to publish an anthology someday."

"I'd love to read one of your short stories."

"They're only handwritten . . . not even typed yet."

"I don't care. It'll give me a diversion from the stress of my nursing duties. How many have you written?"

"Four since coming to Fort DeRussy. I write most evenings after work. This is my first date with a real woman."

Helen didn't correct him for his comment about it being a date. She took his hand. Pulling it into her lap, her heart began to beat faster. The surf splashed on the wooden pilings throwing foamy water onto their feet as their silhouettes merged.

Later that night, Helen struggled to fall asleep. Kissing Ray had stirred feelings that she was not ready to have so soon after learning of Tommy's death. She felt guilty for necking with Ray on the same beach where she had accepted Tommy's proposal of marriage. Weren't buddies supposed to respect each other's girlfriends, fiancées, wives? Ray was no help. It was up to her to put a stop to this budding romance out of respect for Tommy. And what would Tommy's parents think if she started dating someone so soon after their son's death?

She didn't call Ray the following day or return his telephone calls. She would wait another day before calling and firmly telling him it was too early for her to be seeing anyone. She decided not to read his short stories, as it might weaken her resolve, but late that night she was drawn to the handwritten pages, rationalizing that she would soften his disappointment by adding something nice about his short stories. The first story was about a fisherman meeting a girl sketching fishing boats and their blossoming romance. The plot was simple, yet their love was authentic. And the writing familiar. Too familiar.

At nine thirty-seven the following morning, Helen marched into the office Ray shared with three men and a woman, and slammed a shoebox on Ray's desk, along with his short stories.

"Helen, why aren't you at the hospital?"

"Ray, you're a big fat liar." she shouted, drawing startled attention from the others.

"The love letters from Tommy—you wrote every one of them. They're in your handwriting and the same words you use in the stories you gave me."

Ray slumped back in his wheelchair. "I can explain everything."

Helen folded her arms across her chest. "It better be good. And no lies."

123

"Let's go outside to talk." He wheeled himself ahead of her and stopped under a large shade tree at the edge of the beach. "Tommy was deeply in love with you but couldn't express himself in words, so I helped."

"You wrote the letters? Every letter? Every word?"

"I could feel what Tommy felt and wrote what his heart was saying. Is that so wrong?"

"So, are you saying they're Tommy's feelings in those love letters and not yours?"

"They're what Tommy wanted me to write."

"You didn't answer my question. How did you feel writing those intensely romantic letters to someone else's sweetheart?"

Roy took a deep breath and looked into Helen's angry face. "I didn't have anyone like you waiting for me back home. When I wrote the letters for Tommy, I imagined that I was writing to my girlfriend—someone who loved me as much as you loved Tommy. Just a stupid fantasy of a lonely soldier in a muddy, stinking foxhole on Guadalcanal."

"So, the love letters came from the hearts of *two* men?"

Ray didn't reply—the tears in his eyes were his testament. "I guess this is good-bye."

It was mid-afternoon when Helen arrived back at her dorm, still early enough to call Tommy's parents and feel some connection to Tommy. His mother answered, and they chatted about her work at the hospital, the health of Tommy's grandparents, and how the farm was doing. Then there was an uneasy pause.

"Helen, you called for something more than how this year's corn crop is doing."

"Yes, I'm confused, and I need to know exactly how Tommy died."

"Are you really sure? It may haunt you."

"It will haunt me for the rest of my life if I don't know."

"A month ago, we received a letter from Tommy's platoon leader about the medal being recommended for the man who risked his life to save Tommy. According to two eyewitnesses, Tommy had taken extra ammo to soldiers in a nearby foxhole. On his way back, the enemy opened fire, and Tommy was wounded and fell to the ground. It was too dangerous for anyone to try and save him, but one brave soldier ran into enemy fire and pulled our son back to the safety of their foxhole. The heroic man received multiple bullet wounds, but thankfully he's recovering, according to the letter we received. We've been trying to locate him so we can thank him for risking his life to save our son."

"Was his name Ray Griffin?"

"Why yes, that's the young man I've been trying to locate. How did you know his name?"

"Ray Griffin was brought to Tripler Hospital with serious wounds. He asked for me and told me Tommy's last words. Tommy said, 'Tell Helen I love her more than anything.'"

"Helen, I know how Tommy felt about you. There's something more that you need to know. Two weeks ago, we received the last letter Tommy wrote. It was delayed somewhere in the military postal system. It was written four days before Tommy was killed." There was a long pause, and Helen heard soft weeping. "Helen, Tommy wrote about Ray."

There was a stunned silence before Helen could ask her to go on.

"What did he say?"

"Tommy wrote that if he didn't make it back, I should introduce you to his buddy, Ray." They both sobbed.

The revelations were too much for Helen to absorb, and she called in sick the following morning. At two thirty that afternoon, there was a knock on her door. "Who is it?"

"It's Ray."

"I'm a mess."

"I don't care. Please open the door."

She opened the door and pushed aside the hair hanging over her face. "You're not in your wheelchair."

"Doctor Woodbury said I don't need it anymore. But that's not why I'm here. I got a call from Tommy's mother to thank me for trying to save Tommy. She invited me to visit them in Iowa."

"Anything else?"

"Yes, but for once I can't think of the right words to say."

She reached for his hand pulling it to her breast. "You already said them in your letters."

Delayed Letter

D rew Miles flipped through his mail, most of it going into the wastebasket unopened. Bills were paid by auto pay, and most correspondence now was by email and Facebook. So he was surprised to see a letter, especially one stained and wrinkled, with a six-cent postage stamp and a bold post office imprint: LETTER DELAYED. The original postal mark was 2/1/1970. "Delayed!" he blurted out. "That's an understatement. It's 2004." He carefully slit open the envelope, and even after so long, he recognized Dorothy's flowing handwriting on the one-page letter. He hadn't received any communication from her since the divorce and blamed her lawyer for turning what should have been an uncontested divorce into an acrimonious one that neither side had wanted.

Drew regretted his one-night stand that led Dorothy, already depressed after the death of their infant son, to file for divorce. He hesitated before reading the letter that might open old wounds. He had forgiven her in his mind three decades ago and moved on with his life. He had dated several women, three seriously, but had been more successful as a city planner in Mountain View, California. His innovative ideas on better city designs had resulted in several trips to Europe and Asia, which he'd combined with vacations. But he hadn't returned to Hawaii. It was Hawaii where he and Dorothy had spent their honeymoon. He smoothed out the wrinkled letter and took a deep breath before reading.

February 1, 1970
Dear Drew,
   When our precious baby died, a part of me died too. I couldn't explain to you my depression, and I thought I could get through it on my own. I should have confided more in you and sought professional counseling. I'm sorry I was so cold in bed. I know part of the reason for your affair was what was going on at home—or rather what was not going on. I gave you the cold shoulder, but I never stopped loving you. The lawyer I chose was no good, and he made everything so much worse. I just wanted it over with and to escape far away.
   I'm writing this letter because I leave in five days for a job in Waikiki as an assistant manager of a small hotel, and I'm not sure I'm doing the right thing. What I want to say is I forgive you for the affair and maybe you might want to come to Hawaii next summer, and we can see if there's something worth putting back together. Maybe I'm too much of a romantic, still thinking the pieces can be salvaged after such a bitter divorce. Anyway, you can contact me at the Golden Sands Hotel in Waikiki.
Aloha,
Dorothy

Drew leaned back in his chair and closed his eyes. He hadn't wanted the divorce, thinking she would cool down and they would reconcile. But Dorothy's twice-divorced girlfriend had suggested her own tough lawyer, and then there was no turning back. Dorothy's lawyer told her to make no contact without him present, so reconciliation wasn't possible. But what would be the purpose of contacting Dorothy thirty-four years later? She probably was married and had grown children. An apology after so many years would sound disingenuous or worse. Now retired for less than a year, he was planning a trip to the South Pacific and Australia, and he didn't need to return to a sad chapter in his past.

Drew was restless when he set his novel aside and turned off the bedside light. The letter had caused long-dormant feelings to resurface, and perhaps it would have been better if it had never been delivered. After an hour tossing in bed, he took an over-the-counter sleeping pill and tried to think about the trip and not Dorothy.

She appeared at his bedside as a hula dancer in a grass skirt and plumeria lei, but as he reached for her, she floated away, leaving her flower lei hanging in the window. He awoke sweaty at one twenty-three a.m., clutching his damp pillow. It had been many years since he'd had that dream, and it was because of that damned letter. He got up and took a cool shower to wash off the sweat and calm his aroused body.

The following morning, he felt better as he strolled down the steep main street of Carmel-by-the-Sea to his favorite coffeehouse. Over coffee and a peach pastry, he perused one of the colorful brochures about Tahiti he'd been collecting, then he put it down. It reminded him of his honeymoon in Hawaii—where Dorothy might still be living. If he left her letter unanswered, it would be on his mind at a time when he wanted to relax. The solution was to call Dorothy and tell her about the letter. Maybe share a little about their lives, and most of all bring closure to the past. Even though it was no longer important, she would at least finally know why he never responded, and perhaps would want to stay in touch by email or Facebook.

He checked Honolulu telephone numbers for Dorothy Miles, then also under her maiden name, Maxwell, but found no listings. He called the Golden Sands Hotel, but no one remembered her, and their records didn't go back that far. Most likely, she either didn't live in Hawaii any more or had remarried and changed her surname. He should have felt relieved that he'd made the effort to contact her. But once the search was started, he couldn't let it go without resolution. He searched the web, but neither Dorothy Miles nor Dorothy Maxwell turned up the woman he was searching for.

He dropped the search effort and continued preparing for his month-long trip to Tahiti, Fiji, and Australia, but the next day he called the airline to determine the additional charges to change the routing to include Hawaii. It was more expensive than he was expecting, a good reason to stick to the original flight arrangements. But hours later, his heart thumping, he added a seven-day stopover on Oahu as his first stop on his journey to the South Pacific. He rationalized that it would feel good to return to the place with such wonderful memories—and that the main reason wasn't to search for Dorothy.

Drew found himself feeling both exhilarated and anxious as his flight swooped low past Diamond Head and Waikiki Beach. He kept repeating to himself, like a mantra, that he should keep expectations of finding Dorothy low. As his taxi pulled under the white-pillared portal of the historic Moana Surfrider Hotel, nervous perspiration drizzled from his armpits. Outside, the Moana Surfrider appeared unchanged, frozen in time as he stepped from the cab, and inside, he saw the lobby had been redecorated but retained its stately elegance. He found himself flooded with nostalgia as he stepped into the same third-floor room he had stayed in on their honeymoon.

Dorothy had chosen the Moana Surfrider Hotel because of its historical significance. Opened in 1901, it was Hawaii's first luxury hotel, referred to as *the* First Lady of Waikiki during its heyday, when its famous visitors included presidents, movie stars, writers, and European royalty. He remembered Dorothy had wiped tears from her eyes when they walked onto the veranda overlooking the magnificent banyan tree in the hotel's rear courtyard. Drew had not understood why a tree would make his new bride cry, but this time, when he gazed over the courtyard, he blinked and wiped a tear away himself as he recalled sipping Mai Tais with his new bride under the banyan, and he remembered wondering why she requested hers without alcohol.

Indelibly etched in his mind was their wedding night, when Dorothy hung her flower lei in their hotel room window. When he asked why, she embraced him, kissing both cheeks then his lips, and murmured that it was so angels could find the room and bless their baby. This was the surprise Dorothy had kept until their wedding night in the Moana Surfrider, and it explained why she was so teary-eyed under the banyan tree. The lei remained in the window for the entire week, and during their evening strolls on Waikiki Beach, they always paused below the lei in the window and embraced.

Still adjusting to the three-hour time difference from California, he was wide awake before sunrise and was the first customer in line at the Surfrider Café next to the courtyard. It was a surreal feeling, sitting in the courtyard with his coffee and white-chocolate macadamia scone. Everything he remembered from his honeymoon appeared the same, even the shrill chatter of mynah birds in the banyan at daybreak and twilight. He drew up a plan: he would spend the first day searching for Dorothy. Then, if he didn't find her or get a solid lead, he would spend the remaining days sightseeing.

Dorothy had wanted to study art in college, but with pressure from her parents, she chose a dual major in art and business to assure them she would have a marketable degree. He remembered her style of art was painting historic buildings in the setting that existed when they were built. It wasn't much to go on, and perhaps she never returned to art. He waited until ten to begin calling the twenty-three art galleries on Oahu, asking if they knew of an artist named Dorothy, possibly with a last name of Miles or Maxwell, who painted historic hotels and buildings. He got one hopeful lead of an artist living in Kailua, but when he called her, he quickly discovered that it was not the Dorothy he was searching for. Several people suggested he should check with amateur artists who exhibited their works on the Honolulu Zoo fence on weekends.

That gave him a free day, and he joined a whale-watching cruise and saw two humpback whales and five dolphins less than a mile off of Waikiki Beach. He was told that about ten thousand whales travel the three thousand miles from Alaskan to Hawaiian waters every year between December and April, and he was guaranteed whale sightings or he could return again for free.

Saturday morning, he sat at the window of Honolulu Coffee, in the front of the Moana Hotel, sipping their side car, which included a small cappuccino, a half espresso, a small glass of seltzer water, and three tiny chocolates served on a carved wooden tray. He wasn't alone; there was a steady stream of tourists and a few regulars who came for the good coffee and ambiance. He couldn't help noticing an older man with a straw hat sitting at a nearby window with a laptop and a pile of loose notes on the table—maybe a writer. A few minutes later, a middle-aged woman approached him and said she loved *Reunion Promise* and hoped he was writing a sequel. Drew mused to himself that if he ever wrote a book, this would be the perfect place to write.

His plan was to walk over to meet the local artists along the zoo fence at ten, then continue around to the tunnel into Diamond Head Crater and climb to the top. He read every section of the *Honolulu Advertiser* and finished the crossword puzzle before returning to his room to brush his teeth and get his small backpack and water bottle.

He strolled on the beach side of Kalakaua Avenue, surprised at the number of homeless, something he didn't remember from his honeymoon. Then he followed Monsarrat Avenue around the Diamond Head side of the zoo, where he saw at least a hundred paintings, prints, and photos hanging on the fence. Back from the fence, under shade trees, sat the artists in beach chairs, expectantly eyeing every passerby. There were more artists than potential buyers, and he attracted attention as soon as he entered the twelve-foot section of fence allocated to each painter.

His eyes were on the artists, not the art, as he systematically asked each if they knew a Dorothy Miles, Dorothy Maxwell, or any local artist with Dorothy as a first name. No one knew an artist with the name of Dorothy, but all asked if he was interested in a piece of art. He reached the end of the fence dedicated to local art and paused to check his map to see how far it was to the tunnel entrance to Diamond Head Crater. A little more than a mile. Maybe twenty minutes.

There was no specific reason for turning back—perhaps just intuition; even if she had changed her name, he might recognize her style of painting or the way a painting was signed. He retraced his steps, this time looking closely at the paintings. But he was distracted by the honking of mostly pickups flying Hawaiian flags—a protest of some sort—and he almost missed the painting that caused him to freeze. On the fence were four paintings of historic buildings—the Royal Hawaiian Hotel, the 1882 Iolani Palace, the Bishop Museum, and the Moana Surfrider Hotel. He stepped closer to the painting of the Moana Surfrider, his heart pounding, not trusting his eyes as he gazed at a tiny lei painted in the third-floor window. He read the artist's name, D. Holt and turned toward the thirty-something woman he had spoken to a few minutes earlier. She definitely wasn't Dorothy, but the painting couldn't be anyone else's.

"Did you paint the one of the Moana Surfrider Hotel?
"No, I'm Jill Stein. The artist that did the painting is Dotty Holt."
"Does she ever go by the name, Dorothy?"
"I've only known her as Dotty. Are you interested in the painting?"
"I'm very interested!"
"Dotty's over there reading children's stories." She pointed to a banyan tree with a group of young children sitting on the grass around a woman seated in a webbed beach chair. Behind the children stood parents, their attention split between watching their children and their smart phones.

"Thanks." He hurried across the street, causing a car's breaks to squeal. "Sorry," he said, waving at the driver. He rushed on, then slowed as he neared the woman with the wide-brimmed straw hat reading to the children. At first, he didn't recognize her. Then, like a photo developing in an emulsion, the familiar features took shape. The glasses were different, but not her eyes, the cute nose, or the mouth that turned up at the edges. Silver hair brushed her shoulders, accenting the slender neck he had nuzzled so long ago. Her voice, now mellowed like a fine wine, reached deep into his memory. The children sat cross-legged and spellbound as she read. She paused occasionally to look up with a range of facial expressions to add drama to her words. It was a story about a whale that protected a girl and boy from a shark, and the children squealed as her voice deepened at dramatic moments.

At the end of the story, hands shot up, and excited children asked questions. She leaned toward each child as she listened, then answered as if it were the most important question in the world, as it was to the child at that moment. Finally, after every child's question was answered, she stood and told the children she would return with another story the following Saturday. Drew stood back until the parents and children had drifted away.

"Can I help you carry your things?"

She glanced at him. "Thanks, but I can handle everything. You have a grandchild here?"

"No. I'm interested in buying the painting of the Moana Hotel, but it didn't have a price."

"That one's not for sale. But I can paint a similar one for you."

"One with a lei in the window?"

"No." She stiffened as her eyes locked on him. "Do I know you?"

"Yes." He took off his sunglasses. "Remember me?"

"Oh, God! Drew! What are you doing here?"

"I recently received a letter you sent me in 1970."

"Is this some kind of a joke? You had thirty-four years to write back, and you didn't. I moved on decades ago."

"The letter was lost in the mail and arrived less than two weeks ago. I brought it with me to prove it's not a lie."

"I better sit down." She unfolded her chair and slumped down and took off her hat. "I don't know what to say. How did you find me?"

"I had a vacation planned to the South Pacific and Australia, but when your delayed letter arrived, I decided to stop in Hawaii to try and locate you. No one knew you as Dorothy Miles or Maxwell, so I came to the zoo fence hoping you still painted. I instantly knew you were the artist when I saw the painting with the lei in the window."

"I switched to a nickname, Dotty, when I came to Hawaii. I was married to Barry Holt for seven years. Drew, it's too late to try and ignite what died thirty-four years ago."

"Dorothy, hear me out. I never wanted a divorce, but once the lawyers got involved, I was pulled along, unable to stop it. Then it was over, and you were gone—out of my life. Can we at least go somewhere to talk? Maybe back in the courtyard of the Moana Surfrider, where I'm staying?"

She bit her lip as she studied his face. "Okay, but I need to put my paintings away and change."

"Don't change. I like you just the way you are."

"I need to go home and shower, and if I'm going to the Moana Surfrider, I want to wear something special."

Drew helped put the paintings and chair in the trunk of her old maroon Lexus. They agreed to meet for tea on the veranda of the Moana at three, and he booked a table at The Veranda, where they served afternoon high tea. He was sitting in a rocking chair on the front veranda when she pulled into the pillared portico for valet parking. As she stepped from the car, he stood, taking in her ageless beauty. Her hair was swept back in a bun held in place with a pearl-studded, turtle-shell barrette. She wore a shiny red Chinese dress on her lithesome body, a daring slit on the side along her thigh. He moved quickly to meet her with a fresh lei, a kiss on the cheek, and a hug, holding her until she gently pulled back.

"Dorothy, you took my breath away."

"Hawaii is a good place to age except for too much sun. You've taken good care of yourself, Drew."

"I try. Anyway, thanks for the compliment. I made reservations for high tea."

"I was hoping you would."

A white-gloved waiter seated them in rattan chairs, reminders of a time when only affluent travelers came on ocean liners and often lingered in the islands for a month or more. The three-tiered silver tray held delectable treats: small sandwich wedges on the bottom level, scones in the middle, and mouth-watering berry tarts on the top. They both chose the house blend tropical tea then nervously began to debrief each other on three decades of life.

Dorothy had sent the letter after the emotions of the divorce had subsided, and she was ready to forgive him for his marital transgression. She had known it wasn't his fault, but she couldn't help blaming him for being away when their infant, not even two weeks old, took his last breath as she held him. He had gone to look at a solar project in Palm Springs, planning to be away only a day and a half. She hadn't answered when he called, so he kept calling, but he hadn't been able to reach her. He'd had no way of knowing that she had rushed to the hospital with Danny.

After the divorce, Dorothy wanted to go far away, and she jumped at the opportunity to take advantage of her business degree and become the assistant manager of a hotel on Waikiki Beach. She stayed four years before moving to a larger hotel with a better salary. By then she was dating an optometrist with a home on Tantalus. Barry Holt was the first man she dated after the divorce, and although she was not strongly attracted to him, with time she was comfortable in the relationship and anxious to have another child. He was twelve years older and had two children from a previous marriage who lived with their mother in New Haven, Connecticut. She and Barry married, and two years later, they had a healthy daughter, Hanna, who graduated from the University of California, Irvine, and now worked on urban development problems in Los Angeles.

Barry had asked for a divorce after seven years, saying he wanted to go back to his ex-wife and try again. He offered Dorothy a handsome divorce settlement, but returned four years later.

"I guess he just couldn't settle into a commitment. But by then, I didn't have the emotional energy to try again."

She, too, had traveled to Asia and Europe, and they laughed as they shared stories about funny events and mishaps in their travels. She had thought about trying to contact Drew, particularly when she visited their baby's grave on his birthday in Monterey. She'd even looked up his phone number but had never placed the call.

"Dorothy, I thought you might be the one that left flowers at Danny's grave, and I came at different times during the day but never saw you."

"I came at sunrise. Remember, that has always been the most spiritual time of day for me. I knew you thought Hawaii was paradise, and I kept expecting you to visit here and perhaps try to contact me, but you didn't."

"I was afraid that returning to Hawaii might destroy the enchanted memories of our honeymoon. But, when the letter came, I realized you had also wanted to try again. I couldn't get you out of my mind, so here I am."

"Drew, I still think about you, but I'm at peace with my life."

"Do you think there's still a chance to rekindle the love we lost thirty-four years ago?"

She tilted her head ever so slightly and smiled. "Yes . . . but where do we start?"

Drew reached for her hand. "At high tea on the terrace of the Moana Surfrider Hotel."

Charming Deception

*A*fter graduation from the University of Wisconsin in Madison, Amy Toyama returned to Hawaii hoping to teach in middle school, but there were no positions available. She took the only interesting job available that paid a living wage, a tour guide, where her fluency in Japanese was an asset. Most days, she took groups of eight to twelve tourists on walks through Waikiki, varying the itinerary according to the group's interests. Japanese and Korean groups usually wanted to spend more time in high-end stores along Kalakaua Avenue and at the Royal Hawaiian Center, while Americans preferred less pricey aloha wear and Hawaiian-themed souvenirs found in ABC Stores and the International Market Place. Families with preteen children wanted to visit the Honolulu Zoo and the Waikiki Aquarium, where they could see giant clams and the quixotic-patterned Hawaii State fish with a tongue-tying name — *humuhumu-nukunuku-a-pua'a* — and stop for ice cream or shave ice. On Thursdays, she usually accompanied a group on an around-the-island tour to popular tourist spots, such as the Dole Plantation, Hale'iwa, North Shore, Sea Life Park, and Hanauma Bay.

The Paradise Art Gallery, on the ground floor of the Royal Hawaiian Center, was a favorite among those discerning visitors willing to shell out thousands of dollars for paintings capturing the charm of Hawaii at legendary prices. The charming, suave manager, Douglas Dowling, offered Amy a commission on sales to people she brought to his gallery, but she declined the offer. Unphased by her rebuff he had pressed his glossy business card into her hand and suggested they have lunch together anytime she was free.

She didn't intend to take him up on his offer. Not because of any outward negative characteristics. Quite the opposite. Douglas was always meticulously groomed, with a perfectly trimmed goatee, wavy black hair, an expensive aloha shirt, and leather shoes with never a speck of dust. What was his real interest in an average-looking, five-foot-three-inch Japanese-American woman with skin darkened by the intense Hawaiian sun? She envisioned him standing in front of a mirror admiring himself and not her.

It was one of those days when everything started off wrong. She had overslept, so she skipped breakfast to catch TheBus, which arrived late, only to discover she had forgotten her bus pass. She was rushing through the Royal Hawaiian Center when she heard someone call her name and turned to see Douglas standing in the door of his gallery. "Today, I insist you have lunch with me at P. F. Chang's after your morning tour."

She had no time to think up an excuse and was hungry. "Okay. But not until one."

"Perfect!" He waved, but she had already dashed on.

By one o'clock, with only a granola bar to keep her going through the morning, she arrived famished at the gallery. Douglas politely shepherded four tourists from his gallery and locked the door. "I hope you're hungry."

"Starved."

It was a three-minute walk to the restaurant, where the maître d' greeted Douglas by name and escorted them to a reserved table. Amy had already gone through the bowl of Asian-flavored breadsticks before the French Beaujolais was poured and the glazed, succulent roast duck was served.

"Amy, you weren't kidding about being hungry."

"I missed breakfast and must have walked six miles this morning."

"If that is what it takes to get you to have lunch with me, then I'm not sorry about your misfortune."

Douglas did most of the talking while Amy ate. His family had moved to Los Angeles from Paris when he was a teen, and he dual-majored in art and economics at Long Beach State. After eight years selling art in Southern California, he moved to Hawaii and started his own gallery in the upscale Royal Hawaiian Center. He was vague about what brought him to Hawaii, but a home on exclusive Black Point, in Kahala, suggested he had done very well in selling art.

Amy revealed what it was like growing up as a first-generation immigrant in Hawaii. Being Japanese, it was easy to blend in with a population that was almost two-thirds Asian, but she was an anomaly at the University of Wisconsin. Even though she didn't have a foreign accent, she was regularly mistaken for a foreign exchange student.

Amy began to date Douglas. Mostly they attended social events together—the Honolulu Symphony, the Honolulu Academy of Arts, and a black-tie event at the Hawaii Convention Center. The romantic side evolved slowly, something that suited Amy as she continued to wonder what her real attraction to Douglas was. He was a good kisser, yet had made no effort to go further, and she began to wonder if he might be gay. At events, he was somewhat solicitous of older women and invariably complimented them on their gowns and jewelry.

Normally, Amy had groups of at least eight on around-Oahu tours, but special tours were arranged for smaller groups. A family of four from Tokyo had requested a visit to Sea Life Park to see the rare *wholphin*—the result of crossbreeding a false killer whale and an Atlantic bottlenose dolphin. Arrangements were made with Hakura Sato, director of guest relations for a half-hour viewing of the wholphin. The groom of the young couple was studying false killer whale behavior at Tokyo University and was interested in seeing the result of the first such crossbreeding in captivity. The challenge was that none of the four spoke English, so Amy would have to translate, even though she was unfamiliar with technical terminology.

The woman at the reception desk took Amy's business card and said Hakura Sato would meet them and take them into the research section, where a marine biologist, Steve Gibbs, would answer their questions about the wholphin. Mr. Sato arrived moments later and greeted the visitors in Japanese, with appropriate bows and exchanges of business cards. Then he had everyone sign liability waiver forms before leading them into the restricted research area.

Sato pointed to a man emerging from a dolphin holding pool. "That's Steve Gibbs, who'll be with you shortly. I apologize, but I have other guests I must attend to, and Mr. Gibbs will answer all your questions. Miss Toyama, I trust you will translate for Mr. Gibbs, as he isn't fluent in Japanese." He bowed to the Japanese guests and left.

Steve waved to them as he peeled off his wetsuit and dried off with a towel. Amy couldn't help noticing his muscular body and the skimpy swimsuit that clung low on his hips. He slipped behind a canvas curtain and reappeared minutes later in a T-shirt and tan shorts, running his fingers through his wet hair as he walked over to meet them.

Formal greetings were made, with Amy translating, then Steve led them back into the area where they kept the rare wholphin. He spent the next hour enthusiastically talking about the challenges of crossing a false killer whale with a dolphin and what it meant to the science of crossbreeding. Amy noted that Steve mentioned he was a graduate student at the University of Hawaii and was working only half-time at Sea Life Park. The young Japanese groom, Akira Ito, asked many questions, while his wife and in-laws stood respectful but silent in the background. When Steve and Akira leaned over the side of the wholphin tank, Amy couldn't help noticing Steve's tight butt. The young bride noticed too, and she demurely covered her mouth when she saw Amy had noticed her gaze. At the end of the tour, Steve walked them to the entrance to Sea Life Park.

Amy couldn't help being disappointed that Steve had given all his attention to Akira and barely acknowledged her presence, except when she would ask about a technical term she couldn't translate and he would rephrase it. At the minivan, he shook hands with the Japanese visitors, then he turned to Amy. "You were a great help today. I, uh, live near the University. Perhaps we could have a coffee sometime."

"It's my job, so there's no obligation for you to repay me. Anyway, I think you'll make a great teacher someday." She quickly hopped into the van, and immediately regretted turning down his offer. It would be unprofessional to lean out of the window and shout that she had changed her mind. She felt better by the time they reached Honolulu. She was in the early stages of dating Douglas and her infatuation with Steve was simply a temporary physical response, and nothing more.

Friday evening, Amy had a romantic candlelight dinner with Douglas and a moonlight drive around Diamond Head to his oceanside home on Black Point. He explained that a close friend was recovering from an operation in his home, and he didn't want to disturb him this late at night and would show her his home on another day.

Amy's heart was pounding when they embraced at the entrance to her apartment building, and he caressed her softly on the side of her face. But he turned away, not asking to come in as she expected. His Jaguar was still parked in front when she peered down from her sixth-floor window. Wondering if he would change his mind, she watched until the sleek automobile pulled away and disappeared into the night.

Amy lay in bed, the gentle shell-chimes on her balcony not enough to calm her anxiety about Douglas. He was handsome and clearly showed an interest in her, yet he didn't advance the relationship to the intimacy she was ready for by now. She was also perplexed about his expensive lifestyle, as she had rarely seen any sales in his art gallery. The modest inheritance he had mentioned must have been much larger than he wished to reveal. Perhaps there was another woman or even man in his life, and that was why he had not invited her into his home.

"Yun, how many do I have for today's tour?"

"Thirteen signed up for the Saturday morning walking tour. Seven from Japan, five from the mainland, and someone from Honolulu. You'll be doing double duty in English and Japanese."

"Not a problem." She took the clipboard, walked over to the tour group, and cheerfully read off names and handed out identifying stickers. She looked up in surprise when she came to the name of the local resident. "Steve, what are you doing here?"

He grinned. "I heard you're the most charming tour guide in Waikiki so couldn't miss your tour."

Instead of simply handing him his sticker, she peeled off the backing and stuck it firmly on his hard chest and patted it. "Mr. Gibbs, you might be disappointed."

Amy gave lively descriptions about famous people who had visited Waikiki, from writers—Robert Louis Stevenson, Mark Twain, and Jack London—to movie stars as far back as

Charlie Chaplin, and singers, including Elvis Presley. When they reached the Waikiki Aquarium, she motioned for her tour group to gather around her. "Today, we are fortunate to have with us Mr. Steve Gibbs, a marine biologist, who I'm sure will enchant you with descriptions of the diversity of marine life in the aquarium."

Steve frowned, bewildered for a few moments, then stepped forward. "Thank you, Miss Toyama, for inviting me to give a few comments about the aquarium's unique marine life. My specialties are dolphins and whales, so forgive me if I'm unfamiliar with some of the marine life you're about to see." He then proceeded to lead the group on an hour-long tour of the aquarium, giving polished presentations about the marine life to the delight of everyone, including Amy.

At the end of the tour, after everyone but Steve had left, Amy faced him, arms crossed over her chest. "Fess up. That presentation was way too rehearsed for someone who just studies whales and dolphins."

"Well, when I saw the brochure for your tour, I brushed up on my notes that I used last summer when I was a tour guide at the Waikiki Aquarium."

"You sure impressed the tour group."

"I did it to impress you."

"Why?"

"I have an invitation to a black-tie dinner to honor outstanding citizens for the past year, and I'm desperate for a date."

"Are you always so melodramatic?"

"Only when I need a date for a black-tie dinner this Saturday night."

"Steve, that's two days from now. And I'm already seeing someone."

"I'm not asking you on a romantic date, but I'm terrified of showing up alone."

"There you go again with your histrionic words. Okay, I'll ask my boyfriend, and if it's okay with him, I'll come so you won't be terrified."

Amy was surprised when Douglas encouraged her to attend the black-tie event with Steve and told her he would be away on a business trip to Los Angeles anyway. She wondered if his lack of jealousy was a good or bad sign for their relationship. On balance, it was probably good that he was not the jealous type and wanted her to enjoy herself.

Steve took her breath away when he appeared at her door in a tuxedo—the beachboy look replaced with that of a dashing movie star. He stepped forward, looping a purple orchid lei over her head, and warmly embraced her, though the image of a Hollywood star was tarnished when they reached his chariot, a VW Cabriolet convertible with dents and scratches and, inside, a faint fish odor.

There were four lines at the entrance to the banquet hall—three for the general public and one for VIPs. They joined the line with a placard labeled A to H and, after waiting almost ten minutes, reached the check-in table. Steve had misplaced his invitation among the piles of papers and books in his apartment, so he gave his name.

The check-in receptionist flipped through the guest list twice before looking up. "Sorry, Mr. Gibbs. I've checked under both Gibbs and Steven, but you're not listed. I can place you on a waiting list, in case there are several no-shows, but there are three couples ahead of you."

Steve shook his head and sighed. "No thanks." He turned to Amy. "I'm sorry about the mix-up. It's my fault for losing the invitation. I, uh, know a really nice restaurant if we can get in."

"That will be fine," she replied, trying to conceal her disappointment. *This wouldn't have happened with Douglas,* she mused.

He pulled out his cellphone, scrolled through his index of names and tapped on one. Five rings, then an answer. "Jacques, it's me, Steve Gibbs. I need a big favor. I have a gorgeous date, and I urgently need a table for two this evening."

Amy could hear Jacques's exclamation, "Steve, you are so difficult! Come, and I'll find something for you—maybe in the kitchen."

Steve's beamed. "Amy, we've got a table. But I'm not sure of the view."

"It'll be fine. What restaurant is it?"

"A surprise."

Amy was stunned when he pulled up to Michel's, the elegant French restaurant in the Colony Surf, near the foot of Diamond Head. "Steve, people make reservations weeks in advance to dine here." She tucked her hand under his arm as they approached the maître d', bracing for a pretentious reception.

The maître d' grinned. "Bonsoir, Mr. Gibbs. It is a pleasure to have you and the lovely lady dining with us this evening."

"Thanks for squeezing us in at the last minute."

"For you, anything is possible."

They were seated at a reserved oceanfront table. Amy looked suspiciously at Steve. "Okay, what's going on here? How does a graduate student in marine biology get a coveted table at Michel's?"

Steve shrugged. "Jacques is my roommate and is working on a PhD in chemistry. He's a graduate student by day and maître d' in the evenings. He makes more than I do at Sea Life Park and needs every dollar he can earn to support himself and a younger brother back in France."

They took Jacques's suggestions and ordered the fresh ono with a black-truffle cream sauce, paired with a lively sauvignon blanc from the Loire Valley. Steve gazed into her eyes as they clicked wine glasses and waves crashed on the rocks a few feet away, evoking unexpected romantic feelings in Amy. "Steve, I can never tire of the melodic sounds and fragrance of the sea."

"Amy, that's why I had to study something to do with the ocean. I hope this will make up for the rough start to our evening."

"Far beyond my expectations."

Steve was careful not to reveal his romantic feelings toward Amy, and she refrained from disclosing her feelings about the handsome man with rough edges sitting across from her. Yet, romantic feelings did not need to be spoken at the candlelight dinner on Waikiki Beach. The evening had begun as an embarrassment to Steve and ended with romantic hope.

When Steve embraced her at the door of her apartment, Amy pressed closer than she intended against his hard body. As she undressed and put away her costume jewelry, the events of the evening reeled through her mind. It troubled her to have romantic feelings for two men when she had already made her choice.

At first, the ringing was a dream, then she jerked up pushing back her covers. Douglas must have forgotten that it's three hours earlier in Hawaii than LA. "Hello."

"It's Steve. I hope I didn't wake you."

"You did. Why are you calling so early?"

"I couldn't sleep in after last night and am about to head to Coffee Talk, a funky coffeehouse on Wai'alae Avenue. I thought you might be up for breakfast."

"You're calling me at seven twelve on Sunday morning to ask me to join you for coffee! For your information, I planned to sleep in today."

"I'm sorry. My apologies."

"Good-bye, Steve."

Just after eight, Amy strolled into Coffee Talk and plopped in the chair across from Steve, who was reading the Sunday *Honolulu Star-Advertiser*. Startled, he blurted out, "You came."

"Keen observation, Sherlock. Since you woke me up, maybe you can get me a large cappuccino and a warm almond croissant."

"Absolutely! Thank you for coming, and I'm really sorry for waking you so early."

Amy scowled at him and picked up the newspaper and flipped to the entertainment section. But minutes later, she was beaming when he returned with the cappuccinos and croissants.

"Is the big grin about me or the cappuccino and croissant?"

"You. There's a big write-up about the black-tie banquet last night."

"Don't remind me of it."

"Shush. Listen to this. Missing from the banquet was Steve Gibbs, a graduate student in marine biology at the University of Hawaii, Manoa Campus. Mr. Gibbs was selected to receive a Citizen Heroism Award for rescuing three people from a helicopter that crashed off of Waikiki Beach." She looked over the top of the paper. "You never told me that."

"It was many months ago, and I happened to be surfing very close to the crash. I wasn't the only one to help."

"I bet we were supposed to go through the VIP line. Did it say that on the invitation?"

"I don't remember. I lost the invitation."

"Anyway, they shouldn't have turned you away."

"I had a better time with you at Michel's."

"Steve, I had a great time, too. But I need to make it clear that I'm dating someone else."

"So why are you here?"

She pursed her lips. "You're impossible."

He smirked. "Pass me the lonely-hearts section in the newspaper."

149

"Steve, I'm not buying your pathetic attempt to get my sympathy."

She turned to another section of the paper and took a sip of her cappuccino. Moments later she shrieked, "Oh, my God!" Then silence, as heads turned toward them.

"Amy, what's wrong?"

"Read this." Her hands trembled as she handed him the paper and jabbed her finger at an article.

DRUG RAID FAILS

HPD narcotics chief, Sago Morimoto, said a tip led to a raid early Saturday morning on a Black Point home. But no one was in the home at the time, and no drugs or stolen jewelry were found. The source of the tip is now in question and being investigated. Mr. Morimoto would give no further details at this time.

"Just a false tip," Steve said, and he handed the section back to Amy.

"Steve! What if it's my boyfriend's home?"

"What makes you think so? There are many homes on Black Point, and he runs a successful and reputable art gallery."

"Before Douglas left for the mainland, he dropped off a large suitcase at my apartment and told me it contained valuables and that he was concerned about recent burglaries in his area. I need to be sure it wasn't his home that was raided."

"It's only a few minutes away, so we can drive by and put your mind at ease."

They drove to Black Point, and Amy gasped when she saw a temporary lock on the front door. "It *was* Douglas's home that was raided," she said.

Steve said nothing and drove on, waiting for Amy to process what she'd seen. "Steve, I'm worried about what might be in the suitcase Douglas left with me. I thought it strange that with all his friends, he would leave it at my apartment."

"Maybe because no one would expect you to have a suitcase full of valuables."

"Steve, what would you do if you were me?"

"If the suitcase has stollen jewelry or drugs, you could be accused of being an accomplice. I would call the police and tell them you saw the newspaper article and that Douglas left a suitcase with you for safekeeping."

"If it gets into the newspapers, I could lose my job."

"Maybe. But I doubt it if you're volunteering information. And silence could be jail time."

Amy called the police, who arrived within the hour to take down her story and Steve's account, then took fingerprints and had Amy sign a release form before taking the bag for testing. Amy was shaking as she closed the door, then she slumped back into Steve's arms.

"I'm afraid to face Douglas. If he's guilty, I'm in danger, and if he's innocent, he'll be furious that I didn't trust him. Steve, I don't want to face him."

"Come to my place. I'll sleep on the couch, and you can have my bed. I just have to change the sheets."

She laughed. "At a time like this, you're worried about clean sheets on the bed."

The following days were traumatic, as Amy's worst fears were proven true. The suitcase held drugs and stollen jewelry worth over a half million dollars. Douglas and an accomplice were arrested at the Honolulu International Airport, and Amy was told she would have to testify in court about the suitcase.

Steve's support for Amy during her months of preparation and testimony at the trial brought them closer together as trusted friends. Yet their romance stalled due to both Amy's anxiety over the trial and Steve's intense concentration on completing his dissertation.

Amy was not prepared for Steve's call on June twenty-third. "Amy, I have great news. I submitted my dissertation today, and the committee will be reviewing it over the next two weeks, so how about going with me to an exotic resort on the Big Island?"

"You're joking."

"No. I have a free trip to the Kona Village Retreat, on the Big Island, where we'll be staying in a little grass shack and go native."

"Steve, . . . what are you smoking?"

"It's the real thing. Remember that black-tie affair? Well, my award included a four-day, all-expense-paid vacation for two at the Kona Village Retreat. But it expires June thirtieth."

"Steve, that's just a week away. And let me get this straight. You're asking me to join you in a grass shack on the Big Island. We're friends, not lovers. And I can't just drop everything and run off to the Big Island with you. Sorry, but you'll have to find someone else. A dinner in Waikiki would be fine, but running off to go native in a grass shack is out of the question."

"Anything I can do to change your mind?"

"No."

Amy was preparing dinner when there was a knock on her door. She thought it might be Steve to try and change her mind, and she walked briskly to the door. "Who is it?"

"Steve."

"I told you no." She swung open the door and found Steve on his knees holding a dozen crimson roses.

As soon as Steve and Amy exited the Hawaiian Airlines flight at the Kona International Airport, they were greeted with flower leis by Kaleki, a pretty Polynesian woman who graciously accompanied them to the secluded retreat. Amy had agreed to come on the trip after Steve accepted her conditions: separate beds and no pressure to consolidate sleeping arrangements. Ten minutes north of the airport, they turned off the paved highway onto a jarring path across a lava field, then onto a sandy road that ended at a high hedge, hiding all but the tops of coconut palms.

Kaleki said, "Now hold hands and close your eyes as I lead you back a century to an enchanting South Pacific village."

Amy squeezed Steve's hand as Kaleki lead them through the arched bamboo gate into another world.

"You can open your eyes now."

Steve had visited Fiji, the Cook Islands, and Tahiti, so he was not expecting to be astonished when he opened his eyes, but he gasped along with Amy. "Steve, it's right out of the set for the movie *South Pacific*."

Quaint thatched bungalows were sprinkled among the coconut palms spread out just steps back from a powdery golden-sand beach that slid gently into the shallow aquamarine sea. Children played on a koa-wood outrigger canoe on the beach while adults relaxed in hammocks and on the lanais of their bungalows. Hawaiian women in muumuus and men wearing lavalavas—the cloth skirt or kilt worn by Polynesian men—were involved in daily chores: mashing taro with stone pounders to make poi (steamed taro root pounded to a smooth paste), weaving baskets with strips of pandanus leaves, collecting coconuts, and repairing fishing nets.

Kaleki said in a soft voice, "Nothing is rushed here, as the main activity is relaxing to the sounds of the surf, the birds, and the subtle rhythms of native village life. Guests are here to totally relax. You should not feel pressured to do anything beyond enjoying the ambiance and delicious meals. There are no telephones, TVs, or radios in the bungalows, and cellphone use is strongly discouraged during your stay. We want our guests to leave behind their worries while here in Kona Village Retreat."

The bungalows were artfully positioned to give the guests privacy, with every lanai having views of the ocean and sunsets. Their bungalow was tastefully furnished with rattan and koa furniture, the walls and ceiling covered in tapa cloth with geometric patterns common among villages in the South Pacific. Next to a basket of papaya, mango, lilikoi, and finger bananas was a tapa-covered folder with their registration form and a list of the week's activities. A wooden bell and rod hung outside the door with instructions of the number of taps for various services they could request.

Complimentary native attire was neatly laid out on their beds. Steve changed into his lavalava and waited for Amy to reappear from the bathroom. "Wow!" he said as she stepped out with her floral sarong accentuating her curves. She didn't comment on his firm chest and whale's tail pendant nestled in a patch of curly hair. They sipped chilled guava juice from coconut shells as they explored the village, with Steve chatting in Hawaiian to native Hawaiians.

"Wow, Steve, I didn't know you spoke Hawaiian. I only learned the Hawaiian words we needed when I studied hula as a girl, but I can't carry on a conversation."

"I had a Hawaiian roommate as an undergraduate at UH. It helps in my research among Hawaiians, who know a lot about where I can find rare marine life species."

By midday, with temperatures hovering near ninety degrees, families were in the warm surf or on hammocks strung between coconut trees. Steve led Amy as they snorkeled out over the scattered coral heads, some close enough to touch. Darting among the coral crevices and crenellations were canary-yellow and magenta cleaner wrasses. Nearby a pair of beautifully banded Moorish idols swayed in harmony like young lovers.

Further out, on the edge of the fringing reef, they came upon a spotted moray eel and a Hawaiian spiny lobster without claws.

On their candle-lit lanai, they dined on fresh opakapaka baked in ti leaves, an avocado salad, and a pilaf of rice infused with local spices. Amy wanted to try a fruity sangria, and although not on the drink list, a flask with wedges of fruit arrived within minutes. She sucked on an orange wedge, then set it aside.

"I'm so glad you didn't give up on me after I turned you down."

"I wasn't going to come alone, and I hated to see the tickets go to waste. So I was willing to give my best shot to change your mind. The last time I got on my knees was when I was a boy and hugged my collie."

After a sunrise breakfast, they strolled over to watch two burly Hawaiians prepare the imu pit for the roast Kalua pig. The men were perspiring profusely from the hot rocks that would layer both the bottom of the imu and cover the top of the pig wrapped in banana leaves. After a few words in Hawaiian, Steve grabbed a shovel and joined in the ancient ritual of preparing the imu. Amy watched with increasing interest as sweat trickled down Steve's body and his lavalava slipped dangerously lower.

She took Steve's sweaty hand as they walked toward the ocean. "Is this how you relax on your vacation?"

He laughed. "I wanted to dig an imu and show off my native skills and muscles." He trotted ahead and waded to his waist, unwrapped his sweaty lavalava and rinsed it in the ocean, seemingly unaware that the water didn't conceal what lay beneath.

They spent the rest of the day learning Hawaiian crafts, taking several iced-tea breaks and a late afternoon dip in the ocean. At the evening luau, Steve was given the first portion of roast pig for his help in preparing the imu and shared it with Amy. Knives were unnecessary, as the succulent meat was pulled apart with the fingers. There were platters heaped with laulau, chicken long rice, lomilomi salmon, white rice, and small bowls of two-finger poi. Desert consisted of baskets of local fruit and coconut custard pudding. Steve's knowledge of Hawaiian did not extend to the hula dancing performance, where it was Amy who wowed the other guests.

The final day was a gentle mix of long walks along the beach, snorkeling, and getting closer. They shared the kind of stories that are important to someone who cares and will listen. Steve was noticeably nervous when they returned to their bungalow. He said he was going out for a short jog on the beach while Amy took a shower and prepared for their final dinner. He returned, panting, with sand on his arms and knees.

"Did, you fall down on the beach?"

He shrugged. "I attract sand like a magnet. I'll take a quick shower and will be ready in a jiffy, and you won't need sandals this evening."

Twilight for Amy was special, when the hues of the day melted into the night, letting stars gradually appear in the arc of the sky. Steve held a tiki torch as they strolled along the beach.

"Am I being kidnapped?"

"Love can't be taken by force."

"Where does a scientist who can't sing or dance and doesn't read romance novels come up with those lines?"

He grinned in the flickering light of the torch on his face. "The sea of course. It casts spells on anyone who dares to get too close."

At first, she thought the lights were from a small fishing boat just offshore, but as they came closer, it materialized into a table and two chairs floating on the water.

"Is that where we're dining?"

"Yes, it's only inches deep at low tide, but, like Cinderella, we must leave before the bewitching hour."

They dined under the mellow glow of torches, soothing surf caressing their feet. They listened to the music of the sea under a star-studded ballroom infinitely grander than the earth. The succulent seafood dishes pared with French wines were the final props in the nautical love story. The tide had risen almost to their knees when they finished the tarts topped with tangy 'ohelo berries picked from shrubs on the slopes of Mauna Loa volcano.

"Steve, put out the torches," Amy whispered. "I'm ready to be led into deeper water."

John/Jon

*I*t was near sunset when Jon Smith rode the elevator to the seventeenth floor of the Sheraton Waikiki. A frequent traveler on the mainland, he carried his own luggage to avoid the nuisance of waiting for the bellhop to bring his bag to the room. He had chosen the Sheraton Waikiki because it was centrally located, on the beach, and earned him Sheraton Reward points.

Jon had jumped at the consultancy with the Hawaiian Electric Company that would give him a paid trip to Hawaii and the possibility of a permanent position with Hawaii's largest electricity company. His success as a private consultant on power-system optimization came at a price—more than two hundred days a year living out of a suitcase and too little attention to his social life. His previous girlfriend had finally thrown in the towel and moved back to Green Bay, Wisconsin, and within months was in a serious relationship. At thirty-seven, he realized he was ready to settle down and focus on finding a marriageable woman and starting a family.

Check-in at the Sheraton went smoothly, and he was in a good mood as he rode the elevator to the seventeenth floor. Stepping into his hotel room, he noticed a large suitcase, something he occasionally encountered when luggage from the previous occupants had yet to be picked up. He headed for the bedside telephone to call for a bellhop to remove the bag.

"What are you doing in my room?" shouted a woman standing in the bathroom doorway.

Startled, he stared at the woman clutching a towel to her breasts, wet tendrils of black hair curling over her bare shoulders. "I'm so sorry."

"Get out of my room!"

He quickly retreated—heart racing. He would see more skin on the beach, but a young woman emerging from a shower, water glistening from her skin, was titillating. The vision, only seconds in the making, revealed a woman with large dark eyes, pronounced eyebrows, and an olive completion that reminded him of women he'd met during his semester in Italy.

He went straight to the check-in counter. "You must have given me the wrong key. There's a woman in my room."

The receptionist took his check-in packet. Keys chattered as she rapidly typed on her keyboard. "Isn't your wife Valerie?"

"I'm not married, and I'm traveling alone."

"Mrs. Valerie Smith checked in earlier and left a message that her husband would check in later today. Oh! I see the mistake. You're Jon Smith not John Smith."

"Yes, j-o-n," he said.

"I'm so sorry. I'll get you another room."

Again, the rapid clicking of keys then the buzz of the printer.

"Mr. Smith, I've upgraded you to a suite on a higher floor with an excellent view, and I'm enclosing a complimentary drink coupon for our oceanfront RumFire lounge."

Jon smiled. "Thank you. It's happened before but never with a woman in the room. That's the problem with having such a common name. Would you kindly call and explain the mix-up to the woman? She was quite upset when I walked in and surprised her."

"I'll call her right away and explain the error."

The view from his two-bedroom suite was as stunning as the brochure, with the iconic Diamond Head volcano at the far end of Waikiki Beach. To the west, the red sails of a yacht appeared to be painted on the horizon. At most hotels on the mainland, he rarely looked out of the window, as the view was usually of other buildings, but Hawaii wasn't any other city.

He stripped and headed to the shower, the fleeting image of Valerie still on his mind. It had only been a glimpse, but it was enough to ignite his imagination. He paused in front of the large mirror, comfortable with his looks. At five foot ten, he had the brown hair and matching eyes of his mother and the firm masculine chin and mouth of his father. He had maintained his physique by forcing himself to exercise every morning, a habit he had started years ago when working on his black belt in judo. His skin was pale, something he hoped the Hawaiian sun would fix on his two free weekends.

Jon headed down to the RumFire lounge, settled into a low chair at a table facing the infinity pool that appeared to flow seamlessly into the ocean, and ordered the local Big Wave beer and the mixed pupu plate. A young Japanese couple sat at a nearby table, the man doing the talking while his bride nodded in the demure way that women in so many cultures hone to a fine art. A twenty-something Caucasian couple were at the outer edge of the infinity pool, toasting with flutes of Champagne, their voices muffled by the sound of the surf crashing into the concrete wall below. He hadn't realized that the beach in the rear of the Sheraton had become a casualty of rising sea levels and more intense storms.

The pupu plate of sushi and garlic tiger shrimp arrived. As he dipped a prawn in the spicy sauce he mused, *I should be paying Hawaiian Electric for this job. The only thing missing is the touch of a woman.*

Jon heard the scraping of chairs behind him and a faintly familiar voice. Glancing back, his eyes locked on Valerie, seated next to a brawny man with a military-style haircut and biceps that threatened to split his sleeves. Jon quickly looked away and hurriedly finished his beer and pupu plate, then he told the waitress to charge the drinks of the couple behind him to his room. As he got up to leave, he glimpsed Valerie's husband's menacing stare and turned to avoid eye contact.

The interview for a permanent position at Hawaiian Electric was set for the last day of his consultancy in order to give their engineers and managers as much time as possible to assess his capabilities. The days were packed with meetings with management and their systems engineers. Jon was impressed by their ambitious goal: making Hawaii the nation's leader in the percentage of electricity generated by renewable energy. The challenge, and the reason for his consultancy, was load-balancing, while the less-predictable solar and wind gradually became the dominant source of electricity.

On the fifth day, he took a forty-five-minute flight to the Big Island to review the status of the long-troubled geothermal project. The potential geothermal energy from an active volcano was far beyond the electricity needs of the thinly populated Big Island, and studies had been completed on an undersea cable to the major market on Oahu, but the cable would be expensive and posed serious technical risks. Jon discovered that another major barrier to large-scale commercial development of geothermal power was the opposition from native Hawaiians. It came from two factions, one finding it offensive to their religious beliefs and the second not wanting any commercial developments. Jon could easily see that it would be perilous to jump into a debate with such strong social and cultural ramifications, so he took a neutral position on the role of geothermal generated electricity in Hawaii's future.

Back in Honolulu he gave a briefing to management outlining steps to better optimize their electricity system. Phase I would not be difficult to implement. But as renewables became a larger share of the electricity supply, Phase II would require major capital investments in battery storage facilities. He was impressed with the desire of management to introduce more renewable energy, something he often found lacking in mainland utility companies.

Friday evening, Jon left the Hawaiian Electric headquarters after dark and was surprised to see fireworks over Waikiki.

"A special occasion?" he asked his cab driver.

"Nope. Happens every Friday evening at this time behind the Hilton Hawaiian Village. Popular with tourists."

The fireworks display only lasted a few minutes and was over before he reached the Sheraton. He changed into shorts and a polo shirt and headed out to see the Friday night activities along the beach and grab a beer and sandwich at one of the beachfront restaurants. Leather sandals in hand, he stepped onto the beach, surprised at how fast the crowd had dissipated after the fireworks. He leaned over and scooped a handful of sand and let it sieve through his fingers, evoking a feeling of contentment.

"Mr. Smith, I need help."

Startled to hear his name, he turned to see a shadowy figure. "Who are you?"

"Valerie Smith. You accidentally stepped into my room a few days ago."

"I'm sorry for walking in on you."

"The hotel receptionist called and explained the mix-up, but that's not my problem. My husband hit me, and I have no one to turn to."

"You should call the police."

"That would make matters much worse. I don't want him arrested."

"Why me?"

"You picked up our bar tab, and not many men would do that. Can we go somewhere away from this hotel and I'll explain?"

"Sure." He hesitated. "But, Valerie, I don't want to get in the middle of your marital problems."

"I understand." She gripped his arm, and they continued down the beach, stopping at one of the quieter beachfront bars, where Valerie pulled aside her hair to show the bruise on her left cheek. Over drinks she tearfully told her story.

"I met John five years ago, when I accompanied a girlfriend to a sports bar to watch the football team of her alma mater play in the Orange Bowl. John had played football in college and told me he was a senior sales representative of a sports equipment company. He was handsome and the center of attention with his stories about travels to Japan, Korea, and Thailand when he was in the military, and the many exotic places on his bucket list. He pressured me to marry after nine months and proposed a honeymoon in Tahiti, and even though I had reservations, I said yes. We could only afford a honeymoon in Hawaii but that was okay with me. I gradually discovered that John was a habitual liar, had been dishonorably discharged from the Army, and was only a junior sales representative in the sports equipment company. Worst of all, he's abusive when he drinks too much, like tonight.

"I was hoping a stress-free vacation to Hawaii would improve our relationship. But he changed his flight reservations at the last minute, saying he had an important meeting in Los Angeles and would meet me in Hawaii. The argument started this afternoon when I noticed the airline routing tags on his suitcase indicated a stop in Las Vegas, where his previous girlfriend lives. He exploded, saying I was over-reacting, and he hit me."

"Valerie, I feel sorry about your situation, but there isn't anything I can do."

"My wallet is in our room, and I'm afraid to go back until he sobers up and cools down. If you could get me a room in another hotel for the night, I'll pay you back tomorrow."

"Sure, let's try the Sheraton Princess Kaiulani. I'm a Sheraton club member, and hopefully I can get a last-minute room at a reasonable rate." He was nervous about getting involved in a marital dispute, a recipe for problems he didn't need or want. In spite of his misgivings, he got a room for Valerie. He gave her a twenty for incidentals and said he would stop by to check on her the next morning. Valerie teared up and gave him a hug.

Valerie looked much better the following morning when he met her for breakfast in the Pikake Terrace garden restaurant. She had covered the bruise with makeup, and her hair was neatly wrapped in a bun on the top of her head.

"Are you the woman I met last night on the beach? Where did you get the makeup?"

"Thanks for the compliment, and I feel a lot better this morning. The receptionist had seen the bruise and thought you had hit me, and after you left, she appeared at my door with a small makeup kit." She paused, nervously twisting her hands together. "I called my husband, and he apologized, and . . . I'm going back after breakfast. I'll leave a check for you at the front desk. I know what you're thinking, but I've invested so much in my marriage." Valerie had barely touched her coffee when she stood, leaned over, and kissed his cheek, lingering for a moment.

He watched her walk away, his fingers touching the spot she had kissed.

Jon felt uneasy about Valerie's decision, yet he knew it wasn't his concern. He spent Saturday in his room, writing his consulting report so he would be free to be a tourist on Sunday. He woke early on Sunday morning, and by six fifteen, he was on the H-1 Freeway, following his GPS map to Haleʻiwa, on the north Shore. An hour later, he entered the local Café Haleʻiwa. The waitress recommended the local favorite, loco moco, a hamburger patty on white rice, smothered in gravy, and topped with two fried eggs. It was filling, but even two cups of coffee didn't wash away the aftertaste of the greasy dish.

The best part of the breakfast was listening to the lively local banter between the waitress and the locals—a mix of three languages: English, pidgin, and Hawaiian. Topics were local, as if the rest of the world didn't exist, and even Waikiki was referred to as if it was far away. It was strangely comforting to escape the news of the world, if only for a day.

He drove along the tropical windward side of Oahu, stopping briefly at picturesque beaches, but he felt restless, as images of Valerie crowded into his thoughts. Was she all right? Why hadn't he given her his cell number, just in case? By the time he reached the H-3 Freeway, he was ready to return to Waikiki, even though there was enough daylight to complete the round-island drive.

To avoid the chance of encountering Valerie and her husband at the Sheraton Waikiki, he drove to a recommended takeout restaurant on Monsarrat Avenue, at the base of Diamond Head. The woman in front of him helped select a Hawaiian meal of pork laulau with sides of white rice, sweet potato, poi, and a beer. He parked in the free parking area around Kapiolani Park and ate his meal on San Souci Beach while watching surfers catching the final waves of the day.

The sun had just dipped below the horizon when a deeply tanned surfer passed with his surfboard under one arm. He paused and advised, "Put da beer in paypa bag. No troba."

"Thanks." Jon slipped his bottle of beer into a bag to avoid the possibility of being ticketed for having an open bottle of alcohol on a public beach. He remained until the last of the pink hues on the clouds had disappeared, then he held up his beer bottle wrapped in a paper bag. "Here's to you, Valerie," he said, and he drained it.

The briefing of Hawaiian Electric management on Monday morning was to be followed by his interview after lunch. The briefing went well; three of his five recommendations were tentatively accepted, and two were deferred for further study. What Jon liked most about the meeting was the openness to fresh ideas on how to improve the company's performance. Many of his consulting jobs were meant merely to confirm the managing director's thinking and not to rock the boat with new ideas. The interview lasted two hours and, he was fairly sure an offer of a position would come shortly.

He returned to the Sheraton, changed, and headed down Kalakaua Avenue looking for a gift to take back for his mother and a place to eat. He was drawn into a restaurant serving Dungeness crab ramen with a garlic-butter sauce and Tsingtao beer. The overpriced meal was below expectations but not a surprise in the middle of Waikiki. In nearby Duke's Lane, he bartered with a wily Vietnamese woman for a gold necklace with a turtle pendant for his mother.

It was early evening when he reached the beach and strolled toward the Sheraton Waikiki, pleased with how the interview had gone and his prospects for a job offer. He watched a dinner cruise a mile offshore and the flashes from cameras as people took picture of Waikiki Beach. Pant cuffs rolled up and loafers in hand, he moseyed toward the surf, then he paused as he spotted two people struggling on the beach.

"Let go! Leave me alone!" a woman cried out.

The voice was unmistakable, and he sprinted toward the couple shouting, "Let her go!"

Rotating to face him, his hand gripping Valerie's arm, the man scowled. "Butt out. This is none of your business."

"I don't want trouble, but hurting a woman *is* my business."

The guy threw his wife down and lunged. Stepping to the side, Jon shoved him sprawling on the sand. He got up slower than Jon expected and staggered toward Jon with fists raised.

"You've had too much to drink. Let your wife go and go back to your room."

John paused, turned toward the hotel, then spun with a roundhouse swing at Jon, who deflected his fist, thumped him to the sand, and twisted a thumb back. "Go back to your room and sober up."

John shrieked. Valerie screamed, "Please don't hurt him."

Jon let go, and her husband slowly got up, snarled at him, and staggered toward the Sheraton. Valerie moved to Jon's side, placing her hand on his forearm.

"Thank you. Everything was going fine until he started drinking. I can't take it anymore, and told him I'm going to file for a divorce."

"Valerie, you can't go back."

"I know now. It seems destiny keeps throwing us together."

"I'll get you a room."

"I already took care of that and had my bags moved to the Ilikai Hotel, where he won't find me. I'm pretty shaky, so maybe you could walk with me and listen while I talk things out."

After checking her into the Ilikai, they walked behind the hotel to the Ala Wai Yacht Harbor. At first, Valerie talked about the yachts, as if nothing else were on her mind. Growing up, she had sailed on the family's thirty-foot yacht on Chesapeake Bay. It was not just Sunday outings with the family. For her and her brother, the yacht was the Jolly Roger pirate ship, and they were searching for treasure. Their parents bought them an inexpensive metal detector and let them off in small coves to search for booty.

"Yachts bring back great memories."

"Did you find any treasure?"

"My heart raced every time our metal detector buzzed. We found a few recent coins, scraps of rusty metal, a silver spoon, and, best of all, a dagger with a jewel-encrusted handle."

"Shiver me timbers," Jon said.

Valerie laughed. "So, you're a pirate fan too?"

"When I was a boy, I loved pirate movies, and I still do, particularly ones set in exotic places, like the Caribbean."

"Our jeweled dagger handle apparently came from a pirate movie filmed in the cove. The rubies and emeralds were glass, but to us they were real gems. I hoped that when I had children, they would have some of the same experiences. Now I don't know. I'm going through with the divorce this time."

At the door to her hotel room, they embraced, and she gave him a feathery kiss on the lips. "You're a man I will never forget."

Almost a year passed with no word from Valerie. Jon's address changed when he moved to Hawaii to take the new job, but his email remained the same. He thought it best for her to contact him if she was interested in staying in touch. He wondered if she had gone back to John, as so often happens with abused women. He had been attracted to Valerie, and in another setting would have asked her for a date. But his romantic attraction to her was apparently not reciprocated.

He rapidly clicked through his daily emails, deleting those that required no action or were meant to extract money from his wallet. A strange email message popped up.

Ahoy Jon,
In the light of the full moon on May 11
I'll be searching for pirate treasure on Waikiki Beach
Yo Ho Ho

"Some kind of joke," Jon blurted out and tapped DELETE. That night, as he readied for bed, it popped into his mind. *Could it be Valerie?* He was about to call her when he realized that probably wasn't what she intended. She must have found out that he had moved to Honolulu or she wouldn't have sent such a cryptic message. Yet, if she had a serious romantic interest, why did she wait almost a year to contact him?

On May eleventh, he went to work as usual, trying to put the strange email out of his mind. If she was truly interested, she would follow up with a call or email. He returned to his Waikiki condo as the sun hung low in the sky. He poured a glass of rosé, took the cheese plate from the refrigerator, and stepped out onto his twenty-ninth-floor lanai. The steady breeze had brought forth more than the usual number of yachts, their colorful triangular sails appearing like chips of stars on the sea. He'd catch the BBC news at six, then the PBS news a half-hour later, and warm up the leftover Korean meal. Everything was in order for a relaxed evening. He finished the wine and cheese and checked his email as the PBS news came on, and one message caught his eye.

Ahoy, Matey. The Jolly Roger sails tonight.

He didn't recognize the email address, but it had to be Valerie. His heart raced in anticipation as he showered and slipped on his black cotton slacks and an old white dress shirt with a wide collar. He fastened a red bandana around his head and looked in the mirror. If only he had a black patch over an eye, but . . . not enough time.

He reached the Sheraton Waikiki in ten minutes and walked through the long lobby looking into Honolulu Coffee and the RumFire lounge. Then he followed the narrow sidewalk left, toward the beach. He rolled up his pant cuffs and strolled near the surf's edge toward Diamond Head for a mile before turning back. Doubts replaced hope as he realized the email was probably a prank, not from Valerie at all. She wouldn't have expected him to search the entire two miles of Waikiki Beach for her. As he reached the steps to the concrete walkway into the Sheraton, he paused and took a last look back at the empty beach.

The voice came out of the darkness. "I'm looking for a scallywag to help me search for treasure." A shadowy figure emerged from the shadows.

"Aye, aye, Captain. I'm an old seadog ready to sign on to the Jolly Roger to search for treasure."

Perfect Match

Among the thousands of profiles and photos on the singles website, one was a near-perfect fit for him.

Debra Wagner, female, age 30, 5 foot 11 inches.
Single, nonsmoker, university degree.
No children, but love children. Residence in Sausalito, San Francisco Bay Area.
Likes: hiking, reading books with substance, old bookstores, good coffee, stage plays, tropical destinations, and international travel.
Dislikes: smokers, heavy drinkers, and men who won't say they are sorry.
Partner: optimistic, playful, university education, similar interests, respectful of my views.

The email reply included a photo with his daughter.

Dear Ms. Wagner,
My name is Martin Kingsley. I'm thirty-four and have a cheerful, loving, seven-year-old daughter, Becky. I found your profile and photo on the dating website. I believe I could be the man you're looking

for. I have a master's degree in biology and have worked at the Hawaii Department of Fisheries for the past six years. Between university degrees, I spent two years with the Peace Corps in Fiji. I love international travel and have been to Asia twice, once to Europe and to four South Pacific countries. I don't smoke, drink lightly, and also am into great coffees. I love kayaking and snorkeling. I'm not muscular or a great athlete but I stay active. Most important to me is finding a compatible woman who also will be a loving mother for Becky. I look forward to hearing from you and will answer any questions you have.

Aloha,

Martin

Over the following two months, they exchanged dozens of emails and photos but did not talk on the telephone. Martin explained he wanted to hear her voice the first time they met. Debra accepted his offer of a paid trip to Oahu for a week and a room for her in the Halekulani Hotel, on Waikiki Beach. She checked online and found that the Halekulani Hotel was one of the most expensive hotels in Waikiki and suggested that a more moderately priced hotel would be fine, but Martin's reply was that he could get a special *kama'aina* (resident) rate, and it was his favorite hotel for sunset drinks.

Debra expected to spot Martin and his daughter as soon as she stepped off the Hawaiian Airlines flight. But she saw no one resembling him, and a chill ran down her spine. Was this a trick?

"Debra Wagner," a woman called out as she hurriedly approached with a fragrant orchid-and-tuberose lei. "Aloha, and welcome to Hawaii. I'm Lori. Martin is stuck in a meeting and sent me to greet you and drive you to your hotel." She nervously arranged the lei around Debra's neck and gave her a warm hug.

"Lori. Martin assured me in an email last night that he would meet me at the airport."

"I know. It was a last-minute meeting that he couldn't miss, but you'll see him soon enough, and he's exactly like the photos and description he sent you."

"How do you know what he sent me? "

"We're very close."

"Lori, you look familiar. Have we met before?"

"It's possible. After you check in, we can meet in the cocktail lounge for a drink. I'm sure you'll find Martin everything that you expect."

Debra wondered why Lori was giving a big sales pitch for Martin. She would make up her own mind after meeting him. It was troubling not to be met by the man she had flown half-way across the Pacific Ocean to meet. If it was such an important meeting, why didn't he mention it in his last email sent the previous night?

They were greeted in style at the hotel, and Debra was escorted to her room to register. Lori suggested Debra freshen up in her room and then meet her for drinks and a chat before Martin arrived in the open-air House Without a Key, named after the famous Charlie Chan novel. As Debra entered the terrace lounge, she saw Lori wiping her eyes with a handkerchief. Strange? Lori jumped up as soon as she spotted Debra.

"Please sit down, and I'll order you a drink. Mai Tai okay? It's a Hawaiian favorite."

"An iced tea would be better for my stomach. It was a bumpy flight." Unsaid, she was anxious about Martin not showing up.

Lori ordered an iced tea and, as the waiter walked away, broke into sobs and covered her face with a handkerchief.

"Lori, what's going on? Has something happened to Martin?"

Lori shook her head and wiped her face, smearing her heavy makeup. Then she blew her nose. Her hand shook as she lifted her drink and emptied it in two gulps. She slumped back in her chair. "Debra, please hear me out before you jump up and run to pack." She took a deep breath. "Martin is my husband and knows nothing about you. I sent the emails."

"Oh, God, you must be crazy!" Debra pushed back her chair, and Lori lunged forward grabbing her arm.

"I'm dying."

Debra froze. "What does any of this have to do with me?"

"Nothing and everything. At least, everything to do with why you're here. Hear what I have to say, then I'll leave, and you can spend the week in Hawaii doing whatever you want. Your room is prepaid, and I'll never try to contact you again."

Debra hesitated, then sat back in her chair and crossed her arms over her chest. "I'm listening."

"I have an aggressive brain tumor. They tell me I have no more than four months to live. My cancer is not treatable. My husband and daughter don't know; they think I'm being treated for a female urinary infection."

"Lori, you need to tell your family so you can get the love and compassion needed at this time. And plans need to be made for—"

"You are the plan. Because once I tell them, everything will change. They will be worried and will hover around. Their smiles and laughter will be forced. Nothing will be normal. It's worth everything to me to have two, maybe three, extra months of normalcy and happiness before I have to tell them. It's my life, and that's what I want."

"Lori, that's your choice, but it can't include me. You can't just go to a dating site and pick out a wife like in a mail-order catalogue. It doesn't work that way."

"I know it sounds awful, but it seemed the best way. I know Martin, and he'll put off searching for a wife, maybe for years, when our Becky needs a mother now. When I met Martin in graduate school, he missed all of my hints that I was interested in him, so I took the initiative and asked him out. He's so loving and trusting and can be easily tricked by some assertive woman with less than honorable intensions. I know Martin better than he knows himself, and I did my best to be a matchmaker for this great man and Becky. I was petrified about meeting you at the airport and trying to explain everything in a way so you would understand. I'm truly sorry."

"And how were you going to introduce me to Martin? Something like, 'Martin, I want you to meet your future wife.' How do you think that would go over?"

"Not like that. I told Martin and Becky that you're a college friend coming to spend a week in Hawaii and we would be showing you around the island, have a few meals together, go to the beach and maybe a luau. It would give you time to get to know Martin and Becky and for them to see your best qualities. There would be no pressure, and at the end of the week, you fly home. A friendship will have been established, and in the coming time of need, you could be there if you wanted to pursue a relationship."

"Lori, even if I agreed to your diabolical plan, starting a relationship through deception is a recipe for disaster. I couldn't be myself knowing I was trying to make Martin fall in love with me while the one he loves is sitting beside him. Count me out of your scheme."

Lori's demeanor changed. Lips pursed, she fumbled through her handbag and pulled out a packet of tourist brochures and tossed them on the table as she rose from her chair.

"These will help you have a pleasant vacation in Hawaii. Good-bye." She hurriedly walked away, bumping into a table and knocking over two empty glasses.

Debra immediately checked on the cancelation policies of
the Halekulani Hotel and was told that all but the first day's
charges would be refunded to Lori Kingsley's credit card. She
didn't intend to let Lori pay for her vacation when she wasn't
going to participate in her scheme as matchmaker. She found
a room at less than half the rate at the nearby no-frills Waikiki
Shore Hotel and moved in the next morning.

Debra spent the day on the beach near the Waikiki Shore,
enjoying drinks and snacks from one of the three takeout cafés
in the rear. At sunset, she walked to the end of the rock-and-
concrete pier, where several people were peering into the water.
A man in a straw hat and pink polo shirt pointed out the two
adult green sea turtles feeding on the seaweed. He was a writer
and said he had recently retired in Waikiki and came daily to
see the sunsets and turtles to remind him of why he'd moved
here from Ohio.

Like most visitors from the mainland, Debra woke early
the following morning, her internal clock set three hours later,
to California time. She strolled past the Halekulani to the
Sheraton Waikiki and bought coffee and a chocolate croissant
at Honolulu Coffee in the rear of the hotel. Then she settled in
at a small table with a view across the mirror-smooth infinity
pool that appeared to flow into the ocean. Debra mused, *I'll
have a worry-free week in Hawaii without getting involved in
someone else's family problems.* She leaned across, picked up
a copy of the *Honolulu Star-Advertiser* from the next table,
and turned to the entertainment section to check out the local
events. There was a play about Japanese-American immigrants at Kumu Kahua, the theater specializing in plays about
Hawaiian life; an outdoor concert at the Waikiki Shell on
Friday night in Kapi'olani Park; and an outrigger canoe race
on Saturday, ending on the beach behind the Hilton Hawaiian
Village. She was about to flip back to the front page when she
saw a familiar name.

Noted marine biologist and photographer Martin Kingsley, of the Hawaii Fisheries Department, will give a talk on Hawaiian fish species at the East-West Center, followed by a viewing of his Hawaiian photos. The talk is open to the public and will be held in Burns Hall, 4:00–5:00 p.m. today.

Debra shrugged and flipped to the front page. She didn't believe in fate, fortune tellers, serendipity, or an invisible hand guiding her life, and coincidences happen all the time, as she had learned in her statistics class in college. Ignoring the DO NOT FEED THE BIRDS sign, she tossed bits of her croissant to the sparrows. She left a trail of footprints in the wet sand as she strolled toward Diamond Head, enjoying the solitude before the arrival of the daily crowds. Deeply tanned men were opening beach kiosks, their surfboards lined up like soldiers in formation, and shiny outrigger canoes were being wiped and readied to take tourists out to ride the waves.

She took a midday swim, then returned to her room for an afternoon nap, the consequence of the time-change and lack of a good night's sleep. It was three ten p.m. when she rolled over and looked at the bedside clock. Hours before, she had dismissed the idea of attending Martin's talk, but now, for no compelling reason, she suddenly felt an urgency to attend. Pulse racing, she slipped into a summer dress and pulled her hair into a ponytail. The taxi driver didn't need directions to the East-West Center. He told her about its international reputation of attracting dignitaries, including presidents and prime ministers, to present talks. She told him she wasn't going to hear anyone important, just a marine biologist talking about fish. The gray-haired Japanese driver's final words were, "Scientists seek the truth, and politicians seek reelection." They both laughed.

She entered the packed conference room as Martin was about to begin his talk. He was about six feet tall, with a tan that matched his unruly hair and eyes, slightly magnified by his round glasses. He paused when he saw her standing at the back of the room. "Miss, please have my chair." He moved his to the right side of the front row.

Debra appreciated the unexpected gesture and was pleasantly surprised to find his talk lively and informative. He clearly loved his research, though he tried to cover too much in an hour. Most compelling was his infectious smile and how excited he appeared when answering questions from the audience. He was humble in his replies to questions, readily admitting when he didn't know an answer.

At the conclusion of the session, Dr. Barry Cord, the host for the talk, invited everyone to view Kingsley's marine photographs in the ground floor exhibit hall, but Debra decided not to stay and risk meeting Kingsley or, worse, Lori, if she showed up. The East-West Center receptionist told her it would be a wait of at least forty-five minutes for a taxi during the Friday evening rush hour and suggested she remain to have some punch and enjoy the photo exhibit.

She moseyed over to the beverage table for a glass of Hawaiian guava punch, and she entered the crowded exhibit room. The twenty-four-by-thirty-inch photos were professional and reminded her of ones she'd seen in *National Geographic* magazines. One improbable photo of a dolphin jumping over the setting sun caused her to move closer. "Can't be real," she murmured.

"It is. It was just a lucky shot."

She turned, brushing Martin, who was standing so close she could detect the tropical scent of his cologne — unusual for a man but right for Hawaii.

"I was out past the coral reef on my kayak trying to catch the green flash at sunset. I didn't realize until the next day that a dolphin had jumped at the moment I snapped the photo. It's my daughter Becky's favorite." He studied Debra's face. "You look familiar, but I don't recall meeting you before."

"I'm Debra Wagner. I'm vacationing and staying in Waikiki."

Martin laughed. "You're here in Hawaii on vacation and came to listen to a boring talk about fish. You must be a biologist."

"No. I'm an English teacher. I really must go."

"Did you come by taxi?"

"Yes."

"Well, the East-West Center reception desk is closed, and it's rush hour, so you'll have a long wait for a taxi. I'm meeting my wife and daughter in Waikiki for dinner, so if you can wait a few minutes I'll drive you."

Trapped, she fidgeted with her watch band. "I don't want to trouble you, and I can wait for a taxi."

"Nonsense. It's the least I can do for someone who gave up an afternoon at the beach to listen to my talk."

Martin was chatty during the ten-minute drive to Waikiki Beach. He mentioned how he and his wife, Lori, had come here on their honeymoon and never left. He seemed in another world as he talked about her and how she was always at his side when he needed some encouragement. Debra had rarely heard a man speak so fondly about his wife, and to a stranger no less. She was becoming increasingly anxious as Martin unknowingly spun a web drawing her into the situation she had adamantly decided to avoid.

The evening passed at a glacial pace as she replayed the series of missteps that got her into this mess. She should have known better than to come to Hawaii to meet a man she had communicated with only by email, and that the offer to stay at the deluxe and expensive Halekulani was too good to be true. *After discovering Lori's ruse, what was I thinking when I went to Martin's talk? I was curious about Martin, but I should have known I was entering dangerous waters that would complicate my feelings—and compromise my objectivity.*

After a restless night of sleep, she waited until nine thirty, after Martin would have left for work, before calling. "Lori, this is Debra. Are you alone?"

"I'm at the doctor's office."

"I met Martin at his talk yesterday."

"I know. Martin was amazed that a woman on vacation would come to his talk. I didn't have to ask the name because I knew it must be you. So why are you calling?"

"I really don't know."

"You see something in Martin, huh?"

"He's smart, good looking, and considerate, as you said."

"Debra, Saturday morning we're going to Kapiʻolani Park to watch Becky's soccer match. We'll stay for a picnic and swim at Sans Souci Beach across the street. You could just happen to walk by on the beach, then let things evolve naturally. Since Martin knows you're staying in Waikiki, he won't be surprised to see you. It will give you a chance to see the family dynamics without anyone thinking it's a job interview."

"I'm not sure. I don't feel good about all the deception."

"Do you have a better idea?"

"Yes. Don't get involved."

"That train has already left the station. I hope you decide to come."

Doubts flooded her mind as she wrestled with her inner warnings about getting mixed up in a life-and-death issue between a husband and wife. As an interloper in a couple's marital issues, she could end up receiving the wrath from both sides. She walked aimlessly along Kalakaua Avenue, the sidewalk chatter, a polyglot of English, pidgin, Japanese, Chinese, Korean, and Vietnamese, fading in and out like the radio on a drive around the island. She had to move to the side to let two happy Japanese children pass with inflated beach toys larger than themselves, and blindly accepted the flyers that were handed to her on street corners, tossing them in the nearest trash bin unread.

At the Waikiki Aquarium, she turned back, following the undulating reach of the surf for over a mile to her hotel, where she spotted a crowd around a green sea turtle on Fort DeRussy Beach. She had a sandwich and beer at a beachside bar as she watched the sunset, trying to keep her mind away from Martin, but everything seemed to provoke thoughts of him. The setting sun reminded her of the photo of the dolphin jumping over the sunset, and even the fragrant scent in the breeze was faintly like Martin's cologne. She didn't like him crowding into her consciousness when she was trying to enjoy the beauty of a sunset on Waikiki.

A shrill police siren woke her at five forty-three a.m., and she lay in bed trying not to face the decision. Forty minutes later, she dressed and walked to the end of the concrete pier behind her hotel and joined a small crowd waiting to see the sunrise over the Koʻolau Mountains. It should have been an exhilarating way to start the day, but the sun and ocean evoked thoughts of Martin.

Debra struggled, unable to make a firm decision until midmorning, when she walked on autopilot down Kalakaua Avenue toward Diamond Head and Kapiʻolani Park. At the corner of Kalakaua and Kapahulu Avenues, she stopped at the Starbucks and ordered an iced coffee flavored with two pumps of hazelnut. She nervously rattled her iced coffee, drawing stares from other patrons, then at exactly eleven, she walked across to Kapiʻolani Park and scanned the two soccer fields. She easily spotted Martin, as he waved his arms and yelled encouraging words to his daughter's team. To be safe, Debra joined the parents of the opposing team on the opposite side of the field. The seven-year-olds ran after the soccer ball with more zeal than skill, and Becky's team was trounced seven to two. As they turned toward the beach, Martin's arm around his daughter's shoulders, Lori looked directly at Debra, smiled, and gave a quick thumbs-up.

Debra watched as they stopped to get three folding beach chairs and a cooler from the trunk of their car, then crossed to Sans Souci Beach. Even at a distance, she could hear Becky excitedly talking to her parents. Debra circled to the War Memorial Natatorium, the once-elegant memorial to the First World War that had been used for swimming competitions but was now all but abandoned. She proceeded up the beach, sandals in hand, pausing frequently to pick up bits of coral, hoping Martin would see her and make the first move. She passed directly in front of them and was about to turn back when she heard her name and turned, trying to appear surprised when she saw Martin waving.

"Debra, what a surprise. You must come and meet my wife and our budding soccer star."

Becky poked her dad in the side. "I'm not a soccer star!"

Debra put on her best smile and walked across the beach, not sure what to say.

Lori took the lead. "You must be the woman Martin told me about." She offered her hand.

"Pleased to meet you," Debra replied, her stomach churning.

"Becky's our soccer player. She almost made a goal this morning."

"Mom! We got clobbered," Becky protested.

"Hi, Becky. I'm delighted to meet you. I also played soccer."

"When you were my age?"

"I started at six and didn't make a single goal for the first two years. I wasn't good at anything and mostly substituted for the other girls when they needed a rest. Then a coach took the time to teach me how to position my feet when kicking and how to strike the ball, and I started making goals. I played through high school, then got a scholarship to play for Westmont College in Santa Barbara."

Becky looked up at Debra with her big brown eyes. "Will you teach me how to play better?"

"I'd love to. If you have a soccer ball, I'll show you how to take control of the ball and position your feet when kicking. Then maybe you can give me some pointers on snorkeling and where to see fish."

"Deal!" Becky vigorously shook Debra's hand.

"Becky," Lori said, "I'll get the ball from our car while you three get acquainted."

They started with lunch of cold KFC chicken and chilled bottled water; afterward, Debra worked with Becky for an hour, showing her how to receive the ball, set her non-kicking foot so it pointed where she wanted the ball to go, then strike the ball in the center with the other foot. Later, Becky took Debra snorkeling hand-in-hand. They went almost to the red flag at the outer edge of the coral reef, then they followed the north side of the channel to the beach. Becky smoothed lotion on Debra's sunburned shoulders while she chatted as if she were a close friend. Martin commented to Lori on how lucky they were to meet Debra on the beach.

Debra declined Martin's offer of a ride back to her hotel, saying she wanted to walk along the beach, and Becky and Lori gave her hugs before they parted. It had been her most memorable day in Hawaii, and her trepidations about meeting Martin and Becky had proved to be overblown. But while Becky was a delight to be around, Debra couldn't look either Martin or Lori in the eye without feeling a sickening feeling for getting involved in Lori's deceitful plan. That night, she made up her mind that deception was the wrong way to start any romantic relationship. She wouldn't contact them again.

Over breakfast, Debra was looking through some tourist brochures when her cell phone rang. She stiffened when she saw Lori's number on the screen. On the fourth ring, she answered. "Hello, Lori."

"Sorry to bother you, but Becky's out of school today and Martin's in a conference all day. Becky wants to see you again, and my usual babysitter's not available. Any chance I could leave her with you for a couple of hours while I go to the doctor?"

Debra clutched the phone, as this was exactly what she was trying to avoid. "Okay, for two hours."

Lori must have already been on their way, because she arrived within minutes. Becky bounced out of the car and Lori took her full beach bag and soccer ball from the back seat. "Debra, I told Becky it was only for two hours, but she packed enough for a week."

Two hours later, Lori called back, her voice weak. "Debra, I'm not feeling well and need to go home to bed. Could you keep Becky until five, when Martin will pick her up?"

"That'll be fine. We're about to build a sandcastle, something I haven't done since I was her age."

Debra and Becky were eating shave ice when Martin arrived at five nineteen.

"Sorry I'm late. There were so many questions from the audience, and I was the last speaker. Lori called and said she wasn't hungry and for us to get a bite before coming home. Any chance you can join us? I was thinking of Becky's favorite restaurant."

"California Pizza!" Becky squealed.

Over a large pizza, Becky excitedly described their day. "We snorkeled and saw two humongous turtles behind Debra's hotel, and we built the best sandcastle ever, and we decorated it with plumeria blossoms that we picked up from the ground in Fort DeRussy. Some people took pictures of our castle. Debra, can you show Daddy the picture you took just before a big wave knocked it flat?"

The day hadn't gone as planned, yet she had to admit that playing on the beach with Becky had brought back happy memories of her youth. The pizza dinner with Becky and Martin had also been fun. Yet once she was back in her room alone, the guilt resurfaced. When Martin found out about the ruse, he would be angry, and that would kill any chance for a genuine romance.

Debra joined tours during her last two days in Hawaii, but her times with Becky stood out as the highlights of the trip. Lori, Martin, and Becky came to the airport to see her off, and Becky cried, clinging to Debra until the last minute. Debra looked from the window of the plane as it taxied away, hoping to see Becky waving.

The email came sooner than expected. Debra sent flowers and called to give her condolences to Martin and comfort little Becky. She offered to fly over and help with Becky for a couple of weeks, but Martin said it would make it harder when she had to leave again. His voice was monotone and emotionless, as if he were reading a script. She knew men hid their grief, yet there was little she could do unless he asked for help.

Debra wondered if Martin would contact her, but as the months slid by, her hopes dwindled, and she began dating an old high school flame who had recently been divorced. A year passed before a letter arrived. She didn't open it immediately, taking time to make a fresh cup of coffee and sit down on her small patio before carefully slitting it open.

> *Dear Debra,*
>
> *I apologize for not writing sooner. After Lori's death, I kind of pulled into my shell like a turtle. It wasn't good for Becky or me, and her grades suffered. I didn't want to discuss my pain with anyone—men are not as good as women in letting out their inner feelings. Becky asks often about you and when you'll return.*
>
> *Lori told me everything just before she died, and I know all about how she searched dating sites and pretended she was me to bring you to Hawaii. She knew it was going too far, and I forgave her for everything. But Lori knew me better than I know myself. And she's right that Becky needs a loving mother. But it's so hard getting started. I went to the dating website where you and Lori met, but you're no longer on it. Maybe I'm too late.*
>
> *I don't know the right way to ask, but if you're not seriously dating someone, can I call?*
> *Aloha,*
> *Martin*

Debra replied by email that she was dating someone but would be happy to talk anytime.

Ten minutes later, she was just about to enter the shower when her cell phone rang. At first, she wasn't going to answer, but she did on the fifth ring. "Hello, Martin. I didn't expect you to call so soon. I was just about to take a shower."

"I'm sorry. I'll call back later?" The tone was apologetic.

"No, Martin. This is fine. I want to hear what you have to say."

"Debra, last night I had a dream that Lori returned as an angel and made me promise I would ask you out on a date."

"Martin, you called because you had a dream and Lori asked you to call me?"

"It was a dream about Lori coming back as an angel. It brought me a feeling of closure, so I can move on with my life. I didn't feel right about revealing my feelings about you so soon after Lori's death. What I want to say is you're on my mind all the time, and I want you to come back to Hawaii. I promise that this time it'll be me waiting when you step off the plan."

Pink Bows

*C*indy Maki had only attended a church service once, with her girlfriend while a teenager in Seattle. She'd felt awkward when a gold-plated tray was passed to her and she didn't have any money to offer, and she'd wondered if God noticed. Back home, she tried to read the Bible but felt little connection to the ancient stories and gave up.

Fifteen years later, on a balmy Sunday morning on Waikiki Beach, Cindy had a spiritual experience that changed her life.

To early risers like Cindy, Waikiki offered a pristine beach—the sand smoothed and glistening wet below the reach of the high tide, and above, the beach leveled by giant machines that visited in the dead of night to erase the swarms of footprints of the previous day. Far offshore, larger waves broke over the barrier coral reef, leaving gentle ones to roll onto shore.

Some would say that the melodic sounds of the surf were the same on every beach around the world. But on a balmy Sunday morning, as Cindy sat on a beachside bench eating Spam musubi and sipping oolong tea, a sensuous sensation surged through her body, tingling the tips of her fingers, and leaving her with Zen-like feelings of happiness and contentment. Thereafter, her Sunday morning visits to Waikiki Beach became a form of spiritual meditation to cleanse her mind of worries of the past and prepare her for the week ahead.

Cindy had grown up in Seattle in a traditional first-generation Japanese family. Her parents spoke broken English, and during the hysteria after the bombing of Pearl Harbor they were interned for the remainder of World War II by the US Government—a period of their lives they never discussed with her or their friends. Her high school graduation gift was a week's vacation in Hawaii, where she was seduced by the beauty and aloha spirit of Hawaii and the richness of its Asian-American culture. When Cindy returned after her second year of college, her friends told her she would miss the seasons and that the smallness of living on an island would annoy her. They predicted she would soon return to Seattle. But they were wrong. That had been over two decades ago.

Cindy worked at first in a sandal shop, where she met and fell in love with a local Japanese-Hawaiian man. A year later, they were married at sunrise on Waikiki Beach. But his passion for surfing took precedence over married life, and eventually his life. The surfing community gathered on the North Shore for a ceremony and returned his ashes to the sea. His small insurance policy paid enough for Cindy to buy out the owner of the sandal shop on Kalakaua Avenue in the heart of Waikiki. It was not very profitable financially, but she felt the rewards of meeting people from around the world made it worthwhile.

She never traveled to the tropical beaches of the South Pacific, the Caribbean, the Mediterranean, or the Indian Ocean, but countless visitors told her that nowhere else could match the friendly aloha spirit of Hawaii—something she shared with every person who entered her sandal shop.

Twenty years had slipped past, and many changes occurred in Cindy's life. Yet her Sunday morning ritual on Waikiki Beach stayed the same. It was warmer than usual as she twisted off the cap from her aqua-and-fuscia thermos, unwrapped the cellophane from her Spam musubi, and noticed an older man with gray-streaked hair appear on the beach with a four- or five-year-old girl. The child was swinging on his arm and wearing a frilly white party dress with a big pink bow in her curly blond hair. The fusion of sounds from the surf and passing cars muffled their voices, except for her occasional squeals. The man knelt in the sand and removed her shiny red shoes and white socks. Then he watched as she pranced to the water's edge, looked back, and cautiously entered. He called to her when she reached her knees, and she waded to shallower water and tried to catch fingerling fish. When she returned to the beach, she dug her fingers in the wet sand and playfully tossed it into the air.

Cindy was surprised that the man only had to call her once before she skipped across the beach and took his hand. Her giggles were infectious, and Cindy smiled. The child squealed again as he held her around the waist at the outdoor shower, her little feet kicking in the spray. She nibbled on a cookie, offering him a bite while he dried her feet before putting on her socks and shoes. He carefully fastened the pink bow in her hair, then he held her hand as they crossed Kalakaua Avenue and disappeared up Uluniu Avenue.

The following Sunday, at a few minutes after eleven, they appeared again. Today, under her dress she wore a blue swimsuit with a pattern of pink flowers. The man helped pull the dress over her head and neatly folded it before setting it on a towel next to the pink bow. She ran to the water, then stopped to look back at the man before entering. This time, Cindy heard him call her name.

"Tammy, sweetie, don't go in past your chest."

She gave him a compliant thumbs-up. He never took his eyes off her as she splashed around in the ocean.

The pattern was repeated every Sunday morning at the same time, except on stormy days. Sometimes they arrived with a McDonald's meal and drink that they shared. She would tease him with French fries, usually giving him a bite, but sometimes snatching it away and popping it in her mouth and giggling. Watching their playful interactions became the highlight of Cindy's Sunday mornings. Eventually, she discovered that they attended Saint Augustine's Catholic Church, a five-minute walk away. She guessed the girl's reward for being good in church was a trip to the beach. The gray hair and crinkles around his eyes suggested the man was in his fifties, probably her grandfather. He didn't wear a ring, and they were never accompanied by a woman.

Weeks became months, then years, as she watched the girl grow. As time passed, Tammy ventured deeper into the water and eventually began swimming—duck-paddling at first. The dresses changed as she grew, but never the pink bow in her hair, which he handled as if it were a rare flower. He always watched from the beach, only once rushing in fully clothed when she screamed. She was crying, arms around his neck as he carried her across the beach to the outdoor shower, where he carefully washed and examined her foot before sitting her on a towel. Kneeling in the sand, he dried her feet and kissed the injured one, and she stopped crying.

Cindy never would forget the overcast Sunday in December when they stopped coming to the beach. The girl would have been eight or nine. At first, she assumed they might be visiting friends on the mainland over the Christmas break. Months passed. Then they reappeared on a breezy Easter Sunday. Tammy wore the same pink ribbon, but the dress Cindy had seen many times hung loosely, and she seemed unsteady as she gripped the man's arm. They stopped in the shade of the rock retaining wall nearer where Cindy sat and she heard the man telling her she would be fine and not to be afraid. He smiled and kissed her nose, then he took off her pink bow and blond wig. She had lost weight and looked sickly. Her curly blond hair was gone. In high school, Cindy had volunteered to read stories to children with leukemia; she had learned to control her feelings, but seeing Tammy was too much, and tears streamed down her face. The man looked much older; his hair had turned almost totally gray in just three months.

Cindy wanted to go over and offer words of sympathy, but there was nothing she could say that would make things better, and this was a special time between a grandfather and his sick granddaughter that should be respected. After they left, Cindy noticed the pink ribbon hanging on a bush, probably blown off by a gust of wind. She picked it up and brought it back every Sunday for a month, hoping they would return. But they didn't.

Years passed, and Waikiki changed. Improvements were made to cater to the tastes of wealthier tourists, mainly from Japan, Korea, and China. The concrete sidewalks were replaced with more picturesque cobblestones and bricks, and ponds with small waterfalls and plants were added. The local shops were gradually replaced by larger upscale ones with international reputations. Cindy married a divorced man from Philadelphia, but he struggled to adjust to Hawaii's intense heat and the more laid-back culture, and he longed to be near his children. Finally, Cindy suggested he go, and they remained friends until he passed away.

Next to the register of her sandal shop, Cindy posted her only photo of the man and girl, along with the pink bow and a note asking if anyone recognized them. Several people said they looked familiar, but none led her to them. Each Sunday morning, Cindy said a prayer for Tammy and wondered. Her sandal shop expanded to a second one in a deluxe hotel, and she took on a young partner to lessen her work load. She down-sized and sold her home in Kaimuki and bought a two-bedroom condo in Waikiki close to the beach. While she had had a superb view of Waikiki from Kaimuki, it wasn't the same as being there, surrounded by happy voices and the sounds and scents of the ocean. Cindy never gave up hope of seeing Tammy and her grandfather again—her heart racing every time she saw a gray-haired man and young girl on the beach. The man would be old, maybe deceased by now. And the girl—did she survive the cancer? Cindy wanted to know to find closure for the unsettling uncertainty.

She rarely missed her Sunday mornings at the same bench with her thermos of oolong tea and something to nibble on. She had given up her long-time favorite, Spam musubi, on doctor's orders—too much fat in the Spam.

One cool morning, Cindy had debated whether to go to the beach, as the weather report predicted a passing cold front bringing a high of only seventy-three degrees. She had just sat down on the bench when a child squealed. She felt as if her heart stopped when she saw a girl of four or five swinging on the arm of an elderly man dressed in an aloha shirt and tan slacks. The child had on a frilly party dress with a big pink ribbon in her hair. For a minute Cindy thought it must be a dream, as Tammy by now would be in her late twenties. He had snow-white hair, yet there was a strong resemblance to the man in the faded photo taped next to her cash register. She had looked at the photo thousands of times and knew every facial detail, but was less certain about the girl, who was not clear in the photo, and many young children look similar.

The man put down his beach bag and stiffly knelt in the sand to take off the girl's shiny red shoes, while she steadied herself with fingers in his hair and giggled as she messed it up. He didn't seem to mind, and she gave him a hug before running to the water's edge, lifting her dress above her knees and wading in. "Emi, sweetie, don't go in past your knees," the man called out as he watched her, his hands on his hips.

Cindy couldn't miss her only chance after decades of wondering, and she walked over to him. "Excuse me. This may sound silly, but you resemble a man and little girl who used to come here a long time ago. It must have been about two decades ago."

He tilted his head as he gazed into her face, then nodded and grinned, his worn, off-white teeth revealing the passage of time. "You're the fetching woman who always sat on the bench over there."

She couldn't help blushing. "I'm Cindy Maki. I have a sandal store nearby."

"I'm pleased to finally meet you." He grasped her hand with two hands, giving her goosebumps. "I'm Randy Snyder, originally from Des Moines, Iowa, but I lived in Hawaii a long time ago. I have often wondered about the mystery woman I saw sitting in the same place every Sunday morning. I wanted to meet you, but I had to stay focused on my daughter, Tammy, who wasn't a good swimmer. I had moved to Honolulu with Tammy shortly after my wife, Emi, died. The pink bows are in memory of her. When Tammy was diagnosed with leukemia and the treatment wasn't working, I moved to Boston, where a new treatment was tried, and she recovered. It was the greatest miracle in my life. I don't know what I would have done if I lost her."

"So, you're visiting Waikiki?"

"I moved back two months ago; I always wanted to return to Waikiki. My daughter, Tammy, and her husband, Chad, are visiting now with their daughter, Emi. She insisted I bring my granddaughter to the beach after church, just like I used to do with her. Tammy's sentimental, so she dressed Emi in a dress like she had worn when she was five. I never thought I'd see this day."

Emi came running across the beach. "Grandpa, I found a pretty shell."

"Can I see your treasure?"

She carefully placed it in his hand. "Is it valuable?"

He held the fingernail-sized cowrie close to his eye and examined it. "Priceless!"

"I'll keep it forever," she squealed. "Grampa, is the lady a friend?"

"Yes . . . an old friend."

Before, they left, Cindy told Randy she had something to return to his daughter, Tammy.

"I can't imagine what it could be."

"The pink ribbon that fell from Tammy's hair the last time you were at the beach with her before moving to Boston."

For more than a decade an elderly couple could be seen holding hands on the same bench every Sunday morning. The man eventually began showing up with a cane, a big pink bow tied to it. They always sat close, with the woman resting her head against his shoulder. They would stay for an hour, maybe a little more, and share cups of tea from an aqua-and-fuchsia thermos, then amble away, her arm always around his waist. They didn't appear for several weeks, then on a balmy Sunday in December the man appeared and sat on the bench—two pink bows fastened to his cane.

Sixteenth Birthday Party

*C*helsea nervously sucked on her "Sweet 16" gold and diamond pendant as she stood next to the double doors to the reception room for her birthday party at the Royal Hawaiian Hotel. Thirty-seven adults were inside sipping champagne and eating canapés, each fashioned in the shape of an animal. Her parents had invited prominent friends and professional colleagues, and Chelsea had invited her entire eleventh-grade English literature class to arrive at five thirty. But it was six twenty-four p.m., and not a single classmate had shown up.

It had been difficult making new friends in the elite private school during her first semester. Cliques were well-established, and there was little room for a shy, bookish newcomer with an Australian accent. Her mother, Lauren Tucker, was sure that having Chelsea's sixteenth birthday party in the famous Waikiki hotel would be just the ticket to getting her daughter accepted. Just as important would be the opportunity for her and her husband to show off to their distinguished new friends in the world of business and politics. To that end, the lavish buffet was heavily tilted toward adult tastes, with imported escargots, the finest fresh ahi sashimi, and Sydney oysters on the half-shell.

Chelsea insisted on remaining by the door, not wanting to face the surreptitious glances from the adults inside. She did not want to overhear the whispers asking why no one her age had come to the party. She was already self-conscious about her beanpole figure, and now she was facing the humiliation of being stood up by her entire class.

She was about to give up waiting when a boy appeared at the lobby entrance. At first, she didn't recognize him as he hurried toward her, his hair sticking out over his ears. Then she realized it was Cory Porter, the quiet student who sometimes arrived late to the first class of the morning, AP Calculus, yet aced every exam. She had only spoken to Cory a couple of times when she needed help on a calculus problem and there was no one else around. When he'd sat across from her at lunch, the other two girls at the table had immediately left. Like Chelsea, he was thin. Worse, he often had a disheveled appearance that didn't go over well in their preppy private school. She had overheard classmates speaking disparagingly about Cory not belonging at the school. They made cutting remarks speculating that he'd only gotten in on a special scholarship for the poor.

Chelsea was glad to see anyone her own age. She waved and gave a welcoming greeting. "Hi, Cory."

"Sorry I'm so late. The bus didn't arrive, so I had to hitch a ride from Waimanalo." He took out the damaged plumeria lei from a Long's plastic bag. "Maybe you shouldn't wear this one I made. You already have two really nice leis."

"Don't be silly. It's special because you took the time to make it for me."

He nervously draped it over her head and gave her a tentative hug that she finished with a kiss on his cheek.

"You must be thirsty after the long ride." She took his hand and pulled him toward the punch bowl. As she handed him his drink she whispered, "you are about to be interrogated by my nosy parents. Be careful what you say."

"Chelsea dear, you must introduce me to your classmate. I want to know all about him," Lauren said in the syrupy-sweet voice Chelsea knew so well. She proffered her hand, which Cory cautiously shook.

"Mom, Dad, Cory Porter is in my English literature and AP Calc classes. He's the top student in calculus."

"A future engineer," her father said. "What college are you hoping to attend?"

"Um, I live in Waimanalo so probably will start at Windward Community College, then, hopefully, transfer to the University of Hawaii. A lot depends on whether I can get a scholarship."

"Oh, I see," Lauren replied with a faux smile. "How, may I ask, can your family afford a private high school education?"

"We can't. I got a scholarship for promising students from low-income families."

"That's nice," Lauren replied. "Well, you have an enjoyable time. Chelsea, dearie, make sure he tries the escargots. He's probably never had them. Well, we must get back to the other guests." She spun and quickly merged into the crowd, her loud voice a beacon to her location.

"Cory, don't pay any attention to my mother. She's an insufferable snob and only mentioned the escargots to embarrass you."

"I like escargots with garlic butter and a dusting of finely chopped parsley."

"Really?"

"Yes, last summer, when I turned sixteen, I had a job busing dishes at Kipuka 888 and got to try the leftovers at the end of the evening. Their French chef, Jean Martell, took a liking to me and introduced me to some of his favorite French dishes, including escargots. If I can't get a scholarship to a university, I'll try to become a chef."

Chelsea nervously adjusted the satin sash on her dress. "Do you know why no one in my class came except you?"

He pursed his lips. "Uh-huh."

"Why doesn't anyone like me? I want to know."

"Jill Peterson, that blond who's so popular, invited the entire class except you to her home for a big bash. Her parents are away, and she promised booze and night-time games in her swimming pool with the pool lights off. I'm thinking she chose tonight because it's the night of your party."

"So why didn't you go?"

"You know as well as I do. I'm not welcome in her crowd. No one would even talk to me."

"So why did you come to my party?"

"You're different."

"Just different?"

Cory shifted from one foot to the other. "Well, I think you're really cute."

"No boy ever said that to me before." She insisted that Cory sit with her at the head table and made sure to sit between him and her parents. It was not enough of a buffer, and her mother leaned over to further her inquisition.

"Cory, your parents must be very proud of you."

"My mom is, but I don't know about my dad. He left when I was three."

"Oh. I suppose your mother works?"

"Yes, at McDonald's in Waimanalo. She hopes to work her way up to store manager someday. I often go there on her evening shift to do my homework and eat."

"So is McDonald's your favorite food?"

"No, but that's what we can afford."

"I see. And, Cory, how do you like the escargots?" she said with a derisory smile.

He finished chewing the snail before relying. "Um, Ms. Tucker, it's okay."

"You can tell me the truth, you're among friends."

"Um, there's too much garlic in the butter sauce and it overpowers the delicate flavor of the escargots."

Lauren's eyes narrowed. *He didn't learn that at the McDonald's in Waimanalo.*

"Mom, Cory is here to see me, and it's my birthday party!"

"Yes, of course, sweety."

Chelsea reached under the table and took Cory's hand and leaned forward to shield him from her mother.

Her father, Philip, stood and pinged his wine glass. "As all of you know, we are here to celebrate our daughter Chelsea's sixteenth birthday. Lauren and I have only been in Hawaii for six months, and because of all of you, we feel totally at home in your beautiful, welcoming state. We were concerned about the public schools in Hawaii and are delighted that Diamond Head Prep School made an exception and accepted Chelsea when we moved here too late to meet the deadline for applications. I see the headmaster, Dr. Eugene Tilling, is here this evening. So, let's all give him a hand for his fine leadership." He went on to acknowledge most of the adults in the room, before mentioning his daughter again.

Chelsea whispered to Cory, "Sounds like a campaign speech."

At the end of the meal, her mother led everyone in singing "Happy Birthday," then it took two puffs for Chelsea to blow out the candles on her birthday cake, molded in the shape of the island of Oahu.

Chelsea's father asked her for the first dance, followed by several other men. Finally, after the obligatory dances, Chelsea pulled Cory onto the dance floor.

"I'm not a good dancer," he muttered.

"But you're the only one I want to dance with tonight." She held him close, and by the second slow dance, her head was resting on his shoulder.

Turning to her husband, Lauren whispered, "I don't want Chelsea mixing with his kind. She's never had a boyfriend, and I'm not going to let her get mixed up with a boy with his background and no future."

"Lauren dear, her infatuation is because he's the only boy at her party. Let her have fun tonight."

As the guests quickly left just minutes after the mayor and his wife departed, Chelsea asked Cory to stay. Under the watchful eyes of her parents, Chelsea opened their gift, tickets for a three-week family vacation in Europe. She threw her arms around each and kissed them on both cheeks. "Mom, Dad, that's what I've dreamed of."

"Chelsea, as soon as school's out, we'll all go to Paris, then to Venice to ride a gondola and dance in San Marco Square, and finally to the enchanted cliff village of Ia, on the Greek island of Santorini."

Chelsea handed the tickets to her mother. "You better keep these so they don't get lost. I want to open one more present, and the rest can wait until tomorrow."

"Chelsea, it's been a long day. Why not open the presents tomorrow?"

"But Mom, Cory was the only one from my school who came to my party. So I must open his gift. Then I want to go for a walk on the beach before going home."

Lauren glanced at her husband and forced a smile. "Sure, honey. It's your sixteenth birthday."

Lauren had a perverse interest in Cory's small gift, wrapped in what was clearly reused wrapping paper. At first, they saw only the rough exterior of a large oyster shell, then Chelsea turned it over. "Oh, my gosh! It's so beautiful." The mother-of-pearl interior shimmered in the light of the chandeliers. There were two cranberry-sized, rounded bumps where pearls had formed under the mother-of-pearl, making it a curiosity, but of little material value. Inscribed below the pearls were the words:

Two roads diverged in a wood, and I—
I took the one less traveled by,
And that made all the difference.

"Cory, I remember those lines. They're from the poem by Robert Frost that we read in our English literature class. The handwriting appears professional."

"My handwriting looks like chicken scratches, so I had a jeweler inscribe the words that I want to live by."

She leaned over and kissed Cory on the cheek. "Let's go for a walk on the beach. I can't have my sixteenth birthday in Waikiki without a walk on the beach." She kicked off her white satin dress shoes and held Cory's hand tightly as they followed the undulating reach of surf. Her parents watched the teens venture into the ocean, the water eddying around their knees as they turned into each other, their bodies merging into a single silhouette.

Lauren swirled her martini, lips pursed. "We better make sure that boy doesn't foil our plans for Chelsea. She's young and vulnerable and not prepared for the feelings that might be unleashed by that boy."

"Lauren, it's just a kiss on a romantic beach on her sixteenth birthday. Remember back on Bondi Beach when we first met?"

"Yes, but you were already a successful businessman on your way up in the world."

"But you were twenty, unmarried, with a baby girl."

"Philip, sometimes you're so hurtful. It's Chelsea, our daughter, I'm talking about. She's very impressionable. And let's admit it, she's not nearly as beautiful as I was at sixteen. Chelsea might fall for the first boy who gives her any attention. And it's not going to be that boy."

"Lauren, she's a late bloomer, and in another year or so she'll be off to an Ivy League college. And with a little help from you, she'll find a rich boy to marry."

Lauren kissed her husband on the cheek. "That's what I like about you. You're such an optimist. And, of course, you provide the lifestyle that I want."

The following morning, they took Chelsea out to breakfast at the deluxe Kahala Hotel & Resort, where Lauren outlined their dating expectations and rules. "It was nice of Cory to come to your party. But we're firmly against it going any further. It's not his fault, but he comes from a different world—one that's simply unacceptable. Do you understand?"

"No, I don't. He's smart and the only one in my whole class who cared enough to come to my party. Doesn't that tell you a lot about his character?"

"It tells us that he's attracted to you, and your party was probably the only one he'll ever be invited to at your school. It's unfortunate, but boys like Cory don't have the opportunities you do and will fall behind in life, settling for mundane jobs with little future. These are the hard facts of life. Even if you aren't convinced, your father and I forbid you to see Cory again. Do you understand?"

"Yes, I understand! How do you know *you're* not ruining my life, huh?"

"Trust me. I was impetuous at your age and got pregnant with you. Fortunately, I had a second chance when I met your dear father. I won't let you repeat my mistake. Now, promise me you won't see Cory again."

She paused, her hands under the table, fingers crossed. "I promise."

Chelsea told Cory she was not allowed to see him again, but he kept pursuing her, writing little notes and poems and dropping them on her desk as he passed. Soon they were having lunches together, then meeting after school, Chelsea telling her mother she was at club meetings. By the spring semester, they were sneaking off to a hidden beach behind Diamond Head to play in the ocean and make out. Chelsea was careful in what she said but made the mistake of writing everything in her diary, believing the little heart-shaped lock would keep it from her mother's prying eyes.

A bent paperclip easily opened the lock, giving her mother access to Chelsea's secrets.

Lauren was furious when she read that Chelsea was regularly seeing Cory after school and even slipping off to a secluded beach together. She confronted Chelsea and grounded her for a month. But predictably, the worst was yet to come. When Lauren and Philip returned early from a conference on the mainland, they caught Chelsea topless in their swimming pool with Cory. Philip physically threw Cory out of the gate in his bathing suit, and Lauren slashed his clothes with a knife before tossing them over the fence.

Four days later Cory was expelled from school for unbefitting behavior. The following week it was announced that Philip and Lauren Tucker had made a substantial donation to the private school, and Philip was being appointed to the school's governing board.

Chelsea mailed a letter to Cory's home, leaving a faint ray of hope for the future.

> *Dear Cory,*
>
> *I cannot see you again, and I am so sorry my parents got you expelled from school. My mom snooped in my diary and made a photocopy of something I wrote about you and me. It was about us making love, but she didn't copy the part that said it was a fantasy. She showed it to the principal of the school, and that is why you were expelled. It's all my fault because of the fantasy I wrote about us in my diary. I'm really, really sorry.*
>
> *I'm being sent to France as an exchange student for my senior year, so there is no way I can see you again. You are so smart, and you'll do well back in a public school. My parents don't see your potential, but I do. Just like you wrote on the shell gift, "Take the road less traveled," and maybe our paths will*

cross again. I know for sure I will never forget you,
no matter where our roads lead.
Love,
Chelsea

After his expulsion from the private school, Cory enrolled in Kailua High School, the nearest public high school to Waimanalo. His Advanced Math teacher recognized Cory's ability and encouraged him to enter the state math competition. Cory entered and, in spite of little preparation, came in second place, winning a scholarship to the University of Hawaii, where he majored in math and statistics.

Cory's senior thesis at the University of Hawaii was a simple statistical algorithm that might determine the effectiveness of unproven vaccines before the results of controlled human trials. This resulted in a scholarship to do a master's degree to further develop and test his algorithm on data supplied by a pharmaceutical company. The mathematical equations underpinning his algorithm were so encouraging that he was transferred into the PhD program, turning the master's degree into a mere formality. Cory's algorithm was tested on several trials that had been previously run and was able to demonstrate, with a probability of between 81.6 and 87.2 percent, whether a vaccine was effective within three to four months, rather than the six to twelve months usually required. The results were insufficient for FDA approval of new vaccines, but they allowed drug companies to determine at an earlier stage whether to proceed or abort human vaccine trials, saving tens to hundreds of millions of dollars that would otherwise be spent on drugs likely to fail. Cory was paid an undisclosed amount for the joint patent filed by his PhD advisor.

Cory's work garnered national recognition—and six-figure employment offers from pharmaceutical companies. Yet he accepted a joint position with Information Technology and the School of Medicine at the University of Hawaii at less than half the salary he could make in the private sector. In interviews, Cory simply said his heart was in Hawaii, and he wanted to give back to the university that changed his life and to be near his mother.

Chelsea followed in her father's footsteps and attended Brown University, where she lost her virginity after a fraternity party in her freshmen year. After dating several men, she got engaged to Edmond Frazer III in her junior year. Her mother approved of Frazer's pedigree and began talking to friends about possible locations for a wedding in Hawaii. Before their senior year at Brown, Chelsea and Frazer spent the summer traveling across Asia, but at the end of the summer, Chelsea returned alone to the United States and gave no explanation to her nosy mother, except that she would not be seeing Edmond again.

She completed a master's degree in political science at Georgetown University in Washington, DC, then, with the help of her father, she spent two years as a legislative assistant for a congressman before abruptly resigning, returning to Hawaii, and abandoning politics. She eventually took a position in Admissions at the University of Hawaii.

It had been sixteen years to the day since Chelsea celebrated her sixteenth birthday in the Royal Hawaiian Hotel and walked on the beach with Cory—memories frozen in time. Ashamed and guilty about abandoning him in his time of need, she hadn't tried to contact Cory. She could have saved Cory by showing their school principal her diary, which clearly stated what she wrote was a sixteen-year-old girl's fantasy and not the truth.

Chelsea knew that Cory had obtained a PhD and developed an algorithm that had given him national and international acclaim, and she occasionally spotted him on campus but always turned away.

Cory frequently drove to Waikiki Beach on weekends for a thirty-minute swim, followed by a cup of coffee and a freshly toasted bagel slathered in cream cheese. He had been tempted many times to search for Chelsea online, but he stopped himself. If she wanted to contact him, he was easy enough to find.

It was twilight on November 18, 2014, when Cory walked down the narrow alleyway on the side of the Sheraton Waikiki to the beach. He thought about the changes over the past sixteen years since he had kissed Chelsea after her birthday party. It was half their lifetimes ago. Professionally, he had already achieved far more than his dreams. But success came at the expense of having the family he wanted. It wasn't that there was a lack of eligible women on campus he could marry. Rather it was his own lack of effort to find and court one.

He slipped off his sandals and sank his toes into the sand, still holding the warmth from the heat of the day, and turned toward the Royal Hawaiian Hotel. The beach was deserted except for a woman sitting so close to the ocean that the surf was swirling around her. She was holding something against her cheek as she gazed toward the horizon. Curiosity drew him closer. Then he paused. She had, after all, come alone, so she must want the solitude of the sea. He turned and continued a few steps. Then he glanced back and saw something glimmer in her hand, like a mirror. Curious, he approached her, the surf muffling the sound of his footsteps.

"Excuse me. Are you okay?"

She shook her head then looked into his face. "Oh, God! Cory, it's you!"

His mouth dropped open. "Chelsea? I thought you were married and living on the East Coast."

She wiped her eyes. "I'm not married and have been here for five years."

"Chelsea, why didn't you contact me?"

"I couldn't face you after not standing up for you when you were expelled. And I suppose the fear that the magic of one's first romance can never be recaptured."

Cory sat down beside her, the surf soaking his shorts. "You were just sixteen. You couldn't go against your parents for me or anyone else. I never blamed you for what happened. Anyway, going to Kailua High School and finding a teacher who believed in me changed my life. That couldn't have happened in the preppy private school. Nobody believed in me there." He paused and gazed into Chelsea's eyes. "I came here tonight because it was exactly sixteen years ago that you had your birthday party at the Royal Hawaiian Hotel and we kissed here on the beach."

"That's also why I came." She handed him the oyster shell. "I take it everywhere to remind me that I should have taken the road less traveled instead of the one my parents wanted me to take. I really messed up my life. I slept around in college. Even slept with Sally, my roommate. Then I had an affair with a married congressman. Finally, I had a breakdown. I abandoned politics and returned to Hawaii. I searched online for you, hoping you got a degree from college. I discovered you not only went on for a PhD but developed an algorithm that made you famous."

"Fame is in the eyes of the beholder. I still feel a lot like that boy from Waimanalo. But it's hard to know, when a woman flatters me, if it is me or my status that she's attracted to. You knew me when I had nothing, and still you fell in love with me."

Chelsea handed the engraved oyster shell to Cory. "I found a skinny boy from Waimanalo long ago, and he gave me this shell engraved with life's instructions, but I didn't follow them, and now it's too late."

Cory ran his fingers over the engraved words. "These words aren't just for teenagers. Let me join you on the road less traveled. And that will make all the difference." He took Chelsea's hand. He pulled her to him, and they fell back as the surf swirled around them.

A gray-haired man watched from the lanai of the Royal Hawaiian Hotel. "Marge, come and look at the couple making out in the surf right in front of our hotel. Disgraceful!"

She joined her husband on the lanai and sighed. "Howard, they're in love."

Cory asked Chelsea to come to his home.

"Maybe this is just a dream," she said. "The dream I've had a thousand times. I want to sleep in my bed alone tonight. Then if the dream doesn't go away, I'll come."

At even forty-nine a.m., Chelsea's iPhone rang, and after the fourth ring she answered. "Hello, Mom. You're calling kind of early."

"Yes, sweety. Remember, Alexandra Steinberg is bringing her son, Joseph Emmet Steinberg II to our brunch at the Kahala Hotel & Resort at eleven thirty today. He's a Yale graduate and already vice president of his father's insurance company, and he's only thirty-five. Alexandra told me he recently broke off his engagement to another woman and is anxious to find a refined marriageable lady. And she told me her son checked your Facebook page and liked what he saw."

"But, Mom, I don't need your help to find a man."

"You're thirty-two and can't afford to pass up the best opportunity you may ever have."

"You're so right, Mom. That's why I'm not coming to lunch."

Homeless Lady

*Y*oshi Shimoda was on his morning jog along Kalakaua Avenue when he noticed a woman sitting at a concrete table next to the beach. He paused when he heard sobs as she struggled to sing "Happy Birthday." She blew out the candles stuck into a plastic cup filled with sand. As she put her head down, her broad-brimmed, frumpy hat knocked over the cup, one candle still flickering at the edge of her straw hat. He ran over and blew out the candle as she jerked up her head.

"What are you doing?" she shrieked.

"I was afraid the candle would catch your hat on fire."

"That's not your concern." She put her head back down.

He stood for a few moments, his eyes taking in the unusual scene. There were eight candles lying on the table, and nearby, a red shopping cart was filled with her possessions. Strangely, they appeared neatly stacked, something that was rare among homeless people, who were frequent in Waikiki and along major streets. "Well, have a good day," he said, and he continued jogging toward Diamond Head.

Yoshi had dated a social worker who worked with the homeless and had heard her sad and frustrating stories. She had explained that homeless people varied widely in their problems, from the mentally ill to those who had encountered unbearable stress or tragedy in their lives and just dropped out. Many, she had told him, could be saved if they had early intervention, but the Department of Social Services was overwhelmed by the most severe cases, leaving little time for the less urgent ones. In any case, Yoshi was a banker and felt he could do little to make a difference beyond contributing to the food drives and meals programs.

But ten minutes later, he placed two cups of McDonald's coffee and a biscuit on the table and sat on the concrete stool across from the woman. "Do you prefer sugar and creamer in your coffee?"

Silence, just the sounds of the surf. Then there was a faint movement of the droopy hat.

He stirred in the sugar and creamer. "You can't drink the coffee with your head down," he quipped.

Slowly she raised her head, revealing a tear-streaked, mud-smeared face that looked as if she'd used mud for makeup. Her wide-set, sparkling blue eyes suggested that beneath the mud was beauty, and that intrigued him.

"Butter and jelly on your biscuit?"

A nod. "What do you want from me?" she hissed and pursed her lips.

"A smile would be nice."

The smile wasn't forthcoming as she studied him. He carefully sliced the biscuit and spread butter and grape jelly on each half and placed them on a napkin in front of her. She took half and pushed the other half across to him. She didn't wolf it down as he expected but took measured bites, as one would see at a high tea at the Moana Surfrider in Waikiki or Tea at 1024 in Chinatown.

"My name's Yoshi Shimoda. And yours?"

"You're either an undercover cop or pimp," she retorted.

"Try a loan officer in a bank," he replied. "It's just that I jog here every morning before work." He pushed his half biscuit back to her. "Well, I've got to get on with my run. Have a nice day." He paused a hundred yards away and looked back, catching her gaze before she turned away.

He couldn't shake the encounter from his mind. He guessed that beneath the mud-smeared face was a woman in her early thirties. The strands of hair that escaped her hat were silky and chestnut, and although she hadn't stood, he estimated she was taller than his five foot six inches. The eight candles suggested someone eight or eighty—child or grandmother. What was the purpose of mud on her face? Perhaps a disguise. Was she running from the law?

The following morning, she was at the same table, gazing toward the ocean, when he jogged past. He stopped at the Starbucks on the corner of Kalakaua and Kapahulu Avenues and returned with two coffee lattes and a warm blueberry scone.

"Good morning, I thought you might like to try my favorite scone and a latte."

She tiled her head and lifted the droopy edge of her hat and looked into his eyes. "I know you want something from me."

"Just talk to me. That's all."

"I don't have anything to say and don't want to hear what you have to say," she said, and she turned away.

He silently drank his latte, and as he got up to leave, he said, "Better drink your latte before it gets cold."

When he looked back, she was sipping the drink, her eyes on him. He waved, then continued on his morning jog.

The next day, she took the drink without complaint and drank. She didn't reply when he again asked her name.

"I think your name is Mona Lisa, because you have her enigmatic smile."

"Linda," she said, and she picked up the scone, broke it into two, and pushed half to his side of the table.

He was perplexed. He'd seen homeless people sharing food among themselves but never giving it to someone like himself who didn't need it.

Days merged into weeks as he slowly peeled away layers of her defenses, seeking the real Linda. Finally, one morning she revealed that the eight candles were for an eight-year-old girl named Natalie. She remained tight-lipped about whether it was her daughter, another relative, or just a friend. It was like a game of charades. He made guesses, hoping for a nod or a change in her expression. He determined that she was thirty-four, or almost thirty-four, and when she stood, he could see that she was about two inches taller than he was. Her face was always smeared with mud, yet the three dresses she rotated were always clean. She didn't have an odor that sometimes accompanied a homeless person, so he knew she must be bathing somewhere. She revealed nothing about where she disappeared to at night.

He became convinced that Natalie was the key to something important in her past. Maybe she was related to her present condition, and he tried several angles to get information. But he received nothing but blank stares. Finally, he tried a direct approach. "I'm sure Natalie misses you."

Her response was instantaneous. She threw down her half-eaten pastry, jumped to her feet, and shook her finger in Yoshi's face. "Liar! I killed her!" Then she spun and headed off, pushing her shopping cart erratically down the sidewalk, scattering tourists.

He was rattled by her outburst and the claim that she'd killed Natalie. Should he go to the police or the Department of Social Services? But maybe it was just an angry outburst. He had no evidence nor insights as to what was true. He needed to know more before deciding what to do.

Linda wasn't at the usual table the following day or the next. He figured she must have moved somewhere else. But she couldn't have gone far with a wobbly shopping cart filled with her possessions. He called his ex-girlfriend, Gail, the social worker who worked in Maui, and asked for advice. She said that without a full name, she couldn't check the Social Services list of homeless people on Oahu, and as long as the woman wasn't in serious need of medical attention or harassing people, little could be done. She warned Yoshi to stick to banking and not get directly involved with homeless people, where he might do more harm than good.

But he was already too involved to take Gail's advice, and he returned to Waikiki after work. He walked block after block, hoping to spot her, knowing she had to reappear to search for food unless someone had taken her in. On the fourth night as he drove down Kalakaua Avenue, he spotted her in front of the Sheraton Princess Kaiulani Hotel, but by the time he parked and returned, she had vanished. Still, he now knew the search area, and the following evening he was sitting across the street from the Sheraton Princess Kaiulani watching from the window of Honolulu Coffee. He could see everyone who passed without being conspicuous. But she didn't appear, and after a week, he gave up the nightly vigils.

Back at home, he brought his lanai furniture inside after hearing the weather alert warning of a major tropical storm bearing down on Oahu. Flooding was expected in low-lying areas, and wind gusts could reach seventy-five miles an hour by morning. He had a restless sleep, his windows rattling loudly as the storm hit in full force just before daybreak. He sat up. Linda was in danger, but where was she? He had to try to find her. He jumped from bed, dressed, grabbed an umbrella and his heavy yellow raincoat, and dashed out the door.

Even with his windshield wipers on high, the visibility was so poor that he had to slow to twenty miles an hour, and he still couldn't avoid the plastic garbage can that rolled erratically across the street into the side of his car. He drove north-west on Kuhio Avenue, then he turned back along Kalakaua Avenue, searching for a red shopping cart. Just past the Duke Kahanamoku Statue, he spotted one under a massive banyan. A figure crouched against the trunk. He pulled into the zoo parking lot and waited for a break between gusts before getting out and opening his umbrella. He didn't make it a block before a blast of wind turned the umbrella inside out, shredding the material. He stuffed it into a refuse bin and, clutching his rain poncho to his chest, hurried toward the banyan tree, his yellow poncho flapping loudly like a flock of geese taking off from a lake.

"Linda," he called as he rounded the twenty-foot wide banyan.

No answer, then mournful sobs as he reached her, a garbage bag over her head. "Linda, I'm here to help you." He reached down and pulled her up, then started pushing the shopping cart back toward the zoo. Linda clung to the side. The shops were closed and dark. He spotted the familiar Starbucks green logo and hoped it was open. It was. He lashed the shopping cart to a street sign with bungee cords, and Linda retrieved a garbage bag of clothes. They were the only patrons, and the manager greeted them warmly.

"You can freshen up in the bathroom while I fix you something hot to drink. The lights have been going on and off, so no promises."

Yoshi began to worry when Linda didn't come out for twenty-minutes. He knocked on the door. "Linda, are you all right?"

"I'm coming."

The door opened. Yoshi gasped. "Linda, you're beautiful." Her dress was wrinkled but clean, her hair in a ponytail, and her face washed, with color on her lips.

"It's the least I can do for coming out in the storm to help me when the whole world was crashing down on me. I wanted to die, then I heard a heavenly voice. And it was you."

They sat at a window table. Irregular shadows and flashes of lightning enhanced her beauty, adding a sensual dimension that she had kept hidden. The lights flickered, then went out. The manager walked over and set a plate of pastries on their table.

"Usually we send everyone out when there's no electricity, but that makes no sense in this storm. Stay until it's safe. The pastries are on the house."

She slowly stirred her second cup of coffee. "I don't really understand why you came out in this storm to find me. I have nothing to give you."

"I can take you to a warm shelter until the storm is over. In a day or two, everything will be back to normal."

"I can never be normal." She pressed her right hand against the window, fingers splayed like the spiky shape of the palm frond stuck on the other side. Her expression softened.

"It was Natalie's seventh birthday. My husband, Larry, said we had more than enough for the party, but I didn't listen. I grabbed Natalie and raced off to get the Neapolitan ice cream that she loved. It happened in an instant. A boy chased a ball into the street, and I swerved—head on—into a garbage truck. I woke in an ambulance and heard the paramedics talking, and when one said the little girl didn't make it, my life stopped at that moment. In my rush, I hadn't even checked to make sure Natalie had buckled herself in properly. I couldn't face anyone. Especially not my husband. I escaped from my hospital room, withdrew money from an ATM, and bought a one-way ticket to Hawaii. I threw the ATM card away because if I used it in Hawaii they'd know where I had gone and come after me."

Yoshi reached over and took her hand. "That was an accident that can happen to anyone, and you have a husband who needs you."

"Larry adored our daughter, maybe even more than me. I can't bear the thought that every time he looked at me, he would be thinking, 'You killed our daughter.' I will never go back. That is final. Do you understand?"

"No. Because running away doesn't solve your problems."

She jumped to her feet. "I'm leaving, and don't try to follow me."

"Linda, please let me help you."

"You can't bring back my daughter."

"Linda, take my raincoat." He wrapped it over her shoulders as she headed to the door. He followed her out to the shopping cart and helped her take off the bungee cords while pleading for her not to go. Then he stood, as sheets of rain lashed his face, watching her walk away and out of his life.

Yoshi didn't try to find her. He'd done what he could to help, and he'd failed. He wished he had accepted Gail's advice and not meddled in something he didn't understand. He changed his jogging route so he wouldn't pass by the beach table where he'd first met Linda, and as months passed, she faded from his daily thoughts. He was walking across to Sans Souci Beach for a late-afternoon swim when he saw two teens taunting a woman. He stepped closer and recognized Linda kneeling on the sand.

"Leave the woman alone," he yelled as he closed the distance.

"Yeah. What'cha gunna do 'bout it?"

"Boys, it's not worth finding out."

They eyed Yoshi, who didn't blink. "Jason, let's go," said one of them, and they sauntered away laughing, their pants hung low, showing their butt cracks.

"Linda, did they hurt you?"

She shook her head as she held a hand over a piece of cardboard. He knelt and righted the acrylic paint bottles. There was a cobalt splotch in the sand. "I didn't know you were a painter. Where's your canvas?"

She slowly turned over a jagged-edged piece of cardboard to reveal a painting of Waikiki Beach entirely in shades of blue with touches of opal-white on the crests of waves.

"Wow, you're a really good painter. Why didn't you mention it before?"

"It's not important."

"Did you study art in college?"

She shrugged—a wry smile.

Again, another piece of useful information—she had attended college. "Linda, you could sell your paintings and make some money. I can buy you some canvases to get you started."

"I use only discarded cardboard to save the environment." Yoshi guessed that Linda came from a middle or upper-class family, as most homeless people were far too worried about survival to care about protecting the environment.

She produced three paintings on cardboard the first week, each in hues of blue, except for opal-white on wave crests. Yoshi was able to get an exception to the rule that only Art Club members could post their paintings on the zoo fence. They allowed one of their members to display her art to help a homeless person. All three sold on the first day at $40 dollars each. In June, Yoshi got Linda to agree to enter an 18- by 24-inch painting in the State Art Contest, and she took first place in the creative materials category. The work sold for $320 at auction. Yoshi was pleased that with his help, Linda was now able to make a little money from her art.

While he had gradually filled in some of the pieces of Linda's hidden past, he still didn't know where she disappeared to every evening. She couldn't be sleeping on the streets or in a homeless shelter, and she didn't have enough income from her paintings for even a cheap room. Yoshi was leaving a retirement dinner for a friend at the Outrigger Waikiki Hotel when he spotted Linda pushing her red shopping cart west on Kalakaua Avenue, and he followed her, staying on the other side of the street. At the entrance to Duke's Lane, she looked back, then turned into the alleyway lined with stalls selling cheap imported goods to tourists. He ran across the street and reached the narrow lane in time to see a Vietnamese woman pull back a canvas tarp at the side of her stall, and a moment later, Linda and her cart were gone. The woman secured the tarp and walked his way, carrying a large handbag over her shoulder.

"Excuse me. There's a woman named Linda staying next to your stall?"

She held her handbag tightly to her chest. "Why you ask'n?"

"I'm a friend and want to help Linda find her family."

"She find her own family if she want. She no trouble. You cop or someth'n'?"

"Just a friend who buys her coffee and pastries and wants to help her. All I need is her last name. I know it starts with *B*, and I promise not to do anything to hurt her."

She shifted from one leg to the other as she studied his face. "You Japanese, huh?"

"Yes, and you're Vietnamese, aren't you? We're both emigrants to America."

A slight smile. "Name, maybe Burnet or Barnett. From Palo Howto. Now must go or miss bus."

"Thank you for your kind help."

In nine days, it would be exactly a year since he had first spotted Linda blowing out candles in memory of her daughter. He had enough information to find her husband, assuming the name was Barnett, Barnet, or, less likely, Burnet, and the city was Palo Alto, California. He called the *Palo Alto Daily* and asked if they had an article in their paper of an accident between a car and garbage truck in June or July of the previous year. Thirty minutes later he received an email with an article attached.

PAGE MILL ROAD ACCIDENT

Under investigation, a head-on collision between an Acura and a Palo Alto garbage truck resulted in the two occupants of the car being taken by ambulance to the Palo Alto Hospital. The young girl sustained a serious concussion and is in an induced coma. The mother, Linda Barnett, suffered a minor concussion and mysteriously disappeared from the hospital less than an hour after being admitted. Anyone with information on Mrs. Barnett's whereabouts should contact the Palo Alto Police Department or her husband, Larry Barnett. The family is offering a reward of $10,000 for her safe return.

Yoshi easily found Larry Barnett's telephone number and called several times but got no answer. Finally, he left a message that Linda was in Waikiki, with details on how to find her. Yoshi felt sure he knew where she would be on Natalie's birthday, as Linda had agreed that he could bring a small cake. Still, he was frustrated that none of his calls were returned. Various explanations streamed through his mind. Barnett could be away on travel or could be dating someone else; perhaps reconciliation was not possible.

Yoshi was apprehensive as he carried the eight-inch boxed birthday cake, thermos of coffee, and knapsack filled with paper plates, cups, and forks to the meeting spot. He planned to share the cake with tourists that he hoped would gather around to sing "Happy Birthday." Linda was sitting at the table, her face washed and hair in an appealing ponytail—but missing any sign of a smile.

"Aloha, Linda."

Her glassy eyes belied her smile.

"Let's start with a cup of hot Kona coffee that I brewed myself."

She said nothing as he poured her a cup and added sugar and Hazelnut creamer. She held the cup with both hands and watched as he inserted nine candles around Natalie's name in pink letters. Several people paused to watch as he lit the candles, then he motioned for them to join them in singing "Happy Birthday." As Linda leaned in to blow out the candles, a girl dashed forward and blew them out, startling Linda and Yoshi.

"Mommy, I missed you so much!" she cried as she turned and threw her arms around Linda's neck. "Please come home, we need you so badly."

A man stepped forward, engulfing them in his arms. "Linda, it's time to come back and make our family whole again."

Yoshi asked that the $10,000 reward be donated to help the homeless people in Waikiki. They stayed in touch through the years, particularly on Natalie's birthday, when he always stopped at the concrete table to have a cup of coffee and remember. He followed the same running route into his seventies but had long ago given up jogging. On Natalie's fiftieth birthday, he returned with two cups of McDonald's coffee and a muffin, as he had brought Linda the first time they met. He thought his mind was playing tricks when he saw Linda sitting at the concrete table with a small cake.

As he approached, the woman turned and smiled warmly. "Mom said you would come. Will you sing happy birthday with me?"

As he stepped closer, he saw the letters written in cobalt blue icing on the cake—*In Memory of Linda*.

"When did Linda die?"

"She wanted to be here, but God called her home last week. Mom asked me to give you this."

Yoshi couldn't hold back his tears as he looked at the painting on carboard of two people sitting at a concrete table on Waikiki Beach. Everything was painted in shades of blue, Linda's favorite color—except for the red shopping cart.

Flip-Flops

"*You* ou want me to pay for your vacation in Hawaii so you can write a story about a woman who repairs flip-flops? Sheryl, what have you been smoking? I need stories with broad personal appeal—success stories with substance. The answer is no. You can go on your nickel, and if you can come back with a publishable story, *then* we can discuss reimbursing you for the trip."

Ed Wu was the tough, no-nonsense editor in chief of *Asia-Pacific Life*, a magazine that published success stories of immigrant Asian-Americans. He was particularly tight-fisted about out-of-state travel, with Hawaii out-of-bounds except for exceptional stories.

But Sheryl's friend Alice Mayeda had sent a postcard from Hawaii with a cryptic note: "Auntie Chu repairs flip-flops (they call them 'slippahs' here) in Waikiki's International Market Place and has a story worth telling."

Alice, an award-winning freelance travel writer with a nose for good stories, had led Sheryl to two publishable stories in the past year, so Sheryl took her friend's tips seriously.

The appeal of visiting tropical Hawaii tipped the balance in favor of the trip. Online she found a deal that included the flight and a week at the Sheraton Princess Kaiulani Hotel. In addition to the 35 percent savings, the hotel was adjacent to the International Market Place, where Auntie Chu had her sandal repair stall. At check-in, when she told the receptionist that she was a writer for *Asia-Pacific Life*, she was given an upgrade to a fifteenth-floor room with a view of the ocean and coupons for two buffet breakfasts.

It was midafternoon when Sheryl entered the International Market Place and looked up in wonder at the thatched hut nestled in the branches of a giant banyan tree—unexpected in the middle of high-rise condo buildings and the densest concentration of hotels in the Pacific. She walked deeper into the maze of tiny stalls selling cheap imported tourist trinkets, amused by the chatter of Vietnamese venders.

"Come look," a Vietnamese woman beckoned, her hand motioning to the display of gold jewelry marked down thirty percent. "Business slow today. Give you extra twenty percent off. Best deal in Waikiki."

"No thanks. I'm here looking for a woman called Auntie Chu. She mends sandals and slippahs."

"Where's your broken sandal?" the woman asked in a suspicious tone.

"I flew here from California to interview her for a magazine article."

"Why want interview woman that repair rubbah slippahs?"

"I've heard she has an interesting story to tell about the life of an immigrant to Hawaii."

"Look around. Everyone immigrant. Why you want bother Auntie Chu? You tax person or somethin'?"

"Sorry for bothering you." She continued deeper into the warren of stalls, stopping several times to ask where to get a sandal repaired. Stall owners eyed her suspiciously, some shaking their heads and others pointing deeper into the complex until she spotted an old woman hunched over a battered wooden chest repairing a sandal. An obese Hawaiian woman sat on a stool hidden by her muumuu. Sheryl paused a few feet away and listened.

"How Jimmy-boy do?" Auntie Chu asked as she mended a cheap flip-flop.

"Jimmy, he work hard, but when surf up, he forget eva'thin fo' surfin'."

She pulled up an armful of her muumuu material as she slipped on the flip-flop, then gave Auntie Chu a hug and shuffled away.

"Miss Chu, I'm Sheryl Li, from Los Angeles."

"You got sandal fo' repair?"

Sheryl gazed at the woman she had flown halfway across the Pacific to interview. Her face was a roadmap of creases framed by square-cut, straight gray-hair. A piece of black electrical tape was wrapped around one stem of the spectacles that hung low on her nose. Her eyelids allowed a sliver of her sparkling eyes to show, and her hands were gnarled, with chipped black fingernails like those of a mechanic or coal miner.

"No. I'm hoping you'll let me interview you."

She frowned. "Fo' what? I pay taxes and no bother anyone."

Sheryl stepped closer. "I write stories for *Asia-Pacific Life* magazine and was told you had an interesting story to tell. I flew all the way from Los Angeles to interview you."

"You jokin' wiff me. Nobody want story 'bout woman who repair rubbah slippahs."

"So why does everyone know you here and want to protect you?"

"All good people. Work hard. Help each otha'. No story here."

"Okay if I just watch you work?"

"I think you crazy. Sidewalk free."

"Miss Chu. The last customer didn't pay."

"April have no money. Five keikis. Big heart. Sometime bring sweet papaya. How she work with broken rubbah slippah? Huh?"

A woman in a body-hugging short dress stepped past Sheryl and handed Chu an alligator-skin shoe and a broken five-inch heel. "How much to repair the heel?"

Chu took the heel and quickly examined it. "Four dolla'. Take ten minutes." Without waiting for the woman to agree, she began working on the shoe.

The woman stood back and took out her rhinestone-studded cellphone and scrolled through messages, frequently flipping back her bleached-blond hair. She paid with a five-dollar bill, took the change, and walked briskly toward Kuhio Street.

"Miss Chu, you charged so little. She was rude and didn't even give you a tip."

Chu smiled, revealing her crooked, deeply yellowed teeth. "She hooker. New here, tryin' to make livin'. Shoe fake knock-off like her handbag. I give everyone second chance before decide. I had ten dolla' when arrive. Strangers help me, give food and loan money, no interest. Eva'one call me Auntie Chu."

Sheryl remained until closing, watching her work. Most called her Auntie Chu. they ranged from a shabbily dressed homeless man to the general manager of a hotel who left a tip as large as her repair charge. All got the same treatment. She scolded two teenage surfers for not being in school as she repaired one's slippahs. They didn't talk back, and she shooed them away after accepting hugs for payment.

Every morning, after breakfast at her hotel or across the street for lighter fare at Honolulu Coffee, Sheryl returned to observe and extract fragments of Auntie Chu's story. She brought tea to Auntie Chu, who protested, then accepted the drinks. Nearby stall owners gradually revealed slices of Chu's life and the people she had helped through the years.

Her Buddhist parents had fled China to Vietnam to escape religious persecution, then, as South Vietnam crumbled, she escaped with her daughter on a harrowing journey across Cambodia into Thailand and eventually to Hawaii. Four years later she received news that her husband, son, and parents had been killed in the final days of the collapse of South Vietnam.

Her daughter, Hua, had been always at her side until she started school. She would weave strips of palm fronds into dolls and animal shapes and pretend to read children's books to her mother. When she learned to read, she would sit next to her mother and teach her words from children's books. Hua often studied and played with a Vietnamese girl from a nearby stall. They played hide-and-seek among the hundred stalls and spied on customers, watching for shoplifters and earning the nickname the Detective Twins.

On the last day before returning to the mainland, Sheryl flipped through her notes, shaking her head. Her boss was right, there wasn't a story that would excite most readers. Auntie Chu was one of hundreds who eked out a living in America with little to show for it. When she died, she might be remembered by the stall owners but would not warrant more than three lines in the local paper.

She arrived minutes before noon with two broccoli-and-beef plate lunches. "Auntie Chu, as this is my last day, I thought we could have lunch together."

"Why you do this?" she complained.

"I came for a story but got something better. Every day I've witnessed how you help people in small but meaningful ways. I want to show my appreciation for letting me stand around and observe you for the past week. I must have irritated you."

Chu cocked her head and stared at Sheryl. "You not much bother. You have keiki?"

"A boy, seventeen, who lives with his father in Texas so he can get a private education that I can't afford. I miss him a lot.

He used to call every week but now only on holidays. He has a busy life." Sheryl's eyes brimmed with tears. "I'm hoping he'll go to a college in California so I can see him more often. But his dad wants him to stay in Texas."

Auntie Chu gazed into Sheryl's eyes—a connection made. "Business slow today. You come my place. I fix Chinese meal—tell story."

"I'd love that."

"Who should I give these lunches to?"

"All are family, so no matter."

Sheryl followed Chu onto TheBus to Chinatown, a thirty-minute ride from Waikiki, and into a world where English was a foreign language and the air was infused with a mélange of Asian scents. Storefronts overflowed with salted jellyfish, fermented eggs, fresh octopus, eels, pig's heads, and unrecognizable spiky fruits and vegetables. Chu was picky, examining each item and sniffing or palpating for freshness.

They turned down River Street, encountered a man screaming that they were all going to hell, then they stepped around a man passed out on the sidewalk. She turned down a narrow alley that reeked of urine and unlocked a steel door into a large storage room. A second steel door opened into what appeared to be a hallway with a skylight, but when Chu switched on an overhead light, Sheryl realized this was Chu's home. It was clean, but so narrow that her three-foot-wide bed had to double as their seat. Along the opposite wall was a bench with a two-burner electric stove, a small steel sink, and, underneath it, a mini-refrigerator. At the end of the room, a red plastic curtain separated the toilet and cramped shower. The bright spot in her depressingly confined room was the wall covered in colorful art, photos, and award ribbons. They started at the door with stick figures and progressed across the wall to an 8- by 10-inch photo of Hua in her graduation gown in front of Stanford University.

"You must be very proud of your daughter."

Chu frowned. "Every parent proud. You know that."

"But how did you afford an education to get her prepared for Stanford?"

"She go Iolani private school—best education."

"But how could you afford a private school?"

She added vegetables to her sizzling wok. "Save everythin' to change life for daughter. Why my story different from any Asian parent? They care same. Story only because I repair rubbah slippahs. I help few people, but many help me when I come Hawaii with ten dolla in pocket. No story to tell. Help cut vegetables so we can eat Chinese meal."

On the flight back to Los Angeles Sheryl read the story she'd typed about the woman who repaired rubbah slippahs. It was a touching story, worth remembering. She paused, her finger wavering over the delete button, then clicked it and closed the laptop. *Priceless things should not be sold.*

Footprint Thief

*N*icole Peterson dropped off her husband, Melvin, and their two teenage children at the Interisland Terminal, then drove to Waikiki. She parked at Kapiʻolani Park near the Diamond Head end of the famous beach. The choice was easy, as there was free parking, and it was away from the over-crowded section of Waikiki. She rarely crossed the island from the windward side, where they lived in a church-owned home adjacent to Melvin's church. Their life was woven into church activities. Suffocating at times, she reflected. Every summer, the family flew twenty minutes over to Molokaʻi Island to assist with the maintenance of one of Hawaii's oldest churches in a poor Hawaiian community.

This year, Nicole had conjured up a believable excuse for not participating in the eight-day church mission. It had turned out to be easy; all she had to tell Melvin was that she had a minor infection of a female nature, and he didn't ask any ques-tions. The real reason was that she needed time to herself to take quiet walks on the beach, have a few cappuccinos and decadent pastries in coffee shops, and read a romance novel or two—things that were anathema to Melvin. To him, they were here to serve God, not to dally away their time in places like

Starbucks or the Honolulu Coffee, spending money that could be used in doing the Lord's work.

When she'd met him at Westmont, a small Christian college in Santa Barbara, he'd seemed like a great catch—tall and handsome, with a winning smile and plenty of ambition. His parents were devout Christians, yet his father had made millions by taking over struggling oil companies, ruthlessly slashing staff and benefits, and selling them at a handsome profit. Melvin seemed different. He had just returned from a summer trip across Eastern Europe and talked of the missionary work he planned to do in Africa.

His passion and charming personality attracted eligible women. Yet she was the first and only woman he asked out. He was not as romantic as the other men she'd dated, insisting they wait until marriage to consummate their nuptials. She didn't reveal that she wasn't a virgin, and she believed he would make a great pastor and husband. But only the first proved true. After their short honeymoon to Cancun, it was all about building his career as a pastor; she was to be his partner to help him at every step—without pay, of course, because it was God's work.

After seminary in Orlando, Florida, Melvin was offered a position as assistant pastor at a church in Hawaii. They both agreed it was a dream place to live, so he jumped at the offer. They moved into a small three-bedroom home on the church property in Kailua, and both plunged into church activities that consumed all of their time. After seven years, Melvin became the pastor, and Nicole continued tirelessly building the youth program without pay. There was no time or money for travel to distant countries, and Melvin's thoughts of missionary work in Africa proved to be a fantasy. Their two children, Mark and Mary, added joy to her life, but, combined with church activities, gave her little time for herself.

At thirty-seven, Nicole's light brown hair tumbled in luxurious waves over her shoulders, thanks to touch-ups from a hair salon, an expenditure Melvin thought frivolous. She worked hard to maintain her figure and enjoyed adding brighter shades of lipstick and eyeliner when Melvin was not around.

Nicole walked across the wide expanse of grass in Kapi'olani Park to Sans Souci Beach, the favorite of locals. She slipped off her sandals and stepped onto the golden sand. The feeling between her toes sent a sensuous shiver through her body, and she inhaled the soft Kona breeze that twirled strands of her hair. The tide was low, leaving an undulating strip of wet sand unblemished by footprints. She followed the beach toward the center of Waikiki, planning to turn back at the Sheraton Waikiki. Waikiki Beach encompassed a series of beaches with individual personalities and names known by locals. One was Kuhio Beach, where the water was gentle, protected by an off-shore concrete wall. It was a perfect place to wade, and she raised her skirt above her knees and entered the calm water. Suddenly, she screamed. She dashed back to the beach, dropped to her knees, and rapidly rubbed sand over her leg.

"This will relieve the pain." She turned into his smile that took her breath away. His locks of hair tumbled across his brow to heavy black-rimmed Cary Grant glasses and penetrating eyes. He dug his long fingers into the fleshy orange pulp of half a papaya, squeezed it into a mash and smeared it over the red streaks on her leg. Holding her breath, she cautiously pulled her dress higher than necessary as his fingers spread the fragrant, soothing paste all around the affected area.

"You appeared from nowhere. You must be local to know the enzymes in papaya neutralize jellyfish stings."

"No. Just on a stopover on my way to Asia. I've been stung several times by jellyfish and found papaya a quick remedy. I was watching you from the bench and knew immediately what happened when you screamed. I'm Joshua Beckman. I come from Washington, DC." He held up his sticky hands. "I better not shake your hand. Anyway, please call me Josh."

"I'm Nicole. I'm, uh . . . married to a pastor." *Why did I say that?*

"Is the papaya helping?"

"Yes. Oh, no! The birds have gotten into your breakfast."
He turned and shrugged as several pigeons pecked at his
paper plate of rice, scrambled eggs, and Portuguese sausage. "I
was trying a local breakfast from McDonald's. I guess I could
say it's for the birds," he jested.

"Josh, the least I can do is buy you a fresh cup of coffee
and a pastry."

He stared into her eyes. "I'd like that. If your husband
wouldn't mind?"

Her heart raced. *Melvin wouldn't approve, but he doesn't
need to know.* "There was a nice coffee and pastry shop in the
front of the Moana Hotel when I was here a couple of years ago
to attend a wedding ceremony. I wanted to stop in, but Melvin
said the coffee was just as good at home. It's a five-minute
walk along Kalakaua. Hopefully it's still there. Things change
fast in Waikiki."

"Let's try it." He washed his hands in the outdoor shower
while Nicole rinsed and then wiped her leg with his towel.
"Nicole, I've heard in Hawaii a proper introduction requires a
hug and a kiss on the cheek."

"Only when giving a flower lei." She offered her hand and he
held it several seconds too long as he gazed into her eyes. Josh
didn't reveal much about himself until they were seated with
their cappuccinos and white-chocolate macadamia-nut scones.
He was a freelance photographer, specializing in ancient ruins
across Asia. He told her his favorite Asian sites were Bagan in
Myanmar, Angkor Wat in Cambodia, and cliff-hanging mon-
asteries in Bhutan and Tibet. She noticed he described them in
terms that could equally fit a beautiful woman, using phrases
like "entwined with sensuous" (vines), "burnished honey-gold
at sunrise," with "curvaceous, radiant domes."

"Sounds so exotic. I would love to see them someday, but
here is where I've made my life."

"Things are changing rapidly since the end of the Vietnam War and the ouster of the ruthless Khmer Rouge in Cambodia. Thousands of priceless artifacts have been looted, and swarms of tourists are coming and further damaging the fragile ruins at Angkor Wat and Bagan—many ignoring signs to stay off of the intricately carved surfaces that survived over eight hundred years only to be worn smooth in a decade or two. Popular sites are already fenced in by hundreds of stalls selling cheap trinkets and T-shirts that shrink from adult to a child's size in one washing. I'm addicted to photographing these sites before it's too late."

"So, what brings you to touristy Hawaii?"

"A friend offered to let me stay at his condo in Foster Tower across the street. He's on a month-long trip to Europe, so I thought I'd take him up on his offer and perhaps meet a maiden in distress on the beach."

A little corny, she thought as she twisted a strand of hair. "How long is your stopover?"

His answer was unexpected and solicitous. "Depends on how long you suggest I stay."

She turned away from his penetrating gaze. "You know I'm married."

"I know. You told me when we met on the beach. I'm not asking you for a date."

"You'll need a week to get a sense of Oahu. The natural beauty is high in the Ko'olaus and on the windward side so you'll need a car and good walking shoes."

He nodded. "You said your family was on another island fixing up a church. Any chance you would have a free day to show me a few places not in tourist brochures? I'll pay you as my personal guide."

"It would be better if you go with a tour group. I have nothing to offer that they can't do better. And I haven't seen much of the island either."

"Well, then we can enjoy exploring new places together."

"You know that's not what I meant."

He stirred his cappuccino, then licked the foam from the lip of his cup. "Okay. If you don't mind. So tell me, what's it like being a pastor's wife?"

"Nothing like your life. There is never-ending work at the church organizing events and doing whatever Melvin needs me to do. I can never let down my hair, as I'm the pastor's wife, and I'm expected to be an exemplary member of the congregation. If someone saw me having coffee with you, there would be gossip."

"Sounds dreadfully stifling. Are you happy?"

"I have the two children I wanted, and Melvin is a faithful husband, and he's helping people find purpose in their lives. I guess I'd say, in the spectrum between happy and unhappy, I'm on the positive side of neutral. I'd never leave my husband for another man." She sipped her drink, avoiding eye contact.

"Of course. I understand. You know, I was thinking of going to the Bishop Museum today to see their collections from across the Pacific. Would it be too far out of your way to drop me off at the museum? I can catch a taxi back."

"Sure, I can do that, but my car's a twenty-minute walk from here."

He chuckled. "I think I can walk that far. What would you suggest I see there?"

"I've never been inside. Melvin says it's too expensive and has lots of pagan stuff."

"Maybe it's time for you to have a look and decide for yourself. Why not join me as my guest? I bet you'll be surprised."

She tapped on the tabletop with her fingernails. "Okay. But we need to keep our distance."

"You mean I can't put my arm around your waist?"

"No! I'm serious."

"Deal."

The Bishop Museum lived up to its reputation, having the most extensive collection of Pacific artifacts in the world, including irreplaceable capes and kahili of Hawaiian chiefs. They lingered for most of the afternoon in the three-tiered Hawaiian Hall, surrounded by hundreds of heirlooms from the royal Kamehameha family. It was Nicole who touched Josh's arm frequently as she excitedly pointed at exhibits. Both agreed that the Starbuck Cape was among the most striking artifacts— its geometric pattern made from thousands of canary-yellow, red, and black feathers from small *'o'o* and *'i'iwi* Hawaiian honeycreepers. Nicole had read about the Starbuck Cape and told Josh that when Hawaiians were making a royal cape, they would only pluck a few feathers from each of the hundreds of now-rare birds before releasing them.

The sun was low in the sky when they pulled in behind Foster Tower. "Nicole, I had a great day, thanks to you. I will feel just awful if I can't at least give you a peck on the cheek."

"I already told you it's not acceptable without a lei."

"Where can I buy a lei?"

She griped the steering wheel with both hands, shrugged, and leaned over, presenting her cheek.

His kiss, gentle as a morning sea-breeze, brushed her ear-lobe, then he pulled away. "Nicole, if you can free yourself from church duties tomorrow, I'd be most grateful to have you as my guide."

Her heart pounded. "I, uh, can't."

"Okay. I'm eating alone tonight. Any chance you can stay for dinner?"

"I have other plans. Now I really must go."

An hour later, Nicole sat at her kitchen table, picking at left-over chicken and rice, trying to convince herself she'd done the right thing. She called Melvin, and he told her of the important work they were doing for the Lord; she was relieved that he didn't ask about her day. As she showered, she fantasized about Josh's gentle hands rubbing papaya on her leg. Later, she prayed for forgiveness for having impure thoughts.

A light rain splattered the vehicle as she drove up the Pali Highway, her headlights cutting a silvery swath through the predawn indigo. She didn't have a plan, except to return to Waikiki Beach and complete the walk she'd started the previous day. There was a risk of meeting Josh again, but the chances were remote so early in the morning. Anyway, she rationalized that it was a public beach, and she had as much right to walk on it as anyone else.

The sun had not risen above the Koʻolaus when she started her walk, her footprints the first on the beach as the tide receded. As a girl, on the few times they had gone to the beach, she'd imagined she was on an uninhabited island, and hers were the only human footprints. As she approached the spot where she had met Josh the previous day, she looked toward the bench, feeling both relief and melancholy that he wasn't there. She quickened her pace after passing the spot, turning back at the concrete steps to the walkway fronting the Sheraton Waikiki. As the sun cleared the Koʻolau Mountains, it illuminated the shades of blue in the ocean and sprinkled gold dust on the sand. She retraced her footsteps, concentrating on stepping on each one to reverse the imprint in the sand, as she had done as a child.

Nicole paused and frowned when her footprints were suddenly replaced by much larger ones wiping out hers—something a child might do, but hardly an adult. She looked down the beach but didn't see the footprint thief. Then, further along the beach, the prints turned up higher on the sand, leading to a towel and sandals, then down again to the surf. She spotted the culprit snorkeling back toward shore and waited to see if her suspicions were true. Who else but Josh would have purposely stepped on her footprints?

He didn't stand up until he was in two feet of water. He pulled off his mask. "Well, what a surprise!" Josh said as he swept back his soggy locks.

"You stole my footprints."

"I did, indeed. You're pretty possessive."

She crossed her arms over her chest. "I didn't expect you this early."

"I didn't expect you either, but, alas, fate has thrown us together again. Now that you're here, we can have breakfast and discuss where we'll go today."

She didn't say anything as he strolled past her to the outdoor shower where the spray fractured sunlight over his muscular body. Her eyes followed the rivulets of water down from his broad shoulders to his rippled abs and the skimpy trunks that sucked to his body. She turned away, picked up his towel, and closed the distance, waiting for him to step from the shower. He grinned as he took the towel and she stepped back, her eyes following it as it moved over him.

"Where shall we eat?"

She avoided eye contact. "I've heard Duke's serves a good breakfast on the second floor. But you can't go like that."

"I'll do a quick change in my room. If you want, you can come up and see my photos."

"You mean your etchings," she chided.

"Suit yourself. You can wait in the lobby. It'll only take a few minutes to change."

At Duke's, it was a twenty-minute wait, but it was worth it to get a seat next to the railing with a view overlooking the pool and the ocean. Josh ordered a hearty breakfast of pancakes, Portuguese sausage, and eggs, while Nicole stayed with a healthier avocado sandwich.

"Josh, were you watching for me this morning?"

"Last night, I dreamed that you flew with me to Asia to photograph the two thousand temples in Bagan Valley, Myanmar."

She licked a bit of avocado from her lip. "Sounds more like a fantasy. Or is that your standard pickup line?"

"You are very cautious, Nicole. Anyway, I hope you can spare a few days to see sights with me."

"I told you yesterday that I can't drop everything to be your tour guide for a week. There must be a hundred trained tour guides on Oahu."

"But I want you as my guide."

"Why?"

"When I travel with a friend, the colors are brighter, the sights more memorable, and the food more enjoyable."

Nicole sighed. "I'll give you one day. Then you're on your own for the rest of the week. How about a hike into the center of Oahu's rainforest to give you a taste of what exists twenty minutes from touristy Waikiki Beach?"

"Sounds perfect."

Nicole drove past elite Punahou School and up Manoa Road to the trailhead to Manoa Falls. Their ambitious plan was an eight-mile hike to the top of the Ko'olau Mountains and return, ending the day with a swim at the base of 150-foot Manoa Falls.

Within minutes, the forest canopy filtered out the sounds of the city, replacing it with the gentle harmony of the tropical rainforest—babbling Manoa Stream, creaking tree branches, strange bird calls—and fragrances of wild ginger, lilikoi, and damp leaves on the ground. The trail was muddy and slippery, laced with exposed roots to trip hikers, and Nicole had to hold Josh's hand more than she intended.

Near the crest of the mountain, they entered an enchanted forest. Four-inch-thick bamboo chimed in the breeze, accompanied by the liquid whistles of a white-rumped shama. The overlooks gave great views back toward Honolulu and Waikiki to the south, but clouds pushed against the windward side of the Ko'olaus, allowing only glimpses of what lay to the east. Nicole tried to point out where she lived, but Kailua remained shrouded by clouds. As they were about to turn back, the clouds parted, and for a few minutes, Josh snapped photos of the rippling green Pali cliffs. Then he turned his lens back to Nicole.

"Josh, you can't sell photos of the hidden secrets of tropical Hawaii with me in every frame."

"Some special images are not for sale."

They reached Manoa Falls in the late afternoon, just as it began to drizzle and the last couple was packing to head down the trail.

"It's beginning to rain, Josh, so I think we'd better skip the swim and head back to the parking lot."

"We're already wet and muddy. I'm going in."

Nicole followed, and they swam to the falls as the clouds opened up, causing the surface of the water to dance. "This is so exhilarating. I feel like a kid again, Josh." She swam to a clump of wild ginger overhanging the water and squeezed a cone-shaped vermilion flower. Sticky fluid oozed into her hands.

"Nicole, what are you doing?"

"I read that Hawaiians used the liquid as a shampoo." She rubbed it in her hair, producing a fragrant ginger shampoo, then swam under the waterfall, letting frothy foam flow down her body and fan out over the water.

Josh swam to shore and, shielding his camera from the rain, snapped several shots of Nicole under the cascading water. "Superb! Publishable."

"Better not. What would the church delegation think?"

"No one will ever guess it's you, a proper minister's wife shampooing under a waterfall."

The rain passed, leaving the trail slippery; they both fell several times, pulling the other into the mud. At the car, Nicole said, "We're total muddy messes! You're going to have to help me clean the car when we get back to your place. Melvin would be very angry to see mud all over his car, and he'd ask questions."

"Agreed, but you'll need to get your clothes washed or the car will get dirty again on your drive back to Kailua. And there just happens to be a washer and dryer in my condo."

"How convenient," Nicole retorted.

"Suit yourself. I was hoping we could have a nice meal in Waikiki, but we need to shower and change into clean clothes."

A meal of leftovers at home or a fine dinner in Waikiki. "I'll think about it."

She parked in a visitor stall at the Foster Tower garage, then she surprised Josh by taking a set of clean clothes out of her trunk. "Here's the deal. I still need to shower and freshen up, so I'll take you up on the offer of a shower. But I want to be assured privacy."

"I'll wait downstairs in the lobby."

"Not necessary." She had never done anything so daring, but no one needed to know. Anyway, she wasn't going to his room for anything more than a shower and change—a lot better than changing in the dirty bathrooms along the beach. She suggested he shower first, as she needed more time.

He opened the sliding glass door to the lanai and returned with a folder and glass of chilled rosé. "While I'm taking a shower, you might want to glance at my recent photos of Hindu temples in Kathmandu. Conditions weren't great, with clouds shrouding much of the Himalayas in the background."

His cheerful singing in the shower kept her mind on him— weakening her resolve. He emerged in a terrycloth bathrobe. "I'll change while you're taking a shower. Do you need my bathrobe?"

For an instant she was tempted to say yes. "No, I'll dress in the bathroom. I like your photos. Do you usually shoot in black and white?"

"Depends on the magazine. Mostly color, but sometimes the mood can only be captured in black and white."

"How so?"

"Black and white filters out the distracting colors. It's a little like an X-ray that sees what lies beneath."

"Were the photos you took of me in color or black and white?" she teased.

"In color. But I dream in black and white."

His words gave her a strange, fuzzy, warm feeling. "Well, I better shower and change." The lack of a lock on the bathroom door made her heart beat faster. *What if he opens the door? Should I yell for him not to peek?* Nicole's years in the church choir gave her a distinct advantage when singing in the shower and took her mind off of Josh for a few minutes.

Josh swayed to her tune as he slowly clicked through the photos of her.

They dined in the Pacific Beach Hotel next to their 280,000-gallon, three-story oceanarium, with hundreds of fish swimming among towering coral reef formations. Josh raised his wine glass. "A toast to you for becoming a friend as well as a charming travel guide. May these days never be forgotten."

Nicole clicked her glass to his. "And to you for getting me to let down my hair today." She sipped, then turned to view the fish through the massive oceanarium window, afraid Josh would notice that she was blushing. She had long ago stopped dreaming about such romantic dinners; they were too extravagant for Melvin. The most she could expect was a meal at a family restaurant in Kailua, usually using discount coupons. She had learned to accept that there were more important things to consider, like saving for the children's braces and a Christian college and donating to the missions. Yet there was a part of her that yearned for more. Tonight was her chance.

It was after ten when they strolled along Waikiki Beach, their silhouettes etched into the darkness by the moon over the Ko'olaus. She didn't pull away when Josh turned her into him and held her close and nuzzled her hair. They did a slow dance, their toes sketching the lyrics in the sand. Later, as she got into her car to drive home, he leaned in and kissed her as the French do.

Nicole returned each day to meet Josh and explore hidden places on Oahu and in her heart. She knew she was betraying her marriage vows and promised herself it would end the moment Josh left on his flight to Asia, an hour before her family arrived back from Moloka'i.

He took pictures, mostly with her in the frame, and she repeatedly scolded him, saying they wouldn't be publishable. Yet sometimes she posed provocatively, hitching her skirt above her knee or leaving an extra button or two undone. When syrup from a shave ice dripped from her chin, he licked it slowly, then moved down her neck until she stopped him at the second button of her blouse.

On the final evening before Josh's departure, he asked her to stay the night and she did. They spent the evening on his lanai sipping wine, nibbling *poke* (diced raw fish), and reminiscing about their lives with no reference to the future, until he gently took her hand and led her inside. Before sunrise, she woke and repeated in her mind, like a Hindu mantra, that she would never leave Melvin and the children, regardless of her intense feelings for the man lying beside her.

Nicole embraced Josh moments before he boarded his flight to Asia. "Josh, promise you won't try to contact me. I'm sorry. But that's the way it has to be." Eyes awash in tears, she turned and hurried across to the Interisland Terminal to meet Melvin and the children. She needed time to rinse her face in the bathroom and compose herself before facing her husband.

She didn't realize their flight had arrived early, and they were already waiting in the baggage area, the children sitting on suitcases. "Mom, where were you?" they asked in unison.

"I had to stop at the restroom." She hugged and kissed both children before turning to Melvin. "Welcome home." She embraced him.

"I'm exhausted," he responded, and he quickly turned to pick up a suitcase. "I need a good shower, and then I've got to prepare my Sunday sermon." He paused and stared into her eyes. "I heard from the assistant pastor that he didn't see you all week."

She was ready with a reply that would shut down further questions. "I had a bad period and a touch of the flu that I didn't want to spread to the congregation. I feel better now."

The church grew, but Nicole pulled back from total commitment to the church, taking more time for herself, especially photography, something Melvin thought frivolous. Both children finished high school, attended Christian colleges on the mainland, and then found better jobs on the mainland than they could get back home in Hawaii. Melvin began working evenings at the church and frequently visiting members of the congregation at night. Several times, Nicole had seen lipstick on his shirt collar. She wasn't concerned, as parishioners often gave him hugs. But traces on his underwear couldn't be dismissed. When she confronted him, he replied with little emotion that he had met someone and wanted a divorce. She received little from the divorce settlement; the home was church property, and most of their savings had been spent sending the children to college on the mainland.

The church congregation blamed Nicole for the breakup of the marriage, and she moved across the island and rented an efficiency apartment in Waikiki. Her photography and organizational skills helped her land a job as a wedding planner and backup photographer.

It had been nine years since Nicole stepped onto Waikiki Beach and met the man who would sometimes creep back into her dreams to beckon her. She had resisted the temptation to contact him, settling for copies of travel magazines where Josh's photos appeared. One of the first ones included photos of hidden Oahu. The lead photo was of a woman under a waterfall, her head turned so she couldn't be recognized. She hid the copy and would take it out whenever she felt alone and unwanted, and she'd reminisce.

Nicole was now free to contact Josh. Afraid that trying to relive a magical week in her past would be a disappointment, she decided it was better to hold onto her memories unblemished by time. It was better not to know that he was probably married or had changed in ways she wouldn't like. More likely there had been many women in his travels, and Nicole didn't want to spoil the illusion that she had been as special as the words he'd whispered when making love.

The morning sun had not cleared the Ko'olaus when Nicole paused at the spot where she had met Josh nine years earlier. She never forgot how his fingers had soothed the jellyfish sting and awakened feelings that frightened her. She scanned the empty bench where he had been sitting, then turned and continued toward the Sheraton Waikiki, where she would turn back, still early enough to be the first to leave footprints in the sand. She came across two sets of prints heading directly into the ocean and saw the surfers padding out to catch waves beyond the barrier coral reef.

She turned back at the Sheraton Waikiki, following her footsteps, stepping on each print to reverse its direction, bringing back memories of meeting her footprint thief. She looked ahead as far as she could see and saw a handful of early risers—mostly couples. There was a man in shorts and a broad-brimmed hat slowly walking toward her. She fantasized that it was Josh who had miraculously appeared and was coming to sweep her up in his arms. Of course, it was impossible that the first time she walked on Waikiki Beach in nine years she would meet Josh again. The man was about the right build, but too far away to make out his face.

As she watched he raised a hand and waved, and she glanced behind to see who he was waving at, but there was no one. He began trotting, then running toward her, and she knew it could only be Josh. She quickened her pace. "Josh," was all she could say before they came together and embraced as he spun her around and kissed both cheeks, then her lips.

"Josh, this isn't possible!"

"Not at all. Nicole, after we parted, I couldn't get you out of my mind, so when my friend who owned the condo in Foster Tower offered to sell it to me, I jumped at the opportunity. I have used Hawaii as my home base for almost eight years."

"But you didn't try to contact me?"

"You made me promise not to. I didn't even check the web, because the temptation to go to the next step and contact you might have been irresistible. I wondered if you would ever return to Waikiki Beach, then this morning, when I came down for a swim, I saw footprints following the edge of the surf. And at the spot where we met, they turned toward the bench where I'd been sitting nine years ago. Who would do that at the same spot, and at sunrise? I guessed it was you and followed your prints."

"Josh, I didn't try to contact you for the same reason. But I checked travel magazines in Barnes and Noble every month and bought all the issues that carried your photos. I recently moved to Waikiki. I have a small efficiency apartment facing the Ala Wai Canal. This morning is the first time I've walked on Waikiki Beach since our fateful meeting nine years ago."

"You said 'I.' What about your husband, Melvin?"

She took a loose strand of her hair and tucked it over her ear. "If you have time, I'll explain everything."

He reached for her hand as he gazed into her eyes. "I have the rest of my life."

Angels

*T*en-year-old twins Ricky and Sarah were the envy of their fifth-grade class when it was announced that they were going to Hawaii for a week. Such breaks in the middle of a term were frowned on by the school administration, except for special cases. But arrangements were made for them to keep diaries of their activities and to do a limited amount of homework.

On their honeymoon, Seth and Pat Zorn had stayed in the Rainbow Tower of the Hilton Hawaiian Village in Waikiki Beach. As near as they could calculate, the twins were conceived in their hotel room or while frolicking in the ocean late at night. They had planned to bring the twins earlier, but finances kept them pushing the trip back until changed circumstances made it a priority.

They were an unusual-looking couple. Seth was six foot four, with bushy eyebrows that moved to express his moods like the comedian Groucho Marx's. His curly dark-brown hair formed a hedge around the university baseball cap he wore on family outings, a reminder of the baseball scholarship that put him through college. He was biracial, his mother from Jamaica and his father from Norway. Petite Pat had tawny hair the color of a lion's main, which suited her ferocity when she played soccer in high school. A bubbly extrovert, she had to entice

Seth to parties, where he was unusually reserved. Yet he was the opposite at home when playing with the twins.

They were the last to exit the plane at the Honolulu International Airport. Seth pushed Pat in the wheelchair to the elevator and down to the baggage claim area, while the twins raced ahead to tug the suitcases off of the carousel. They paused near the exit while the children collected glossy tourist brochures. Then, at the taxi stand, they waited for a limousine with room for their bags and the wheelchair.

"First time Hawaii?" asked the gray-haired Filipino driver as he drove out of the airport.

"We came on our honeymoon eleven years ago," Pat said.

He smiled as he looked in the rearview mirror. "Maybe, keikis Hawaii-made."

Pat blushed.

Their driver gave them a 10 percent discount from the meter reading. "Second time Hawaii give you local *kama*'aina special," he said, and he handed Seth his business card with his name, José Lopez, in gold lettering. "If you want island tour, I give you kama'aina special price."

"We might take you up on your offer."

Nancy, the desk manager at check-in, upgraded them to a newly refurbished two-bedroom suite on the ninth floor of Rainbow Tower and gave them four complimentary breakfast-buffet coupons. Their room overlooked two swimming pools and Waikiki Beach, with Diamond Head looming at the far end of the famous beach. The needed rest was not to be, and thirty minutes after arrival they were at the pool, Pat relaxing on a shaded lounge chair, sipping sweetened tea, while Seth played Marco Polo with the twins.

They arrived just after sunset at the hotel's Tropics Bar and Grill at the edge of the wide beach. Across the sky, a trail of cottony clouds brushed pink were pierced by the silver glint of a plane heading to Asia. Below were the twinkling lights from a sunset dinner cruise ship and the scarlet sails of a sleek yacht returning to the Ala Wai Yacht Harbor. For Seth and Pat, the setting and memories exceeded their seafood dinner, but it was the opposite for the twins, who devoured their hamburgers and French fries smothered in ketchup.

"You know, Seth . . . I've dreamed about returning since our honeymoon."

"Even with hyperactive ten-year-olds?" he said in fake indignation.

She stroked his forearm. "You're as excited as I am to have all of us together where it all started."

He nodded and turned toward the ocean, seeking a few moments to compose himself.

After the meal, they toured the hotel's tropical gardens and animals, the night and soft lighting adding intimacy to the setting. The penguin pool was quiet, with the tuxedoed entertainers statue-like at the entrance to their tiny caves. Farther on, the flagstone walkway curved left, following a shallow meandering pond filled with orange-and-black-mottled koi and a sprinkling of ducks. At the edge, a black-crested night heron surveyed his buffet. Standing stoically on a grassy patch, an imported flamingo balanced on one leg, its head and oversized beak tucked under a wing. Farther on stood an empty parrot perch.

"Dad, where are the parrots?" Sarah asked.

"They're worth thousands of dollars, so they're taken in for security at night."

"Can we see some in the wild?" asked Ricky.

"No, they're from Central and South America, not Hawaii."

"Mom, can we go there someday? Benito in my class is from Costa Rica and said there are lots of pretty parrots in the rainforest."

Pat gave Seth a flitting glance, then she reached for Sarah's hand. "I'm sure you can go someday."

A woman standing nearby turned to them. "There are lovely wild parrots in the zoo at the far end of Waikiki. They're smaller than those multi-colored ones on men's shoulders in Waikiki, but they're a brilliant green, with long tails and Christmas-red beaks."

"We'll go see them." Seth smiled and thanked her.

Back in their hotel room, the extra-long day ensured the twins would go to bed without complaints. Seth and Pat moved to the small balcony. During the day, the glare of the sun reflecting off the beach and thousands of hotel windows washed away the bright colors, but in the soft light of the night, the colors returned, muted, with blurred edges like an Impressionist painting.

"Seth, do you feel the same as when we were here on our honeymoon?"

"No. Then our roots were just taking hold, but now they've become so intertwined that they can never be separated in life. And even in death it will only be temporary."

She leaned back against his shoulder and whispered, "I feel the same."

Seth rolled over and reached for Pat, his hand finding an empty pillow. Sitting up, he could see the curtain swaying with the morning breeze and Pat's silhouette. He didn't rush to her but took time to make a cup of sweetened tea.

"Morning darling," he said cheerfully as he leaned in to kiss her cheek. "You're up early."

"I don't want to miss a second of this day. I feel like I'm already in heaven."

Seth struggled to hold back his tears. "I can't think of any other place I'd rather be at this moment."

She stroked the back of Seth's neck the way she did when inviting him to bed. "I want to take the drive around the island today and see the places we saw on our honeymoon."

"We had a long, tiring day yesterday. How about lying around the pool today and going tomorrow when we're fully rested?"

She took a sip of her tea and handed the cup back to Seth. "We need to go today."

Her words frightened him. "Okay, darling. I'll make the arrangements. We'll have a wonderful day to remember. I better call José and see if he's available." He made it to the bathroom before sobbing.

José answered on the second ring and gave them a fixed price below those listed in *This Week Oahu*. He arrived at eight in his spotless stretch limousine and presented them with a box of warm malasadas and drinks—guava juice for the children, Kona coffee for Seth and Pat.

José spoke in broken English, enriching his descriptions with personal insights that would not come from more polished tour guides. As they passed Pearl Harbor, he explained that his father had watched from the roof of his home as waves of Japanese planes released bombs on December 7, 1942. The following day, he had stood for two hours in the long line of men and women to sign up to serve in the military. He told of the Japanese-Americans in Hawaii who immediately joined the military after the bombing, yet were viewed with suspicion. Most were sent to fight in Europe and not against Japan.

Beyond Pearl Harbor, they veered onto the H-2 Freeway that cut across Oahu between the Koʻolau and Waiʻanae Mountains, a region that had once been the center of the island's pineapple industry. Today, visitors zoomed through the broad U-shaped valley, stopping at the touristy pineapple-themed Dole Plantation before continuing to Haleʻiwa and the North Shore, where the world-famous championship surfing contests took place.

José believed Hawaii was the best island destination to live in and retire to because it offered two things that could not be found on other island destinations. "You see, *aloha* not just say *hello, welcome, good-bye*, but something more meaningful in Hawaiian culture—*love*. Second, *hula* have deep meaning to Hawaiians, not just dance for tourists. You go Caribbean, see nice beaches, hear calypso music, while empty wallet with big smile, no care you come back."

Pat remembered the tasty pineapple soft ice cream cones at the Dole Plantation, but time was short, so they continued to Hale'iwa for shave ice at Matsumoto's, which sold a selection of over twenty flavors. Hale'iwa still retained touches of old Hawaii, with its one-story clapboard buildings and wooden porches, although they now attracted droves of tourists. Matsumoto's was a favorite stop, with a double-line of customers snaking out the front door and along the side of the building. José parked in front so Pat could watch Seth and the kids in the line and the stream of smiling faces emerging with their shave ices. Seth and the kids returned with shave ices in extra-large plastic cups with wide rims to catch drips. The children had chosen familiar flavors—cherry, banana, and strawberry—while Seth went for local flavors—lilikoi, mango, and guava.

Pat nudged Seth. "Remember when I spilled a few drops on my front and you licked it off? You were so naughty that day."

"Mommy, what did Daddy do that was so naughty?" Sarah asked.

"It's a secret, Big Ears."

Beyond Hale'iwa, they followed the Kamehameha Highway that hugged the shore as it snaked along the tropical Windward Coast. It was a slice of Oahu that maintained more of the natural Hawaii that existed before it became a state and the dominant tourist destination in the Pacific. To the left of the highway, beaches appeared in secluded coves, and to the right, the tropical forest swooped up to corrugated cliffs crowned with wispy clouds. Roadside homes and stores varied from quaint plantation houses to shacks, and the stone ruins of the 1863 Kauloa Sugar Mill were reminders of the sugarcane and pineapple industries of the past.

Their first stop was above Waimea Bay, with a stunning view of the U-shaped bay and wide beach. José explained that calm waters of the summer were replaced by dangerously high waves, sometimes reaching thirty feet in the winter, when international competitions attracted surfers from around the world. With no beach access for wheelchairs, they continued past Sharks Cove.

The children were anxious to snorkel, and José suggested the deluxe Turtle Bay Resort, which was wheelchair accessible. He knew several of the Filipino staff, a plus, as this got them special treatment. Their table was moved closer to the beach so Pat and Seth could watch the twins snorkeling.

"José, why is this the only deluxe hotel in this beautiful part of Oahu?" asked Pat.

"Too far from popular activities in Waikiki, plus local opposition to large commercial developments."

"What do you think about resorts like this?" asked Seth.

"I have three keikis, and they need jobs. Oldest son already leave island. No work here, so local people, investors, and politicians need to work together—find compromise. Some people use religious reason to block change. Then no room to agree."

They were still too full to stop at the tempting shrimp trucks near Kahuku, so José suggested they stop a little later at a colorful shack selling local fruit, corn, coconuts, and plate lunches. The Hawaiian woman behind the counter wore a garish turquoise muumuu with crimson hibiscus flowers matching her lipstick. She greeted José cheerfully, each asking about the other's family, followed by laughter about a boy named Kekoa. Turning to the twins, she asked, "You like poi?"

"What's poi?" Ricky replied.

"Auntie Lily's poi the best. All keikis like and must try when come Hawaii." She scooped the gray, purple-tinged, pudding-textured poi into small cups and handed them to Sarah and Ricky. "No spoons needed, just two fingers."

Their expressions were of befuddlement. "Um, tastes like paste, but not too bad," Sarah tactfully replied. Pat dipped her fingers in Sarah's cup and licked them. "It brings back memories of grade school when I ate paste when the teacher wasn't looking."

"Gross!" said Ricky.

A larger cup of poi was given to Pat, along with a ripe papaya and a hug.

As they drove on, Seth asked José how Auntie Lily made money with so little business and giving away so much.

"Hawaiians very generous if you treat them with respect. Never rush. First, talk story 'bout family and keikis before open wallet."

As they approached Kaneohe, José pulled into Kualoa Beach Park, where Pat's wheelchair could be pushed across the level, palm-tree-studded grass to the narrow beach. Offshore was Mokoli'i, commonly called Chinaman's Hat because of its cone shape. While the twins waded in shallow water, trying to catch fingerling fish, José told Pat and Seth about the role of Chinese, Japanese, and Filipino laborers who were brought to Hawaii as early as the 1850s. Conditions were only slightly better than slave labor, but gradually, the industrious immigrants gained an economic foothold, starting with tiny clapboard shacks selling Asian food and traditional medicines. It was a constant struggle to educate their children, as they were not accepted at most schools. But today, evidence of the rewards of their struggles was everywhere, with Asians prominent in government, the law, business, and the universities.

As they left the park, Pat whispered to Seth that it was time to return to their hotel and prepare for the sunset.

The plan had been to complete the full circle-island tour as they had done on their honeymoon, but Seth didn't need to ask why they were cutting the trip short. "José," he said. "It's time to head back to our hotel." The twins cheered, as they preferred the hotel's pools and waterslides, and Seth said nothing as he gently caressed the back of Pat's hand.

They took the cross-island H-3 Freeway. It was among the costliest sections of freeway ever built in the United States. The expense had been justified by the claim it would provide a critical link between the Kaneohe Marine Base and Pearl Harbor naval facilities. But by the time it was completed, its strategic importance had been eclipsed by new technologies and strategies for war, and now it was mostly tourists who were the beneficiaries of the highway into the clouds, with breathtaking views of the jungle-encrusted Pali cliffs. José turned on the headlights as they entered a tunnel three-quarters of the way up the Koʻolau Mountains, and a minute later they emerged to views of Pearl Harbor, Honolulu, and a hint of Waikiki Beach hidden among towering hotels.

Back at the Hilton Hawaiian Village, Pat rested in their room while Seth took the children to the hotel's small Paradise Pool, with its waterslides and Jacuzzi next to the saltwater lagoon. They returned to find Pat sitting on the side of their bed dressed in her wedding gown.

"Mom, why are you wearing such a fancy dress?" asked Sarah.

"Because this is a special day with my family, back where it all began. You little darlings will have a babysitter tonight while your father and I go out."

"We're old enough to stay by ourselves," the twins complained in unison.

"It's already settled. You two can order what you like from room service and see any kid's movies you want."

Seth noticed the weak unsteadiness of her voice. "Honey, are you sure you're up to going out tonight? I can have a special meal served on our balcony."

She smiled. "No. Tonight is just for the two of us."

Seth put on the pair of nice slacks he'd brought. He wore his linen sport coat over an aloha shirt. He assisted Pat with her lipstick and gently smoothed rouge on her sunken cheeks. She told him their destination was a secret, then beckoned Ricky and Sarah to come to her wheelchair for a hug. She kissed both of them and gazed lovingly into their eyes. "I'll love you forever." She looked back longingly as Seth wheeled her to the door, but the children were already checking out the movies on the TV.

As they exited on the first floor, Pat asked if it would be possible to go to the water's edge and repeat their wedding vows. Seth looked at the wide expanse of beach. "I'll find a way." He scanned the couples strolling along the sidewalk and asked a husky Hawaiian man if he could help carry the wheelchair to the water's edge.

"E brah, no prob'um. Lesgo."

Each gripped a side of the wheelchair, and they carried her across the sand as the big guy's petite girlfriend followed, holding up layers of Pat's wedding dress. At the surf's edge, the young woman neatly spread out Pat's wedding dress, then took the hibiscus flower from over her right ear and tucked it over Pat's left ear, signifying a married woman. Before leaving, she leaned close to Pat, smiled, and said, *"Aloha nui loa"* — very great love.

They were just in time to catch the setting sun. The surf swirled around Seth as he knelt next to Pat, his arm snuggly around her as she tilted her head against his shoulder. Seth could barely hear Pat's words as they said their vows, but that didn't matter.

"Pat, remember we watched the last time for the rare green flash at sunset that promises you will never be disappointed in love, but we didn't see it. Maybe this is the moment."

"We don't need it. My love for you is already flashing the colors of the rainbow in my heart."

The sun appeared to melt like a ball of butter on a griddle. Then it was gone.

"Did you see them?" Pat whispered, her voice as soft as a mother's lullaby.

"The green flash?" He smiled.

"Angels," she murmured.

He held her head against his shoulder as twilight added deeper blues to the heavens, then indigo, studded with a million guiding lights. Holding her frail hand, her head tucked under his chin, he repeated their wedding vows as tears blurred the stars. The surf whisked away his words but left untouched those locked forever in the vault of his heart.

Extra Settings

*H*is father's faded aloha shirts hung on the left and his mother's dresses on the right. The shelf above had a straw hat, a dried *haku lei* (crown of flowers), and a shoebox decorated with holiday stickers. He took down the shoebox and was surprised to see not his father's but his own name, David Kang, neatly printed on the top. Curious, he lifted the lid and found a glossy photo of himself in his graduation robe and a bundle of envelopes neatly held together with a red satin ribbon. He untied the ribbon and thumbed through the twenty-two envelopes, one for every year since he'd married Brynn in 1984. They ended in 2005, the year after their divorce. He wondered why he had never seen them—why they had never mailed any of the letters.

He set aside the bundle and studied the photo taken on the football field after his high school graduation ceremonies. He was wearing a dozen flower leis that piled as high as his nose. At five foot nine, he was two inches taller than his father, Andy, and a half-foot taller than his mother, Meihua. He had the best features of both parents—his mother's lighter complexion and naturally even teeth, and his father's height and squared chin. His parents were second-generation Chinese emigrants and proud to be Americans. Fluent in both Mandarin and English, they preferred Chinese food, except for Thanksgiving, when the meal was traditional American.

David paused before opening the first letter, dated 1984. It was a year that had held so much promise—and also warning signs he'd failed to see. He'd grown up in Waikiki and had been surfing since he could carry a surfboard across the beach. He'd became a surfing instructor at eighteen, earning enough money to cover his tuition at the University of Hawaii, where he majored in business. An important side benefit of his job was the attention he got from lovely young women, and he'd dated several. But none of them were serious; they were mostly here on vacation and not looking for more than a summer fling with a beachboy.

It was a typical July morning, though the air was sultry without the usual trade winds, when he spotted her strolling his way, maneuvering around the patchwork of mats and beach towels. She stopped a few feet away and spread out her luxurious beach towel with CAPRI embroidered in large gold letters. His heart almost stopped when she took off her exquisitely woven wide-brimmed hat and shook free a rain of golden-red curls, then turned, her green eyes locking on him.

"Would you mind watching my things for a few minutes while I take a little dip? The sun makes me so hot."

"Uh . . . sure," he replied as his fingernails dug into the bar of surfboard wax he was holding.

"Thank you. You're so kind," she said in a solicitous voice. Then, in a swirling motion, she flipped off her wrap to reveal a bikini with little space for the flower pattern. "I'm Brynn," she purred over her shoulder, then she trotted down to the surf.

After her dip, she rented an umbrella and surprised him by asking if he would mind rubbing lotion on her back. She had a spray of light freckles on her dimpled cheeks. She revealed that she was home on summer break from Stanford and asked which university he was attending. He thought it strange that she presumed he was a university student; as a kama'aina, she would have known that few beachboys attended college.

Brynn returned the following day with a stunning brunette, who soon showed herself to be an unabashed snob, talking agonizingly about her rich boyfriend back at Stanford. David ignored her until she made a derogatory comment about the older Hawaiian man who managed the surfboard rentals. "Miss," he said. "Your comments are offensive. Konane, my boss, is a great guy, and he's saved several people from drowning over the past twenty years. Please don't talk like that about someone you don't even know."

The brunette glared at David as she grabbed her beach towel and bag. "Brynn, I'm leaving. Are you coming?"

Brynn shrugged and gathered her things, gave a furtive glance at David, and left with her friend. Late in the afternoon of the following day, Brynn reappeared to apologize for her friend's rude behavior.

"You don't need to apologize for your girlfriend. You did nothing wrong."

She nodded, grateful he let her off the hook, though she realized that doing nothing *was* what was wrong. She fastened her gaze on David's eyes. "Can I buy you a drink after you get off work?"

"Sure. How about Duke's? It's five minutes away and overlooks the beach. The crowd is mostly young singles, and the service is good—as well as the drinks."

David was greeted warmly by the waitress, and over the next hour, several women stopped by to chitchat with him, while Brynn pretended to be nonchalant about the other women's interest.

"You seem to know a lot of women around here," she said coyly, her finger slowly circling the lip of her margarita glass.

"I've been around Waikiki Beach all my life, so I've met most of the men and women who work on the beach, particularly during summer vacations. The last two women I talked to go back to my high school days. One's attending UH and the other Chaminade University."

"No shortage of dates?"

David scratched his chin. "Why do you ask?"

"Because I want to know about the competition."

That was the start of a whirlwind romance through July and into August, when Brynn returned to Stanford. David had many unanswered questions about her, yet his romantic feelings took precedence. She revealed that her parents lived in exclusive Kahala, but she was reluctant to have him meet them. Two days before her departure to the mainland, he gave her a 14-karat gold chain with a turtle pendant that cost him almost a month's salary, and she accompanied him back to his apartment. He had planned to see her off at the airport, but Brynn was adamant that he not come, saying that it was too early to introduce him to her parents.

Two weeks after her departure, the necklace was returned with a short Dear John note. He was hurt. But he realized on reflection that their relationship had been doomed from the start. They came from different worlds and had very different expectations. She was looking for a prominent man to bring her wealth and status, someone who could be acceptable to her class-conscious parents, Fredrick and Miriam Truscott, while he hoped eventually to own a store in Waikiki. After nine drafts, he finally settled on a short reply telling her he would never forget their romance but understood that he couldn't meet her parent's expectations. He closed with the words, "Be faithful to your hopes and dreams."

Three weeks later, David was surprised and hopeful when she called.

"Brynn. Everything back to normal at Stanford?"

"No. You bastard, you've ruined my life!"

"What are you talking about?"

"I'm pregnant, and you've destroyed everything. I'm not ready for a child—particularly yours!"

"Are you sure it's me?"

"You were the only one I slept with this summer, and I don't believe in immaculate conception."

"Have you considered an abortion?"

"Abortion is out if the question. I'm a strict Catholic, and it would be murder. I already talked to my parents, and they said my only option is to marry you. They are furious with you for seducing me."

The reaction of the two sets of parents to the pregnancy couldn't have been more different. His parents were delighted that they were going to have a grandchild and looked forward to the wedding. Brynn's parents saw David as the one who had destroyed their daughter's carefully planned and orchestrated future, and they only begrudgingly accepted him into the family. Without consulting with David, Brynn's parents planned a luncheon at the Kahala Hilton to discuss the wedding plans, insisting the wedding take place before the baby bump became noticeable.

David had premonitions of an awkward first meeting between the respective families, but the event turned out to be worse than expected. Miriam made it clear that she and the wedding planner were in charge and needed no help from David's family, quickly rejecting each of their suggestions. The small wedding that David had hoped for turned out to be a hundred and eighty-eight guests, of which twenty-eight were from his side.

They had made it almost to the end of the tense, four-course luncheon when Miriam swirled her second martini and blurted out that the International Market Place was a fire hazard filled with illegal Vietnamese selling fake Chinese goods and not paying taxes.

Meihua set down her silver-plated dessert spoon and glared at Miriam. "We've had a café next to the International Market Place since before the Vietnamese came in the 1970s, and I can assure you that they are hard-working people who pay their taxes and are putting all their hopes into their children's education and future. They are more trustworthy than the unscrupulous land developers who bribe officials for sweetheart deals and exploit immigrant workers."

Meihua, of course, was unaware that Brynn's father had made his wealth from such land dealings. Twice, he'd even had to pay hefty fines for illegal transactions. He had left the islands under a cloud of suspicion and started a chain of stores on the West Coast. Then he'd returned, after quietly paying a six-figure fine, to launch stores on Oahu and Maui.

The gala wedding at the Royal Hawaiian Hotel came off without a hitch and the new couple moved into Brynn's parents' home until after David's graduation from UH. While at UH, he worked half-time in her father's Waikiki store, then he managed it after graduation, eventually managing three stores in Hawaii. Holidays were spent with the in-laws in Kahala or at their chalet in Aspen, Colorado, and even on trips to Europe. They bought a three-bedroom home in Nui Valley, a twenty-minute drive from Waikiki, and their son was accepted at the exclusive Punahou School. Outwardly they were a happy, successful family, but there were tensions from the beginning. David was aware that their lives were controlled by her parents, and he was frustrated that Brynn wouldn't visit his parents' apartment in Waikiki.

In 2004, David was sent to Florida to open one of his father-in-law's stores in Orlando, near Disney World. Brynn's refusal to accompany him did not surprise him, as their marriage had turned markedly cooler. A month after David's move to Florida, he was served divorce papers, and the following day, he was fired by Brynn's father. He was disheartened but, again, not surprised by the ruthless efficiency of Brynn and her father to expunge him from the family. The first person he called was his son, Nicholas, now nineteen years old, to explain.

"Dad, I've expected this for years, given the tension between you two and the ceaseless meddling of Mom's parents. I'm not going to let them do the same with my life. Dad, just remember, I love you no matter what."

Those words lifted David's spirits, and he quickly set out to find a new job. Within a month, he was hired to manage three sportswear stores in Florida, delaying his plans to move back to Hawaii to open his own store and be near his aging parents and his son.

David sat on his parent's bed, opened the first envelope, and unfolded the single sheet filled with his mother's distinctive cursive writing. Then he took a deep breath before reading.

November 22, 1984
Dear Son,

Your wedding was the most beautiful one I've ever seen. You looked like a prince and Brynn a princess. You warned me that Brynn was having morning sickness and you two might not make it to our place for dessert today after the Thanksgiving dinner at her parent's home.

I told your father that our mismatched set of dishes was okay, but he bought a new set on sale at Sears. We set two extra places at our table, just in case, and had your favorite macadamia-nut ice cream and apple pie for dessert. We said a prayer for you two and for a healthy baby. Hope you can make it next Thanksgiving.

With a pretty wife and baby in the oven, as your
dad likes to say, you have even more incentive to
graduate from the University of Hawaii. We are
so proud of you and full of high expectations for
your future.
Love,
Mom and Dad

He wondered again why they never mailed any of the letters, then, as he read them, it became obvious. His parents
didn't want to cause friction in his marriage. Yet they could
not help expressing their unrelenting hope that he would appear
with his family to share in a Thanksgiving meal.

He still remembered that first Thanksgiving at Brynn's parents' home, when she wanted to just relax around the pool after
the meal, claiming she was very tired. They had been married
less than a month, and he didn't want to argue over something
so small. Yet if it wasn't important, why did he remember it
twenty-one years later?

He slipped the letter back into the envelope and opened
the next one. He thought he knew the message it contained,
but he didn't.

November 28, 1985
Dear Son,
We weren't sure baby Nicholas could sit in a high
chair, but I borrowed one from our neighbor to be
safe. Your silly father bought two blue helium-filled
balloons and tied them to the highchair. In addition
to your macadamia-nut ice cream, we bought
Neapolitan ice cream for our grandson, who might
choke on nuts.

We set three extra places at the table, and when
you didn't show up, we thought it would be a
shame to eat alone when so many people weren't

*having a Thanksgiving dinner. We walked three
blocks to Waikiki Beach and spotted two Chinese
students sitting on a bench. They are studying at the
University of Hawaii. At first, they were hesitant to
accept our invitation. We had so much fun serving
them and explaining about the Thanksgiving
tradition in America. As you know, Chinese prefer
dark meat, like duck, which is more flavorful. So we
served them the turkey legs. They enjoyed speaking
Mandarin and were curious about life for Chinese
in Hawaii. A half-hour after they left, they returned
with a bouquet of flowers.*

*I'm sure you had an enjoyable Thanksgiving
dinner with baby Nicholas at the table. We see so
much of you in the photo you sent. It's next to your
wedding picture on our dining room wall. I can't
wait to hold our grandchild.*
Love,
Mom and Dad

David leaned back on the headboard of his parents' bed
before opening the letter for 1986, the year he graduated from
the university. Both of his parents and his both in-laws were at
the graduation ceremonies, and they even sat together. Miriam
had *accidentally* forgotten to send an invitation to his parents
for the graduation party at their Kahala home. An awkward
invitation was made, one that his parents politely declined,
saying they were too tired after the graduation ceremonies.
David remembered wanting to run to his parents as he watched
them fade into the crowd. He knew where he should be, yet he
let Brynn and her parents lead him away.

The letter was written in his father's scratchy handwriting.

November 27, 1986
Dear Son,

Your mother asked me to write this year's Thanksgiving letter, as she was a little woozy and went to bed early. Nothing to worry about. As you know, Meihua rarely drinks alcohol and had a little too much wine. She'll be fine in the morning.

When we didn't hear from you after two telephone messages, we suspected you were away on a trip with Brynn and Nicholas. Just in case you returned and surprised us, we set places for you two and borrowed a high chair for Nicholas. We moved the breakable things out of reach, as we remembered that you were already getting into things at his age.

When you didn't show up, we walked down to the beach but saw no likely candidates, so we strolled toward the Waikiki Aquarium, and guess what? We found a middle-aged man sitting on the sand with his back against the seawall and, a short distance away, a woman walking slowly our way. You can guess what your matchmaker mom did. She talked both of them into joining us for Thanksgiving dinner. Both brought a bottle of wine. That explains your mother's wooziness and is the reason I'm writing the letter this time. By the end of the meal, they had plans to go sightseeing together. Meihua, the romantic one, said she could tell there was chemistry between the two.

Your bedroom is just as you left it, and Meihua dreams that, someday, Nicholas will spend the night with us. Hope all is well with you and your family and you can come next Thanksgiving.
Aloha,
Dad and Mom

Each envelope contained a different story reminding David of how lucky he was to have parents willing to share what little they had with strangers. There were always place settings for three extras and undiminished hope that David and his wife and baby would come, yet there was no bitterness when they failed to arrive. The places were always filled by people needing more than a Thanksgiving dinner, and they weren't disappointed.

The guests were as varied as if selected from a global telephone directory; there were even a few street people with no address or telephone. There was a newlywed couple from Idaho who had lost their wallet on the beach. Meihua gave them forty dollars when they left and invited them for free meals at their café. Then there was a seventy-six-year-old woman who had brought her husband's ashes back to Waikiki, where she had met the young private fifty-six years earlier during the Second World War. And strangest of all were a homeless artist and a social worker, who connected and, a year later, were married. Finally, he reached 2004, the year his world fell apart. He held the letter to his forehead, wondering what his parents really thought about the divorce. When he called his mother from Florida, she expressed sorrow for everyone. But were her real feelings in the letter?

> *November 25, 2004*
> *Dear Son,*
>
> *We were sad, yet not surprised, to receive the news from you about the divorce. We have always hoped that, eventually, Brynn would accept us and that we would hear a knock on our door one Thanksgiving. We do not have anger in our hearts toward Brynn, just sadness that even here in paradise, with such a kind husband and smart child—well, Nicholas is not a child anymore—she couldn't find happiness. With your new job on the East Coast, we knew you might not make it home for Thanksgiving. But*

there will always be extra settings at our table. It seems that an invisible hand has guided so many wonderful souls to us every Thanksgiving to give us more than we gave.

When you didn't arrive, your father and I were about to walk to the beach, but there was a knock on the door. I was shaking when I opened the door, thinking it might be you, and for a moment it was you. There stood a very handsome man with a cute waif of a young woman at his side. I can't hold back the tears as I write. He said, "Hello, Grandma. I'm Nicholas. Do you have space for two more at your table?" The last time I saw Nicholas, he was attending Punahou and had stopped by our café with two of his friends for a plate lunch. Made us so proud to have a grandson attending Hawaii's best private school.

Well, Nicholas had flown home from Stanford to spend Thanksgiving with his girlfriend, who is hapa—half Vietnamese and half Chinese. He has been secretly dating Grace Lee for three years but hasn't told his mother, as he knew she wouldn't approve. They plan to be married after college graduation and are both studying to be teachers. Nicholas said they will have a small wedding, and he will not let his grandparents turn it into a gala affair. We were thrilled to be the first to be told about the planned marriage and be invited to the wedding.

Oh yes, Grace gave me a beautiful haku lei that she made herself. I'll keep it forever. Today, I feel my life is complete.
Love,
Mom and Dad

David closed his eyes and massaged his forehead. His son had come to his parent's apartment for Thanksgiving, yet he had stayed away all those years because Brynn didn't want to come. He couldn't hold back the tears.

The funeral two days earlier had moved him more than anything but the birth of his son. Over a hundred people came, representing a cross section of Waikiki, from homeless people to executives, and a potpourri of nationalities—Chinese, Japanese, Indonesian, Thai, Caucasian, Portuguese, and Hawaiian. They had helped many over the years, and these people remembered their generosity. After the service, when he stopped by their closed takeout café, he found flowers, leis, balloons, and incense candles stretched across the storefront. An elderly Vietnamese shopkeeper approached him and asked if he were the son who never visited. When he said yes, she said he must keep the takeout café open for everyone, and David said he would, and he meant it.

The last envelope was the most difficult to open, as it was written just days before the fatal accident. He thought that if only he could set back the calendar two weeks, he could have attended their last Thanksgiving dinner, and maybe the ripple of events that followed would have had them crossing the street a minute before or after the reckless driver.

November 24, 2005
Dearest Son,
    We saw Nicholas and Grace three times during the year. They're so much in love and have set the wedding date for Saturday, June tenth, in Waimea Valley. We met Grace's parents. They now live in Hale'iwa, where they recently opened a giftshop selling Hawaiian-made swimwear and muumuus.

They are such a nice couple. They are as delighted as we are that David and Grace are getting married.

Back to the Thanksgiving dinner. Actually, I should start on my birthday, on October 15, when your father took me to the Royal Hawaiian Hotel's Mai Tai Bar next to the beach for drinks and Hawaiian music. When we stopped to admire the hotel's large orchid display, you'll never guess who we met—Minami Wang, director of guest relations at the hotel. We were glad to see her, as we remembered Minami was your high school sweetheart. She's divorced and lives at Iolani Court Plaza with her seventeen-year-old daughter, who attends Iolani School.

We invited them to our Thanksgiving dinner, and they came. She told stories about the funny things you two did that made us laugh so hard, tears were running down our cheeks. She said you were the first boy she ever kissed, and she still remembered the tingling feeling that no other man ever gave her. She said you called her nani, the Hawaiian word for beautiful. Before she left, she gave us two complimentary brunch coupons for the Royal Hawaiian Hotel. We're planning on going to the New Year's Day brunch.

I'm getting wordier each year, but every word comes with love for you.

Love,

Mom and Dad

PS: If you ever have a spare moment, you might give Minami a call. She said she would love to see you again, even if it's only for a cup of coffee.

"Aloha, Royal Hawaiian Hotel. How can I direct you call?"
"Calling for Ms. Minami Wang, manager of guest relations."
"May I ask who's calling?"
"A friend looking for *Nani*."

Secrets

"*I* can't come to the phone right now. Please leave your name, phone number, and a short message, and I'll get back to you as soon as I can."

"I'm Scott Tilton and hope you're the Lynn Namura that I dated when I attended the University of Hawaii in the mid-1990s. I'm in Waikiki for a week and would be pleased if you have time to meet me for sunset cocktails and pupus at the Moana Hotel's Beach Bar tomorrow evening at six. And I hope you can stay and watch the Friday night fireworks. If your sister Ann is still in the area, bring her along, and we can catch up on the past two decades and reminisce about old times at UH. I've always wondered if you and Ann took the around-the-world trip you talked about. You can call to confirm or surprise me and just show up."

Scott was not tall by mainland standards, but in Hawaii, where the population was dominated by Asian-Americans, he was above average. His stocky build, dark wavy hair, and olive complexion came from his mother's Sicilian side of the family. The main physical attribute from his Scottish father was his hazel eyes, which captured the hues of the surroundings.

Friday morning, he rented a surfboard and paddled out beyond the reef to see if he still had the dexterity for riding waves. After a few wobbly attempts and less-than-graceful spills, he regained the knack and was able to stand, but he still lacked the nimble maneuvers of the locals. It was exhilarating and brought back the carefree days at the university, when the siren call of the surf often drew him away from his studies.

Even with sunscreen, by midmorning he could feel the sting of a sunburn. Reluctantly he returned his surfboard and headed back to the Marriott Waikiki Beach Resort to shower and change. The afternoon was spent exploring Waikiki to see how many of his favorite haunts were still there. While Waikiki had the same feel that he remembered from his university days, now it had moved upscale to cater to affluent Asian visitors. The classy aloha shirts in the window of a Tori Richard store drew him inside, but the price tag on the one he liked quickly sent him to a nearby ABC Store for a twenty-dollar aloha shirt.

He had met Lynn at a Hawaiian slack-key guitar festival at the Waikiki Shell, in Kapiʻolani Park, across from Waikiki Beach. After the festival, they had walked along the beach, then, with surf swirling around their ankles, kissed. It wasn't a romantic moonlit night, as the sky was overcast and threatening to rain, yet that didn't matter.

The following day, he spotted Lynn on campus and sauntered over and cheerfully greeted her—provoking a who-the-hell-are-you? stare.

"Lynn, remember me? From last night?"

"I'm Ann. You must be thinking of my sister." Lynn hadn't mentioned that she had an identical twin at UH. The three began studying together in Hamilton Library and going to Waikiki on weekends, until he and Lynn paired off, and Ann dropped out of most of their weekend forays.

Scott graduated a year before Lynn and was offered a position with an import company in Washington, DC. He had hoped

Lynn would follow him after graduation, but she accepted a teaching position at Mid-Pacific Institute, adjacent to the University of Hawaii. The romantic calls gradually decreased, and by spring, they mutually agreed that the long-distance relationship wasn't working. Scott had asked Lynn if something he'd, done or hadn't done, was the cause of their breakup, and she quickly said no. The Christmas cards with friendly notes continued for nine years. Then his card came back stamped RETURN TO SENDER. He assumed she had probably married and no longer wanted to stay in contact with a former boyfriend. He checked the internet and discovered her Facebook page had been deleted.

He arrived early at the Beach Bar and took a seat facing the rear stairs, where Lynn would appear if she came. He slipped her photo from his wallet, and even after so long, her beauty sent a shiver through him. Her oval face and wide set green eyes were accented by tortoise-shell framed glasses and auburn hair that cascaded to her shoulders. People could change a lot in two decades, and he tried to keep his expectations low to avoid disappointment. She was three inches shorter than he was, and both twins had enjoyed wearing high heels when they went to parties. They often wore each other's clothes, and the only sure way to separate them was the Hawaiian names on their gold bracelets.

Six o'clock came and passed, but no one appeared who faintly resembled Lynn. Then, as he was about to order a drink, she appeared like a mirage, lifting her floor-length floral muumuu as she descended the steps and floated across the courtyard, an orchid lei over her arm.

"Aloha, Lynn," he said cheerfully as he rose with his pink carnation lei. "I wasn't sure you would come."

"Neither was I until the last minute."

He ignored her curious reply, and they exchanged leis and kisses on cheeks, then he helped her be seated.

"I called the Moana Surfrider Hotel to confirm, but you weren't registered."

"Sorry, I forgot to tell you in the phone message that I'm staying at the Marriott Waikiki Beach Resort. It's only about a ten-minute walk toward Diamond Head on Kalakaua Avenue."

Scott took in the subtle changes to the woman he had thought he would marry two decades ago. Her hair was shorter, the tips curled forward just below her diamond-studded ear-lobes. There were a few light freckles on her forehead that he didn't remember. The added touch made her face more radiant than he recalled.

"Lynn, you're more attractive today than twenty-one years ago."

"Thanks for the compliment. Muumuus are great for con-cealing the imperfections of age. You know, Scott, the touches of gray on your temples make you more distinguished."

There was an awkward pause as they gazed at each other across the small table.

"Lynn, where should we start?"

There was a flicker of tenseness in her face as she adjusted the Chinese barrette in her hair. "I want to start from this moment as if we just met for the first time."

Scott was caught off guard with her strange request. He had expected to spend much of the evening reminiscing about their time together at UH, and perhaps learn why she had abruptly stopped writing, leaving no forwarding address.

The waitress arrived at their table with the drink and pupu menus. "Aloha, we have a two-for-one Mai Tai special when you add any pupu plate." They ordered the Mai Tais with the crispy crab roll pupu.

"Well, Lynn, why don't we start by telling a little about our-selves, as if we just met. You go first."

"I'm teaching math to seventh-graders at the Mid-Pacific Institute. I'm divorced and have a son, Shane, at the University of Colorado. I belong to a hiking club, and, oh yes, I teach Sunday school. Shane and I recently returned from Cebu, in the Philippines, where we swam with thirty-foot whale sharks. I read a lot and enjoy most classical Hawaiian music and dance. Overall, I feel comfortable with my life." She paused. "With the exception of not having a soul mate."

She hadn't indicated a significant other, so maybe. . . . "Well, I didn't last long in Washington, DC, Lynn. I moved to the San Francisco Bay area to partner with a woman importing paint pigments from China. I've never been married, but I have a lovely daughter, Kayla, attending UC Davis. It's a convoluted story that I'd rather not discuss right now. I raised my daughter alone and haven't heard from her mother, Charmaine, since Kayla was three. I also like hiking. Kayla and I have hiked in the Sierras and the Rockies, and we're planning to climb Mount Whitney this summer. I wrote a mystery novel several years ago, but after a dozen literary agents rejected it, I gave up on the idea that I might be the next Clancy."

Lynn twisted her napkin as she gazed at Scott. *Never married and a daughter in college, so he also has secrets.*

It wasn't hard to segue into other topics, and it was almost seven forty-five when they strolled onto the beach. Lynn took off her sandals, then hitched up her muumuu to wade into the surf. "I love the soothing feeling of the ocean on my feet."

Scott rolled up his pant legs, tossed his loafers on the sand, and followed her into the frothy surf as the first boom of the fireworks lit the sky. He slipped his arm around her waist. She leaned into him as they watched sparking bursts in the sky, mirrored on thousands of hotel windows and the ocean. Their bodies swayed to the rhythm of the surf and when she turned to embrace him, her tears caught the sparkles in the sky.

The only time Lynn's voice lost its melodic tone that evening was when he asked about Ann, and she bristled.

"Remember, we're supposed to have just met? So you don't know about my twin."

As they strolled back to Lynn's car, they discussed the sights they would see together. At her car, he mused aloud, "I wonder what would have happened if I had stayed in Hawaii?"

"Scott, it wouldn't have turned out the way you think."

"How can you be so sure?"

"Good night!" The wheels squealed as she sped away.

The following morning, Scott was waiting when she pulled up in front of the Marriott Waikiki Beach Resort in her faded red Volkswagen Cabrio convertible. "Aloha. Hope you had a good sleep."

"Like a baby. I left the sliding glass door open to let in the ocean breeze, and the Mai Tais helped. I woke up thinking about you."

Lynn laughed. "I woke up thinking about breakfast. Hope you're hungry?"

"How about Coffee Manoa in the Manoa Market Place? That was my favorite back in my university days."

"Gone. Once Starbucks opened across the street, they couldn't compete, and they closed. I know a great option near Diamond Head that serves a mean bagel with cream cheese, Maui onion, local tomato, and avocado. The only problem is finding parking on Monserrat Avenue."

They parked two blocks from the café and squeezed into a table, shoulder-to-shoulder with others. The cappuccinos came in widemouthed porcelain cups with a dolphin design in the foam. Scott surprised Lynn when he reached over and wiped away her foam mustache, then licked his finger.

She quickly pulled back. "So early in the morning and you're already mischievous. We only met last night, remember," she scolded.

"So, Lynn, where are you taking me today?"

"I'm thinking that we start with a climb to the top of Diamond Head for a 360–degree view of Waikiki, Honolulu, and the Ko'olaus. But you'll have to behave, as we'll be in close quarters in a dark tunnel."

"I'll try."

"Try what?" she replied with a coy smile.

"To kiss you."

She shoved his hand away. "Everyone's looking. We better go."

They drove through the tunnel on the north side of the volcano into the half-mile-wide crater. "Lynn, this reminds me of a miniature version of the Ngorongoro Crater, in East Africa. It would be a great place to let Honolulu Zoo's African animals roam free."

Lynn frowned. "And eat tourists. Even if it was a super idea, here in Hawaii, things move at a glacial pace, and there's strong local resistance to change. The good thing is that Diamond Head no longer has any military significance. It has become a favorite tourist attraction, at least for those healthy enough for the steep climb."

The moderate slope of the switchback trail belied what waited ahead—a pitch-black tunnel, then steep concrete stairs leading into a dungeon-like room at the base of steel stairs. Midway through the tunnel, Scott pulled Lynn against him and kissed her with passion as his hands slid under the back of her shirt, but his ardor was quickly doused when a noisy Boy Scout troop entered, flashlights blazing.

"Now I have a whole troop of bodyguards," Lynn said with a laugh.

A backlog of hikers filled the dark, musty bunker at the base of the spiral stairs, as people going in both directions bumped and pushed. In the darkness, they didn't see the heavyset man lumbering down the stairs until he knocked Lynn backward into Scott, who struggled to hold her as he straight-armed the man.

"Careful buddy!" he snapped as he steadied Lynn. Then, realizing he had grabbed her breast, he quickly apologized. "Sorry, I—"

"Don't apologize for keeping me from a nasty fall."

From the concrete bunker at the top, they crawled through the narrow opening where cannons once protruded, then circled around to the lookout platform.

Scott stood behind Lynn with his arms snuggly around her waist. "The view is as stunning as I remember. Can we see UH from here?"

"Yes." She pointed mauka (toward the mountains) where the University of Hawaii buildings stood at the entrance to Manoa Valley. "Behind the university is the Mid-Pacific Institute, where I teach."

Waikiki rose up to the west, a glass-faceted concrete forest of high-rise hotels and condos, bounded by a ribbon of golden sand, the variegated blue sea on the left, and the arrow-straight Ala Wai Canal on the right. Beyond the canal, houses, condos, and shops filled the low areas, then gave way to the tropical forest on the slopes of the Ko'olau Mountains.

She pointed to the darker blue channel through the barrier reef off Sans Souci Beach. "That's the start of the annual two-and-a-half-mile Rough Water Swim that ends at the Hilton Hawaiian Village. I entered a few years ago and finished in the middle of the pack of a thousand swimmers. That day, the current beyond the reef was unusually strong, and dozens of swimmers had to be picked up by surfers and boats. But the highlight for the crowd on the beach was a Japanese woman who, at the finish, danced out of the ocean sans swimsuit."

Back at the trailhead, they paused for bottles of cold water from the drink machine, then took down the canvas top of her car.

"I was thinking, Scott, that we might drive around the southeast side of Oahu as far as Makapuu Point, and on the way back, we could stop in Hawaii Kai for a late lunch."

"I'm ready."

The drive past Kahala and Aina Haina was not particularly interesting, with houses crowding the Kalanianaole Highway and blanketing the hillside. But finally the view opened up to Hawaii Kai, set in a valley with a picturesque marina and orderly canals giving it the look of a 1950s Hollywood movie set. Beyond Hawaii Kai, the highway rose up the side of Koko Head, another extinct volcano crater, and passed Hanauma Bay, Oahu's famous and crowded snorkeling spot, which many found the most scenic coconut-palm-fringed beach on Oahu. A few miles of winding, narrow highway carved into barren volcanic cliffs brought them to a congested parking lot overlooking the Halona Blowhole, where ocean sprays sometimes reached thirty feet, producing rainbows when the sun was at the right angle.

"Scott, we're not here to see a water spout. That's something you can see in many places."

Lynn pulled him to the far overlook, away from the crowds. Below was a crescent beach bounded by vertical, craggy cliffs. "Do you know what makes this tiny beach special?"

"It's just big enough for the two of us."

"Good guess. It's where the great kissing scene was filmed in *From Here to Eternity*. I've seen the movie at least five times and get goosebumps every time I see Burt Lancaster kissing Deborah Kerr on the beach."

"Maybe, we should try it tonight."

"You're not Burt Lancaster," she said, laughing.

They continued on to the Makapuu Point at the eastern end of Oahu, where they had breathtaking views of the velvety-green Pali cliffs, which seemed to hang like giant stage curtains from the clouds, in stark contrast to the two small, barren islands just offshore. From their high vantage point, they spotted a pod of dolphins. Lynn told him it was a good place for whale watching during the winter months.

It was midafternoon when they returned to Hawaii Kai. They bought plate lunches at a Korean barbecue café and ate at an outdoor table next to the yacht harbor. Lynn was surprised when Scott asked for chopsticks and used them with dexterity to pluck morsels from his Styrofoam plate.

"After all these years away, you still prefer chopsticks?"

"I always ask for them when I'm in a restaurant that has them because it brings back memories of my time in Hawaii. Remember how we used to snatch pieces of food from each other's plates?"

"No. Everything started yesterday." While he found her behavior perplexing, he also found it refreshing to have a fresh beginning to their relationship.

Days and nights slid by as they explored the island and each other, gradually peeling back layers of their past. Scott felt the relationship was better than the first time, when he was young and unsure of what he really wanted or needed. There were small differences that he noticed in Lynn. She loved sashimi and poke, yet he remembered her gagging the first time she tasted raw fish. Then, she was not a morning person and wouldn't sign up for any early classes, but now she was up at the crack of dawn, probably the result of two decades of getting up at daybreak to teach classes. He remembered Lynn was less decisive when they dated in college but now quickly made decisions. He liked the more mature and decisive Lynn and hoped this restart to their relationship was real.

Two nights before Scott was to leave, he took Lynn to the Chart House, overlooking the Ala Wai Yacht Harbor, for their famous escargots à la Ernest and stuffed ahi. He was careful not to mention that they'd eaten there on the twins' twenty-first birthday, as Lynn was in a chatty mood and he didn't want to spoil the romantic atmosphere.

"Scott, I'm so happy you called and we got together this week. The days have gone by so fast." She paused and nervously sipped her wine. "I'm not ready for it to end yet, and I'm afraid."

"Why afraid? We've had a wonderful week together, and I hope there's more to come."

"When things are perfect and my left eye twitches, it's before something bad happens. It has been twitching today, and I'm afraid to leave you tonight, frightened that something will change our relationship."

I hope she means what I'm thinking. "Then why not stay with me tonight?"

She smiled and reached across the table and caressed the palm of his hand. "I don't do one-night stands."

"Neither do I."

The middle-aged receptionist greeted them with a cheerful aloha. "How can I help you this evening?"

"Any messages for Scott Tilton?"

The receptionist studied the computer monitor, noting that only one person was registered. "No messages." Then she shot a furtive glance at Lynn and smiled. "Have a pleasant evening."

As they entered the elevator, Lynn pinched his side. "You really didn't need to stop and ask about messages. You should be thinking of *us*."

"I wanted to make sure there was nothing urgent, so we won't be bothered."

"Acceptable answer. Mind if I take a shower first?"

"Not at all. Do you need me to wash your back?"

"I'll call if I need help."

She did call, and he joined her with a bar of soap. They took turns soaping each other, then she leaned back against the tiled wall as Scott slid to his knees, warm water splashing off his head and broad shoulders as he passionately kissed her. They made love a second time in his bed and again the next morning. Scott wanted to tell Lynn that when they were dating, he'd never doubted his love for her, yet that wasn't entirely true.

Lynn stood at the mirror in her underwear, brushing her hair, her dress draped over a chair. "Scott, as this is your last day, you choose the destination."

He picked up her dress and walked to her side. "I don't want you to get mad, but I really would like to go back to the beach at the base of Diamond Head and try and find the messages we buried two decades ago."

Lynn stiffened and stopped brushing. Without turning, she said in a firm even voice, "Everything started when we met this week under the banyan tree. Your wish puts everything at risk."

"Lynn, I'm trying to understand you. But we did nothing back then to be ashamed of. It was your idea to have each of us write down a secret that the other two didn't know and bury it for twenty years. You must be a little curious about what Ann and I wrote, and I'm curious about what you two really thought about me. Lynn, remember our thoughts were those of immature college students, and a lot changes in twenty-one years."

"Scott, what if the secrets ruin everything?"

"Lynn, nothing can change the way I feel about you. I promise."

"That's a promise I doubt you will keep." She threw down her brush and grabbed the dress from his hands. "Let's go, but remember, I warned you."

Scott was upset by Lynn's angry outburst and at a loss as to how to respond. He was sure that Lynn's worries were unfounded and suspected she might have written something derogatory about him. Still, that was twenty-one years ago, and they were not the people they were now—not the couple who had just slept together.

They parked at the overlook near the lighthouse. She didn't hold his hand as they walked down the zigzag paved path to the beach and turned right toward Waikiki. She stood back with arms crossed tightly over her chest as Scott carefully searched the cliff face. He remembered using mortar to conceal the hole he'd chiseled into a soft sandstone layer above a black lava bed in the cliff. He told Lynn that the jar could be long gone due to cliff erosion or, more likely, discovered by a beach visitor. He had almost given up the search when he spotted an irregular circular discoloration in the rust-colored sandstone bed.

"Lynn, I think I've found it."

Lynn sat on a lava boulder, raking her fingers through the sand as she watched Scott use his Swiss Army knife to pry out the four-inch-wide mortar plug and remove a peanut butter jar. The lid was heavily corroded and had to be pried off with the knife's can-opener attachment. He knelt on the sand next to Lynn and handed her the cellophane bag containing the three notes.

"Which one should we read first?"

"Scott, I suppose yours, since this is your idea." She opened it, and they read it together.

> *Dear Lynn,*
>   *This is my secret. I love you and plan to ask you to marry me. My confession is that, a few weeks ago, I had a romantic dream about Ann and have been thinking about her when I should be thinking about you. I know my crush on Ann is just an immature fantasy and that you're the only one for me.*
> *Love,*
> *Scott*

"So, you secretly had the hots for Ann?"

"Yeah, there was something about Ann that made my heart pitter-patter faster. But it was you that I chose."

"Outside of her body, was there anything else that attracted you to Ann?"

"That was long ago." He shrugged. "Maybe it was her lugubrious poetry that moved me. I don't remember, and anyway, I came back to Hawaii looking for you."

"Are you sure?"

What a strange question, he thought, and he didn't reply.

Lynn's hands shook as she unfolded Ann's note and handed it to Scott to read.

> *Dear Scott and Lynn,*
> *My secret is I'm attracted to Scott. Last week, when we were playing in the ocean, a wave pushed me into him. He held me close momentarily, and I felt a tingling all over. Probably just imagining things. Anyway, Sis, I know his heart is in your court.*
> *Love,*
> *Ann*

"I never knew that Ann had those feelings about me. Would be fun if all of us could get together someday. Is she still in the islands?"

Lynn looked down, clawing her fingers through the sand. "Let's read *Lynn's* note next."

"It's your note."

"Oh yes. *My* note."

Lynn took a deep breath and began reading her note—her voice barely audible.

> *Dear Scott and Ann,*
> *If you're reading this note, you know the secret that I haven't told you. I'm dead. Sorry, Sis, for not telling you that I took the test and discovered*

I was the twin that carried the fatal gene. I know I have eight, maybe ten years, and I want to live as normally as I can without people feeling sorry for me because I'm dying. Scott, now you know why I didn't follow you to the mainland.
I have a second secret that only a close twin can see. Ann, when you and Scott look at each other, there is more than friendship in your eyes. I'm not going to marry Scott, and I hope romance blooms between you two.
Love,
Lynn

Scott gazed into Lynn's eyes. "But you didn't die?"

Tears streamed from her eyes. "I wanted to tell you before things got serious, but it was easier to live with the lie for our week together. I planned to write you a letter and explain everything."

"What are you talking about?" He took her hands and pressed them to his chest.

"Scott, my parents shared our names. Lynn's full name was *Lynn Ann* Namura, and my name is *Ann Lynn* Namura. In honor of Lynn, I dropped Ann and began using my middle name, Lynn. I never expected you to call. At first, I was going to tell you, but I didn't." She paused. "I'm sorry."

"So, you're really Ann."

"Yes."

"Did you know what Lynn had written in her note?"

"She told me the first secret of why she didn't marry you but not the second, as I was dating someone else at that time."

"Ann, I'm so sorry that Lynn had to die so young. I need to visit her grave and tell her I would have married her for the years we could have had together."

Ann scooped up a handful of sand and carefully poured it into his palm then folded his fingers. "Lynn, thank you for giving me permission to fall in love with Scott." She leaned over and kissed his fingers. "Lynn's with us now. She asked me to spread her ashes here on the beach."

No More Moves

"*C*an I help you find something?" the manager asked as he straightened a pile of T-shirts.

"Mister, I need a job. I'm really a good worker, and will work any hours."

Bernardo Kita-Rodrigues paused and took a measured look at the teenager. He was skinny—looked hungry, and had a hack-job haircut that wasn't from a barber. His clothes were clean but worn, with mismatched buttons on his shirt. His glasses were too small for his head and were probably several years old.

"What's your name?"

"Danny Gallagher. I'm sixteen."

"Sorry, I don't need additional help at this time. Maybe in the summer." He turned to assist a customer holding two sun-screen lotions. "They're both the same price but I'm not sure which one is more water-resistant."

"Excuse me, Ma'am," said Danny. "Surfers prefer that one because it lasts longer, so better value and protection."

"Thank you. I'll take two bottles of the one the young man recommended."

Danny turned to leave. "Mr. Gallagher," said Bernardo. "Wait while I finish with my customer."

After the woman left, Bernardo scratched his chin as he studied the teen. "How about I try you for four hours this Friday and Saturday nights, but no promises?"

Danny grinned and stood straighter. "You can pay me whatever you want."

"You'll get minimum wage. I need someone to help customers find what they're looking for, so you'll need to learn the location of items. Also, there's restocking to do. And keep a watchful eye out for shoplifters. If you see one, don't confront the person; just tell me, and I'll handle the matter."

Friday evening, Danny showed up two hours early and went down every aisle, writing down the items in a school notebook. At first, he was overly helpful to customers, so Bernardo showed him how to be less intrusive and to offer assistance only when a customer appeared to need help. By Saturday night, Bernardo could see the kid was a fast learner and highly motivated. He extended his work hours to six on Saturday and Sunday, and four on Friday night, giving him sixteen hours work a week.

At the beginning of summer vacation, Danny's hours were increased, and he worked five days a week and received a fifty-cent an hour wage increase. He consistently arrived at least fifteen minutes early, and after closing didn't leave the store until everything was in order. By July, he'd already spotted four shoplifters.

Though Bernardo knew Danny took the Number 2 bus that passed through Kalihi, the boy remained evasive about his family and where he lived, saying little except that he lived with his mother and little sister, named Abby. Sometimes he brought her with him, and she would sit quietly in a corner reading a children's book or doing her second grade homework. She was shy and wouldn't answer questions or even take a treat from

Bernardo without getting a nod from her brother. Bernardo knew from the street address Danny gave on his employment form that he lived in a rough neighborhood.

It was a humid August evening when Danny arrived late for work, something he had not done since starting four months earlier. His clothes were disheveled and soaked with sweat, and his fingernails were dirty. Bernardo took a new shirt from the sale rack and handed it to him. "Go to the bathroom and clean yourself up, and then we need to have a chat."

Danny returned ten minutes later wearing the new shirt and combed hair. "Mr. Bernardo, I'm sorry I was late. It won't happen again."

"Danny, it's important to know what's going on with you. I can't let your personal life interfere with work. Is it something I can help you with?"

He shook his head. "You can't help. And I'm not supposed to tell anyone."

"Danny, silence doesn't solve problems. You can trust me."

He looked down at the floor. "We were evicted from our apartment today and have nowhere to go."

"Where's your family now?"

"My mom's afraid that if the authorities know we're homeless, they'll put Abby and me in foster homes."

"Danny, I won't report anything to the authorities."

"I, uh, don't know who to trust," Danny replied in a pleading voice.

"I knew you were fifteen, not sixteen when I hired you. I called the high school near where you lived and found out you're a fifteen-year-old, ninth grade honor student."

Danny bit his lip. "They're hiding under a banyan tree next to the Waikiki Aquarium. Mom's scared and doesn't know what to do." He looked away to avoid Bernardo's gaze.

"I happen to have an empty cottage behind my home that you can use for a month or two."

"We have no money. Mom had to spend everything on her operation. She hurt her arm in a bicycle accident, and she's a piano teacher and can't work until the cast comes off, and the doctor said she may never play again."

"The cottage is free, but you can help maintain the lawn and flowers. Business is slow tonight, and we have more important things to attend to." He announced to the two shoppers that he was closing early.

In the darkness, there was no sign of life among the massive, tangled roots at the base of the banyan tree.

"Mom, it's me, Danny. Mr. Kita-Rodrigues has offered us a place to stay for free."

Silence, then a rustling noise and a small beam from a flashlight as a woman and young girl emerged from the darkness.

"Ms. Gallagher, I'm Bernardo Kita-Rodrigues. I'm the one who hired your son to work part time in my shop." He extended his hand, and she reached with her left hand, awkwardly shaking his hand.

"I'm Kelly Gallagher. Danny has told me a lot of good things about you. I appreciate your giving him a job."

"I've never had an employee with so much enthusiasm, and I don't want to lose such a good worker. I have a vacant cottage behind my home, about twenty minutes from here, in Aina Haina. It isn't much, and it needs a good cleaning, but it should be suitable for a month or two, until you can get back on your feet."

"Mr. Kita-Rodrigues, anything at all will be a great help," Kelly quickly replied.

"Please call me Bernardo."

Everything they had was stuffed into three battered suitcases that easily fit into Bernardo's SUV. Bernardo got a closer look at Kelly when he turned on the vehicle's cabin light. Even in her stressed state, with messy black hair escaping from the loose bun at the back of her head, he could see the slightly angular, sophisticated features of a fortyish Katharine Hepburn—minus the raspy voice.

Abby squealed with delight when Bernardo switched on the garden lights to reveal the overgrown backyard, thick with banana and papaya plants. Bougainvillea covered the walls of the cottage. "Mommy, it's a fairy tale cottage, and I can even pick bananas from the porch."

Bernardo laughed. "Abby, I'm appointing you official caretaker of the banana plants."

The cottage was compact, with two small bedrooms, a toilet, and shower, plus the kitchen and dining area in one room. It was musty, with cobwebs around the windows and cockroaches floating in a dishpan of green water and in the toilet bowl.

"Sorry, about the condition. It hasn't been occupied since my mother passed away four years ago."

"Bernardo, this place is perfect. We'll turn it into a cozy home in no time," Kelly cheerfully replied.

"You must be hungry?"

"You've done enough. We'll be okay tonight."

"Mommy, my stomach's growling."

"Well, Abby," said Bernardo. "We better calm down that tiger with a little tiger food." He returned a few minutes later with leftover cold chicken, macaroni salad, Maui potato chips, and two-thirds of a gallon of milk. "That should hold you until we can go shopping in the morning."

It was after eleven when the cottage grew quiet and Kelly switched off the kitchen light. A glow in the garden attracted her attention. Thinking Bernardo had forgotten to turn off the outside light, she stepped onto the porch. As her eyes adjusted to the darkness his silhouette took shape, framed by banana leaves. She slowly approached. "Bernardo, I want to thank you again for rescuing us at my lowest point in life."

He looked up and smiled. "Kelly, it was you who rescued me."

"I don't understand."

"Join me for a nightcap, and I'll try to explain?"

"I'd love to." It wasn't the bottle of Bailey's Irish Cream but the two glasses that surprised her. "Were you expecting me?"

He poured the cordial into the second glass. "No." He paused. "Maybe, we should talk later after you're rested. You've already had more than enough stress for one day."

She lifted the glass and swirled the honey liquid. "If talking to me makes you feel better, I can sit here all night." She touched her glass to his.

"I don't know where to start. My wife, Melanie, vanished seven years ago. Her car was found in a cane field off of Highway 99, a few miles from the North Shore. She had driven to Haleʻiwa to see a friend and never arrived. To this day, there hasn't been a single piece of evidence found to indicate what happened—no blood, no solid tips, nothing. That night, I was waiting in the garden with the cordial and two glasses when I got the call from the police. At first, I thought it must be a mistake and she would arrive home. Then, as days turned into months, hope faded. But hope has no expiration date. It's hard to let go of hope for someone you love deeply, even when there is none. My work keeps my worries away during the day, but at night, I set out two crystal glasses and Bailey's Irish Cream and wait. Crazy, huh?"

"Crazy people lack empathy for others, but you have it, or I wouldn't be here tonight. Not getting closure makes it harder to move on." Kelly put her drink down and reached for his hand. "You can move on and still hold Melanie close to your heart."

Bernardo nodded. "Tonight, I feel happier than in months because I found purpose in Abby, Danny, and you, and that feels good."

"I worry most about little Abby, who doesn't understand when I cry and why we have no food. Tonight, Abby was the happiest I've seen her since my accident. To her, this is a fairyland. When I tucked her into bed, she talked about the secret hideaway she wants to make in the bushes. Hope it's okay with you."

"Of course. Your coming here is a needed breath of fresh air for this place. It's been a long time since laughter came from the cottage." He paused. "Mind if I ask about your husband and why he isn't helping?"

"Simple story from a trashy novel. Woman escapes with two children to get as far away as possible from an abusive, alcoholic husband. Then she breaks her arm and can't work while bills pile up and the children go hungry. I taught piano lessons and played in the symphony, so breaking my arm put my career on hold, maybe forever. I stopped believing in fairy tales when I was ten, but when you showed up tonight with the offer of the cottage, it was like a fairy tale, and you were the prince in shining armor." She wiped her eyes with her left hand, then downed the last of her drink. "I needed that."

"Kelly, my armor needed a shine." Bernardo stood when she got up, and they briefly hugged. He remained and watched until the lights went out in the cottage.

One month merged into a second and third as they shared meals and outings together. Bernardo began letting one of his employees manage the store on Sundays so he could take excursions with Kelly and her children. They weren't romantic outings, and there were no dates with just the two of them. Often, Kelly and Bernardo prepared meals, with Abby squeezing in to help. Kelly's cast came off, but she needed therapy to get the feeling back into her fingers, and the doctor warned that full use of her fingers might never return.

Abby spent much of her play time in her fairy-tale garden. She hollowed out a secret hideaway in a thicket of vines. Bernardo discovered it when he heard Abby talking to her dolls. He followed the trail of popcorn and cookie crumbs to the hidden entrance. Abby made him cross his heart and hope to die if he told anyone about her secret place.

They had several picnics on the grass next to Sans Souci Beach and three trips to Hanauma Bay, where Bernardo taught Abby to identify reef fish and to pronounce their local names. The one fish Bernardo couldn't pronounce was the official state fish, humuhumu-nukunuku-a-puaʻa, and when he tried, Abby would bend over holding her stomach as she laughed. On Kailua Beach, they entered a sand-sculpture contest and spent two hours shaping an eight-foot dragon that Abby was sure would win a prize. It didn't, but she proudly told the tourists who stopped to take photographs that it was her design.

To celebrate the end of Kelly's physical therapy, Bernardo said they would all go to the Moana Hotel for high tea. He bought Abby a new dress and shoes, and Kelly fixed up her hair. As they were shown to their table on the veranda overlooking the courtyard at the rear of the hotel, Kelly paused at the grand piano.

"Kelly, would you like to try a few notes?" said Bernardo.

"Bernardo, I'm scared. It's been almost five months, and I'm afraid I've lost the touch."

"How do you know without trying?"

"Failure in front of all these people would be embarrassing."

"Not as embarrassing as being homeless under a banyan tree—and you snapped back from that quickly."

"Only because you rescued us."

After they were seated and had ordered, Bernardo excused himself and walked to the maître d'. Kelly could see the two men talking and glancing back toward their table.

"Mommy, I bet Bernardo is asking if you can play the piano."

"I fear that you're right."

"Don't be afraid, Mommy. Danny and I will clap, even if you're not so good."

Bernardo was grinning as he returned to their table. "The maître d' will be pleased to have you play two or three light classical pieces."

"I bet you didn't tell him I broke my hand and haven't played for almost a half a year."

"True. Do it for us."

Kelly looked at Bernardo and her children's expectant faces. "Okay," she said, and she stood.

She paused at the grand piano before sitting on the padded seat and adjusting its position. Her fingers touched the keys. The notes were discordant, and people looked up, curious. Kelly hesitated, hands poised over the keyboard as she gazed toward the expectant faces of Bernardo, Danny, and Abby, who gave a thumbs-up. She gave a slight nod, then, like magic, her fingers moved across the keyboard. The melodious music wafted onto the beach, and as if it were the music of Homer's mythical sirens, beachgoers were lured nearer to listen. When she finished and stood, the applause stretched to the water's edge. She bowed graciously to those on the veranda and the crowd on the beach.

"Kelly, I've never heard anything like it!" Bernardo said as he helped her be seated at their table.

"You have too much wax in your ears," she replied with a wry grin. "I missed several notes."

Later, as Bernardo waved his hand for the bill, the manager of guest relations approached their table. "High tea is on the house for your wife's captivating performance. Miss, I was inside, and people began drifting to the open windows, and I could see people on the beach gathering around to listen. Would there be any chance that you would be willing to consider playing at our high teas?"

Kelly remained poised as she first looked at Bernardo and her children. "I would be honored to play at your high teas."

The fifteen-hour-a-week position at the Moana Surfrider Hotel was soon supplemented by a second part-time job giving piano lessons at a private school. It was a difficult decision to move from the cottage that gave her and the children more than a roof over their heads, thanks to the friendship and support of Bernardo. But Kelly needed to prove to herself that she was a capable and responsible mother. She told Bernardo first, and he asked her to stay longer but understood her feelings, and he offered to assist her with the move. She asked him to be present when she told Danny and Abby.

Kelly made the announcement a week before Thanksgiving, telling Abby and Danny that they would have Christmas in their own apartment and would be starting in a new school in January.

Abby screamed, "I don't want to move again. I never had a real friend at school until now."

"Honey, it's the best for everyone."

"Not for me. I won't go." She jumped from her chair crossed her arms over her chest as tears welled up in her eyes. "All we ever do is move, move, move. I never have friends. Nobody invites me to their birthday parties. I don't have a daddy!" She knocked over her chair and ran out of the door slamming it so hard a picture crashed to the floor.

Kelly jumped to her feet. "Abby, you come back here immediately."

Bernardo grabbed her wrist. "Let me talk to her. She probably ran to her secret hideout in the bushes that you're not supposed to know about."

"Okay. But explain that I'm trying to do what's best for everyone."

Bernardo stood in front of the thicket of bushes for a couple of minutes, listening to Abby tell her terrible news to her doll, Sunshine. "Abby, it's Bernardo. Can I come in?"

"You don't know the password."

He knelt by the low entrance, and slowly said, "Humuhumu-nukunuku-a-pua'a."

"Who told you the password?"

"Sunshine."

She giggled. "Dolls can't speak."

He crawled in, and as they talked, she scooted closer and leaned against him. He put his arm around her shoulder. Bernardo crawled out first, followed by Abby clutching her doll. He gathered everyone around the table.

"Abby has agreed to do whatever her mother decides, but first everyone should have a chance to express their opinion on whether to move or stay until summer vacation. We all should think carefully about what's best for the three of you, and after the Thanksgiving dinner, everyone will present their views on whether to stay until summer or move now, then your mother makes the final decision."

"Okay," Kelly said. But her mind was made up.

Everyone participated in preparing the Thanksgiving meal, with turkey and traditional trimmings. And there were apple and pumpkin pies with vanilla and strawberry ice cream for dessert. Bernardo brought out the special dishes, silverware, and candelabra that he hadn't used since Melanie had disappeared. Kelly, Abby, and Danny each lit one of the candles, and they all held hands around the table as Bernardo said the short Thanksgiving prayer.

"Thank you, Lord, for bringing these three wonderful people into my life and making my house a home again, with laughter and muddy footprints on the floors. I pray for good health and happiness for Kelly, Danny, and Abby in the year ahead."

"And Bernardo," added Kelly.

"Mommy, why does Bernardo like muddy footprints on the floor and you don't?" asked Abby.

"Bernardo means he loves to have you staying here even though you make a mess."

After the meal, when the pots, pans, and dishes had been washed and dried, they moved to the garden table, bringing their drinks with them. Bernardo refilled Kelly's wine glass, then asked her to speak first.

"Caring for my children is the most important thing in my life, and every time we had to move because of my financial difficulties, I lost part of my dignity as a mother. Now I have enough income to fulfill my role as a mother and provide a stable home with, hopefully, no more moves after this one."

Danny said he was happy where they were and liked his school but would do whatever his mother felt was best for the family, and he hoped the new apartment was not too far from his job in Waikiki.

Abby didn't look up from the table as she spoke. "I'm so happy here but want Mommy to be happy too. I will try to make friends at the new school and hope someday Mommy will find a daddy as nice as Bernardo."

Bernardo sat his untouched glass of wine on the table. "When my wife, Melanie, disappeared seven years ago, part of my heart died. Yet I knew I needed to move forward. I didn't realize when Danny showed up at my store with that hack haircut that he would change my life. When I first set my eyes on Kelly, my heart started to beat again in ways I thought were gone forever. Kelly, what I want to say is, will you go out with me on a *real* date?"

Kelly gazed into his eyes. "Are you sure?"

He lifted his glass. "I was sure that first night, when you stepped into the garden and let me fill the glass that had sat empty for too long."